BEDLAM AND BREAKFAST

As Judith set the serving plate down, she saw Joe Flynn come through the swinging doors between the dining room and the kitchen. He looked annoyed and was motioning to her.

"What's wrong?" she asked, hurrying around the big oak table that had belonged to her grandparents.

"Some jerk just flipped me off in the driveway," Joe said, keeping his voice down. "Kind of a burly guy, maybe a little younger than I am. The woman with him was pretty burly, too." Removing his lightweight summer blazer, Joe shrugged. "I guess he thought I was going to run them over when I pulled into the drive."

Joe usually took of his jacket and holster in the back hallway, but the incident had changed his routine. With alarm, Judith noticed the holster and shoved Joe back through the swinging doors.

She was too late. Barney Schwartz had come into the dining room. He saw the gun in the holster, let out a yelp, and grabbed Judith around the waist.

"If you shoot," Barney yelled, using Judith as a human shield, "the broad with the striped hair gets it! My number isn't coming up yet."

Other Bed-and-Breakfast Mysteries by
Mary Daheim
from Avon Books

MARY DAHEIM

LEGS
BENEDICT

A BED-AND-BREAKFAST MYSTERY

AVON BOOKS, INC.
1350 Avenue of the Americas
New York, New York 10019

Copyright © 1999 by Mary Daheim
Excerpts from *Just Desserts* copyright © 1991 by Mary Daheim; *Fowl Prey* copyright © 1991 by Mary Daheim; *Holy Terrors* copyright © 1992 by Mary Daheim; *Dune to Death* copyright © 1993 by Mary Daheim; *Bantam of the Opera* copyright © 1993 by Mary Daheim; *A Fit of Tempera* copyright © 1994 by Mary Daheim; *Major Vices* copyright © 1995 by Mary Daheim; *Murder, My Suite* copyright © 1995 by Mary Daheim; *Auntie Mayhem* copyright © 1996 by Mary Daheim; *Nutty as a Fruitcake* copyright © 1996 by Mary Daheim; *September Mourn* copyright © 1997 by Mary Daheim; *Wed and Buried* copyright © 1998 by Mary Daheim; *Snow Place to Die* copyright © 1998 by Mary Daheim
Inside cover author photo by Tim Schlecht
Published by arrangement with the author
Library of Congress Catalog Card Number: 98-93760
ISBN: 0-380-80078-0
www.avonbooks.com/twilight

First Avon Twilight Printing: April 1999

AVON TWILIGHT TRADEMARK REG. US. PAT. OFF. AND IN OTHER COUNTRIES, MARCA REGISTRADA, HECHO EN U.S.A..

Printed in the U.S.A.

WCD   10 9 8 7 6 5 4 3 2 1

LEGS
BENEDICT

FLOOR 2

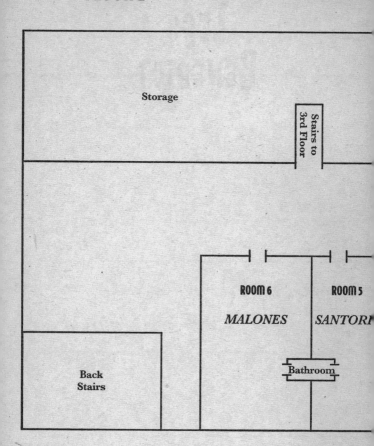

Storage

Stairs to
3rd Floor

ROOM 6

MALONES

ROOM 5

SANTORI

Bathroom

Back
Stairs

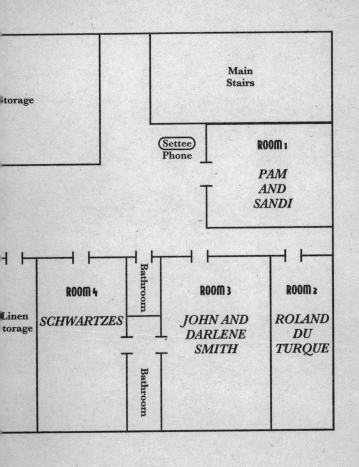

ONE

JUDITH MCMONIGLE FLYNN stared at the blank computer screen, hit several keys in succession, and swore out loud. "I'm ruined!" she exclaimed, running frantic fingers through her silver-streaked dark hair. "I'm helpless! All the B&B reservations for the next two weeks have fallen into a big, black hole!"

"No, they haven't," her cousin Renie said in a matter-of-fact voice as she came to stand behind Judith. "Move it, coz. Let me show you something." Renie pressed a single key, and the screen scrolled down. "There you go. Somehow, you put a bunch of white space at the top. We delete that . . ." Renie pressed another key. "And here comes the Hillside Manor guest list."

"Ah!" Judith put a hand to her bosom and leaned back in the chair. "Thanks, coz. I was really upset there for a minute. This thing has been giving me fits the last few days."

"You're still learning," Renie said, gazing at the names, addresses, and phone numbers that now appeared on the screen. "Even after all these years of working with a computer, I still hit something by mistake, and weird stuff happens. Frankly, you should be using some kind of B&B program. Your system is pretty clumsy."

"No, it's not," Judith said, on the defensive. "I use E-mail for almost half my reservations, and all the ones from overseas. Then I type them in and can use the word-processing part of the computer for letters and Christmas card lists and all the other stuff. How is that clumsy?"

Renie shrugged. "You'd make life easier if you had a real program," she insisted, still looking at the screen. "I'm sure they're available for B&Bs. Why don't you call . . . Hey, since when have you been reserving rooms for Mr. and Mrs. John Smith?" Renie pointed to the names on the middle of the screen.

"That's Mr. Smith's name," Judith replied. "Your last name is Jones. Some people really are named John Smith."

"With a P.O. box in New York City?" Renie was skeptical.

"He explained that on the phone," Judith said in a reasonable tone. "He lives in an apartment in Manhattan and it's easier for him to pick up his mail at the post office."

Renie shrugged. "I thought people in Manhattan had doormen to take in the mail. But you know best. You've been in the B&B business for nine years. There can't be many surprises left."

Judith studied the screen. "Actually, there can be. That's one reason I enjoy innkeeping. But most of all," she added, more to herself than to Renie, "I love the people."

Renie was smiling. "We may be as close as sisters, coz, but we're different in a lot of ways. I prefer to conduct my graphic design business from the basement where no one can find me."

"Right . . . yes." Judith was still peering at the screen. "You know, this is sort of weird. Five of the six rooms booked for next Monday are for two nights. They all booked within hours of each other, and none of them used E-mail. They phoned." She ran a finger down the screen, indicating the reservations for Doria, Perl, Santori, Schwartz, and Smith.

"Why is that weird?" asked Renie. "They're for the

third week of June. School's out, everybody's on the move. When did the requests come in?''

Judith glanced up at the old schoolhouse clock. ''Between eight and eleven-thirty this morning.'' It was now a few minutes after noon. ''The sixth reservation was made a month ago, by a couple from Minneapolis.''

Renie shrugged, then lighted a cigarette. ''As far as I'm concerned what's weird is that you had any openings this time of year. Aren't you usually booked solid from Memorial Day through Labor Day?''

Judith winced as Renie exhaled. ''Not in mid-June. Generally, there's about a ten-day lull. The locals know and the tourists have caught on that it always rains in the Pacific Northwest right after school gets out. Coz,'' she continued, unable to hide her exasperation, ''do you have to smoke in *here*?''

''Why not? Your mother does. And Joe has his cigars.'' Renie flicked ash into the sink.

''I almost never let Mother smoke inside, and Joe never smokes anywhere but up in our family quarters on the third floor. Sometimes I wish you'd go back to eating like a disgusting pig.''

''Not me,'' Renie replied breezily. ''My dry cleaning bills have gone way down. You know how messy I am when I eat. Now I just drop live ashes and set my clothes on fire. That way, I never have to clean them.''

Judith uttered a beleaguered sigh, though she knew that Renie was more or less speaking the truth. Her cousin's obsession with food had often driven Judith crazy over the years, in part because no matter how much Renie ate, she never got fat. Conversely, Judith was always watching her weight. ''Statuesque'' was her favorite self-description, and at five-foot-nine, she could afford a few extra pounds. Or so she told herself when she dared to get on the scale.

''If you go on smoking here,'' Judith threatened, ''I'll have to bar you from the house.''

''If I go on smoking,'' Renie countered, ''you're afraid you'll start again. Besides, since Bill retired from the university at the end of this past quarter, we're trying out hobbies we can share. He's started smoking, too.''

"Aaargh!'' Judith twirled around, arms covering her head. "I don't believe it! Bill's like Joe, he never smokes anything but cigars!''

"He does now. We may even take up pot.'' Renie flicked more ashes in the sink. "Got to go, coz. I have a meeting downtown at one.''

For once, Judith was relieved to see Renie depart. The phone was ringing; the cleaning woman, Phyliss Rackley, was yelling from the basement; and Sweetums had scooted through the open back door where he was sitting in the pantry, batting at cans of cat food.

The call was from a Mr. Harwood, asking for Judith's mother. He sounded like a salesman, but Gertrude Grover could deal with him. Indeed, Judith's mother probably would make him wish he'd gone into an easier line of work, like guiding climbers up Mount Everest in a blizzard. Judith gave Mr. Harwood her mother's separate number and hung up. Phyliss was still yelling.

"What's wrong?'' Judith called from the top of the basement stairs. Behind her, Sweetums was reaching for the cat food tins.

"There's a mouse in your dryer,'' Phyliss yelled back. "He's deader than a dodo, and gone to see the Lord.''

Judith turned to remonstrate with Sweetums, who had just managed to knock three of the cans off the shelf. The cat leaped out of the way and began rolling one of the cans with his forepaw.

"I'll get the mouse,'' Judith said wearily, and headed down the stairs.

Phyliss, her gray sausage curls more disorderly than usual, was standing on a discarded kitchen chair. "There might be more than one,'' she declared with a grim expression.

"If there is,'' Judith assured the cleaning woman, "Sweetums will catch them. He's a good mouser.''

"He's Satan's spawn," Phyliss retorted. "That cat is Beelzebub's familiar."

"That cat is a cat," Judith said, using a paper towel to scoop the mouse out of the dryer. "I'll put this in the garbage." She started back up the stairs just as a can of cat food rolled past her and hit the concrete basement floor with a clatter. "Okay, okay," Judith muttered. "I get the hint." She glared at Sweetums as she went out the back door.

"Knucklehead!" The raspy voice came from the door of the converted toolshed. "Where's lunch?"

"Jeez." Judith tried to ignore her mother until she had dumped the dead mouse into the garbage can at the side of the house. "I'm coming. It's been a hectic morning."

"Not in here," Gertrude Grover called, motioning inside the toolshed with her walker. "Nothing happens in my so-called apartment. Mold is growing between my toes."

"Didn't you just have a phone call?" Judith asked.

"I hate the phone. Okay, okay," Gertrude admitted, "so what? It was some census taker or something. I told him I was dead. I might as well be. In this boxy place, I feel like I'm already six feet under."

Judith also tried to ignore her mother's complaints. They weren't new, but they were annoying. Seven years earlier when Judith had finally married Joe Flynn, the great love of her life, Gertrude had gone into self-exile in the backyard. Although she'd despised her daughter's first husband, the late and usually unlamented Dan McMonigle, Gertrude had never approved of Joe, either, and refused to live under the same roof. She griped endlessly about the toolshed, but preferred it to sharing space with her son-in-law.

"I'll be right back," Judith called over her shoulder.

In the kitchen, she hurriedly opened a can of cat food for Sweetums and spooned it into a dish in the rear hallway. The cat eyed her coldly, then, with his long, plumelike tail waving with disdain, he pranced away to consume his meal.

Five minutes later, Judith appeared at the closed toolshed door. "Lunch," she called, trying to sound cheerful.

There was no response. Judith balanced the tray in one

hand and knocked with the other. "Lunch!" she called again, this time louder. "Open up!"

Judith was about to knock again when the door opened just a crack. "Who is it?" Gertrude hissed.

Judith sighed. "It's me. Your daughter. With lunch."

"Lunch?" Gertrude's small, wrinkled face displayed confusion. "What about breakfast?"

Judith sighed again. "You ate breakfast at seven-thirty. Now it's after twelve. You asked for lunch. Here it is."

"Lunch." Gertrude shook her head in a bewildered fashion. "If you say so, Toots. Come on, don't just stand there like a tree stump."

Gritting her teeth, Judith entered the small sitting room and set the tray down on her mother's cluttered card table. "Liverwurst sandwiches, lemon Jell-O with mixed fruit, carrot sticks, sweet pickles, and coconut bars I made this morning. Oh, and coffee. Okay?"

Warily looking at the items on the tray, Gertrude struggled to set the walker aside, nudged the card table, and eased her frail body into the shabby old orange and yellow armchair.

"Phew!" she exclaimed as Judith tried to help her get settled. "That was quite a trip! I'm all worn out."

Judith didn't ask her mother what trip she had been on. Maybe Gertrude referred to the trek from the door; maybe she was recalling some long-ago journey with Donald Grover, Judith's father. As age eroded her mother's mind and body, Judith often didn't know what Gertrude was talking about. And neither did Gertrude.

"All set?" Judith asked with a forced smile.

The watery eyes suddenly sharpened. "Huh? If you mean do I like this slop, guess again, kiddo. Since when did I eat liverwurst you can slice? You know what I like— the kind that comes out of one of those tube things, and you smear it all over everything, including your elbows."

"Falstaff's is carrying this new brand," Judith explained. "It's supposed to be healthier."

"Healthier?" Gertrude made a slashing gesture with one

arm. "How can eating sliced liverwurst give me new organs? Or," she asked slyly, "do I get a new liver?"

Judith had to smile. It was always a relief when Gertrude showed signs of her perverse old self. "If you don't like it, I'll go back to buying the other kind," she told her mother. After all, what was the point of serving low-cal, nonfat, high-fiber foods to a ninety-year-old woman who had been raised on lard and bacon grease?

Buoyed by Gertrude's temporary lapse into sanity, Judith returned to the house. Phyliss was running the vacuum cleaner in the living room, and two more calls had accumulated on the answering machine. One was a reminder from the dentist for a cleaning and checkup, the other, a reservation request for the Fourth of July. Hillside Manor was already full during the holiday weekend, and had been booked since early April. In its location on the south slope of Heraldsgate Hill, the B&B had a perfect view of the annual fireworks out in the bay. Guests who were in the know always made their reservations well ahead of time.

The rest of Friday was spent on the usual tasks. When Phyliss left at one o'clock, Judith finished up the housework that the cleaning woman hadn't quite managed to get done during her four-hour daily stint. A woman called to cancel the Doria party of one for Monday, but within fifteen minutes a man phoned to reserve the room for a Mr. du Turque. Judith returned other calls that had backed up on her answering machine, computer requests were checked, and the appetizers were created for the incoming guests who began arriving around four. All six rooms were occupied by the time Joe Flynn arrived home from his duties as a homicide detective with the metropolitan police force.

"The rain stopped," he said in a cheerful tone after kissing Judith hello. "Dare we barbecue tonight? I'll take over."

Judith considered. She had the meal planned and had just begun to peel potatoes. The menu would keep. "Why not? If it starts raining again, we'll come inside."

"I'll thaw the hamburger," Joe announced, heading for

the refrigerator. "Will your mother be joining us or will her broom have landed by dinnertime?"

"Joe . . ." Judith started to remonstrate, then shut up. It was so pleasant of late to have her husband come home in a good mood. It was also unusual. "Mother likes hamburgers," Judith said instead. "But she'll probably eat in the toolshed. I take it you had an easy day?"

"A snap," Joe replied, putting a pound of hamburger in the microwave. "Wife whacks husband with fireplace shovel. Wife confesses. Woody and I get home on time," he said, referring to his longtime partner, Woody Price. "That's the way I want it until I retire at the end of the year."

Originally, Joe's prospective retirement had been a bone of contention between the Flynns. Judith felt that deep down, under the complaints and the grouchiness, her husband loved his job and knew that he was doing something worthwhile. But spurred by Bill's example, Joe had decided that as soon as he could take Social Security, he too would bid farewell to the workplace. He was tired, he was burned out, and murder on a daily basis ravaged the soul. Judith understood her mate's attitude.

The weekend progressed smoothly, or as smoothly as it could with the usual difficult demands of the guests. A couple from San Jose demanded a futon. Fortunately, Judith kept one stored in the big closet on the second floor. A woman from Des Moines fell in love with the baby grand in the living room and played old favorites, none of which were Judith's. The honeymooners from Houston got into a big fight and the bride ran out of the house. Her groom found her two hours later, sitting on the next-door neighbors' front porch, pouring her heart out to Arlene Rankers.

Monday dawned with the usual mid-June drizzle and dreary gray skies. Around noon, Judith received a call from Earl and Donna Eckstrom, the couple from Minneapolis who had made their reservation some weeks earlier. They had had car trouble east of the mountains and would have to cancel. Judith graciously accepted their apologies, and wished she had a more stringent policy on last-minute can-cellations. On the other hand, true to her good heart, she felt sorry for the Eckstroms. But their defection left a vacancy.

Renie arrived late in the afternoon with a large sheet cake. "The gas company gave me this when I went in to consult on their revised customer newsletter. Some vice president was retiring and they were having a party, but the guy got drunk at lunch and passed out, so they had to cancel. They thought I'd like the cake, but we'll never eat all of it. I figured you could serve it to your guests instead of the usual hors d'oeuvres."

Judith regarded the cake with "It's been a gas, Omar!" etched in orange frosting. "Well . . . I suppose. Maybe I could serve it later, after everyone has come in from their night on the town."

Renie shrugged. "If not, give it to the Dooleys. They've still got about fourteen kids living at home, don't they?"

"At least," Judith laughed, referring to the large brood in the Dutch colonial on the other side of the back fence. "I can't figure out which are children and which are grandchildren these days. Sometimes I wonder if people don't drive by and drop off a spare kid. Corinne and her husband would never know the difference."

The front doorbell rang, a signal that either a guest or a tradesperson had arrived. Family, friends, and neighbors always used the back door at Hillside Manor.

"Time to play hostess," Judith said, heading through the swinging doors to the dining room. "Stick around, I'll make us something to drink."

The man and woman on the front porch appeared to be son and mother. "Barney Schwartz," the short, burly man said, and used his left hand to wring Judith's until she winced. As he let go, Judith noticed that the index and middle fingers of his right hand were missing. "This is my ma, Min," Barney said, flicking the three remaining fingers at the older woman.

Min towered over her son. "That's short for Minerva,"

she said in a deep, faintly accented voice. "How do you do, Mrs . . . ?"

"Flynn," Judith replied and cautiously offered her numb hand.

But Min Schwartz merely waved. "Arthritis. My fingers are very stiff."

So, Judith observed, was her spine. Minerva Schwartz was not only tall, but ramrod straight, and possessed of a sharp, aquiline profile that age hadn't quite undermined. The eyes matched the steel-gray hair, which was swept back from her face and arranged in a tight little topknot. She reminded Judith of her piano teacher, Mrs. Grindstein.

"You'll be in Room Four," Judith said. "It has twin beds and a very nice view of the bay. Here, Mr. Schwartz, I'll help you with your luggage."

Barney Schwartz put his foot down in front of the two suitcases and the train case. "I'll manage," he said with a crooked smile. "Hey, what's with the parking? We pulled up in that cul-de-sac out front."

Judith glanced outside and saw a brand-new Cadillac parked at the curb. "That's fine. We all have garages, although one of our neighbors, Mr. Porter, tinkers with cars in his free time. We try to leave him a couple of free spaces. You drove from . . ." Judith paused, trying to recall the Schwartzes' point of departure. ". . . Royal Oak, Michigan?"

"Yep," Barney answered, gathering up all three suitcases. "Just outside De-troit. Motown. The Motor City. You been there?"

"Ah . . . no, unless it was at night on the train." Judith managed a half-smile. "Years ago, my cousin and I took the train to New York before we sailed to Europe."

The cousin had inched her way into the entry hall. "I'll pour," Renie said in an undertone as Judith headed up the stairs with the Schwartzes.

Judith gave a slight nod as she led her guests to their room. "We had new wallpaper put up this winter," she said, opening the door. "I hope you like it."

Barney didn't bother to look, but Min surveyed the subtle iris design with the air of a connoisseur. "Very pleasant." She moved stiffly towards the nearest door. "Is this the bathroom?"

Judith nodded. "You share it with Room Three. There's also a bathroom just outside which is usually used by Rooms One and Two, but accessible to any of the guests. Rooms Five and Six also share a bath."

Barney was shoving the suitcases into the small closet. "What about a key?"

"Oh." Judith's half-smile twitched. "Here, this is for the room. The other key is for the B&B. If you come in after ten at night, you'll have to unlock the front door."

Barney's bushy eyebrows rose. "You don't keep this joint locked?"

Judith shook her head. "Not during the day. This is a very quiet neighborhood."

Barney seemed amazed. "No break-ins? No burglaries? No crime?"

Judith shook her head. "No, it's very safe." The Schwartzes couldn't see her cross her fingers behind her back. There had, alas, been a murder or two over the years, but only one had occurred on the premises of Hillside Manor. Of course, a killer had once stayed at the B&B. Two killers, actually. Or was it three? The disasters blurred in Judith's memory.

"Wow. It's hard to find a safe neighborhood in a big city these days." Barney seemed overwhelmed as he accepted the keys.

His mother, however, was regarding the bathroom door with misgiving. "I prefer not to share. At my age, I need access to a bathroom at all times, day and night."

Judith heard the authoritarian tone in Min's voice. More to the point, Judith understood the vagaries of the elderly. "Well . . . there's the bathroom just outside the door, and there's one off the entry hall where you came in just now."

Min vehemently shook her head; the topknot didn't budge. "I want this bathroom locked on the other side."

Judith also understood the obstinacy of the older generation. She remembered that Mr. and Mrs. Smith were in Room Three, the largest of the guest rooms. The price was a bit higher, and therefore, the visitors who stayed in Three expected the best of the amenities. Perhaps the Smiths would be sympathetic.

"I'll see what I can do," Judith said.

Min, however, wasn't giving in, nor did Barney seem willing to mediate. Judith understood that, too. Barney probably had given up arguing with his mother forty years ago.

"Lock it now," Min commanded.

Judith hesitated. "I'll make it worth your while," Barney said, finally breaking his silence.

Judith sighed. "No, no. It's my job to make guests happy. I'll lock it, and hope that the Smiths are a considerate couple."

"The Smiths?" Barney's bushy brows quivered again.

The faint sound of the doorbell could be heard from below. "Yes, the Smiths. Excuse me, I'll take care of this right now."

Hurriedly, Judith went into the bathroom and locked the door from Room Three. Then, with a strained smile and a wave, she raced downstairs.

Renie had already opened the door. Two pretty young women in their mid-twenties stood on the porch, each holding what looked like brand-new suitcases and wearing sweatshirts, one of which read "Plays Well With Others." The second shirt was emblazoned with "Runs With Scissors." A blue and white airport shuttle was just pulling out of the cul-de-sac.

"Ms. Perl and Ms. Williams," Renie announced. "Of Newark, New Jersey. This is your innkeeper, the redoubtable Mrs. Flynn."

"Redoubtable?" murmured Judith with a questioning glance at Renie. "Hi," she said in her most amiable voice. "Welcome to Hillside Manor."

Both young women started talking at once, then burst

into giggles. "Stop it, Pam," the willowy blonde said to the plump brunette. "You'll make Mrs. Flynn crazy."

"You started it, Sandi," Pam replied good-naturedly.

"Did not!" Sandi shot back, and they both lapsed into giggles again.

Sandi was the first to get herself under control. "Sorry. We teach preschool, and sometimes, when we're out of the classroom, we get to acting just like our students."

"But we don't wet our pants!" Pam doubled over with laughter.

"Or worse!" Tears of mirth began to roll down Sandi's cheeks.

Judith tugged at her chin. "Ah ... Would you like to take your things upstairs?"

Both young women stopped laughing at once. "Upstairs, downstairs, all around the big stairs, here we go!" they chanted together, and gave each other high fives when they'd finished.

"Sure," said Pam.

"Let's go," said Sandi.

The young women managed to stay composed while Judith introduced them to Room One, a cozy nook next to the stairs. The decor's bright red and pink roses seemed to suit the newcomers' personalities perfectly.

"You'll be sharing a bathroom with the Smiths from Room Three and Mr. du Turque from Room Two," Judith explained. "If it gets too crowded, there's a bathroom downstairs off the entry hall."

"No problem," Pam declared. "We're used to sharing. That's what we teach our students."

Judith felt relieved. Perhaps Mr. and Mrs. Smith would be equally obliging. "Great. The appetizer hour is at six, with wine, sherry, and juices. Is there anything else you need?"

Both young women were eyeing the closet. "Can you lock that?" Pam asked.

No one in Room One had ever made such a request.

Judith tested the knob. "I honestly don't know. I'd have to look for a key. Is it important?"

Pam and Sandi exchanged quick glances. "Not if you have a safe," Sandi said.

"I do." Judith offered Pam and Sandi a reassuring smile. "It's in the family quarters, though, so you'll have to give me whatever you want to put in it."

Again, the two women looked at each other. "We'll get back to you on that," Pam said. "Okay?"

"Sure. I'll be downstairs." Judith left.

Renie was in the front parlor, nursing a bourbon and water. She had prepared Judith's Scotch, but the ice was melting. "Here's to Humpty and Dumpty," Renie said, raising her glass. "I'm glad you're stuck with them and not me."

"I get stuck with a lot of people," Judith said, frowning at her highball. "These two are no problem. At least they're cheerful. By the way, when I mentioned drinks, I meant pop or tea."

Renie cocked her head. "So I'm a mind-reader?"

"You know I shouldn't be sitting here drinking at this time of day," Judith said, then glanced at the venerable grandfather clock that stood next to a tall bookcase. It was almost four-thirty. "Why did I let you talk me into this?"

"I didn't," Renie replied. "Isn't the late afternoon usually a signal for drink 'em if you got 'em?"

"Not for me," Judith retorted as the doorbell rang again. "See what I mean? Now they'll smell liquor on my breath." She shot Renie an annoyed glance.

Pete and Marie Santori of Miami, Florida, looked as if they wouldn't have cared if Judith had appeared stoned out of her mind and in the nude. Their deeply tanned arms were entwined and they only had eyes for each other. *Honeymooners*, Judith thought, and offered the couple a bright smile.

"You're in Room Five," Judith said after Pete and Marie had managed to let go long enough to bring in their two large pieces of luggage. "If you'd sign the register . . ."

"You do it, Pooky-wookums," Marie urged with a poke in the ribs for her beloved.

"No, Diddlyumdoodles," responded Pete, tickling his bride's chin. "Ladies—lovely ladies—loving ladies—first."

After a few more exchanges of treacle, Pete finally signed in. He was tall, dark, and lean, with gold chains around his neck and a gold link bracelet on his right wrist. Judith was about to hand the Santoris their keys when Pam and Sandi came down the stairs. The two young women suddenly stopped just before the first landing.

Sandi screamed and Pam collapsed.

Pete and Marie charged past Judith and ran out through the front door.

TWO

JUDITH'S FIRST CONCERN was for Pam, whose huddled figure lay on the landing. Sandi had stopped screaming, but stood frozen with her fists pressed against her mouth. Renie had rushed into the entry hall, looking stunned.

"Get some brandy," Judith called to Renie. "Pam? Pam?" She knelt next to the young woman, who was making whimpering sounds.

Sandi lowered her hands. "Pam's okay," she asserted in a ragged voice. "She had a shock, that's all. It was a mistake. A big mistake," Sandi repeated more loudly.

Pam opened glazed eyes. "A mistake," she mumbled. "Stupid."

Judith gently pulled Pam to a sitting position on the landing. "Don't exert yourself. Take some deep breaths."

Sandi gave herself a shake, then edged past Judith and Pam. "I must apologize to those people," she said. "They must think we're crazy." She went outside, in search of the Santoris.

Renie returned with a brandy snifter, which Pam waved away. "I'm okay, honest. It must have been the angle coming down the stairs. I thought that man was someone else. An ex-boyfriend. He was a real pain. I'd hate to run into him again." She uttered a little laugh.

"That's annoying," Renie said. "I still run into some of my former boyfriends. In fact, I figure I run into more of them than I realize. I can only recognize the ones who still have most of their hair and some of their teeth."

Pam managed to look interested. "It must have been different when you were dating," she said in a wistful voice. "After ten years, I've yet to find a guy who doesn't have a good excuse not to get married. What's wrong with men these days?"

Renie, who was still crouching by the stairs, folded her hands in her lap. "My husband, Bill, says it's not what's wrong with men, but what's wrong with women. By liberating themselves, they've not only confused men, but robbed them of . . ."

"Here's Sandi," Judith interjected, warding off another of her cousin's parrotings of Bill Jones, Ph.D.

Sandi's smile seemed forced. "Everything's fine," she assured the others. "Those nice folks just laughed it off. I coaxed them back inside."

"Hi again," the voice and the wave were subdued.

Pete and Marie were no longer entwined, and despite Sandi's reassuring words, Judith thought the Santoris looked shaken. Of course they had a right to be upset; the preschool teachers must have frightened them.

"I'm always being told I have a double," Pete said in an amused voice. "I must be a type."

Marie nodded, then looked up fondly at her husband. "It's the chiseled features, the dark hair and skin, the sort of Greek god appearance." She stroked his cheek for emphasis.

"Some god," Sandi muttered, running her hands through her short blond hair. "I mean," she added hastily, "some *kind* of god."

Judith stepped back into her normal innkeeper's role. "If you could move, Pam, I'll take Mr. and Mrs. Santori up to their room. Thank you," she added as Pam got to her feet and came down the last two steps to the entry hall.

Pete and Marie fairly galloped up the stairs ahead of

Judith. She could have sworn she heard Sandi whisper a very un-preschool-teacher-like word that rhymed with pick, crick, and trick. Not to mention lick, wick, and nick. Or click, tick, and kick. At the top of the stairs, Judith shook herself. She was beginning to think like Sandi and Pam.

"I'm sorry for your fright," Judith apologized after showing the Santoris into Room Five with its canopied bed and pink rosebud wallpaper. "Ms. Perl and Ms. Williams teach preschool, and it appears that they're very excitable. Like their pupils."

"No problem," Pete said, placing a suitcase on a folding stand.

"Girls are always swooning over Pete," Marie put in, "but now that we're married, he's all mine." She smiled widely, which made her otherwise plain features light up.

Judith went through her litany, explaining about the keys, the bathrooms, the serving times. She had just finished telling the couple about breakfast when Pete asked who was staying in the adjacent rooms.

"This room is next to the linen storage room on this side," Judith replied, gesturing with her left hand. "Room Six is vacant so far. We may have a late check-in."

Pete seemed relieved. "That's great." He turned to Marie and chucked her under the chin. "We can make all the noises we want tonight, Dooky-pooky."

"You bet, tweety-sweety," Marie responded, still wearing her brilliant smile. "Yum, yum!"

Wondering whether the lovebirds or the teachers would put her over the edge first, Judith went back downstairs. Renie was in the entry hall, speaking with a chunky black man whose bald spot shone like a tonsure.

"Roland du Turque, Kansas City," Renie announced. "Is that Kansas or Missouri?"

"Missouri," Roland replied in a soft, mellow voice, then held out his hand to Judith. "Ms. Flynn?"

Roland's quiet air and courtly manner acted as an antidote to her other guests' more flamboyant behavior. "I'm very pleased to meet you," Judith declared. "You're in

Room Two. May I?'' Her hand swept over Roland's large satchel and briefcase.

"No, no," said Roland, his dark eyes twinkling. He sported a trim goatee and appeared to be in his early forties. "I can manage. Your associate here has been filling me in about the rules and regulations."

"Oh." Judith shot Renie a quick glance. "In that case, I won't bore you with repetition." She gestured at the stairs. "Shall we?"

"Of course." Roland bowed. "After you."

A short hallway between Room One and Room Three led to Room Two. It had been a late addition, carved out of the too-spacious Room Three, and its windows looked out onto the cul-de-sac. Because it was small and narrow, the price was considerably less than for any of the other accommodations. The double bed had been squeezed into an alcove under the eaves, and was draped in gauzy green-and cream-striped material. To give the room a more airy appearance, Judith hadn't used wallpaper, but cream paint that matched the bed hangings.

"Charming," Roland remarked, taking in the details. "Daguerreotypes. Most interesting."

"They came from an old family album," Judith said. "All the pictures were taken in Cincinnati, but they go back so far that I honestly don't know who these people are."

Roland peered at the grouping of a half-dozen posed photographs. "Handsome people. Hearty. German?"

"Hearty," Judith thought, was a tactful way of saying overstuffed and obese. "Probably. They're my mother's family. She was a Hoffman before she married my father, Donald Grover."

"Ah." Roland gave the pictures one last look. "Then I'll be joining you at six for the informal get-together?"

"That's right," Judith replied. "Though I don't actually mingle. I think it's intrusive. Guests seem to do better on their own when it comes to getting acquainted."

Roland du Turque concurred. After he had bowed her out of Room Two, Judith hurried back downstairs. Although it was only five-thirty, Pam and Sandi were in the living room where Renie had poured them each a glass of white wine.

"We're having a hot talk about toilet training," Renie said, getting up from one of the two matching sofas in front of the fireplace. "Now that our three kids can finally go to the bathroom on their own, I wanted Pam and Sandi's advice on how to get them to clean the toilets."

"They should be old enough to read the instructions on cleaning materials," Pam said, now very serious. "Many of those compounds are highly dangerous."

"Pam's right," Sandi put in. "How old are your kiddies?"

"Twenty-nine, twenty-eight, and twenty-six," Renie answered with a straight face.

Sandi covered her mouth with her hands and Pam broke into giggles. "No! We're not much older than that!" cried Pam.

"Older, younger," chanted Sandi, reaching across the sofa to slap hands with Pam, "bigger, smaller, shorter, taller, inside we're all the same!"

Happily, Judith heard the doorbell. She hurried off to the entry hall, and found Mr. and Mrs. John Smith waiting on the porch.

"Just pulled in," said John in a marked New York accent. "We drove all the way from Montana today. It started raining the minute we crossed the mountains, but it's stopped now."

"The weather's like that around here," said Judith. "Very changeable." Guardedly, she studied the pair. John Smith was tall, rangy, and in his mid-forties. He had restless hazel eyes and a manner that suggested he was always on the alert. The suit he wore looked very expensive to Judith, perhaps an Armani, though there was a foot-long tear in the left pant leg.

Mrs. Smith, who also struck Judith as tense, was clad in a deep blue silk wrap skirt and a scoop-necked blouse. She was above average height, pretty in an artificial way, and no more than mid-twenties. Judith began to wonder if Renie's earlier suspicions were correct.

"This is the wife," John asserted, as if he could read his hostess's mind. "Meet Darlene, Mrs. Flynn."

Darlene offered Judith a limp hand and a bogus smile. "Pleased to meetcha," she murmured.

"Yes, of course," Judith stammered. "Now if I could show you . . ."

John waved a bony hand. "We'll manage. Just tell us the room number."

"It's Room Three, but I wanted to explain about the . . ."

"Later," John broke in. "Come on, Darl, let's go." He picked up one of their two large suitcases and headed upstairs, his movements surprisingly graceful. Darl followed with another bogus smile for Judith.

Hearing a dull thump on the front porch, Judith went to fetch the evening paper. As she opened the door, she saw one of the middle Dooleys, O. P., for St. Oliver Plunkett, wheeling away on his bicycle.

"Thanks," she called, waving the paper.

In front of the Rankerses' house, the fair-haired teenager glanced over his shoulder. "Sure, Mrs. Flynn," O. P. called back.

The diversion caused O. P. to lose control of the bike, which went over the curb and directly into the path of an oncoming car.

"O. P.!" Judith screamed. "Look out!"

The car, which had been going very slowly, was able to stop in time. O. P. righted his bike in the middle of the cul-de-sac, took a deep breath, and gave Judith a mortified grin. "That was close," he shouted.

"It was my fault," Judith said in a shaky voice. "I shouldn't have yelled to you. You're sure you're okay?"

"Yeah, I'm fine," O. P. replied, pedaling back toward the sidewalk. "But I need to deliver the Rankerses' paper."

"It's a good thing nobody goes fast in this cul-de-sac," Judith said, then became aware that someone was calling to her from the car that had just missed O.P. Turning, Judith saw that the Ford Explorer bore Illinois plates.

"I said," the pudgy woman in the passenger seat mouthed slowly, as if Judith was an idiot, "where's a place to stay?"

"Oh!" Judith hurried to the car. "Sorry, I was distracted. I'm afraid I caused our newspaper carrier to lose control of his bike."

"This is one confusing neighborhood, especially with all these stupid hills," the woman complained. "Do you know . . . ?"

Judith interrupted. "Yes, Hillside Manor is the light tan house with the dark green trim on the other side of the laurel hedge. I own it. Do you need a reservation?"

The woman exchanged glances with the man at the wheel. "Yeah," she responded. "You got room for us?"

Judith nodded with enthusiasm. "Yes, we had a cancellation. Park in front of the car from New York next to the driveway, and come right on in."

The woman and the man exchanged another glance. *Maybe*, Judith thought, *they think I really am a moron*. She could hardly blame them.

Renie was just taking her leave of the teachers. "Did I hear another scream?" she asked in a slightly bored voice.

Judith explained about the bike, and the newcomers from Illinois. "You usually aren't around when the guests arrive," Judith added as Renie headed for the back door. "How come you're not rushing home to get dinner?"

"Believe it or not," Renie said, grabbing her purse from the kitchen table, "Bill is cooking tonight. If he can find the stove, he may have another new hobby." The screen door swung behind Renie.

The couple from Illinois was in the entry hall, along with their luggage, which consisted of a foldover, a large suitcase, and some kind of satchel.

"Malone," said the middle-aged man, holding out a beefy hand. "I'm Mal and this is the wife, Bea. You got room for maybe a couple of nights?"

"I do," Judith said, offering the Malones a gracious smile. "You'll be in Room Six. And you're just in time for the appetizer hour."

"Appetizer hour?" Mal's leathery face screwed up in contempt. "What happened to the cocktail hour?"

Judith cleared her throat. "I don't serve guests hard liquor at Hillside Manor," she said in her primmest voice. "It's a matter of insurance, not to mention legality."

"Hunh." Bea's jowls jiggled as she gave a disapproving shake of her head. "What kind of a state is this, anyway? Don't you folks out west have fun?"

"Upon occasion." Judith still sounded prim, but felt a bit foolish. "Now if you'll sign in, I'll show you your room. I do serve sherry, however, along with the appetizers."

"Sherry!" Mal was scornful. "What kind of fruitcake drink is that?"

"Shut up, Mal, sign the damned thing," Bea ordered, tugging at the elastic waistband on her brown polyester pants. "I want to put my feet up for a few minutes. It's been a real rough day."

Mal's leathery features softened. "You're right, kid. It's been a bitch. How much?" He pulled a worn leather wallet out of his back pocket.

"Eighty dollars, which includes tax," Judith replied.

"Eighty bucks! No booze! Sheesh!" Mal counted out four twenties and gave them to Judith. Then he put on a pair of thick glasses and bent over the registry. It seemed to take him a long time to get around to signing his name.

"You full up, you said?" asked Mal, putting his glasses away.

Judith nodded. "Yes. The last of the reservations arrived just a few minutes before you did."

Again, the couple exchanged glances. "The Smiths," Mal said in a noncommittal tone.

"How did you know?" Judith asked in surprise.

Mal shrugged his broad if somewhat rounded shoulders. "That's the name on the line above us."

"Oh," Judith responded in a small voice. "I thought perhaps you knew them."

Mal drew back as if he'd been insulted. "Hell, no. Not those Smiths. Sure, I know some Smiths. Who don't? Why should I know these ones?"

"Well . . . No reason," Judith said with an apologetic smile. "I mean, I thought maybe you were traveling together. We often get friends or families who come by car and . . ."

"So which room?" Mal broke in. "Us, that is. I see they're in Three."

Somehow unsettled by the comment, Judith hesitated. In the living room, she could hear Pam and Sandi, singing some of their children's songs to the tune of the baby grand. Judith hoped they'd have the good sense to shut up when the other guests began arriving for the appetizer hour.

Which, she realized, as Roland du Turque came down the stairs, was upon them. "I'll be right back," she informed Roland. "The sherry and juices are already on the gateleg table."

"Sheesh!" Mal muttered. "Juices! You got a decent saloon around here?"

"Yes," Judith replied, starting up the stairs. "There are two nice pubs on top of the hill, and several excellent restaurants, including the Hexagon, although it caters mostly to the young."

"Pubs?" echoed Mal, puffing a bit as they reached the second floor. "*The young*? I'm talking about a place where you can tie one on."

"Try the bottom of the hill," Judith said between clenched teeth. "There are several bars down there."

"Hills!" exclaimed Bea. "Where'd all these blamed hills come from? I thought this city was on the ocean."

Opening the door to Room Six, Judith shook her head. "We're on the Sound. The ocean is a hundred miles away."

"Hunh." Bea pulled at her tan mock turtleneck. "This sure isn't what I expected. We're from Chicago, we got a big lake. No hills. But plenty of saloons. Right, Mal?''

"Right." Mal was surveying the lilac chintz decor. "Jeeesus! This ain't like no motel I ever saw!"

"It's not a motel," Judith said crisply. "It's a B&B. Would you prefer a motel?"

Abruptly, Mal turned to face Judith. "Huh? No, this is just the ticket. A B&B. Right, Bea? And Bea! Ha-ha!"

Bea laughed, though without mirth. "Yeah, Mal, a B&B. That's where we want to be. *Ha, ha.*" She sounded sarcastic, even bitter.

Judith rushed through the usual information, including the shared bathroom with Room Five. "They're honeymooners," she added. "They're very . . . sweet."

Bea made a face. "We were honeymooners—about two hundred years ago. We went to Lake Winnebago so Mal here could fish."

"Didn't catch much, either," Mal said, more to himself than to Judith or his wife.

"You sure didn't," Bea responded with a trace of acrimony.

Judith decided it was time, perhaps past time, to take her leave. "I'll see you downstairs," she said, nipping through the door.

The Smiths were just coming out of their room. Judith gave them a cheery smile. "I'll have the hors d'oeuvres out in five minutes," she promised.

"Don't worry about us," John said, the roving hazel eyes checking out the second-floor hallway, the stairs, and the partial view of the entry hall. "We're going downtown for dinner. You got any recommendations?"

Judith did, not only personal favorites, but a collection of reviews she'd clipped and copied from newspapers and magazines. "My husband and I prefer the Manhattan Grill in the financial district," Judith informed the Smiths as they reached the first floor. "Since you're from New York, you might enjoy one of the seafood establishments with a view. We like Andrew's by the ferry dock or the Bayshore, which is at the foot of the bluff and overlooks the harbor."

"They sound swell," John responded, now eyeballing what he could see of the dining room and living room. None of the other guests were visible from that angle, but Judith could hear the piano. The children's songs had somehow evolved into classic jazz.

"Do you need directions?" Judith asked as the Smiths started out through the front door.

"Naw," John replied, a hand on Darlene's shoulder. "We'll manage." The couple left.

Judith rushed to the kitchen, retrieved the hors d'oeuvres from the refrigerator, and punched in numbers on the microwave. While the crab puffs and miniature lamb kabobs heated, she got out an oval platter for cheese and crackers. Five minutes later, she was balancing the serving dishes in both hands, and announcing that the food had arrived.

So had Barney and Min Schwartz, who were engaged in conversation with Pam Perl by the bay window that overlooked the harbor. Sandi Williams was standing by the piano, while Roland du Turque continued to play a jazz medley.

"Thelonious Monk," Judith said in a worshipful tone as she approached the piano at the far end of the long living room. " 'Round Midnight.' 'Criss Cross.' And . . ." She cocked her ear, then smiled broadly. " 'Epistrophy.' "

His hands still plying the keys, Roland smiled back. "You're a buff."

Judith pointed to the built-in stereo system and storage space on the other side of the bay window. "I have several of Thelonious Monk's recordings, mostly old LPs. I think I discovered him before the rest of the world did, back in the early fifties." Judith laughed aloud. "I remember telling my Auntie Vance I wanted one of his records for my birthday. When I didn't get it, Auntie Vance said that nobody at any of the music stores had records put out by the Loneliest Monk."

Roland chuckled, a deep, rich sound that somehow was in harmony with the notes he was playing. "They found out soon enough who that fine musician was."

Judith nodded in agreement, and was about to add more of her jazz memories when Mal and Bea Malone entered the living room. Reluctantly moving away from the piano, she approached the couple from Chicago.

"I thought you were going out," Judith said, wearing her innkeeper's smile.

"We are," Bea answered, reaching for the appetizers. "But we thought we'd grab some snacks first. We're paying for 'em, aren't we?"

The Malones weren't the first rude guests to stay at Hillside Manor, which, if she had to be candid, was why Judith preferred not joining in during the social hour. Her training as a bartender at the rough-and-tumble Meat and Mingle had inclined her to react strenuously to bad-mannered visitors. In the first three months of her tenure at Hillside Manor, Judith had threatened to break the punch bowl over a foul-mouthed guest's head, called the cops on a couple trying to set the lace curtains on fire, and thrown a woman who had attacked Sweetums with a butter knife into the Rankerses' hedge. She still marveled how she'd managed to stay in business, but assumed the perpetrators were too embarrassed by their behavior to talk about it. Thus, Judith merely inclined her head at Bea Malone, despite the fact that Mal was scooping up half the crackers and cheese.

"Where's everybody else?" Mal asked, stuffing a handful of crackers into the pocket of his windbreaker. "I thought you were full up."

"I am," Judith replied. "Here come the Santoris now."

Pete and Marie descended the stairs arm-in-arm. Mal and Bea both turned to stare, then exchanged yet another glance. Indeed, Judith thought that Mal had given a faint shake of his head.

"You sure this is all of 'em?" Mal asked as the newlyweds approached the gateleg table.

Judith offered the pair a smile. "One of the parties went out for dinner," she replied, then grabbed the hot appetizer plate and presented it to the Santoris.

"The Smiths," murmured Bea.

"Yes," Judith said as Marie oohed and aahed over the selections. "The Smiths."

Mal tugged at Bea's sleeve. "Let's go."

"Sure," Bea responded, filching two puff pastries from the plate. "We might as well."

After the Malones had left the room, Marie nudged Pete. "Will we be like that in twenty years, Tickles-wickles?"

Pete grimaced. "I hope not, Googley-woogley."

Judith said nothing. It wasn't appropriate to criticize guests in front of other guests. As she set the serving plate back down, she saw Joe Flynn come through the swinging doors between the dining room and kitchen. He looked annoyed, and was motioning to Judith.

"What's wrong?" she asked, hurrying around the big oak table that had belonged to her grandparents.

"Some jerk just flipped me off in the driveway," Joe said, keeping his voice down. "Kind of a burly guy, maybe a little younger than I am. The woman with him was pretty burly, too."

Judith gave Joe a quick kiss, then heard the squeal of tires outside. "The Malones, of Chicago," she whispered. "Not my favorite type of guests. Why did they flip you off?"

Removing his lightweight summer blazer, Joe shrugged. "I don't know. I guess he thought I was going to run over them when I pulled into the drive."

Joe usually took off his jacket and holster in the back hallway, but the incident with Mal Malone had changed his routine. With alarm, Judith noticed the holster and shoved Joe back through the swinging doors.

She was too late. Barney Schwartz had come into the dining room. He saw the gun in the holster, let out a yelp, and grabbed Judith around the waist.

"If you shoot," Barney yelled, using Judith as a human shield, "the broad with the striped hair gets it! My number isn't coming up yet!"

Judith's heart sank and Joe's jaw dropped.

But Barney Schwartz's hold remained in place.

THREE

"TAKE IT EASY," Joe said, keeping his voice calm. "I'm not going for the gun. Let go of my wife. Nobody has to get hurt."

Judith tried to wrestle her way out of Barney's grasp. "Please, Mr. Schwartz," she implored, "you mustn't be afraid. My husband is a policeman."

Barney's grip tightened. "Oh, yeah?" he responded. "Back off, creep. I mean business."

Joe held himself in check. "I'm an *off-duty* policeman. Let go of my wife, or I'll be forced to call the neighborhood patrol car."

Little by little, Barney Schwartz relinquished his hold on Judith. He looked shaken, however, and his eyes went straight to his mother, who, along with the other guests, had rushed into the dining room.

"What is this?" Min demanded, rigid with apprehension. "What have you done to my poor boy?"

"Not a damned thing," Joe retorted, finally losing his calm demeanor and reaching out to put an arm around Judith. "Your poor boy tried to take my wife hostage. Guests or no guests, you better have an explanation."

Awkwardly, Barney shook himself and gave his mother a sheepish smile. "It's okay, Ma. I just had a little scare." He turned back to Joe. "Sorry. I thought you were two other guys." Barney took Min's hand and tried to slip it inside his arm. "Come on, let's get a sherry refill."

Min yanked her hand away. "I want to know what's going on."

Barney patted his mother's cheek. "Nothing, Ma, honest. I just . . . screwed up. You know how I get . . . when I *don't take my medicine.*"

"If you say so." Min appeared skeptical as her cold gray eyes swept from Barney to Joe. "You're a policeman?"

"That's right." Joe was removing the offending holster and sidearm. "Just an ordinary civil servant, working a dull desk job, and inching toward retirement."

Min drew back a step. "You need a gun at your desk?"

Joe shrugged. "It's required on the force. What's this about medication?"

Barney opened his mouth, but Min elbowed him aside. "My son has some health problems. Occasionally, he becomes delusional, even paranoid. I'll make certain he takes his pills."

Joe appeared to be reflecting upon Min's words. "Okay," he finally said. "You do that. Now if you'll excuse me, I'm going upstairs to change."

Judith followed her husband up the back stairs to the family quarters on the third floor. "Nice lie," she said, and meant it. The Flynns tried to avoid informing guests that Joe was a homicide cop. Somehow, the job didn't mesh with the romantic image of a B&B.

"Which one?" Joe asked as he removed his highly-polished loafers and put them on a shoe rack in the closet. "Mine or the old bag's?"

"I meant yours," Judith responded. "It's possible that Mrs. Schwartz is telling the truth."

"I wonder." Joe started emptying his pockets. "Who is that jerk, anyway?"

"His name is Barney Schwartz," Judith answered, sitting down on the bed. "That was his mother, Minerva. They drove here from Royal Oak, outside of Detroit. Other than that, I don't know anything about them. You know perfectly well I don't ask for character references when I take reservations.''

"Right," Joe said, but he seemed perturbed. "I don't much like it when a guest sees a gun and thinks there's a bullet in it with his name on it. It tends to make a fellow suspicious.''

"I told you," Judith asserted, "they're from the Detroit area. Don't they have a high crime rate? Maybe Barney has been involved in previous incidents.''

"Previous," Joe repeated, heading for the bathroom. "That's okay. I don't mind previous behavior. It's priors, as in convictions, that I worry about." He closed the door, leaving Judith with an uneasy feeling.

It rained while Joe and Judith ate dinner, but let up shortly after seven. Remembering the cake Renie had left, Judith set it out for her guests on the gateleg table along with a coffee urn. It appeared that everyone had gone out, and the house was quiet. As she tidied up the living room, she noticed a small piece of paper under the piano bench.

It appeared to have been torn from a little spiral notebook. The handwritten words read, "Legs-Hoffa-Provenzano?''

Puzzled, Judith slipped the paper into the pocket of her gray slacks. She not only didn't know what it meant, she wasn't sure who had dropped it. Judith recalled that Pam, Sandi, and Roland had been at the piano, and so might have Barney and Min or Pete and Marie. If the note was of any importance, Judith told herself, the person who dropped it would ask. Over the years, guests had mislaid an incredible number of items, from a portable toilet to an eight-month-old baby. As Renie had said, there couldn't be too many surprises left for Judith when it came to innkeeping.

Then again . . . Judith smiled to herself as she put on her jacket and went out to the garage. She'd had a quibble with Renie's remark at the time. Now, as she headed up to Holiday's Pharmacy on top of the hill, she was anxious to tell her cousin about Barney Schwartz using her as a human shield. If it didn't take long to pick up Gertrude's prescriptions, Judith would drive the remaining six blocks to Bill and Renie's house on the north slope of Heraldsgate Hill.

At ten to eight, Judith was in the Joneses' comfortable green, blue, and off-white living room. "Where's Bill?" Judith asked, surprised at not finding Renie's mate in his favorite chair in front of the TV.

"I sent him out to be reupholstered," Renie said. "After we painted this spring, he was the only thing in the living room that didn't match."

Sitting down in a powder-blue recliner, Judith laughed. "Where is he really?"

Renie scowled at her cousin. "You think I'm kidding? Maybe I should switch job categories, quit graphic design, and go into interior design. Do you realize that of all the permanent fixtures in a house, women complain most about their husbands? Every time, they tend to screw up the decorating scheme. You're lucky—you get to keep Joe in the attic."

Reaching for the footrest on the recliner, Judith put her feet up. "You don't sound as sanguine about retirement tonight as you did the other day. Don't tell me that after only two weeks, you're having qualms." Though Joe's retirement was still months away, Judith already had doubts about a change in lifestyle.

"Actually," Renie said, "Bill's at a meeting. He's still acting as a consultant to the psychology department at the university. And no, I haven't any qualms. For one thing, I'm used to having Bill home during summer quarter. For another, we live on different clocks. He's a morning person, I'm best at night. He goes to bed early, I get up late. It gives us some time to ourselves."

Briefly, Judith reflected. She and Joe were forced to get up at the crack of dawn. Maybe that would change when he retired. But Judith didn't want to think about that now. Though she was a worrier, she sometimes tended to bury her head in the sand and avoid dealing with potential problems.

"How was dinner?" Judith asked, changing the subject.

Renie's eyes roamed the off-white ceiling. "It was something with leeks. One of the kids gave Bill a Welsh cookbook for Christmas last year. Everything in it seems to have leeks. It's the national fruit or flower or . . . *bulb*, I guess, of Wales."

Judith gave Renie a knowing smile. "You're cooking tomorrow night?"

Renie nodded. "Grandma Grover's greenie noodles with lamb steaks."

"I make that every so often," Judith replied. "Thick egg noodles fried with cabbage in about half a pound of butter. Mother loves it."

"So do Bill and the kids," Renie said, then tapped her can of Pepsi. "You want something?"

Judith declined. "I can't stay, I never like leaving the B&B alone too long when guests are coming in and out. Which is sort of why I came. This is a really odd crew."

Since Renie already knew about the preschool teachers' reaction to Pete and Marie Santori, Judith described Barney Schwartz's panic and the rude behavior of the Malones, who seemed more than a little interested in Mr. and Mrs. John Smith.

"Oh," Judith added, "I almost forgot Mr. du Turque. You met him—it turns out he's quite a piano player. Jazz, especially Thelonious Monk."

"Right up your alley," Renie commented. "Nice."

Judith agreed. "So why do I have the feeling that some of these people know some of the other people from someplace else?"

"Because you want them to?" Renie paused to light a cigarette. "Solving puzzles is your avocation, coz. Connect the dots."

"There may not be any," Judith admitted. "But almost all of them act strangely. The Smiths, for example, don't seem anxious to run into the other guests."

"I don't blame them from what you've told me," Renie said dryly. "And yes, I know you've had some very peculiar—and dangerous—guests on occasion in the past. Which is why I'm inclined to believe you may be exaggerating. History doesn't always repeat itself. Pam and Sandi insisted they'd made a mistake. It sounds like Barney Schwartz did, too. Did you say he mentioned taking medication?"

Slowly, Judith nodded. "Somehow, that didn't sound right. But I tried to tell Joe that Barney comes from Detroit, and may have met up with some tough customers. I don't think I convinced Joe, and now I'm not sure I convinced myself. I'd be willing to bet that tomorrow at work, my suspicious husband will run Barney through the computer."

"He's done that before with some of your guests, hasn't he?" Renie asked, calmly puffing away.

"Yes. For various reasons." Judith hesitated. "There's another thing, which I mentioned to you last week—the time frame in which those reservations were made."

Renie glugged down a large portion of Pepsi. "You said they all came in within a couple of hours of each other. But was it *all* of them?"

"No," Judith admitted, "it was only the Smiths, the Schwartzes, the Santoris, Pam and Sandi, and some guy who canceled later. It was an odd name, like a ship. Doria, I think. He was from Las Vegas."

Renie waved a hand. "So in reality, only four of the parties who checked in today made their reservations Friday morning."

"Well . . ." Judith cleared her throat. "Yes, that's true. Roland du Turque called later and the Malones showed up this afternoon without a reservation."

"I don't think that sounds so strange," Renie said, getting up to adjust the floral drapes at the big front window. "You can't tell me that over the years you haven't had other people call in within minutes of each other for the same date."

"They probably did. This time it just struck me as . . .

odd.'' Judith suddenly snapped her fingers. ''How did the Malones know where to find the B&B?''

Renie wrinkled her pug nose. ''Ever hear of the *phone book*?''

Judith didn't let Renie's comment daunt her. ''When they pulled into the cul-de-sac, they didn't ask for Hillside Manor, they asked if there was a place to stay. Now how would they know such a place existed in a residential neighborhood?''

''Your point being . . . ?'' Renie seemed a bit impatient.

Judith started to respond, then stopped, apparently losing her zeal. ''I'm not sure. It just seems odd.''

''Naturally.'' Renie was obviously humoring her cousin. ''Now try to tell me that a month never goes by when you don't have at least one wacko check into the B&B.''

''Okay, okay,'' Judith said as she stood up. ''I'm going now. You make me feel like an idiot.''

''My pleasure,'' Renie said blithely, then put an arm around Judith. ''I just hate it when you go off the deep end, imagining stuff that isn't really there. To me, it's a sign of some big hole in your life. We all have them, but sometimes I think yours is deeper than most. Maybe it was all those years with Dan. Even Joe can't make up for two lost decades.''

Put that way, Judith could offer no argument. Nobody except Renie understood what she'd gone through during her first marriage. Having taken on Dan McMonigle as a sort of consolation prize for losing Joe Flynn, Judith had always felt as if the package had been booby-trapped. But Renie, who was as close, maybe closer than any sister could be, had ended up as Judith's sole confidante. It would have been impossible for Judith to share the pain—and humiliation—with anybody else.

''Maybe,'' Judith said with a lame little smile, ''what's missing is my common sense.''

Renie gave Judith a little shake. ''Not that. We're all missing a few things.'' Wistfully, she gazed up the stairs in the direction of her children's bedrooms. ''At least you have some hope of posterity. I do not. Yet."

Judith broke into a big smile at the reference to her only child's impending parenthood. "You will. Did I tell you that Mike called over the weekend and said they may have miscalculated, and that Kristin could have the baby a couple of weeks early?"

Renie beamed. "Great! Grandma Flynn! What's the revised due date?"

"July second," Judith replied. "Of course, you never know with first babies."

Mike and his long-time girlfriend, Kristin, had been married exactly two years. As National Park Service forest rangers, they had begun their legal life together in Idaho. But seven months later, the newlyweds had been transferred to a national park site just an hour away from Heraldsgate Hill. They were so close that Judith smiled every time she looked out at the mountain range mere minutes from her doorstep.

"Tell me," said Renie, looking troubled, "does the new addition mean a change in your thinking about . . . you know."

Judith shook her head. "I made up my mind about that when Mike and Kristin got married. I've said it before, I'll say it again—Dan was a crappy husband, but he was a good father, the only father Mike ever knew. I won't take that away from Dan—or from Mike."

"Still," Renie sighed, "that's hard on Joe."

Joe hadn't just left Judith to run off in a drunken stupor with his first wife, Vivian. He had left Judith pregnant; he hadn't known about Mike until Joe showed up as the investigating officer in a homicide at Hillside Manor over twenty years later. Ever since Joe had reentered Judith's life, she had agonized over telling Mike the truth. But when he married, it became clear that his love for the man who had helped raise him must never be undermined.

Judith offered Renie a sad little smile. "You're right. It's very hard on Joe. But I think you were the one who said husbands and wives have to live with—and accept—some heavy loads of baggage.''

Renie made no comment, but gave her cousin an affectionate pat. Judith went out into the June evening. The long days that came with the summer solstice had been foreshortened by the cloudy weather. It was almost dark when Judith arrived home at a quarter of nine.

Joe was in the kitchen, taking a beer out of the refrigerator. As soon as Judith saw his face, she knew something was wrong. The house, however, seemed quiet.

''What is it, Joe?'' she asked as anxiety roiled up. ''Is it Mother?''

''I wish,'' Joe murmured ambiguously. ''No. It's not the old bat. Come upstairs, I'll show you.''

Judith practically ran up the two flights to the third floor. She was breathless when her husband joined her in the small sitting room that had originally belonged to Gertrude.

Joe went to the cherrywood cupboard, removed a false panel, and opened the safe hidden in the wall. As Judith watched with a worried expression, her husband brought out something wrapped in a hand towel. ''I decided to do a little checking up on Mr. Schwartz. I went into Room Three and here's what I found in the drawer of the nightstand.''

Judith stared at the gun. ''Oh, dear! We can't have that! Firearms are prohibited at the B&B. Except yours, of course.''

''It's a nine-millimeter Glock automatic,'' Joe said, at his most professional. ''It's a serious sort of gun, and it's loaded. Tomorrow, I'm going to run Barney through the computer and see what comes up. I can also check out the serial number to see if he stole it or purchased it. I told you there was something damned funny about him.''

''I guess so.'' Judith felt faintly sick. ''But it doesn't mean he's a crook. I mean, lots of people travel with guns, especially when they're driving cross-country. What if he has a carry permit?''

Joe tipped his head to one side. ''If he's from out of

state—Michigan?" He paused as Judith nodded. "Then the permit isn't valid here. But it's still legal to own a gun in this state."

"But I have my own rules," Judith pointed out. "No firearms or dangerous weapons. I'll confront him when he and his mother get back from wherever they went. It's going to be awkward."

"I'll be there," Joe said, putting the gun back in the safe.

Judith gave her husband a grateful smile. "Thanks," she said, rocking back and forth on the red- and white-patterned loveseat. "That's another thing—Barney must be a decent man. He travels with his mother."

Joe's rust-colored eyebrows twitched. "So? Ever hear of Ma Barker?"

Judith made a face. "Minerva Schwartz seems like a proper person, not just old-fashioned, but there's something old world about her. She's almost regal."

"If you say so." Obviously, Joe wasn't in the mood for an argument. "As I said, I'll check her son out first thing tomorrow."

"Okay." Judith tried to resign herself, but she was still fretting. "We still have to confront Barney tonight. Oh! The safe—I just remembered that Pam and Sandi wanted to put something in it."

"Like what?" asked Joe, joining Judith on the loveseat.

"I don't know," Judith replied. "They said they'd get back to me on it. I guess they forgot."

Turning on the TV, Joe shrugged. "People tend to do that."

"Yes. And they seem a bit . . . ditzy." Judith decided she might as well forget about the preschool teachers' request. "Oh, dear—I wish you hadn't found that gun. I hate making a scene with a guest."

"Barney already opened the act," Joe said, then glanced at his watch. "Some of your motley crew should be coming back soon. I don't imagine Barney and Ma are night owls."

"Probably not," Judith agreed. "Like so many elderly people, Min isn't in the best of health. She has arthritis, and also mentioned that she had to be near a . . . Oh!'' Judith snapped her fingers. ''I forgot to tell the Smiths about not being able to share the bathroom. Good grief, I'm getting as addled as Mother. Anyway, Mrs. Schwartz wanted the bathroom all to herself.''

Joe had settled down on the loveseat next to Judith and found the channel that was carrying baseball. ''Didn't you go through the usual spiel?''

''No,'' Judith replied. Despite Joe's muffled curse as the left-fielder dropped an easy fly ball, she continued, ''Mr. Smith said he and Mrs. Smith could manage without me. Then, when I saw them just before they left for dinner, I didn't remember. I wonder if they tried to get into the bathroom and found it was locked from the other side. They didn't say so, but they'd only been here about an hour before they left again. Still, you'd think that after a long car trip, they'd need to . . .''

Joe didn't hear a word of his wife's ramblings. He was accustomed to Judith's verbal fussing about the B&B guests, which he'd learned to tune out early on in their marriage. But his attention was caught when Judith suddenly grabbed his arm and let out a little yip.

''Joe!'' she cried, her dark eyes wide. ''Did you say you found that gun in Room Three?''

Reluctantly, Joe turned away from a bases loaded, two men out situation. ''Yeah, right. Why?''

''Are you sure?'' Judith gave her husband's arm a little shake.

''Of course I'm sure. Room Three, the big room that looks out over the bay.'' Covertly, he tried to watch the three-and-two pitch.

''But Joe,'' Judith said in a rush, ''Barney and Min Schwartz aren't in Room Three. They're in Room Four.'' She swallowed hard. ''John Smith and his wife are in Room Three. He's the one with the gun.''

The grand slam that sank the home team didn't seem half as bad to Judith as the sinking feeling she was beginning to have about John Smith.

FOUR

As THE WINNING run crossed home plate, Joe switched off the TV in disgust. "You say the *Smiths* are in Room Three?" he asked, turning to face Judith. "I thought they were in Room Four. I checked the registration."

"You must have read it wrong," Judith said, still sounding shaken.

Joe grimaced. "Maybe I reversed the room numbers. Damn! It's pointless to run a John Smith through the computer."

"Can you ask for his ID?"

"Smith's?" Joe looked at Judith over the can of beer. His green eyes with the gold flecks weren't dancing. He was wearing his official face, all business under a seemingly mild exterior. "He may have phony ID," Joe said. "Then again, while it's a long shot, John Smith could be his real name. As you may recall, it happens."

Judith definitely recalled the man who really was John Smith. He had been a disc jockey who had tempted fate once too often and come to a tragic end. "Are you still going to check up on Barney?" Judith inquired, putting her memories of the encounter aside.

"Probably. His reaction today set off bad vibes." Joe finished his beer and glanced at his watch. "But first, we'll have a word with the current John Smith. It's al-

most nine-thirty. The guests should start straggling in
soon.''

Judith stood up. ''Let's go. Drat, I'm really dreading
this.''

The Flynns waited in the cozy front parlor with its stone
fireplace and matching wingback chairs. Through one of
the two doors, they had a partial view of the entry hall, the
other door looked out into the living room. Joe appeared
absorbed in a western novel. Judith used the wait to sort
through her collection of jigsaw puzzles. Usually, she had
a puzzle set out on a card table near the baby grand, but
the most recent one had been completed over the weekend.
In a desultory manner, she rejected Mad Ludwig's Bavarian
castle, the changing of the guard at Buckingham Palace,
and a herd of cows grazing in Wisconsin.

Shortly before ten, the Malones arrived. Joe turned, but
Judith shook her head. ''Not Smiths,'' she mouthed.

Bea and Mal had discovered the cake. ''Sheesh! Who
the hell is Omar?'' grumbled Mal from around the corner.
''Are we supposed to eat this thing?''

''Why else would it be here?'' Bea asked, sounding irritated. ''There's coffee, see? And paper plates. Dig in.''

''I dunno,'' Mal said. ''I feel kind of guilty. Here we
are, stuffing ourselves, and poor Corelli is . . .''

''Stop!'' Bea broke in. ''Don't even talk about Corelli.
I never want to hear his name again. We got to keep going,
forget the past. Eat some cake, before I start blubbering
again.''

The couple went silent, except for the sound of loud
chewing and a punctuating belch by Mal. Then, through
the partially open door, Judith saw the pair head up the
stairs. From the glimpse she managed to get, it looked to
Judith as if the Malones had taken almost half the big sheet
cake.

''Hogs,'' she muttered to Joe. ''Who's Corelli?''

''Who knows?'' said Joe. ''A relative? A friend? Mal's
barber?''

Pete and Marie Santori arrived next, a few minutes after

Judith had locked up at ten. "How do we lock up?" Marie asked her husband.

Judith could hear Pete fiddling with the locks. "I think I got it. Let's go to bed. I'm beat."

"Sure," Marie replied, her voice flat. "This hasn't come up all roses." They proceeded up the stairs.

Judith gave Joe a curious look. "What happened to all that newlywed exuberance?" she asked, keeping her voice down.

Joe snorted. "As I recall, I broke my leg in a dune buggy on our honeymoon. That wasn't all roses, either."

"But Pete and Marie are all in one piece," Judith pointed out.

"Physically," Joe responded. "Emotionally, they may be fractured. First fight. Do you remember ours?"

Judith grinned. "I sure do. You wanted to donate Mother to medical science. While she was still alive."

"The hell I did," Joe grinned back. "I only wanted to send her away for some tests."

"In the Gulag Archipelago?" Judith's laughter was interrupted by the arrival of Barney and Min Schwartz. The Flynns sat very still as mother and son went into the living room.

"Hey, Ma, want some cake?" Barney asked from the living room.

"No, thank you," Min replied in her inflexible manner. "I've had my fill for the evening. That torte was a bit stale, if you ask me."

"I didn't mind," Barney replied. "It was kind of a small slice, though. Maybe I'll take some of this cake upstairs."

"You should watch your diet more closely," Min said with reproach in her voice. "As I've told you many times, your father was quite stout."

"Aw, come on, Ma, just a little piece," Barney wheedled. "It won't kill me."

There was a pause. "Oh . . . very well. Sweets didn't kill your father, after all." There was a note of bitterness in

Min's voice. "I don't suppose they'll kill you, either, will they?"

"Ma . . ." Barney sounded aggrieved. "Cut it out. I know what I'm doing."

"Do you?" Chilling sarcasm dripped from Min's words, but Barney kept mum. A moment later, the Schwartzes went up to the second floor.

"What did *that* mean?" Judith whispered.

"Barney's health?" Joe whispered back.

Selecting a puzzle featuring a tropical island paradise, Judith put the rest back in the cupboard. "If Barney's taking medicine," she noted, "it's not for diabetes."

Half an hour passed before Pam and Sandi returned. "Wow," Judith heard Sandi say, "that Hexagon gets pretty wild! Are you sure you got all your underwear back, Pam?"

"I got *somebody's* underwear back," Pam replied with a giggle. "I'm just not sure it's mine. Boy, I'm glad our students' parents couldn't see us tonight! I loved it when you kept yelling, 'On your bottoms, hands to yourself, all eyes on me!' "

Sandi also giggled. "Those guys who came on to us— don't you think they were a little young?"

"They had to be twenty-one," Pam replied as the two young women started up the stairs. "That's the legal drinking age in this state."

"Still," said Sandi, "I wonder if they didn't sneak in. I thought they looked like college freshmen."

"So?" retorted Pam. "We deserve a little fun. Between us, we've had more misery than . . ." Her voice faded as they turned the corner on the second landing.

Judith sat back in her chair. "Goodness, they sound sort of bitter."

"Cut them some slack," Joe said. "How would you like to be in charge of spoiled brats who have to be spoon-fed and wet their pants?"

Judith scowled at Joe. "I am. Have you forgotten Mother?"

Joe sighed. "I try, but it doesn't happen. Every time I go out the back door, I see the toolshed, squatting there like some poisonous toadstool."

"Joe . . ." The reproach in Judith's voice was tempered by amusement, but she broke off as the front door opened again.

John and Darlene Smith entered. Neither spoke as one of them, presumably John, locked the front door. Then Judith saw the couple start up the stairs. Joe, who was already on his feet, moved quickly into the entry hall.

"Excuse me," he said in the deceptively congenial voice he used when interrogating suspects. "Could I have a word with you in the parlor?"

"Sure," John responded without betraying any curiosity. "What's up?"

Darlene followed her husband, while Judith smiled politely. Joe offered Mrs. Smith the chair he'd vacated; John lounged gracefully against the mantelpiece.

"There's a rule against weapons at Hillside Manor," Joe said without preamble. "I've had to confiscate your gun, Mr. Smith."

John's hazel eyes narrowed ever so slightly. "What gun?"

"The Glock nine-millimeter," Joe replied. "The gun I found in the nightstand next to the bed in Room Three."

Retaining his careless air, John looked straight at Joe. "Who are you? The night watchman?"

Joe didn't blink. "In a way. I watch out for my wife, Mrs. Flynn." He gave a nod in Judith's direction. "Are you saying you don't own a gun, *Mr. Smith*?"

"That's what it sounds like," John replied, then looked at Darlene. "When did you start packing, babe?" he asked in an amused tone.

Darlene's crimson lips curved into a smile. "Like never? What's he talking about?" She patted her copper-colored curls and gazed soulfully at Joe.

John gave a careless shrug. "Then I don't know what to say. Somebody else must have left it there. Or," he added, his tone vaguely sinister, "do you always go through the rooms when your guests are out?"

Getting to her feet, Judith stepped between Joe and John Smith. "We *never* do that. Guests know the rules and regulations, or should, since they're in the guidebooks and posted on the Internet. Thus, we have no occasion to snoop. But this was an unusual situation, what with Mr. Schwartz's strange behavior this evening."

For a split second, John Smith's eyes seemed to glitter. "Schwartz? What happened?"

Judith had forgotten that the Smiths weren't present when Barney had panicked at the sight of Joe's holster. "It's a long story," Judith said, with a quick glance at her husband.

Joe nodded once. "The incident forced me to search Schwartz's room. I made a mistake, and went into yours. Let's leave it at that. You can have the gun back when you leave. It's perfectly legal to own a gun in this state."

"But it's not my gun." A thin smile played at John Smith's mouth. "Keep it. Or sell it. It's nothing to me." He gestured to Darlene, who wore a bored expression. "By the way, why was the bathroom door locked in our room?"

"Oh!" Judith was embarrassed. "I forgot to tell you. Mr. Schwartz's mother is elderly and requires privacy. There's another bathroom just outside your door in the hall. I'm so sorry I didn't mention it earlier. I promised Mrs. Schwartz she could have the connecting bathroom to herself."

"Not anymore," John Smith smirked. "Before we went out, I picked the lock. Come on, Darl, let's head for bed. We can have a nightcap up there."

Judith winced. Guests weren't officially permitted to bring liquor into the B&B, but the rule was virtually unenforceable. Given the gun issue and her own oversight about the bathroom, she let the infraction slide.

"Sure, why not?" Darlene rose from the chair, shaking out her copper curls. "G'night, all." Judith caught a whiff of jasmine as the young woman wriggled her way out of the parlor.

"Well?" sighed Judith. "What do you think?"

Joe turned out the Tiffany dragonfly lamp that sat on the small table between the wingback chairs. "I think John Smith is one slippery character who's not above picking locks and lying about guns. Unless . . . Who stayed in that room Sunday night?"

"The Coopers, from South Dakota," Judith replied. "They're in their eighties. Anyway, Phyliss goes through the drawers and everything else after guests check out, just in case they've forgotten something."

Always the gentleman, Joe stepped aside to let Judith precede him from the parlor. "Then Smith's definitely lying. I thought so all along. But I don't see what we can do about it."

"No," Judith said, then suddenly remembered the note in her pocket. "Drat. I found a slip of paper under the piano. I should have asked the guests about it. Maybe I'll just pin it on the message board by the registration book." She went to the little desk and used a pushpin to attach the note to the small piece of corkboard framed with Victorian hearts and flowers. The names—"Legs-Hoffa-Provenzano"—boldly stared out at her, and set her spine a-tingle. Hastily, she removed the note and put it in the pocket of her slacks.

"What did the note say?" Joe asked, waiting by the gate-leg table in the living room.

Damping down the inexplicable spurt of alarm, Judith lifted one shoulder as they went into the living room. "It's gibberish to me." She reached behind the table. "I'm going to unplug the coffee urn and put the cake away. There's no reason to stay up for Mr. du Turque. He may have gone to some of the local jazz clubs."

"I'll carry the urn," Joe volunteered. "Jeez, there's not much cake left."

"Good," said Judith, scooping crumbs into her hand.

"I'll give the rest to Mother. By the way, you didn't mention to the Smiths that you're a cop."

"Of course not," Joe replied, getting a grip on the urn. "They weren't here when the rest of the guests found out. It might be a good thing if Mr. and Mrs. Smith don't know. You said they aren't mingling with the rest of this bunch."

"True," Judith agreed, leading the way into the kitchen. Then, as she covered the cake with cellophane wrap, she turned to Joe. "Why wouldn't John Smith admit having a gun? It's not as if we'd fine him or report him. We'd just hang onto it until they checked out."

"Good question," Joe said, pouring out what was left of the coffee. "That's why I didn't tell him I was a cop."

It rained again during the night. When Judith got up at six o'clock she felt sluggish. Maybe it was the weather: As a native Pacific Northwesterner, rain during the fall, winter, and early spring didn't bother her. But in June, gray skies and relentless drizzle could get depressing.

Or perhaps she was tired. Because they waited up for the Smiths, she and Joe hadn't gotten to bed until almost midnight. Judith didn't feel rested. Indeed, she had a sense of having her sleep interrupted, though she didn't recall waking up during the night.

Listlessly, she prepared breakfast for the guests as well as for Joe, Gertrude, and herself. The fare would be simpler than usual. Instead of pancakes or waffles, Judith would serve toast, rolls, an egg dish, ham, fresh fruit, three kinds of juice, and coffee and tea. The informal sit-down breakfast for guests in the dining room started at eight, though often stragglers didn't show up until going on ten.

Joe, also looking sleepy, came down at seven, his usual time. He seemed uncharacteristically quiet as they ate, concentrating on the morning paper.

"The front door was unlocked this morning when I went out to get the paper," Judith remarked, pouring more coffee. "Mr. du Turque must have forgotten."

"Remind him," Joe murmured over the local news section.

"I will." Judith removed her plate and put it in the dishwasher, then began to put Gertrude's meal together. "Mother won't like this egg dish with the cheese and bacon in it. She'll say it's too fancy for breakfast. Scrambled eggs are about as exotic as she likes."

"Then give her the ham and scramble some eggs," Joe suggested.

"No. It's a matter of principle. Though," Judith allowed, filling a carafe with coffee, "it's hard enough these days to get her to eat anything wholesome. She'd probably prefer the rest of the cake."

At the back door, the screen rattled, signaling Sweetums's arrival. "He's early," Judith remarked. "That probably means Mother is up and has already thrown him out."

Sweetums entered the hallway looking wet and bedraggled. He mewed angrily, and tried to claw Judith's leg. "You look like you've been out all night," she said in reproach, then reached down to pet the cat. "Joe, we've got to fix that little flap out here so Sweetums can get in when Mother ignores him. The pet door has been broken since Memorial Day when Auntie Vance tried to kick Sweetums and got her foot stuck."

"Okay, come the weekend," Joe said without looking up from the paper. "Tell me about it then."

Judith hurriedly got out a can of cat food and poured milk into a bowl. Sweetums was shaking himself, sending wet drops all over Judith's shoes. She reached down to wipe them off and let out a little shriek.

"Yikes! I must have cut myself opening that cat food." Peering at her hand, Judith started for the sink, then stopped. "It's not me. It must be Sweetums." She grabbed the cat and pulled him onto her knee. "Did you get into another fight, you bellicose little beast?"

Sure enough, there was blood on Sweetums's fur. But upon closer inspection, Judith saw no sign of a wound. "Weird," she breathed. "Where did this come from?" Setting the cat back on his feet, she quickly washed her hands. "Could it be Mother?" Her voice had risen. "Good God, what now?" Without bothering to grab Gertrude's tray, Judith raced out of the house.

Oblivious to the rain, she ran down the porch stairs and along the walk to the toolshed. She got only halfway when she saw a huddled form in front of Gertrude's door.

"Mother!" Judith screamed. "Mother!"

Judith fell to the ground, reaching out to the prone figure. Then she blinked and uttered a strangled cry.

It wasn't Gertrude Grover who lay at the toolshed's door. It was John Smith, and judging from the blood that soaked his body, he was very dead.

FIVE

JOE HEARD JUDITH scream. He came tearing out of the house, holster in one hand, .38 Special in the other.

"What the hell . . . ?" he shouted.

Judith swallowed hard. "It's John Smith. He's dead."

Joe let out a stream of obscenities. The toolshed door flew open, revealing Gertrude, leaning on her walker.

"What's all this caterwauling?" she demanded. "Hey!" she snapped, narrowing her eyes at Joe. "How come *you're* here? Where's my breakfast?"

"Mother . . ." Judith began, struggling to her feet.

Gertrude finally looked past her walker and down at the ground. "Who's this bozo? He doesn't look so good."

"It's one of my guests," Judith replied, aware that her knees would hardly hold her up. "I think he's dead."

"Hunh," Gertrude snorted. "That'll make two of us if you don't get my food out here, dummy. *Where's my breakfast?*"

Joe, who had knelt beside the body, turned a grim face up to his wife. "You're right. He's dead, and has been for a while." Rising, Joe put the gun in its holster, then glanced around the yard. "I doubt if the killer is hiding in the shrubbery. Go in the house, Jude-girl. Call nine-one-one. I'll wait here.''

''*Wait*?'' Gertrude banged her walker on the threshold. ''Get this stiff out of here, you moron! I can't have a carcass lying around my front door! What next, Armenian war refugees?''

''Mrs. G.,'' Joe began, never having felt up to calling Gertrude anything more intimate, ''why don't you go back inside and . . .''

Judith didn't hear the rest. She was forcing herself to move as quickly as possible, though her feet felt like lead. Finally reaching the hallway by the back stairs, she was startled to see Pete and Marie Santori in their bathrobes.

''What's going on?'' Marie demanded in a harsh voice.

''Ah . . .'' Judith fumbled for words. ''There's been an accident. I'll tell you later.'' Tripping over her own feet, she made it to the phone and dialed the emergency number.

Pete and Marie didn't budge. ''What kind of accident?'' Marie asked in that same sharp tone after Judith hung up. ''Did you tell whoever you called just now that somebody is dead?''

Catching her breath, Judith nodded. ''I'm afraid so. Mr. Smith. I found him outside.''

''I'll be damned,'' Pete said in a tone that bordered on awe. Then, to Judith's amazement, he turned away and covered his face.

''Relax, Pete,'' Marie said, patting her husband's arm. ''It's nothing to do with us. Isn't that right, Yummy-wummy?'' The treacle had suddenly resurfaced in Marie's voice.

''I'd better go outside,'' Judith said, more to herself than to the Santoris. ''Excuse me.'' She brushed past Pete and Marie, grabbing jackets off their pegs as she went.

Joe had managed to get Gertrude back inside, though not without a fight. His mother-in-law had wedged her walker across the threshold, the removal of which had required some strongarm tactics on Joe's part. When Judith returned, Gertrude's muffled curses could be heard from inside the toolshed. Joe was standing in the rain, looking angry and out of breath.

"I don't need this," he panted. "A freaking homicide in my own backyard! How the hell did this happen?"

"To you?" Judith said meekly, trying to avoid looking at the body. "Or to John Smith?"

Joe sighed as Judith handed him one of the jackets. "Both. Mr. Smith, by the way, was shot in the head and chest at close range."

"Oh!" Judith almost dropped her own jacket. "Then he was murdered?"

"Come on, Jude-girl! What else?" Joe's green eyes flashed in anger. "Here I am, thirty-odd years on the force, wanting to end my career peacefully. Even if I'd transferred out of Homicide—which I considered—I couldn't have avoided *this*." His hand swept over the inert body of John Smith.

Judith knew what her husband was thinking. "It's not my fault," she said hastily as sirens wailed in the distance. "I can't pick and choose who stays at the B&B."

Joe didn't reply. He had turned away from Judith, gazing through the rain at the driveway. Sure enough, two patrol cars pulled in almost immediately.

Neither Judith nor Joe knew the officers who were on duty. Mercedes Berger and Darnell Hicks looked very young to Judith, and not long out of the police academy. Indeed, they seemed astonished when Joe informed them there was a homicide victim in the backyard.

"It's so quiet here on Heraldsgate Hill," Darnell murmured.

"We thought it was just a break-in," Mercedes said under her breath.

Darnell, whose cocoa-colored face looked as if it didn't need to be shaved more than once a week, edged nervously toward the body. "Ooof!" he exclaimed, recoiling. "Careful, Merce, there's . . . blood."

"Oh!" Mercedes put a hand over her mouth, big blue eyes staring at John Smith's inert form.

Judith heard Joe heave a sigh. She knew that even the most raw of police officers were prepared for violence before they hit the streets. Perhaps this was the first time that Berger and Hicks had faced reality.

"Rookies?" Joe asked. "How come you're on the same beat?"

"Mike O'Shea is in the hospital," Darnell replied.

"This neighborhood usually doesn't have real crime," Mercedes said.

Joe regarded the pair with irritation that evolved quickly into pity. Maybe, Judith thought, he was remembering his own rookie days as a cop. The sight of his first dead teenager, a drug overdose, had sent him straight to a bar and into the arms of the woman who became the first Mrs. Flynn.

Joe flashed his badge. "I know the drill, okay? So relax. I live here, and this is my wife." He introduced Judith. The ritual seemed to calm the rookie cops. "Now," Joe went on, "here's what we do . . ."

The medics and the ambulance had arrived. Judith went down the driveway to meet them. To her dismay, one of the medics was Ray Kinsella, who had shown up at Hillside Manor when a fortune teller had met an untimely end in Judith's dining room. Ray had also been called in four years later when a neighbor had been murdered.

"Mrs. Flynn?" Ray said, peering at Judith through the rain. "Don't tell me . . ."

Judith gave an impatient shake of her head. "I'm afraid so. It's one of our guests. He's been shot dead."

Kinsella signaled to the other emergency personnel, apparently conveying the message that there wasn't any rush. "Jeez," he said, joining Judith as they walked back to the toolshed, "do you know what happened?"

"No. Joe's here, he's briefing the patrol officers. They're a bit . . . green." Judith gave Ray a sickly smile.

Ray nodded. "Berger and Hicks? Nice kids. I've worked with them a couple of times on traffic accidents at the bottom of the hill."

Joe was still talking to the rookies. Huddled against the backdrop of a wet, gray morning, the trio struck Judith as dismal. John Smith's corpse didn't do much to brighten the scene.

Gertrude had finally shut up. Realizing that she couldn't tend to her mother with the crowd gathering around the corpse, Judith spoke in Ray's ear. "I should go back inside. I have a full house, and already two of the guests are wondering what's going on."

Ray offered Judith a commiserating smile. "You've got some grim business to take care of. I'll check in with Joe, just so he knows I'm on the job."

In the kitchen, Judith could hear noises overhead. She peeked into the dining room, but it was empty. A further look into the living room revealed Mal and Bea Malone, drinking coffee from the big urn that Judith had returned to the gateleg table earlier.

"Who's sick?" Bea asked from the windowseat. "It looks like you got visitors."

Judith glanced through the bay window where the ambulance and the medic van were parked alongside the house. "I'm afraid Mr. Smith is dead," she replied. "My husband and I will explain when everyone gathers for breakfast."

"Smith?" echoed Mal as an unmarked city car pulled into view. "Which one is that?"

"I don't think you met the Smiths," Judith said, watching two plainclothes detectives get out of the white car. "Oh, dear!" She put a hand to her bosom. "I must tell Mrs. Smith! My brain's turned to mush."

Hurrying up the stairs, Judith rushed to Room Three and knocked hard. There was no immediate response. She knocked again. Still, no sound could be heard. After a third fruitless try, Judith got out her master key and unlocked the door.

Darlene Smith was lying in the middle of the queen-sized bed, snoring softly. Wincing, Judith approached the young woman and gently shook her by the shoulder.

"Mrs. Smith? Darlene?"

The young woman nestled further under the covers, a half-smile curving her lips. Without makeup, Darlene Smith looked very young, even vulnerable. Her copper curls were tangled, and a sprinkling of freckles covered her cheeks.

Judith gave the young woman another shake. "Wake up, please," she urged. "Darlene?"

Darlene gave a little jump. "Whaaa . . . ? Laaa . . . ?" Eyes still closed, she frowned and rolled over, burying her face in the pillow.

"Darlene!" Judith was shouting, pounding on the mattress. "Wake up!"

At last, Darlene opened her hazel eyes. For just an instant, Judith saw terror in them. *Does she know?* Judith wondered in amazement.

But Darlene was sitting up, shaking herself, rubbing at her eyes, and making small, animal-like noises. "What's up?" she mumbled, achieving coherence. Then, as her gaze focused, she stared at Judith. "It's *you*? Mrs . . . ?"

"Flynn," Judith put in quickly. There was no point in holding back the grisly announcement. "Darlene, I have some very bad news. John's been shot."

The hazel eyes widened. Clutching the sheet to her partially exposed bosom, Darlene gave a single shake of her head. Her mouth formed the word *No*, but no sound came out.

"I'm so sorry, Darlene," Judith went on after taking a deep breath. "I'm afraid your husband is dead."

Darlene burst into laughter, a high-pitched sound that jarred Judith. *Hysteria*, she thought, and picked up an almost empty glass from the nightstand. "This looks stale," Judith said. "I'll get more from the bathroom sink."

Darlene, however, shook her head. She seemed to be making a tremendous effort to get herself under control. At last, she calmed down, and regarded Judith with a dismayed expression.

"Sorry. Not the reaction you expected, right?"

"Well . . . You never know." Judith set the glass on the

nightstand. "Are you sure I can't get you something?"

Darlene shook her head. "I already got it," she said enigmatically. "Can you go away now?"

"Of course," Judith said, though she couldn't hide her surprise. "Let me know if you need anything." Starting from the room, she glanced at the divan with its cut-velvet rose motif. In years gone by, it had been kept in the front parlor, where Grandma Grover referred to it as "the lounge." Grandma had often laid down in the late afternoon "to rest my eyes," as she had phrased it. Now it served mainly as an added fillip to the more expensive Room Three. But for once, the divan had been put to use: sheets, a blanket, and a pillow covered most of the cut-velvet upholstery. Judith wondered why.

But this was not the time to ask. She left without another word, and as she closed the door, Judith heard Darlene erupt into another bout of laughter.

The Schwartzes were coming out of Room Four as Judith started down the stairs. Turning, she saw mother and son staring at her with curious expressions.

"What's all the ruckus next door?" Barney asked.

"We heard sirens a few minutes ago," Minerva put in. "They woke us up. What kind of a neighborhood is this? I thought you said it was quiet."

Judith swallowed hard. "I did. It is. Usually. But this morning . . ." She made a futile gesture with one hand. "Please. Come downstairs, and I'll explain to everyone in just a few minutes."

By the time Judith had breakfast ready to serve, Roland du Turque, the Schwartzes, and the preschool teachers had arrived. Apparently, the Malones had passed on the news about John Smith's death. Naturally, the guests were agog. Mal and Bea, however, were not fazed, since they were already stuffing themselves with toast, ham, and eggs. Since Pete and Marie Santori had already appeared earlier, Judith assumed they were getting dressed.

"Please, not now—I'll be right back," she promised amid a barrage of questions in the dining room.

Berger and Hicks had given way to the homicide detectives who had arrived in the unmarked city car. Judith recognized the two men from departmental functions, but she didn't recall their names.

Joe, looking wet and irritable, introduced her. "My wife," he said in a tone that suggested Judith might as well be the Grim Reaper. "Do you remember J. J. Martinez and Rich Goldman?"

"Of course," Judith said, as the names clicked in. Jesus Jorge Martinez, a wiry, intense man of about fifty, had been one of Joe's first partners in Homicide; Richard Goldman was a relative newcomer, not yet thirty, with an eager air still undampened by age and experience.

"A real shame," J. J. remarked, with a swift, anxious glance at John Smith's body. "You mind?" he asked Joe.

"Mind?" Joe grimaced. "Do I mind having a stiff in the backyard? Or do I mind you and Rich taking over? Hell, J. J., it's all yours. Besides, I'm a suspect, right?" For the first time, a spark of humor surfaced in Joe's green eyes.

J. J. winced. "Well—technically. Right." He cleared his throat. "The M.E.'ll be along pretty soon. You and Mrs. Flynn want to go back inside?"

"I'll wait," Joe said, then turned to Judith. "Go ahead, feed the guests. I'll . . ."

A fierce pounding resounded from inside the toolshed. Everyone turned, including J. J., who had jumped right off the wet ground. "What's that?" he asked in alarm. "Somebody in there?"

"No," Joe replied with a straight face. "Ignore it."

"It's my mother," Judith snapped, pushing past Joe and trying to step around the corpse. "Mother! Can you wait?"

"I already did," Gertrude yelled back. "That horse's behind you call a husband locked me in!"

J. J. had grabbed Joe's arm. "Is that a witness? Or a suspect?"

Joe brightened. "Both?"

Judith glanced over her shoulder. "Neither. It's *my mother*," she repeated. "She hasn't had her breakfast, and she's upset."

Rich Goldman exchanged a worried look with J. J. Martinez. "We can't move the body until the M.E. gets here. Does this . . . building have a back door?"

"No," Judith retorted. "And it's not possible for Mother to get through a window. She's very elderly and quite frail."

"Is she armed?" Rich asked, his earnest young face still troubled.

"Of course not!" Judith couldn't quite get around John Smith's body. "Oh, drat! I might as well go back to the . . ."

"Moron!" Gertrude shouted. "Idiot! Open this door or I'll torch the place!"

Judith paused. She wouldn't put it past her mother to start a fire. She'd done it before, in extreme circumstances. "Mother, please!" Judith begged. "Try to relax. We'll take care of you in just a few minutes."

"Take care of me, huh? How? Like that pinhead on my doorstep? What's going on around here, mass murders?"

Fortunately, another city car entered the drive. "The M.E.," Joe breathed. "Get back inside, Jude-girl. I'll deal with the old bat."

"She's not an old bat," Judith asserted as she headed for the house. "You be nice, Joe!" she warned from the porch steps.

The Santoris were seated at the dining room table when Judith returned. Popping more bread in the toaster and dishing up more ham and bacon, she listened to the snatches of conversation that floated over and under the three-quarter swinging door.

"We should leave at once," Minerva Schwartz was saying. "This isn't a reputable place."

"We paid in advance," Sandi said. "Preschool teachers don't get paid much. We can't afford to waste our money."

"This John Smith is nothing to us," Mal Malone declared. "What do you say, Bea? Go or stick around?"

"I don't like it here," Bea answered. "Let's pack as soon as we eat. This trip has been a disaster."

"Where's Mrs. Smith?" asked Roland du Turque. "The poor woman must be distraught."

"Oh, yes!" exclaimed Marie Santori. "If anything happened to my Tootsie-wootsie, I'd . . ."

The toast was done. As Judith carried the plates of food into the dining room, everyone went silent.

"Mrs. Flynn," said Roland in what sounded like relief. "Can you tell us what's going on?"

Judith grimaced. "I'd prefer to wait for my husband to fill you in."

Barney leaned around his mother. "Because he's a cop?"

"Yes." If word of Joe's profession hadn't already reached the other guests, it was pointless now to keep up the deception. "He's worked Homicide for most of his career. He's consulting with the other detectives and the M.E."

"But you can tell us about Mr. Smith, can't you?" Pam put in.

Judith started to hedge, then relented. "I can't tell you much. Unfortunately, I was the one who found his body." She explained the situation, adding that the victim probably had been shot a few hours earlier. "Joe—Mr. Flynn—will ask if any of you heard or saw anything unusual."

Glances were exchanged around the table. Pete Santori was the first to speak. "Marie and I heard a commotion this morning. It woke us up. But nothing during the night. Right, Sweet-treat?"

Marie nodded vigorously. "It was screaming. You, probably, Mrs. Flynn."

"Probably." Judith scanned the faces of her other guests. Maybe it was fear, maybe it was resentment, maybe it was because the hour was still early—but it struck Judith that everyone gathered around the oval table seemed guarded.

"Anyone else?" she prodded. "Perhaps you woke up at some point, but didn't know why?"

"That mattress bothered me," Bea complained. "I don't feel rested."

"I was up twice," Minerva acknowledged. "My age, you know. Bladders become uncertain."

"Sandi snores," Pam said, poking her companion. "She won't admit it, but she does."

"Do not," Sandi retorted. "Anyway, you wiggle a lot."

"I stayed awake for a long time," Roland said. "I'd heard some wonderful jazz riffs at one of your downtown clubs. They kept playing in my head."

Judith heard Joe come into the kitchen. She turned, seeing J. J. and Rich behind him.

"Go ahead," Joe said to Judith over the top of the swinging door. "The body's being removed. Go ahead, you can feed the old vulture in the toolshed now."

"Joe . . ." But the reproach died on Judith's lips as he moved past her into the dining room.

"Ladies and gentlemen," Joe said in his most professional voice, "meet J. J. Martinez and Rich Goldman, Metro Homicide. They want to ask you a few questions. The interviews will be conducted in the front parlor."

"Interrogations?" cried Bea. "Hey!"

"Sez who?" muttered Mal.

"We were just checking out," Barney declared, getting out of his chair so fast that he pulled some of the tablecloth with him and upset a cream pitcher.

"Come on," Pete drawled, "we're honeymooners. Doesn't that make us immune?"

"Wild," breathed Sandi.

"Yucky," said Pam.

"Now I've lost it." Roland's mellow voice was wistful. "The phrase, that is, from last night."

Judith didn't stay around for the arguments, which she knew her guests would lose. Of course, she'd also lose the guests. It wasn't likely that this bunch would become repeat customers.

She did, however, hear Joe deliver what must have been bad news. "Someone mentioned leaving. I don't think that will be possible for a while. I'm not in charge here, but as of now, you're all suspects. So sit back, relax, and enjoy your stay at Hillside Manor."

As Judith carried her mother's breakfast out the back door, an eruption of protests, squeals, and curses followed her.

Similar invective greeted her at the toolshed. Gertrude was fit to be tied, among other things. Judith's mother was in no mood to listen to explanations or anything that resembled reason. The blame for her tardy meal rested solely with that boob, Joe Flynn—or, as Gertrude veered off on another tangent—with Judith and her dumbbell guests. Either way, there was a conspiracy to deprive a helpless old lady of her breakfast.

Judith suffered in silence. For once, she had more serious problems than her mother's harangue. As if to emphasize that point, Judith flinched as she exited the toolshed and walked around the outline that the police had made of John Smith's body.

Joe was in the kitchen, making a second pot of coffee. "I'm not going in to work until later," he said, his irritation with Judith apparently quelled. "It's in our—yours and mine—best interests to keep a handle on this."

"Of course, Joe," Judith said meekly as she heard muffled voices in the dining room. "By the way—did you check Mr. Smith's ID?"

"Oh, yes," Joe replied, settling into his favorite captain's chair. "He didn't have any."

"*What*?" Judith half-fell into a chair on the other side of the kitchen table.

Joe nodded. "That's right. He had a wallet, money intact, but no driver's license, no credit cards, zip. How did he pay for the room?"

Judith tried to remember. "I'm not sure. Most people use credit cards, but some send in a money order or check."

She got up and went to the computer. "I can tell by looking up the reservation. Let me see . . ." She clicked the mouse a few times, then scratched her head. "Hmmm. I'm getting that same problem I had last week. Now what did Renie tell me to do . . . ?"

Joe, who hated computers despite his occasional dependence upon them at work, ignored the remark. "What's with Mrs. Smith?" he asked.

"She was hysterical . . . I think." Judith tried deleting extra space, as Renie had showed her. Nothing happened. "Anyway, she wanted to be left alone. You can hardly blame her."

Joe jumped out of his chair. Without a word, he ran to the back stairs and disappeared around the corner. Judith considered following him, but didn't want to lose track of what was happening—or not happening—with the computer. She was still facing a blank screen.

Looking up at the old schoolhouse clock, she noted that it was almost nine. Renie might be up, though not necessarily lucid. Judith decided to take a chance and call her cousin. If for no other reason, the news of a murder at the B&B wouldn't keep.

But before she could get to the phone, Joe came tearing back down the stairs.

"She's gone!" His face was very red and he looked furious. "How the hell did she get out of here without you noticing?"

Judith clapped a hand to her head. "I don't know! But I've been in and out . . . The car! Is that gone, too?"

"Hell, yes! I looked out the upstairs window." Joe clenched and unclenched his fists, then rushed out of the kitchen, presumably to inform J. J. Martinez and Rich Goldman.

With a sinking feeling, Judith returned to the computer. As far as she could tell, Darlene's presence wasn't the only thing missing from Hillside Manor. All the reservations for Monday, June twentieth, were also gone, as if they had dropped into a deep, dark, bottomless pit.

SIX

EVEN AS JUDITH sputtered and muttered, Joe dragged her out through the dining room and past the curious gazes of the guests. In the entry hall, he stabbed at the register.

"License number," he said as Rich Goldman came in from the front parlor. "Quick!"

Judith had already turned the register to Tuesday. She flipped back a page, stared, fingered the page itself, and gasped. "It's gone! Somebody tore out the Monday registrations."

Joe swore so loudly that Rich jumped. "What about the computer?" Joe demanded.

"That's what I was trying to tell you," Judith replied, tight-lipped and annoyed. "Everything's been deleted. At least as far as I can tell. Plus, the backup disk is gone. It was right there on the counter yesterday."

Joe turned to Rich. "You're young, you must know computers. See if my wife screwed up."

The accusation further riled Judith. "I did no such thing," she said coldly. "It was all there yesterday when I entered the Malones into the computer."

Joe ignored the denial, hustling a bewildered Rich Goldman out to the kitchen. Judith started to follow, but retreated a couple of steps. The door to the front parlor was open just a crack. She peered inside to see who was first on the interview list.

J. J. Martinez was pacing the area in front of the small hearth. Leaning forward in one of the wingback chairs was Barney Schwartz. ". . . cross-country tour," Barney was saying. "Ma's never been out west."

Judith slipped into the living room where an extension phone sat on a cherrywood pedestal table. She hurriedly dialed her cousin's number.

Renie answered in a vague voice, which was not a good sign. "Can you come over?" Judith asked without preamble.

"Come over where?" Renie yawned.

"To my house." Judith paused. "Are you awake?"

"Mmm . . . In a way."

"Are you up?"

"Not quite."

"Coz, it's almost nine-thirty!"

"Is it?" Renie made some muffled noises. Judith envisioned her cousin struggling to get a look at the clock. "You're right. So what?"

"So can you come? It's really, really important." Judith's voice had a taut edge.

Renie yawned again. "Have your guests left any food?"

"I think so. Please?"

"Give me fifteen minutes," Renie said, somewhat more alert. "I got to bed late. Bill and I had a key club meeting last night."

Despite her overwhelming anxieties, Judith was taken aback. "Key club? What are you talking about?"

"You know—mate-swapping. It's another hobby we've taken up since Bill retired. See you." Renie hung up.

Maybe Renie was kidding; maybe Judith was crazy. Her head spinning, Judith went out into the kitchen where Rich was apologizing profusely.

"This is a PC—I use a Mac at work, just like you do," the young detective explained to Joe.

"Mac, schmac," Joe growled. "I only use the damned thing when I have to."

"Renie's coming," Judith said. "She may be able to help."

Joe didn't look optimistic. "I don't suppose you noticed the license number on the Smiths' car."

Judith grimaced. "No—just that it had New York plates and that it had three numbers and three letters, like ours in this state."

Joe made a face. "Swell. What kind of car was it?"

"Black?" Judith tried to visualize the Smith vehicle that had so recently been parked at the curb between Hillside Manor and the neighboring Ericson driveway. "Dark, anyway. Very dark."

"Make?" Joe had turned deadpan.

Her husband's professional demeanor was getting tiresome. She paid no attention to makes and models of cars, figuring she was lucky to find her own Subaru in Falstaff's parking lot. "Smaller than a bus, bigger than a bike. Wheels, windows, and whoop-de-doo." Seeing the fire bank in Joe's green eyes, Judith grew more serious. "It had a symbol like some kind of a medal with wings. Red and gold, I think."

Joe and Rich exchanged swift glances. "A Chrysler, maybe," said Joe, giving Rich a shove towards the back door. "Come on, let's radio this in from your car so we can get out an APB."

Feeling insignificant, Judith brought a fresh carafe of coffee out to the dining room. Minerva was now absent, apparently having followed her son as the next interviewee. Barney was nowhere in sight. Judith poked her head around the corner and saw him sitting in the living room, leafing impatiently through an auto racing magazine.

"This is crazy," Bea Malone declared. "Why can't we go? These cops are making us feel like a bunch of cheap crooks."

Pete Santori laughed, an unexpected, rather nasty sound. His bride, however, spoke in a reasonable voice. "The police have to follow procedure,'' Marie said. ''This B&B is now a crime scene, and we're witnesses. Maybe it won't take too long.''

''Ha!'' Mal snorted. ''Cops are dumb. They won't figure this out for months. If they ever do,'' he added with a dark glance at Judith.

''My husband,'' Judith said with dignity, ''has one of the best arrest and conviction rates on the force.''

''All things are relative.'' The comment came from Roland du Turque, and was offered softly, almost apologetically.

''I think it's kind of exciting,'' Pam asserted. ''Though we probably can't use it for sharing time, can we, Sandi?''

Sandi giggled. ''I guess not. We can't share our adventures at the Hexagon, either.''

Both of the preschool teachers embarked on a fit of the giggles. Somehow, the merriment sounded hollow. Judith went into the kitchen just as a wide-eyed Renie came through the back door.

''I can't believe it!'' Renie gasped. ''Joe just told me what happened! Coz, are you okay?''

Judith nodded a bit uncertainly. ''I don't think the horror has quite set in. This has been a terrible, terrible morning.''

Though sympathetic, Renie gave Judith a wry smile. ''But not a first.''

Judith sighed. ''No. But the fortune teller murder seems so long ago. And because of the circumstances, we knew the killer was one of the people in the B&B. This time, it could be anybody. John Smith was shot outside.''

Renie's brown eyes narrowed. ''Do you really believe it was someone prowling the neighborhood?''

''Well . . .'' Judith uttered a weak laugh. ''No. I guess not. This group of guests is all wrong. Oh, maybe not *all* of them. But there's something more than odd about *most* of them. Which is why I wanted you to come over.''

After serving Renie the last of the egg dish, Judith explained about the deletion in the computer and the missing page from the register. "Do you think you could retrieve it?"

"Where's your backup disk?" Renie asked.

Judith grimaced. "It's gone, too."

"Great." Renie looked dismayed. "Even if you found it, whoever took it might have erased that, too."

Judith's expression was pleading. "Can you at least check the computer for me?"

"You've got to get a better system, a program, a more efficient way of handling this stuff," Renie declared. "The half-assed method you've been using isn't practical, even when you're not dealing with a homicide." She sat down and began clicking the mouse. "This way, it's not that hard to dump something from the computer, especially if you know what you're doing. Which, alas, you do not. I'll check, though."

But Renie came up empty. "Sorry," she apologized, leaning back in the chair at Judith's makeshift desk. "I give up."

Judith's hands were clenched into fists of frustration. "Why? To cover up an address or phone number?"

"Maybe." Renie stood up and removed a pack of cigarettes from her purse. "What about checks and credit cards? You have records, don't you?"

"I can't remember who used what," Judith replied, not bothering to reprimand Renie for lighting up. "Of course, I can get copies of the checks from the bank, and the credit card receipts are in my file. Everybody paid in advance, except the Malones, and they used cash."

Renie frowned through a blue haze of smoke. "So why dump the reservations and tear out the register page? It doesn't make sense."

"None of it does." Judith sank into one of the captain's chairs. "I wish I could listen in on the interviews. I feel like a prisoner in my own house."

Renie had wandered over to the swinging door. "The teachers are still in the dining room. So is Roland du Turque. But the detectives must have finished with the rest of them.'' She moved back by the sink and looked out through the kitchen window. ''Where's Arlene? Has she shown up yet? She'll love your latest fatality.''

Judith was well aware of how, despite the kindest of hearts, her friend and neighbor thrived on disaster. ''The Rankerses left early this morning to visit some cousins for a few days. They must have taken off before I found the body. Arlene will be sorry she missed this.''

Renie looked surprised. ''Carl and Arlene are away? Drat. Bill and I were thinking of inviting them to join the key club. Carl would be great. He has all the right equipment.''

''Coz!'' Judith was aghast. ''You have to explain this to me. It simply blows me away that . . .''

Bea Malone had entered the kitchen. ''The coffee urn is dry as a bone. In fact, it's smoking. You want to refill it or call the fire department? They're about the only emergency crew that hasn't shown up yet.''

''Oh!'' Judith whirled around. ''I'll be right there.''

Retrieving the urn, Judith refilled it, then suggested that she and Renie join the guests in the living room. ''We might learn something,'' Judith murmured.

As they passed through the dining room, Judith noted that Sandi and Pam were the only ones remaining at the table.

''Crazy, huh?'' Sandi remarked.

''Is it okay to tinkle?'' asked Pam.

''What?'' Judith paused on the threshold. ''Oh—yes, of course. The bathroom's right off the entry hall, remember?''

The scene that greeted the cousins was like a tableau from some dark Russian play. In the bleak, gray morning light, the Malones huddled on one of the sofas, Minerva Schwartz stood like a sentry in front of the big bay window, her son sat on the windowseat with his head bowed, and, on the other sofa, the Santoris held hands and exchanged whispered words.

''I'll be serving lunch around twelve-thirty,'' Judith announced, surprising herself as well as her guests. "That is, if you can't leave the house, I'm more than willing to provide food. No extra charge."

To Judith's amazement, Bea Malone burst into tears. "I can't stand it! First Corelli, now this. The whole world's out to get us. I want to die."

Mal cradled his wife in his arms. "Hey, hon, calm down. We're okay, we're fine. We'll be out of here by tomorrow."

"Who's Corelli?" It was Barney Schwartz who asked the question with something akin to alarm.

"Never mind," Mal growled. "Keep your snout out of this."

"Now just a minute . . ." Barney was on his feet, punching a fist into his other hand. "You can't talk to me like that."

"Mr. Schwartz," Roland exclaimed softly. "Your poor hands—how did you lose those two fingers?"

Whirling on Roland, Barney hid his hands behind his back. "What kind of a sick question is that? Why do *you* care?"

Roland, who had just come from the front parlor, backed off. "I'm sorry, Mr. Schwartz. It's just that I love the piano so much, and it struck me as terribly sad that someone who wanted to play might be . . . impeded."

Barney snorted. "I'm no music lover." He turned to Minerva. "Am I, Ma?"

Minerva lifted her chin. "You certainly never took to the classics, though you were exposed to all my fine Wagnerian recordings and an occasional touring performance."

"Ma . . ." Barney gave his mother a sheepish look. "All those fat women yelling their heads off with wings on their hats. Besides, they sang so long that my butt went to sleep before the rest of me did."

Marie looked up from her place next to Pete on the sofa. "Don't you live near Detroit, Barney? How about that Motown sound?"

"The Supremes were okay," Barney acknowledged. "But that was a long time ago."

Roland cleared his throat. "Historically, the Motown sound—specifically, Motown Records—was important because their artists' popularity created a new enthusiasm for so-called black music and consistently put their songs on the best-seller charts."

"Really." Pete sounded bored. "Is the coffee ready yet?"

"Not quite," Judith answered as Roland quietly moved the length of the living room and sat down at the piano. Seeing him at the bench reminded her of the piece of paper she'd found the previous night. "Did anyone misplace some notes?" she asked.

"Notes?" Roland fingered a chord. "What kind of notes?"

"Just . . . names," Judith replied. "On a slip of paper that had been torn out of a small spiral notebook."

"What were the names?" asked Marie, looking faintly disturbed.

Judith had left the paper on her dresser. "I don't recall exactly. I think one of them was Hoffa." She uttered a feeble laugh.

"Hoffa?" Barney echoed. "What about him?"

"We don't know any Hoffas," Mal declared.

Bea, who had recovered from her bout of tears, gave a disgusted shake of her head. "Heck, no. Wasn't he some kind of union crook?"

"Teamsters," said Pete. "Hoffa disappeared several years ago. He was probably murdered."

"Tough," Mal grunted, then scowled at Judith. "He wasn't staying here, was he?"

Before Judith could utter an indignant denial, she saw Phyliss Rackley standing in the entrance to the living room. The cleaning woman's sausage curls were practically standing on end and her face was a bright pink.

"I quit," she said, and stalked back into the dining room.

"Phyliss!" Judith rushed after her. "Wait. Let me explain . . ."

But Phyliss was vehemently shaking her head. "Godless doings, murder, blood lust, pillage, and the Lord only knows what else. I tell you, it's that cat. He's in league with the Evil One."

"Phyliss, please." Judith tried to take the cleaning woman's hand, but she yanked it away.

"Don't add lies to the list of sins. I can't be around such infamy. Who knows, I could be next. That cat is always trying to put me under a spell. He wants me to do bad things, like fornicate and tap dance in short skirts."

"Phyliss . . ." Judith felt depleted. "Okay, let me write you a check." She led the way into the kitchen. "Who would you recommend as a replacement?"

"Replacement?" Phyliss seemed taken aback. "I'd never let anyone I know work here. This is Babylon, Sodom and Gomorrah, a den of iniquity. Better watch out, all you who enter here."

"All right." Judith feigned indifference as she started to write a check. "I'll look in the classifieds, especially the Heraldsgate Hill weekly. It comes out tomorrow. Thanks, Phyliss. 'Bye."

"*What*?" Phyliss squawked. "Thanks? Goodbye? *After all these years*?"

Judith assumed a puzzled expression. "You want severance pay? A tip? A going-away gift?"

"Well . . ." Phyliss's weathered face was a mass of consternation. "No. No, 'course not. I just thought . . . well . . . maybe you *might* be able to save me."

"Hmm." Judith concealed a smile. "And all these years, I thought *you* were trying to save *me*."

"I don't mean *that* way," Phyliss said, waving a bony hand. "I mean, from Satan and all these other evil-doers."

Judith sighed. "Are you saying you might consider staying on?"

Phyliss's Adam's apple bobbed. "Well . . . the Good Book says we're to be tested, doesn't it? Isn't this a test?"

If so, thought Judith, *I've passed a few already, but not always with flying colors.* "Life is a test," she replied. "I don't blame you for being frightened, Phyliss. This is a scary situation. But except for its having happened on our property, it has nothing to do with us."

Nothing to do with us. Judith had heard that phrase before, several times, from different mouths. Her guests seemed eager to disassociate themselves from the crime. Judith could hardly blame them.

"I suppose," Phyliss began, tugging her housedress down over the telltale signs of her slip, "I could at least start cleaning. But don't let that cat near me," she warned.

"You were late today," Judith remarked, putting the checkbook back in her purse. "Was something wrong?"

As ever, it was a loaded question. "Wrong?" Phyliss fanned herself. "You bet. I had to call for the doctor. I thought I was heading straight to meet the Lord."

"Did the doctor come?" asked Judith, feigning interest.

"No." Phyliss shook her head. "But he told me how to cure myself. I put my head in a grocery sack, called on the Lord, and the next thing I knew, it was a miracle. I could breathe again." The cleaning woman offered Judith her most beatific smile.

"You were hyperventilating," Judith said.

"What? I was dying, that's what I was doing," Phyliss said with her own brand of tattered dignity. "Couldn't catch my breath. Awful. A step away from the Pearly Gates."

"I'm certainly glad you're better," Judith said in her most sympathetic tone. "I won't keep you, Phyliss. We're running behind this morning, for all sorts of reasons."

"Don't remind me," Phyliss responded, and headed for the back stairs just as Renie came into the kitchen.

"She's gone?" Renie, who had no patience with either Phyliss's hypochondria or her evangelizing, let out a sigh.

"Only temporarily," Judith replied with a droll expression. "She decided not to quit after all. The next thing I know, she'll be trying to save the guests."

Renie didn't comment. "No takers on that note you found?" she asked, rinsing out her coffee mug in the sink. "The guest interviews are over. Joe and that young detective just came from upstairs. They looked annoyed."

"I suppose." Judith was searching the refrigerator's freezer compartment for luncheon possibilities. "Joe can't believe this happened so close to his retirement. I wish he'd go to work and forget about it for a few hours."

"You're right," Renie agreed, looking out through the window above the sink. "There are plenty of reminders. I see some uniforms combing the area."

Judith joined Renie at the window. Two policemen were searching the Rankerses' hedge, while a third was heading for the front of the house.

"Oh, great," Judith sighed. "I suppose they'll mark the entire property with crime scene tape. What will the neighbors think?"

Renie grinned. "That you're at it again?"

"Shut up." Judith set her jaw, then turned as J. J. Martinez poked his head into the kitchen. "Mrs. Flynn? Could I see you for a moment?"

"Oh—certainly." Judith had forgotten that she, too, would have to be interviewed. "In the front parlor?"

J. J. nodded in his jerky fashion. "Afraid so. Should have questioned you first, but Joe filled us in."

Asking Renie to keep an eye on the guests in the living room, Judith followed J. J. into the parlor. "Do you need more coffee?" Judith asked, ever the hostess. "Something to eat? I'm going to fix lunch in a little while."

"Too much caffeine already." J. J. rapped a mug with his knuckles. "Joe says it makes me jumpy. You think I'm jumpy, Mrs. Flynn?"

"Well . . ." Judith bit her lips. She figured that an extra "J" could easily be added to the detective's nickname. "Jumpy," "Jittery," or "Jerky" would work. "Maybe a little. And please call me Judith. I've known you for quite a while, J. J."

"Oh. Yes. That's true." J. J. gave Judith a surprisingly

diffident smile. Still, she couldn't help but wonder if his manner proved effective in unsettling suspects. Or at least throwing them off-guard. "Now tell me exactly how you found the victim, Mrs . . . Judith," J. J. asked in his most serious voice.

It was only eleven o'clock, yet it seemed like much longer since Judith had discovered John Smith's corpse around seven-thirty. Slowly, carefully, she recounted the circumstances, beginning with Sweetums's arrival in the kitchen.

J. J. seemed intrigued. "Does your cat always come in at the same time every morning?"

"No," Judith answered. "He's unpredictable. Besides, my mother and I sort of share him. Some nights he stays with her in the toolshed. Others, he'll come into the house and sleep in the basement. Then again, he might stay out and prowl. He's a very independent cat."

"Aren't they all?" J. J. remarked, then let Judith continue with her story. When she had finished, the detective remained silent for several moments. "You're certain you didn't hear anything during the night?" he finally asked.

"Not that I recall. What did Joe say?"

J. J. shook his head. "Same thing. Mentioned the front door was unlocked. Killer might have gone out that way. What about the thunder and lightning?"

Judith frowned. "What about it?"

"We had some. Not real close. Off in the distance, towards the mountains." J. J. drummed his fingers on the mantel. "None of the guests heard it, either. My wife and I did, but we live across the lake."

The lake separated the city from the suburbs and the foothills of the mountain range. It wasn't surprising to Judith that the ten miles between Hillside Manor and the Martinez home would make a difference.

"A silencer," Judith suggested. "Is that what might have muffled the shot?"

"Sure. Joe and Rich already found two silencers among your guests' belongings."

"What?" Judith jumped in the wingback chair.

J. J. looked equally startled. "Didn't Joe tell you? Your guests have regular handgun arsenals in their rooms."

Judith was aghast. "I knew about the gun Joe found. You mean some of the other guests also came armed?"

J. J. nodded slowly. "You bet. Santoris. Malones. Du Turque. Even the preschool teachers. Joe found silencers in Schwartz's and Smith's rooms. Santoris had a silencer for their weapon, too. Have to wonder if Mrs. Smith wasn't carrying, too."

"Good grief!" Judith sank back into the chair. "Who are these people?"

"Apt question," J. J. responded. "We're having them run through the computer. By the way, the Malones were outside during the night. Found their shoes with damp dirt on the soles. Won't say where they were or why. Might have been them who left the front door unlocked."

For almost a full minute, Judith didn't say anything. She was too overwhelmed by the enormity of J. J.'s revelation about the weapons. Then reason began to set in. "I suppose," she said slowly, "that in this day and age when people travel by car, they often bring along a gun. But what about the ones who came by plane, like Pam and Sandi?"

J. J. shrugged. "You sure they flew?"

"I saw the airporter," Judith said, then realized the fallacy. "You're right—anybody who is willing to pay for the trip can ride the airporter around town."

"And the rest?"

"The Smiths, the Schwartzes, and the Malones arrived by private car. I don't know about Mr. du Turque," Judith admitted.

"He took the train," said J. J. "But the Santoris did fly into town. I saw their airline tickets."

Judith turned a puzzled face to J. J. "Now you've got me worried about airport security."

"Don't. They're good." J. J. was pacing the parlor. "Guns can be put in the luggage compartment if you notify the airline ahead of time."

"Where is the collective arsenal?" Judith asked.

"We're holding onto everything for now, including the one Joe already took from the victim." J. J. paused. "We're done here . . . Judith." The detective gave her his self-effacing, crooked grin. "I still have to interview your mother. Want to come? I hear she's . . . elderly."

Judith smiled back at J. J. "I think you mean 'difficult.' That is, if you've been talking to my husband."

J. J. scratched his head. "That's not quite the way he put it."

Judith stood up. "I didn't think so. Shall we?"

"Sure." J. J. opened the parlor door for Judith. "Don't worry, I've tackled difficult suspects before."

Judith stopped on the threshold and gazed into J. J.'s dark eyes. "No, you haven't."

They proceeded to the toolshed.

SEVEN

GERTRUDE WAS WATCHING a talk show on TV. The sound was so loud that Judith had to shout at her mother to use the remote to turn it down. Gertrude ignored her.

"A real shocker," Gertrude said happily. "Women who married men who turned out to be the women who'd stolen their other men."

Judith hit the power button on the set; the small living room became mercifully quiet. "This is Jesus Jorge Martinez, Mother. He's a detective, and he'd like to ask you some questions."

"Haysoos?" Gertrude wrinkled her nose. "What kind of goofy name is that? Who's your brother—Hay Fever?" The old woman chuckled at her own skewed brand of humor.

"Mother . . ." Judith began, but J. J. had pulled a folding chair next to Gertrude and was sitting down.

"Mrs. Grover," he said, exuding a jittery kind of charm. "I've heard you're quite a scamp."

"Scamp?" Gertrude scowled. "At my age, the only kind of scamp I can be is a canceled one. Get it? Canceled scamp!" She slapped J. J. on the arm.

"Funny," J. J. remarked. "Now let's talk about this morning."

"Let's not." Gertrude was no longer smiling, but

glaring at Judith. "How come I'm having visitors? Nobody ever comes out to this would-be coffin to see me. Today's like a parade. Am I a float?" She broke into another grin. "Am I afloat? Or sinking fast?"

"Mother," Judith said in a voice approaching despair, "*please*. This is serious."

"How did you sleep last night?" J. J. asked, his lean face sympathetic.

"Sleep?" The question seemed to distract Gertrude. "Who sleeps at my age? Who needs to? Pretty soon, I'll be sleeping forever."

"Did you hear anything last night?" J. J. persisted.

"I don't hear so good," Gertrude replied. "What happened?"

"Umm . . ." J. J. winced. "The man who was found on your doorstep this morning?"

The small wrinkled face was a mask of confusion. "I thought it was a woman."

"No," J. J. responded softly. "It was a man."

Gertrude jabbed in the direction of the TV. "How can you tell these days? Men are women, and women are men. It wasn't like that in *my* day."

J. J. remained patient. "Did you hear anything? See anything?"

Gertrude leaned closer to J. J. "Give me a hint."

"A noise? Voices?"

Gertrude appeared to be thinking. "I'd like to buy a vowel," she said suddenly. "When's 'Wheel of Fortune' on?"

"Pardon?" J. J. looked bewildered.

"I'd like to buy a *bowel*," Gertrude said, with another glare for Judith. "My stomach's not so good. Hey, twerp, where's my breakfast?"

"You had breakfast," Judith said wearily. "It's almost time for lunch."

Awkwardly, J. J. got out of the folding chair. "Thank you, Mrs. Grover. It's been . . . nice."

"Who's next?" Gertrude asked with an anticipatory smile. "The president? The pope? Oprah?"

"I'll be back in a bit," Judith promised as she and J. J. exited the toolshed. "I warned you," she said after closing the door and scooting under the crime scene tape. "Mother's mind is very fragmented."

"Is it?"

Judith turned to look at J. J. But she said nothing.

They went back into the house.

"Look," Barney Schwartz was saying to Rich Goldman, "stop getting us all mixed up. We can't leave town, or we can't leave the house? Which is it?"

Considering that all of the guests were talking at once as they crowded around Rich by the bay window, the young detective kept his composure. "We'd appreciate it if, for now, you'd remain on the premises. Maybe by this afternoon, you'll be free to leave the B&B. But we must insist that you don't leave town. If you feel a need to spend the night somewhere else, please notify us."

"Sheesh," said Mal. "So we're stuck here for the time being?"

Rich nodded. "That's right. My partner and I are headed downtown right now, but we're leaving some uniformed officers here to watch the house. We'll get back to all of you as soon as we can."

The guests began to disperse. Mal and Bea trudged up the stairs; Barney and his mother went into the front parlor; the Santoris adjourned to the front porch; Sandi and Pam used the french doors to go out the back way; Roland du Turque remained at the piano.

The rain had lightened to a mere drizzle, with occasional breaks in the clouds. Judith returned to the kitchen, looking for Joe.

"He left," Renie said, "while you were in the tool-shed."

Judith picked up the phone directory. "I want to check

on something," she said. "Which airport shuttle is blue with white letters?"

Renie cocked an eye at the high ceiling. "Hmm . . . the one that serves Boring Field."

Judith frowned at Renie. "That can't be right. None of the commercial flights land at Boring Field. Those are all charters and private planes."

"Not my fault," Renie said with a shrug. "Why do you ask?"

"Because," Judith replied, finding the listing in the Yellow Pages, "that's what brought Pam and Sandi here. I thought I'd check to see if they really did fly in with those guns."

"What guns?" asked Renie, who was making herself useful by loading the dishwasher.

But Judith had already dialed the shuttle's number. "Now I'll have to think of a good fib," she murmured. "Hello? Yes, this is Judith Grover, of Grand Grove Limo Service. We were supposed to pick up a Ms. Perl and a Ms. Williams yesterday afternoon, but they didn't show. Do you know if they arrived?"

The woman at the shuttle service informed Judith that they had indeed landed at Boring Field, shortly before three o'clock.

Judith made a thumbs-up gesture for Renie's benefit. "Was that a private flight out of Newark?"

"Not Newark," the woman replied. "The flight plan was filed out of Chicago." She added that the plane was registered to Pamela Perl. Agog, Judith thanked the woman and hung up.

"Pam has her own plane," Judith informed Renie. "How does a preschool teacher afford that?"

"Her parents have money? Or did, before they had children? Think how well off we'd be if we'd been infertile." Renie jammed a handful of silverware into the dishwasher.

"I think it's peculiar," Judith said.

"But not impossible," Renie noted. "Now tell me about the guns."

Judith explained about the arsenal that had been found in the guest rooms. Renie seemed more amused than alarmed. "So travelers want to feel safe? Big deal. Isn't that the reason the Brits drive on the wrong side of the road? In days of yore, they had to whip out their swords to defend themselves while riding on horseback."

Judith gave Renie a skeptical glance. "But silencers?"

"Not on swords." Renie locked the dishwasher and turned it on. "I'll admit, that's harder to explain. Who had the silencers?"

"The Santoris and Barney Schwartz. That really bothers me. You don't need a silencer to ward off a mugger." Suddenly, she snapped her fingers. "The receipts! Let me get them out of the file."

Judith's filing system was reasonably well organized. She kept receipts filed by the month of the actual stay, rather than when payment was received. But since all the prepaid reservations had come in the previous week, the records were in an envelope marked for June.

"Here's an Amex receipt for Roland du Turque," Judith noted. "And a Visa for Pete Santori and another for Pam Perl, who paid for both her and Sandi. But this is odd, now that I think about it—the Schwartzes and the Smiths sent in money orders, and overnighted them so payment would arrive before they did. The deliveries came together by Federal Express Saturday."

"From . . . ?" Renie cocked her head to one side.

"Drat!" Judith rummaged in the wastebasket under the counter that she used as a desk. "Phyliss must have emptied this into the recycling bin. Let's go outside."

Unfazed by the drizzling rain, the cousins went around the side of the house to the big green receptacle that was collected only once a month. One of the uniformed officers, who turned out to be Mercedes Berger, approached Judith.

"We've checked that," Mercedes said. "Nothing."

"I'm looking for something . . . personal," Judith explained. "How come you got stuck with watchdog duty?"

Mercedes wore a rueful look. "Darnell and I officially

went off patrol at eleven, so they decided we might as well stay here and work an overtime shift.''

"Any luck with the search?" Judith asked.

"I don't think so," Mercedes replied, though she didn't meet Judith's gaze. "No weapon, at any rate."

With a nod, Judith lifted the recycling bin lid. Fortunately, the FedEx envelopes were right on top. Tucking them under her arm, she led the way around the side of the house.

Renie, however, suddenly grabbed Judith's sleeve. "Hey," Renie said under her breath, "check out the garage."

On the other side of Judith's Subaru, in the space reserved for Joe's beloved MG, Pete Santori was talking earnestly with Sandi Williams. Neither Marie nor Pam was anywhere in sight.

"Pete and Sandi?" Judith whispered incredulously.

The couple was so involved in conversation that they didn't notice the cousins tiptoeing around the corner of the house. "It's obvious, isn't it?" Judith said when they reached the sanctuary of the back porch. "The Santoris and the teachers know each other from somewhere else. How else would you explain Pam and Sandi's reaction when they first saw Pete and Marie?"

"What is this?" Renie asked as they went into the kitchen. "Some kind of rendezvous point?"

"I wonder." She hesitated. "I suppose I could ask at some appropriate moment."

Renie smiled. "You'll ask, appropriate or not."

"You bet." Judith smoothed the FedEx envelopes on the counter. "Here's the one from Barney Schwartz. The return address is in Royal Oak, Michigan. That checks out. And this is John Smith's. It was sent from . . ." Judith paused, staring at the printed form. ". . . Royal Oak, Michigan."

Over Judith's shoulder, Renie looked at the address. "It's not the same, though. In fact, it's not really an address, it's an intersection. But there's a phone number in the three-one-three area code. I think that's Detroit and its suburbs, which would include Royal Oak.''

Judith stared at the two envelopes. "John Smith lived in New York. Or so he said.''

Renie tapped the number. "Call it. See who answers.''

Judith dialed the number. After two rings, she heard a hoarse male voice at the other end. "Freddy's Bar and Grill,'' said the man.

Judith was taken aback. "Freddy?''

"Naw. This is Jake. Who's this?''

"This is a . . . friend. Do you know John Smith?''

"C'mon, lady. Don't piss me off. Who is this?''

Judith thought rapidly. "Are you at the corner of . . .'' She glanced at the address on the envelope and repeated the street names.

"Hell, no. That's out in Royal Oak. You got downtown Detroit. You ain't even in the right area code. They changed it last month.'' Jake hung up.

Judith replaced the cordless phone in its cradle. "John Smith gave a phony number, probably off the top of his head. He didn't realize that there'd been an area code change recently and that three-one-three isn't Royal Oak anymore.''

"In other words,'' Renie said thoughtfully, "John Smith was passing through.''

Before Judith could respond, Phyliss appeared in the hallway carrying a laundry basket. "I got a note in the pocket of my housedress. You want it?''

"What are you talking about, Phyliss?'' Judith asked, getting up from the counter-cum-desk.

"I found it under the braided rug in Room Four. You want it or not? Hurry up, this load of wash is heavy.''

Judith reached around under the plastic hamper and pulled a piece of paper out of Phyliss's pocket. The cleaning woman's eyes surveyed Renie over the stack of laundry. "That you, Mrs. Jones? I see you've taken up with fiendish tobacco. Tsk, tsk.''

"Pagan Jones to you,'' Renie shot back, picking two

bananas out of Judith's fruit bowl and wiggling them on her head to look like horns. "I'm a lost soul, Phyliss, awash in sin and decadence."

"A wash is right," Phyliss huffed. "And that's what I'm going to do. You're doomed, Mrs. Jones. There's smoke in cigarettes, there's smoke in Hades. Just wait and see."

Renie watched Phyliss's departing figure. "Does she really think I'm a pagan? Doesn't she know that we're both Catholic?"

"Same thing to Phyliss," Judith murmured, studying the paper that had been torn off the pads provided in each guest room. "Listen to this—'Meet me outside in half an hour.' It's unsigned, but I'm almost certain this is the same handwriting that was on the note I found under the piano."

"Which went unclaimed," Renie commented.

"Barney was supposed to meet this person outside," Judith said, still puzzling over the note. "When?"

"Half an hour after the note was delivered," Renie answered in a reasonable tone. "It could have been at any time, including yesterday or this morning."

"But if it was during the night, it might pinpoint the time of the murder," Judith said in a thoughtful voice. "Maybe John Smith or whoever he is—was—slipped this note under the door."

"You told me his name *was* John Smith."

"That was then, this is now." Judith jutted her chin at Renie.

"Okay, so maybe John Smith, aka whoever, went outside to wait and somebody else came along and shot him," said Renie.

Moving to the work counter by the sink, Judith began dicing cooked chicken breasts. "But Barney doesn't get the note." She paused to stare at Renie. "It was under the rug, remember? Barney doesn't show. Who does?"

Renie, still in a helpful mode, removed a head of lettuce from the crisper drawer. "Maybe Barney got the note and ditched it."

Judith shook her head. "Burn it, tear it, toss it in the

wastebasket." Again she stopped and looked at Renie. "I suppose Joe and Rich Goldman went through the wastebaskets in the guest rooms. But they must not have looked under the rug. You've been in Room Four, you know how the rug is almost flush with the door. In fact, we had to take a sixteenth of an inch off the bottom of the door so it would clear the braided rug. Grandma Grover made them thick."

"Grandma Grover made everything thick," Renie remarked in a wistful tone. "Her gravy, her puddings, her noodles. She was a wonderful cook and seamstress and gardener and craftswoman. Where did we go wrong, coz?"

"We can cook," Judith pointed out. "We garden. As for the rest—well, it's a different era. Who has time to braid rugs and make clothes for the whole family?"

"Who'd wear the stuff if we made it?" Renie made a face.

"Grandma taught us to sew," Judith said, getting two cans of fried noodles out of the cupboard.

"We sucked," Renie said. "Our mothers weren't much better. Mine once broke three sewing machines in two weeks. She's not mechanical."

"Maniacal is more like it when it comes to our mothers," Judith noted. "Or maybe I mean diabolical. My mother isn't going to like this chicken salad. She'd rather have baloney."

"My mother called three times this morning before nine o'clock," Renie sighed. "That's why I was quasiconscious when you phoned."

Judith was well aware of Aunt Deb's obsession with the telephone and her daughter, Renie. If Gertrude Grover was sharp-tongued and hard to please, Deborah Grover was a maternal martyr in the making. It was pointless to dwell on the flaws that drove their daughters crazy. Judith changed the subject.

"Barney and John Smith in Royal Oak, Michigan. Why? John Smith comes from New York—I saw the car, it definitely had New York plates. He and presumably Darlene drive to Detroit's suburbs. Why? To find Barney? The next thing we know, the Smiths and the Schwartzes head west and end up here. Yet they aren't traveling together and act as if they have no knowledge of each other.''

"That's probably untrue," Renie noted, tossing the salad greens under the running tap. "It also seems that though the Santoris and the teachers claim not to be acquainted, they obviously are. Where did they come from?"

"Pam and Sandi are from Newark, New Jersey," Judith replied. "The Santoris come from Miami."

Renie let the lettuce drain in a colander. "What about Roland du Turque?"

"Kansas City, Missouri, remember?" Judith began to make the dressing for the chicken salad. "The Malones are from Chicago. And, just to add further intrigue, the guy who canceled was from Las Vegas." Slowly, Judith's mouth curved into a grim smile. "Doesn't that mean something to you, coz?"

"Let me think," said Renie, leaning against the counter and resting her chin on one hand. "These are American cities with a population over a hundred thousand? They all have tall buildings we can't leap over in a single bound? I know how to spell each one? Come on, coz, spill it."

"Organized crime," responded Judith. "Where are mob movies set?"

"I don't watch many mob movies," Renie replied. "Bill does, but there's too much gore. They need to cut out the shootings and all that violence before I go see them. Besides, I don't think of Kansas City as a hotbed of organized crime."

"It has been, though, over the years," Judith said, getting somewhat sulky.

"Give it up," Renie urged. "You've never gotten over your Al Capone phase. I still remember your term paper in English. 'Scar-Face: Robin Hood or Robbing Hood?' You got a C-minus. The assignment was to write about legendary American heroes."

"That was my point," Judith countered. "Capone did a

lot of good with his millions. He was extremely generous to charity, and . . ."

"Stick it. Almost forty years later, you know better. Who did you write about in your class on Modern Marriage? Bonnie and Clyde?"

Judith dumped the chicken in with the lettuce. "The course was Modern Family. I wrote about Ma Barker." She ignored Renie's appalled expression. "So explain why these people are armed to the teeth?"

Renie admitted that was peculiar. "But why here? We definitely don't live in a city that's famous for harboring gangsters. Unless you count a rascally union boss or two."

"One of whom Uncle Al and Uncle Vince, both being members of said union, thought was a real hero," Judith said dryly, then snapped her fingers. "Maybe we know why the pages were torn out of the register. Whoever did it, wrote that note to Barney. They didn't want it traced to them through their signatures."

"What if it wasn't Barney?" Renie said.

"Huh?"

"What if the note was intended for Minerva?"

Judith considered. "Do you think that's likely?"

"Likely, no," Renie replied. "Possible, yes."

Unhappily, Judith knew that all things were possible. Especially when it came to murder.

All of the guests, except for the Malones, were milling around the living room. At 12:10, Judith announced that luncheon was served. Phyliss immediately descended upon the living room, armed with the vacuum cleaner.

"Hey!" yelled Barney. "We can't hear ourselves think with that damned thing running."

"I didn't know you were the thinking type," Pete remarked with a snide expression.

Sandi leaned forward, her blonde hair highlighted by the unexpected appearance of the sun through the dining room window. "Put magic in your ears, Mr. Schwartz. That's what we tell our students, don't we, Pam?"

Pam nodded. "It means they should listen real hard."

"My, my," said Roland, gazing at Judith. "The rain's stopped. I believe it's all right to stroll the garden?"

"Yes," Judith replied, placing a basket of hot rolls on the table. The noise of the vacuum cleaner had receded as Phyliss moved to the far end of the living room. "Some of the other guests have already been outside this morning." Her glance flitted from Pete to Sandi.

"It's not cold," Marie put in.

"But it's damp," Pam added.

"There's hardly any humidity, is there?" said Sandi.

"It's usually not a problem," Judith said, seeing an opening. "Most of you come from parts of the country where that's not the case. Or am I mistaken?"

"It can get really bad in Miami," Marie said. Then, as an apparent afterthought, hugged Pete. "Isn't that true, Clingy-wingy?"

"It sure is, Jiggles-wiggles. But we worship the old sun god," said Pete.

"I'd become depressed with all this rain," Minerva Schwartz declared. "So much gray. I'm told you have no real change of seasons here."

"We don't," Renie asserted, entering the dining room with the coffee carafe. "Around here, we call the seasons sort of gray, pretty gray, really gray, and damned gray. Coffee black?"

Minerva regarded Renie with distaste. "I shouldn't think you would encourage visitors to this city with that kind of negative attitude."

"I try not to," said Renie. "But then I'm not in the tourism business."

"Attitude," echoed Barney. "That's what it takes to sell. See, I'm in the car business, got a dealership in Royal Oak. Take a look at my Seville parked outside. Right away, you're impressed. That's a positive, not a negative. Everybody wants a Cadillac—it's the American dream. So when a guy wanders onto the lot, all I have to do is . . ."

Judith wasn't interested in Barney's sales pitch. She and

Renie returned to the kitchen. "I'm calling Joe," Judith said. "He must know something by now."

"But it's not his case," Renie pointed out.

"Then he can transfer me to J. J. or Rich." Judith picked up the cordless phone, but her free hand wavered in mid-air. "Malone," she mouthed at Renie.

Mal was on the line, his voice mournful. "Sheesh," he was saying, "we've had more than our share." He paused, taking in an audible breath. "You hear that? Is somebody else on this line?"

Judith stood like a statue; mercifully, the man at the other end said his phone had been acting up. Mal continued, "First, it was Tagliavini, then Albanese and McCormack, now Corelli. You tell me who's out to get us. Talk to ya later." Mal clicked off the upstairs extension.

Renie, who had been listening at Judith's shoulder, asked what the other party had said.

"Not much," Judith replied, finally daring to breathe again. "It was a man, and he just made commiserating remarks. But you heard Mal—didn't that sound like mob members?"

"I didn't quite catch the names," Renie admitted.

"They were all Italian, except for one Irish or Scottish name. He mentioned Corelli, who the Malones were lamenting earlier as if he were dead," Judith explained, then saw the skepticism on Renie's face. "Okay, okay—I know not all Italians are in the Mafia. But given the guns and the fact that Mal and Bea are from Chicago, and we all know that in the past, both Italian and Irish gangsters have been . . ."

Renie, who was peeking over the swinging door, raised a hand. "Here they come. The Malones, that is. Do you suppose that was a long-distance call?"

"If it was, they better not have charged it to my line," Judith said, then started to dial Joe's work number. "I've got to pass this along. At least we've got some names—if I can remember them." But before she could enter the last two digits, a husky female voice called from the back porch.

"Yoo-hoo—it's me. Can I borrow a cup of Scotch?"

Wearily, Judith turned around, though she knew who was standing on the threshold. It was the last person she wanted to see. It was the neighbor to whom she could never apply the adjective "good." It was Vivian Flynn, Joe's ex-wife, and otherwise known as Herself.

EIGHT

JOE'S EX SLITHERED down the narrow hall on a wave of heavy perfume that Judith had secretly dubbed Eau de Muskrat. This week, Herself's hair was a mass of Botticelli gold ringlets that might have been fetching on a twenty-year-old, but looked ridiculous on a woman approaching seventy. Or such was Judith's not entirely unprejudiced opinion.

"Vivian," Judith said in surprise, "I thought you'd quit drinking."

"I did," Vivian said, crimson lips breaking into a big smile. "Joe's been such a help, going to AA with me." The words were purred, not spoken. "But I have a houseguest, and naturally, I don't want to seem inhospitable."

After spending several years living in a condo on Florida's gulf coast, Vivian had returned to the Pacific Northwest and moved into a vacant house on the cul-de-sac. Initially, Judith didn't think she could tolerate her former rival's proximity. But Vivian traveled extensively, and except for the occasional repair job and the AA support from Joe, Judith's worst fears hadn't been realized. So far.

"I'll pour it into an empty jelly jar," Judith said as Herself came all the way into the kitchen and greeted

Renie effusively. "Is your guest staying long?"

"I don't know." Herself emitted a girlish titter. "DeeDee is a will-o'-the-wisp. She and I sang together at a club in Panama City. We called ourselves the V. D. Girls. For Vivian and DeeDee. Get it?"

"I got it," Judith said dryly.

"Well, shame on you!" Herself burst into raucous laughter. "You see," she gasped, "that's how we'd introduce our act. 'We're the V. D. Girls,' we'd say, and then . . ."

"Yes," Judith broke in, unable to look at Renie, who had her head in the refrigerator, "that's very clever. Here, take the whole fifth. Just in case."

"Oh, Judith," Herself beamed, "you're too kind. If DeeDee stays more than a day or two, I'll have to invite you over to meet her. I just know you two would get along famously."

"Really." Judith wondered if Renie was getting cold. She hadn't budged since saying hello to Herself.

"I must dash," Herself announced. "By the way, was someone taken ill this morning? I didn't get up until ever so late—you know me—but I thought I saw some policemen outside. In fact, is that crime scene tape at your mother's apartment?"

"It is," Judith responded, beginning to get nervous. She dreaded having Herself get involved with the homicide case—and with Joe. "We had a bit of trouble with a guest."

"Oh, my." Herself's false eyelashes fluttered. "Did the guest bother Mrs. G.-G.?"

"No, Mother's fine," Judith replied, edging toward the back door in the hope that Herself would follow. "When your friend leaves, you must pay Mother a visit." The invitation was sincere: Whether out of affection or perversity, Gertrude and Herself had hit it off. Though it pained Judith, she appreciated the company that Joe's ex offered to the old lady.

"I'll do that," Herself promised. "I haven't stopped in

for a week or two. And your mother is such fun. We have a high old time, I can tell you that.''

"Wonderful," Judith said, ushering Herself out the door. It never ceased to amaze Judith that not only Vivian Flynn but Carl and Arlene Rankers seemed to genuinely enjoy being with Gertrude. But of course they weren't related to her.

"Is she gone?" asked Renie, finally withdrawing from the fridge. "Can I come out? Am I frozen yet?"

"You do look a little raw," Judith replied. "By the way, it's raining again."

"Of course." Renie gathered up her purse and jacket. "Time to get to work. I've got a tricky design project to finish this week for the Boring Airplane Company. It's something to do with their community involvement regarding sex offenders. I call it, 'Planes, Trains, and Pedophiles.' See you.''

The call to Joe was futile. He and Woody were on a case, and J. J. and Rich were unavailable. Judith readied Gertrude's lunch and took it out to the toolshed.

"I'm not a rabbit," Gertrude declared after turning her nose up at the chicken salad. "And what are those little brown twigs poking out of that lettuce? They look like matchsticks to me."

"Chinese noodles," Judith said, reminding herself to be patient. "Mother, I make a really good chicken salad. And there are hot rolls and some lovely cake Renie brought over.''

Gertrude snorted. "The cake might be okay, unless Serena made it. The last time she sent over brownies, there weren't any nuts.''

"Renie is allergic to nuts," Judith pointed out. "Do you want her to poison herself?"

"Why not? Everybody else around here seems to be croaking." Gertrude used a fork to stab at the salad, then jerked her hand away as if she'd touched nettles. "I don't see a lot of chicken in here."

"There's plenty," Judith responded, then turned sharply

as someone pounded on the toolshed door. "One of the uniforms," she murmured, and went to meet the visitor.

Neither Mercedes Berger nor Darnell Hicks stood within the circle of the crime scene tape. Instead, a boyish-looking man in a dark suit and muted tie surveyed Judith with cool blue eyes.

"Is this the residence of Gertrude Hoffman Grover?" he asked in a soft, polite voice.

Judith laughed. "Residence? Well, yes, it is. How can I help you?"

The man reached inside his breast pocket and pulled out a badge. "FBI. I'm Agent Bruce Dunleavy. May I come in?"

Judith's eyes widened. "Yes . . . certainly. But I think you want to talk to me, not my . . ."

"Mrs. Grover," Dunleavy began, then reintroduced himself. "How are you today?"

Gertrude, who had managed to pick out half a dozen chicken chunks and had placed them on her roll plate, frowned at the agent. "Want to go from A to Z? Let's start with my ankles, which are swollen like Goodyear blimps. B is for bladder, which is faulty, like a leaky sink. As for C, that's my carcass, a poor thing to behold . . ."

"Mother," Judith broke in, "I don't think Mr. Dunleavy is interested in your health problems."

Dunleavy, however, was chuckling softly. "My own mother has her share of complaints. Tell me, Mrs. Grover, is your maiden name Gertrude Hoffman?"

Gertrude was chewing chicken. "Gertrude Hoffman? A long time ago, maybe. You want some crappy salad?"

"No, thank you." Dunleavy cleared his throat and remained standing, a kindly expression on his pleasant face. "Were you born in Boppard, Germany?"

Gertrude stared at Judith. "Was I?"

Judith gave a slight nod. "Of course. You came to this country with your parents when you were a year and a half."

"Okay," Gertrude said. "I was. Boppard. What a goofy

name. I'm glad I moved." She turned to Judith. "Hey, dumbbell—where's my salt?"

"Your salt and pepper are on that TV table right beside you," Judith replied. "Mr. Dunleavy, would you like to sit down? Take this armchair."

But Dunleavy politely declined. "Did you move to Berlin in 1926 and join the National Socialist Party?"

Gertrude's face grew puzzled. "I'm a lifelong Democrat, voted all four times for FDR. Give 'Em Hell, Harry. All the way with Adlai. John F. Kennedy should be made a saint. First Catholic president. But I voted for Al Smith, too, back in twenty-eight. Fine man, Governor Smith. He should have won."

Judith held up a hand. "Wait a minute—what's this all about? My mother has lived in the Pacific Northwest virtually all her life."

Looking apologetic, Agent Dunleavy shook his head. "Please. Humor me. Let's stay with the questions. Did you or did you not join the National Socialist Party in nineteen twenty-six after being dismissed from your civil service post in Munich?"

Gertrude blinked at Dunleavy. "Civil service? I never took the test. I went to work as a bookkeeper, with the old Hyman and Sanford Company downtown. Now the manager, Mr. Skelly—we called him Mr. Smelly—was a staunch Republican and a teetotaler. So one night, when he made us work late with no overtime pay, we brought in some bathtub gin and . . ."

"Mrs. Grover." Dunleavy's tone was kindly. "That's fascinating, but these are serious queries."

"They're ridiculous," Judith interrupted in an irritable tone. "My mother and I don't have any inkling of what you're talking about."

Dunleavy drew himself up even straighter. "I'm here to investigate Gertrude Hoffman Grover on charges of war crimes while supervising the women's concentration camp at Auschwitz."

"What?" Judith shrieked. "Are you crazy? I'm going to

have to ask you to leave. This is outrageous.''

Gertrude leaned forward in the worn armchair. "Hey, Toots, what's the rush? I like him. " She smirked at Dunleavy. "My dopey daughter doesn't want me to have any fun. It's a wonder she doesn't nail a sign over the door saying, 'Pest House' to keep out visitors.''

Dunleavy's gaze shifted to Judith. "I have a job to do, ma'am. Please don't interfere. I'm from the Department of Justice's Office of Special Investigations. FBI agents are assigned by that office to track down and apprehend war criminals.''

"But it's stupid," Judith insisted. "Mother hasn't been in Germany since she was an infant." A grotesque image of Gertrude's tough, wrinkled face looking out from under a lace-trimmed baby bonnet flashed before Judith's eyes and evoked a semi-hysterical laugh. *Am I cracking up? Is this day just one long nightmare? If I poke Agent Dunleavy, will he disappear into a cloud of fairy dust?* "We have all sorts of proof that Mother's lived here almost all of her life," Judith said, regaining control despite a vague sense of dizziness. "Shall I get some of it?''

Dunleavy made a somewhat diffident gesture of dismissal. "I'm afraid those types of proofs are easily forged. You'd be amazed at some of the things I've come across, including photos supposedly taken with General Eisenhower.''

"Ike!" sneered Gertrude. "I wouldn't have my picture taken with that old fart. I have a friend in bridge club whose sister was married to a man whose cousin's best friend used to fly Mamie around, and he said *she drank.* Now what do you think of *that*?''

"I think," Dunleavy responded with an encouraging smile, "we should get back to my questions. When did you first become acquainted with Hermann Wilhelm Goring?''

Gertrude looked blank. "Who?''

"Goring, Hitler's second in command." Dunleavy waited, but Gertrude said nothing. "According to our records, you first met Goring in nineteen twenty-eight, shortly after his election to the Reichstag.''

"I met a lot of people in the twenty-eight election," Gertrude replied. "That's when I was out stumping for Al Smith.''

Judith stepped between Gertrude and Dunleavy. "That's it. I'm not obstructing justice, Mr. Dunleavy, but I can't let you badger my mother any longer. In case you didn't notice, we've had a tragedy here this morning. We're all in a state of semi-shock. My mother is elderly, she's forgetful, she's easily confused. To put it mildly, this isn't a good time.''

Dunleavy's boyish face flushed. "I know there was a homicide on the premises. I spoke with the police who are watching the house. But I'm afraid that's coincidental to my investigation.''

Gertrude thrust her head around Judith. "Are you talking about Hermann Hoover in twenty-eight? A lot you know. His name was Herbert, and he put us into a big fat depression.''

If not depressed, Dunleavy was definitely disconcerted. "It's possible that I could come back later. Mrs. Grover isn't going anywhere, is she?''

"I never go anywhere," Gertrude snapped. "You think this lazy moron of a daughter of mine would bother herself to take me for so much as a trip to the zoo? If it weren't for my neighbors and a few others, I'd sit here and get covered with moss.''

"Mother, you hate the zoo," Judith countered. "You haven't been there in thirty years.''

"You see?'' Gertrude's chin jutted. "If it was up to her, I wouldn't have gone *anywhere* in thirty years. Hold on there, young man. Don't let Her Daffiness scare you away.''

Dunleavy, however, started for the door. "I'll be back this afternoon or tomorrow morning," he said.

"Ha!'' Gertrude cried. "I've heard that one before.'' She shook a fork at Dunleavy. "You better be back. Maybe,'' she added with a coquettish look, "I'll give you some pudding."

Judith led Dunleavy outside. "You're way off base," she said, closing the door behind her. "Your records must be mistaken. If you come back again, Mother will still be addled. Even without the shock of a homicide on her doorstep, she's exactly what you just saw—a very old woman whose mind is in decay."

The cool blue eyes, which seemed in such contrast to Dunleavy's boyish looks, bore into Judith's face. "Is that so?" He turned on his heel, and headed along the walk to the driveway.

Judith stood outside the toolshed in the rain. J. J. Martinez had made virtually the same remark concerning Gertrude.

There were times when Judith wondered whose mind would go first.

Phyliss was annoyed. "The Good Lord isn't giving me any guidance," she complained. "I need a push, a shove, a nudge in the right direction."

An hour had passed since Agent Dunleavy's departure. The guests had dispersed after lunch, mainly to their rooms, though Pam and Sandi were sitting in the porch swing outside the front parlor window, and the Malones were in the living room, griping about the world in general and Hillside Manor in particular.

"A nudge for what?" Judith asked the cleaning woman.

"To find my coat." Phyllis was on her hands and knees, searching under Judith's makeshift desk. "I put it on that peg in the hall, like I always do. Now it's gone. I suppose them godless criminals stole it, thinking to ward off Satan with a cloak of virtue."

"Could be," Judith remarked, her attention diverted by the calls that had piled up while she was out of earshot of the phone.

"I've had that coat for almost ten years," Phyllis went on. "I paid good money for it, too. Thirty-five dollars at a

Belle Epoch sale. Now how I am supposed to get home without a coat? Maybe that young fella who came asking for your mother grabbed it. He looked fishy to me. Mrs. Wartz thought so, too.''

"That's Mrs. Schwartz," Judith said, taking down the telephone numbers. Two requests for reservations, one in July, the other in August; a reminder from the dentist for a cleaning the following week; and, most intriguingly, a call from J. J. Martinez.

"What?" Judith finally gave Phyliss her full attention. "No one would take your coat, Phyliss." Ten years worth of wear on a cheap black raincoat had rendered the garment shabby, baggy, and frayed around the edges.

But Phyliss was right: The raincoat wasn't on its usual peg. "Did you check the upstairs and the basement? You might not have taken it off when you came in. You were a bit late, remember?"

" 'Course I checked the upstairs and basement," Phyliss answered crossly. "Besides, I remember hanging it right here." She grabbed the empty peg and gave it a shake. "My plastic rain bonnet was in the pocket. Now how can I wait for the bus in this bad weather? I'll take a chill and end up with pneumonia."

"You can borrow one of my coats," Judith said. "I may have a rain bonnet tucked away somewhere."

"That's not the point," Phyliss said doggedly. "I want my own coat."

Judith sighed. "Your coat may have gotten moved. We've had so much activity around here this morning, including a thorough search of the house. I'm sure it'll turn up. Meanwhile, I'll go up to the family quarters and get you another raincoat."

Phyliss began to reiterate her stand that only her own coat would do, but Judith was already halfway up the back stairs. Three minutes later, she returned to the kitchen with the navy blue raincoat she seldom wore. Judith preferred jackets and car coats.

"I found a rain bonnet in a drawer," Judith said, helping

a reluctant Phyllis into the coat. "Key Largo Bank gave them away awhile back as a special promotion." Judith had tucked the gift away, preferring to wear a tin bucket on her head rather than a plastic rain bonnet.

With much grumbling, Phyliss exited through the back door. Judith picked up the phone and dialed the number J. J. had left for her on the answering machine.

J. J. wasn't available, however. Neither was Rich Goldman. Frustrated, Judith checked her bookings for the dates that the callers had requested. She was full up for the two nights in July that a Mrs. Carter from Bloomington, Illinois, had wanted, but had one room left for the August reservations that had been required by Ms. Holcombe in Denver. Judith was about to call Mrs. Carter back when Barney Schwartz stomped into the kitchen.

"Where's Ma?" he demanded, his head swiveling in every direction. "You seen her?"

"No," Judith responded, setting the phone down. "She hasn't been in the kitchen that I know of."

Barney was very red in the face as he shifted his weight from one foot to the other and chewed on his lower lip. "This is crazy. I checked all the cans upstairs, the downstairs can, too. I even tried to open that door down the hall that's marked private, but it was locked. Could she have gone in there?"

"That's the staircase that goes up to the third floor," Judith answered, feeling worry build at the pit of her stomach. "I was up there just a few minutes ago. Nobody was around. Besides, we always keep that door locked."

"Are those cops still here?" Barney asked in a raspy voice. "Maybe they know where she is." He started for the front door.

"Mr. Schwartz," Judith called after him. "May I ask you a quick question?"

Pausing at the end of the dining room table, Barney gave Judith a harried look. "It better be quick. What?"

Though the note Phyliss had found was still in the pocket of Judith's slacks, she didn't produce it. "Were you expecting to meet someone out in the yard at any time since you arrived here?''

''What?'' Barney regarded Judith as if she were crazy. ''Hell, no. Why should I?'' He stomped through the entry hall and slammed the front door behind him.

Puzzled, Judith decided to check the basement. She was halfway down the stairs when she realized that a search for Minerva Schwartz might turn up something very unpleasant. Judith had already found one corpse on the premises. Taking a deep breath and gritting her teeth, she continued down the steps.

The basement was used mainly as a laundry room and for storage. The belongings that Mike had left behind were clustered in the old coal bin. The possessions that Gertrude couldn't fit into the toolshed took up the entire far end beyond the furnace and hot water heater. Cartons of holiday decorations stood against another wall. Joe's workshop was nothing more than a wooden counter and shelves, though there were tools everywhere, along with garden implements and a rusty lawn mower last used by Grandpa Grover. Judith, whose sentimental streak ran deep, couldn't bear to throw it away.

But there was no sign of Minerva Schwartz. Relieved, Judith went back upstairs just as someone rang the front doorbell.

Two men stood on the porch. One was tall, stern-faced, and of African-American descent; the other was somewhat shorter, but broad-shouldered and possessing a full head of curly black hair. Both wore dark suits and muted ties. Judith had seen the type, if not the men, very recently. She set her jaw as the black man introduced himself and flashed his credentials.

''I'm Agent Terrill from the FBI,'' the man said, then indicated his companion. ''This is Agent Rosenblatt. May we come in?''

Judith balked. ''I've already told Agent Dunleavy that my mother isn't in any condition to answer a bunch of silly questions right now. I must insist that you come back later.

In fact, it's pointless for you to come back at all.''

''Pardon?'' Terrill's dark eyes seemed to assess Judith, the entry hall, and the rest of the surroundings all at once. ''I'm not here to see your mother. Are you Mrs. Flynn?''

''Yes,'' Judith snapped, ''and I was never a member of Nazi Youth. I would have been about two at the time.''

Without a word, Agents Terrill and Rosenblatt stepped around Judith and entered the house. ''We've no idea what you're talking about,'' Terrill said quietly. ''Where is Bernhard 'Fewer Fingers' Schlagintweit?''

Judith's jaw dropped. ''Who?''

''Bernhard . . .''

''Yes, yes, you don't need to say it again,'' Judith interrupted. ''I've never heard of this person.''

''I think you're mistaken.'' Terrill turned as Barney Schwartz came through the front door.

''Ma's gone!'' he wailed. ''She's been kidnapped! Or worse!''

''Keep calm,'' Terrill commanded as Rosenblatt moved swiftly behind Barney and twisted the other man's arms behind his back.

Rosenblatt spoke for the first time. ''I'm arresting you, Bernhard 'Fewer Fingers' Schlagintweit, also known as Barney Schwartz, for the murder of Alfonso Benedetto, also known as Legs Benedict, and sometimes using the alias John Smith.'' Rosenblatt clicked a pair of handcuffs on Barney, who howled in protest as the Malones rushed in from the living room and the preschool teachers raced from the porch swing to the front door.

''La-la-la,'' sang Judith, twirling around. ''I really am crazy after all.'' With that, she collapsed against the elephant-foot umbrella stand.

NINE

THERE WERE STARS on the ceiling and comets plunging past the plate rail. The ring around Saturn whirled over the glass-topped coffee table, and the cloud that Judith was floating on felt a bit lumpy. She blinked several times, realized her mouth was as dry as an Arizona desert, and tried to sit up.

"Drink this," urged a voice Judith didn't recognize at first. She blinked again. Sandi Something-Or-Other from New Jersey. No, not Sandi; Sandi was blonde. This was Pam, the other preschool teacher, a brunette, a pretty, earnest face. The hand was holding a glass of water. Judith wasn't floating through the heavens. She was on one of the matching sofas in the living room, with several people watching her with worried expressions.

"Aaangs," Judith moaned. She meant to says thanks; it didn't sound right in her ears. But she let Pam hold the glass to her lips, and took a small sip.

"She fainted," Sandi was saying to Roland du Turque. "Right there in the entry hall."

"Poor thing," murmured Roland, then lowered his voice still further. "What happened to Mr. Schwartz?"

"Something bad," Sandi replied. "Two men took him away in a car. He was wearing handcuffs."

"Oh, my!" Roland sounded horrified. "Do you think . . . ? Does that mean . . . ? Did he . . . ?"

Judith's eyes had begun to focus. "Yes," she said in a weak voice. "The FBI agent charged him with killing John Smith. Except he wasn't John Smith, and Barney isn't Barney Schwartz, and . . ."

"Delirious," whispered Pam.

"She's nuts," Mal Malone asserted.

"We should've gone some place else," Bea said to her husband. "I knew it—this place is hexed."

"We couldn't," Mal responded. "Don't be a chump."

Pete and Marie Santori had entered the living room. Sandi rushed over to explain to the honeymooners what had happened. After taking a few more sips of water, Judith managed to sit up. To her surprise, she felt dizzy and nauseous.

"Since Barney Schwartz has been arrested, does that mean we can leave?" Marie asked in an eager voice.

No one answered, including Judith, who knew she couldn't take responsibility for such a decision. Indeed, she couldn't take much of anything, except collapsing back onto the sofa.

"Mr. Martinez is the primary," she finally said. "I believe that the FBI works in tandem with the local police. We'll have to wait to hear from him."

"How long?" Mal demanded.

"I don't know," Judith replied. *And I don't much care.* She was definitely feeling sick; she had to get upstairs. "If you'll excuse me . . ." Leaving the sentence unfinished, she finally managed to stand up with the help of Pam and Roland.

"We'll come with you," Pam insisted. "You might fall."

Judith didn't argue, even allowing the two guests all the way into the family quarters on the third floor.

"This is nice," Pam enthused. "I like dormer rooms. They're so cozy."

"Years ago, I lived in a boarding house in New Orleans," Roland said. "My room was very much like this one, though not quite as charming."

Judith allowed the guests to chatter for a few moments, then thanked them before she indicated a need to head for the bathroom. Roland and Pam left, promising to lock the door at the bottom of the stairs.

They'd barely disappeared when Judith stumbled into the bathroom and threw up, not once, but half a dozen times. Weak and depleted, she knelt on the floor, summoning strength to get back to bed. When she finally felt better, she flopped onto the pillows and considered her options.

With Arlene Rankers out of town, there weren't many. Judith's unsteady fingers dialed Renie's number.

"You're sick?" Renie sounded flabbergasted. "What is it, flu?"

"Maybe," Judith replied. "Or it could be nerves. This has been one hell of a day, and you haven't heard the half of it."

"But I will," Renie said warily.

"Can you bail me out?" Judith asked.

"Me? Ms. No-Tact? Winner of the Ungracious Award for the fiftieth year in a row? The original Big Mouth? This sounds like a real bad idea, coz."

"This crew can't be any more alienated than they already are," Judith countered. "You know I hate to ask—but I'm stuck."

"Shoot." Renie was silent for an ominously long time. "Okay, I'll be over in half an hour. So much for the Boring pedophiles. I've got a jump-start on this project anyway, but I'll have to throw something together for Bill and the kids' dinner. Bill flunked chicken breasts a la Dolly Parton last night. I assume you want me to stay over?"

Judith hadn't thought that far ahead. Joe should be home by six, but sometimes he worked late. In any event, it wasn't fair to ask him to play both host and cop to the current group of guests.

"You can stay in Room Three," Judith said. "It's vacant now. So is Room Four."

"Huh?"

"I'll explain later," Judith said, hanging up and making another dash to the bathroom.

Renie arrived shortly after four, but didn't come up to see Judith straight away. "The guests filled me in on some of what's been going on," Renie said, sitting at the far end of the bed. "How do you feel?"

"Better," Judith said. "I honestly think it's the flu. If it's a twenty-four-hour bug, I should be okay by tomorrow. Is everybody still here?"

"Everybody who hasn't been murdered, fled, kidnapped, arrested, or otherwise disappeared," Renie said. "I heard about Minerva Schwartz, who still hasn't turned up. She'll have a fit when she finds out her son was arrested."

"*If* she finds out," Judith replied in a worried tone. "Did you notice if Barney's Cadillac was still parked out in the cul-de-sac?"

"The white Seville?" Renie frowned. "No, I didn't see it."

Judith stared at Renie. "Minerva must have taken it. That means Barney never checked to see if the car was gone. Of course, he didn't have much time after he discovered his mother was missing. And," Judith added with an ironic expression, "I know how Minerva got out of the house without being stopped. She grabbed Phyliss's raincoat and whoever was on duty assumed it was the cleaning lady, heading out from her daily stint."

"That's possible," Renie agreed. "Phyliss isn't quite as tall, but she's got gray hair, more or less the same shade."

"Which," Judith noted, "Minerva probably hid under Phyliss's rain bonnet anyway, to disguise the fact that her hair isn't sausage curls, but a topknot. One older gray-haired woman in a raincoat and a plastic bonnet looks pretty much like any other. And speaking of the older generation, let me tell you what happened to Mother today."

Renie bared her prominent front teeth in an evil grin. "Was it horrible?"

"It was, actually," Judith responded, and proceeded to tell Renie about Agent Dunleavy's visit.

After Renie stopped rolling around in a fit of unbridled mirth, she held her head. "That's really about the dumbest thing I ever heard. How could the FBI make such a lamebrained mistake?"

"It *is* the government," Judith said. "And they do make mistakes. Do you remember the time the IRS thought *your* mother was a taxidermist?"

"Wrong Deborah Grover, right address," Renie said. "We didn't know until then that somebody by the same name had lived in her apartment ten years earlier before she moved in. Mom had always wondered why the living room had outlines of wall mountings. The super shouldn't have allowed the other Deborah Grover to put up all those stuffed heads in the first place."

"I doubt Dunleavy will be back," Judith said, then gave her cousin a diffident look. "I hate to ask, but I think I could drink a cup of tea."

"I'll get it." Renie rose from the bed. "Am I supposed to fix dinner for this bunch?"

Judith grimaced. "I guess so. Sorry, coz. I didn't even think about that. But as far as I know, they still can't leave."

"That's fine. I'll make shrimp dump," Renie said, referring to her all-purpose creamed seafood recipe, which wasn't quite as bad as it sounded. She headed out of the bedroom.

Renie hadn't been gone a minute, when O. P. Dooley appeared in the bedroom doorway. "Mrs. Flynn? Mrs. Jones let me come up. Is that okay?"

Judith nodded. "I feel better. What's up?"

Under his unruly fair hair, O. P.'s face was very serious. "I'm just starting the evening paper route, and my mom asked if I could get you to tell your guests to move their car. It's blocking our driveway."

Judith stared at O. P. The Dooleys faced the other side of the block, behind Hillside Manor. To her knowledge, none of the B&B guests had ever parked a car so far away.

"How do you know the car belongs to one of my guests?" Judith asked.

"I saw it parked in the cul-de-sac yesterday," O. P. responded. "It's black, a new Chrysler Concord with New York plates. The license number is . . ."

"You know the license number?" Judith broke in.

"Sure. I like to memorize license numbers, especially out-of-state ones. Sometimes they're really weird." O. P. gave Judith a self-effacing smile.

"That's great, O. P.," Judith declared, breaking into her first real smile since she'd passed out in the entry hall. Then she started to recount what had been happening at the B&B.

O. P., however, knew most of what had gone on. "One of those nice ladies told me when I came to the door. She didn't know if she should let me in until I explained who I was. Then she and the other nice lady—I guess they're friends, huh?—let me come inside."

Judith assumed that O. P. was talking about Pam and Sandi. "Did you memorize the plates on the Michigan car, too?"

O. P. nodded. "Want me to write the numbers down?"

Judith did, handing the young boy a small tablet and pen she kept on the bedside table. "The police will be thrilled." Abruptly, Judith's enthusiasm faded. "The only problem is, they're going to want to take that Chrysler in to search it. I'm not sure how soon they can get it towed."

O. P. made a face. "They better do it quick before my dad gets home from work. Mom says he'll be mad if he can't get into the garage."

"I'll call right now," Judith promised.

O. P. started for the door, then swerved on his heel. "Wow—I almost forgot. This morning I subbed for Rob Simon. He's got the flu, too. Anyway, I came by with the morning paper around five-thirty. I had to get a real early start 'cause I like to take a shower before I go to school, and with so many of us in the house, we sort of have to line up."

Judith gave O. P. an encouraging smile. "And?"

"I remembered not to deliver the Rankerses' paper, so I cut across the cul-de-sac from the Porters' house," O. P. continued, his young face very earnest. "It was getting kind of light, but not real light, because it was cloudy this morning. Anyway, I saw those people I almost ran into rummaging around in their car. You know—the Ford Explorer from Illinois."

"The Malones?" Judith rubbed her chin. "At five-thirty in the morning? How odd. Did you see them take something out?" *Like a gun*, thought Judith, but didn't want to lead O. P.

The boy shook his head. "No. I had to come up on the sidewalk to deliver your paper, and then go on to the Ericsons'. Those people—the Malones?—were still at their car when I headed for the other Mrs. Flynn's and Mrs. Swanson's. Mr. Malone was looking under it, like maybe he was checking for an oil leak."

Judith nodded. "Of course. That's extremely interesting, O. P. Did you happen to see—or hear—anything else?"

O. P. made a face. "Not really. I wish I'd sort of—you know—hung out more. But it was raining, and I had to get the route done. I didn't know it might be important to notice stuff."

"Nobody could know that," Judith consoled him. "You did wonderfully well as it is, especially memorizing those license plates."

O. P. brightened at the praise. "Should I still keep looking around?"

"Definitely. But be careful," Judith cautioned. "Even if Mr. Schwartz has been arrested, some of these other people might be dangerous."

"Really?" O. P. beamed. "Like those nice ladies who let me in?"

"Well . . . maybe they're not," Judith amended.

Then again, she thought after O. P. left the room, *maybe they are.*

*　　*　　*

"Your guests don't seem too excited about eating shrimp dump," Renie said an hour later.

Judith, who had been drifting in and out of a restless sleep, roused herself. "Where'd you get the shrimp? I didn't think I had any."

"You didn't," Renie responded, sitting on the bed. "I used a couple of cans of sardines."

The concept sent Judith's stomach into revolt. But at least she didn't feel like throwing up anymore. "It serves them right," she finally said, then reconsidered. "Actually, the teachers seem nice enough; so does Roland du Turque. I can't quite get a read on the Santoris. What do you think, coz?"

Renie rested her short chin in her hand. "Phonies. Pete and Sandi not only know each other, but from what we saw in the garage, I'm guessing said knowledge could be intimate. *Ergo,* Pete and Marie are faking it. They're not on their honeymoon, and maybe they're not even married—at least not to each other."

"But why the charade?" Judith asked, sipping at the hot tea refill Renie had brought.

"Let's start with John Smith," Renie said, reclining at the foot of the bed. "Who did the FBI guy say he really was?"

"Alfonso Benedetto, otherwise known as Legs Benedict. And," Judith went on, "don't ask me what Barney's real name is—I couldn't possibly pronounce it, though I think his nickname is Fewer Fingers, for obvious reasons."

"Which means the missing Minerva isn't Mrs. Schwartz," Renie noted.

"Assuming that Minerva is really his mother," Judith added with a sly expression.

"And the other missing female, Darlene Smith? Who is—was—she?"

"Who knows?" Judith responded. "A girlfriend, I thought. But they didn't sleep together last night. Grandma Grover's lounge had been made into a bed."

"Ah." Renie clasped her hands behind her head. "So the car was found by Dooleys' house?"

"That's right. As I told you, J. J. has requested that it be towed downtown. But I doubt that they'll find anything to tell them where Darlene has gone."

A short silence passed between the cousins, who were each lost in thought. Then Judith remembered to tell Renie about O.P.'s sighting of the Malones. "It may not mean anything," she admitted, "but it's suggestive, don't you think, coz?"

"Could be," Renie said. "I'll tell you one thing—the Malones are jerks. Judging from what you've told me, they could also be crooks, and thus, not the Malones."

"J. J. is checking them out through their license plate," Judith said. "Until he's got a rundown on everybody, they're all stuck here. Sorry, coz, but so are you."

"Hm-mm." Renie seemed unperturbed. "Roland *seems* okay, but what do we know about him except that he likes jazz?"

"We don't know anything," Judith admitted. "The only personal information he's volunteered is that he once lived in New Orleans."

"J. J. and his partner must be coming up with something by now," Renie said, sitting up. "Will they share?"

"With Joe, maybe. Not with me." Judith's tone was wry.

At that moment, Joe entered the bedroom. He was surprised to see Renie, astonished to find his wife in bed. "What happened?" he asked, hurrying to Judith's side.

"Flu, I think," Judith said, holding up a hand. "Don't kiss me. I might be contagious."

"Well, damn," said Joe, looking helpless as men do when faced with insoluble problems such as illness, birth, death, and women's obsession with shoe sales. "Is this your backup?" He gestured at Renie.

"Yes, thank goodness," Judith replied. "She's made some nice sardine dump for dinner." Ignoring the aghast expression on her husband's face, Judith turned to Renie. "How did Mother like it?"

"Loved it," Renie replied, slipping off the bed. "Why not? It's her recipe." Renie left the room, presumably to check on the guests.

Removing his tie and keeping his distance, Joe glanced at Judith. "So when did you get sick?"

Judith touched only lightly on her collapse after Barney Schwartz had been cuffed by the FBI. "I think I was coming down with this bug all day," she said. "That was the last straw." Judith paused, giving Joe a kittenish look. "I don't suppose you'd want to relieve my mind by telling me what happened after they took Barney away?"

"It's not my case." Gingerly, Joe sat on the edge of the bed and took off his loafers. "You really think you're contagious?"

"Probably."

"It didn't seem to bother Renie."

"She's a woman."

"What?" Joe frowned at Judith.

"Never mind. Do you mean you haven't heard *anything* about this case?"

Going to the closet, Joe shook his head. "Not really, except that J. J. is still checking out the other witnesses. He's also got two missing persons on his hands, including a possible suspect in Darlene Smith."

"Who is actually . . . ?" Judith prompted.

"I don't know. Honest. Woody and I had a hair dryer homicide today."

"A what?" Judith raised her voice as Joe went into the bathroom.

"A hair dryer fryer," he shouted. "You know, husband's in the tub, wife tosses hair dryer at him. Sizzle, zap, hubby's got a permanent perm."

"Oh." Judith waited for Joe to return. "No sign of Minerva or Darlene?"

Joe was toweling off his face. "Not that I know of. I think I'll fix myself a steak."

"Good idea." Judith finished her tea. "Speaking of food, tell Renie I might be able to eat some toast a little later."

"Will do." Joe finished changing in a hurry, then escaped to what he hoped was a germ-free area. Renie reappeared ten minutes later, bearing more tea and two slices of lightly buttered toast.

"J. J. and Rich Goldman just arrived," she announced. "They're grilling the witnesses again in the front parlor."

"Damn!" Judith exclaimed. "I wish I felt better. I'd eavesdrop."

"I could do that," Renie volunteered. "Shall I take notes?"

"Would you?" Judith gave her cousin a grateful smile.

"Sure," said Renie. "I'll start right now."

"Wait," Judith called. "One thing—ask the guests to reregister. I want to compare their handwriting to those two notes."

Renie frowned. "Why not ask J. J. to do that?"

Judith looked mulish. "Because he isn't telling me anything. Thus, I'm not telling him. Not yet, anyway. Get it?"

"Of course," Renie replied. "I know you." She left on her mission.

Judith felt restless and frustrated, but knew she still wasn't sufficiently recovered to get out of bed. After finishing her toast, she dialed Chicago information on a whim. After going through at least three area codes, she finally came up with an address for Malachy Malone in the suburb of Winnetka. Next, she tried Miami, for the Santoris' address.

"That's a nonpub, nonlist, at the customer's request," the soft female voice informed Judith.

"But there is such a person?" Judith asked.

"As I told you, the number is unlisted at the customer's . . ."

"Thanks," Judith said, trying to sound like she meant it.

She already had an address on the FedEx envelope for Barney Schwartz, but decided to check with Royal Oak directory assistance anyway. Sure enough, there was a listing in the 248 area code. As an afterthought, she asked about a Schwartz Cadillac dealership.

"There's no such listing," the nasal-sounding operator replied, "but there is one for Barney's Buick and Cadillac in Royal Oak."

Judith was appropriately grateful. So even if Barney wasn't really Barney, he did live in Royal Oak and owned a car dealership. Judith felt as if she were getting somewhere. Her problem was that she didn't know where.

Joe kept away for most of the evening, except to check from the doorway on the status of Judith's health. Renie, however, returned around eight-thirty.

"I'm not a very good eavesdropper," she confessed. "I kept going from one door of the front parlor to the other, but I got caught twice by J. J. and once by Joe, who doesn't approve of my sleuthing methods. My notes are a shambles." Renie spread several sheets of spiral notebook paper onto the bedclothes. "I couldn't hear a damned thing during the Santori interviews. Both Pete and Marie—not to mention J. J.—kept their voices down. Fortunately, Mal and Bea tend to shout."

"They also tend to be real," Judith put in. "I checked them out through Chicago information."

"Hmm." Renie rubbed at her pug nose. "Then maybe they're as innocent as they claim to be. That was the gist of it—they own a dry-cleaning business in one of the suburbs . . ."

"Winnetka," Judith filled in.

"Right, that was it," Renie went on, "and they were on vacation, heading out here and then down to the Oregon Coast and back home through Reno and Salt Lake. They left their nephew in charge of the shop."

"So why has the trip been such a downer?" Judith asked. "Mal and Bea are always complaining about bad things happening to them, not to mention those references to Corelli and the mob-type names I heard on the phone."

Renie grimaced. "No names were brought up that I could hear. But they did say the vacation had been a disaster. When J. J. asked about their gun—which I gather he'd inquired about earlier—Mal said he always brought a weapon along when they traveled by car. Just in case. He said he usually keeps it in the shop.''

"Is that it?" Judith asked.

"For the Malones," Renie answered. "Roland was sort of a surprise, though not necessarily in a bad way. I didn't get to hear everything—he speaks so softly, you know. However—you'll love this, coz—Roland du Turque is not his real name."

"Oh, great." Judith threw up her hands. "Who is he— the Kansas City Bomber?"

Renie grinned. "Nothing so sinister. He's a writer who specializes in jazz. His real name is Orlando Turquette, but he prefers to travel anonymously so he calls himself Roland du Turque."

"Which name does he write under?" Judith asked.

Renie ducked her head. "I don't know. That's when I dropped my Pepsi and J. J. shooed me away."

"Oh." Judith sat up straighter, noticing that the dizziness finally seemed to have passed. "What about the teachers?"

"Pam was hard to hear," Renie said. "J. J. was questioning her about somebody named Isaac. That seemed to upset her, and after that, I didn't get much except that I gathered he's the late Isaac. Then another name came up, somebody called Rick. Pam's tone was defensive, but I couldn't hear more than a few words at a time."

"Such as?" Judith pressed.

Renie sighed and studied her notes. "Pam said something about Rick and honor, then J. J. asked a question that sounded like, 'Why didn't he stay?', and Pam got huffy and said, 'He's no half-assed wiseguy, he's my . . .' " Renie gave Judith an apologetic look. "I didn't get the last part. That's when Joe came along and yanked my chain."

Judith snatched at Renie's notes. "Let me see that. 'Half-assed wiseguy'? That doesn't sound like Pam, our sweet preschool teacher."

"You bet it didn't," Renie agreed. "But wait 'til I get

to Sandi.'' Renie grabbed the notes back. ''Joe went up to check on you, so I got in after J. J. started with Sandi. She cried a lot, especially when this Rick's name came up again. 'No headcrusher,' '' said Renie, reading her notes. '' 'Not on the pad.' 'Serious headache.' 'Hit the mattress.' And then—maybe the only big news I got out of all this— Sandi said, and I quote, because she wasn't blubbering anymore and I could hear her more clearly, 'Legs was a real stone killer.' ''

''Wow!'' Judith's eyes were huge. ''Sandi! And Pam! They're not such innocents after all. Maybe that might explain why they have a private plane.''

Renie was looking grim. ''Maybe. What's a stone killer?''

Judith fell back against the pillows. ''What's a headcrusher? What language is this?''

''I think,'' Renie said with a little shiver, ''you were right all along. The language is called 'mob.' ''

TEN

"THEY CAN'T ALL be tied to the mob," Judith declared, reaching for the Diet 7-Up Renie had brought her.

"They're not," Renie replied. "I mean, Roland's a writer, and the Malones may be exactly what they say they are—a pair of pain-in-the-ass dry cleaners."

Judith, however, shook her head. "No. I'm not ruling out the Malones, not with all those mob-style names they mentioned. Besides, what were they doing outside at five-thirty this morning nosing around their car?"

"It *is* their car," Renie pointed out. "Maybe they get up early at home. Though I can't imagine why anyone would do such a thing, I've actually heard of people who rise before ten. Some of them haven't even been institutionalized yet."

Judith hadn't listened to most of Renie's peculiar lack of understanding for people who didn't sleep in. "I get up at six," Judith said, more to herself than to her cousin. "But why go to their car?"

"I woke up once at five-thirty," Renie was musing. "There was this funny pink streak in the eastern sky. I thought there must be a huge forest fire in the mountains. Then I saw cars and buses and trucks driving on the bridge over the canal. To top it off, somebody in the neighborhood slammed a door and drove away. It was amazing.''

"The real question is," Judith continued, "when was John Smith—Legs Benedict—shot? Was he already dead when the Malones were in the cul-de-sac?"

"So then I thought maybe it would be interesting to see what went on in the middle of the night," Renie continued. "Sure enough, more cars, more people—right on our own block. I was flabbergasted. Most of our neighbors seem like sensible folk.''

"What if Mal had two guns?" Judith was still mulling to herself. "The one that was found in their room and another stashed in the Explorer. Have J. J. and Rich searched the cars? You'd think so. But I've heard that criminals can be very clever about hiding their weapons in automobiles.''

"The pink streak over the mountains got brighter and turned to gold, and after awhile the whole sky was light." Renie was looking vaguely awestruck. "Bill told me later that was what they call a sunrise.''

Judith turned to Renie. "Go watch the sunset. And while you're at it, take a peek at the Malones' car.''

"Huh?" Renie shook herself. "Is that the Ford SUV?"

"Right, Illinois plates. I told you, O. P. memorized the numbers.''

"What am I looking for?"

Judith's expression was sly. "Whatever the Malones were looking for. And," she called as Renie started to leave the bedroom, "check on Mother, would you? I'm worried about her. She might be upset about that screwy FBI guy who showed up today.''

"Not as upset as he is," Renie said over her shoulder.

To Judith's surprise, J. J. Martinez knocked on the door a few minutes later. "May I?" he asked, poking his head in.

"As long as you're not terrified of germs like Joe is," Judith said with a smile.

"Well . . ." J. J. didn't sit down, though he could have pulled up the bench from the dressing table. "Sorry to hear you're not feeling so good. Thought I'd let you know we're making some progress. Maybe we can let your guests leave later tomorrow.''

"That would be wonderful," Judith said. "I've got more coming in Wednesday. Of course the ones who are here paid through tonight, so nobody's out of pocket." She paused, giving J. J. what she hoped was her most ingratiating smile. "You mentioned progress. What kind exactly?''

"Too soon to go public," J. J. responded. "Background stuff, mostly.''

"You mean evidence that points to Barney as the killer?''

In front of the old cherrywood bureau, J. J. shifted from one foot to the other. "In a way. Can't explain just yet. Oh—we're still keeping two uniforms on duty. Checked it with Joe, they'll stay mostly inside tonight. Lon and Don, last names, Chang and Lang. Young. Sharp. 'Course Joe will be here, in the other bedroom.''

"What?" Judith frowned at J. J.

"Well . . . he doesn't want to get sick," J. J. replied. "He'll bunk in your son's old room. That okay?''

Judith sighed, then suppressed a smile. "Sure. Renie can stay in one of the empty guest rooms.''

"Renie? Oh—your cousin." J. J. moved jerkily around the room, edging ever closer to the door. "Can't stay in the guest rooms. Still off-limits.''

"I see." Judith considered. Renie would have to sleep in the master bedroom, germs and all.

"So that's it," J. J. concluded, opening the door.

"Wait," Judith called to the detective. "What about this Legs Benedict? Who was he?''

J. J. looked surprised. "You heard that? Who said?''

"The FBI agents who arrested Barney Schwartz. Come on, J. J. You really need to fill me in." Judith gave the detective a reproachful look.

J. J. winced, but closed the door behind him. "We're working with the FBI on this. Our hands are tied. Honest.''

"Not entirely," Judith asserted, annoyance bringing back a trace of dizziness. "I have a feeling some of this will be in the morning paper. When a disaster like this happens under my own roof, I shouldn't be the last to know."

"We're keeping your name out of it," J. J. said, on the defensive.

"Thanks. Now tell me about Legs and Fewer Fingers."

J. J.'s face contorted as he apparently argued with himself. "Okay. Guess you can't say or do much, since you're sick. Legs Benedict was a New York hit man for the Fusilli family. According to Terrill and Rosenblatt, there was a leak in the organization. Legs was sent to Detroit to kill Fewer Fingers, but he—that is, Barney—heard he was a marked man and skipped town. Didn't do a very good job of it, since Legs followed him all the way here. Barney got to Legs first. Barney's gun had been fired in the last twenty-four hours. Haven't got the full ballistic report, but that's a real start. Good thing Joe had already put it in the safe. Open and shut case."

"So it is." Judith started to congratulate J. J., then gave a little jump. "Hold it—how could the gun in the safe have killed Legs? Joe put it there last night."

"What?" J. J. looked shaken.

"Didn't he tell you?" Judith asked, trying to sort through the confusion. "Joe confiscated that gun earlier in the evening. Legs was still alive. Besides, the gun belonged to him—we think—and not to Barney."

Bewilderment enveloped J. J.'s lean face. "I don't get it. Joe handed over the gun, said it came out of Room Four. It had been fired recently."

"That gun came out of Room Three," Judith asserted. "Joe got the rooms mixed up from the get-go. The Smiths were in Room Three, the Schwartzes in Room Four. I thought Joe had it straightened out in his mind."

J. J. flopped down on the dressing table bench. "Damn!"

"Were there powder marks on Barney's hands?" Judith asked.

Forlornly, J. J. shook his head. "No. Figured he wore gloves."

"Look," Judith said earnestly. "That gun was in our safe in this very room last night. It couldn't possibly have been used to kill John . . . I mean, Legs."

J. J.'s olive complexion had gone pale. He was clutching at the dresser scarf as if it were a lifeline. "Impossible," he muttered, then bolted from the bench. "That safe—did you and Joe ever leave the room at the same time?"

Judith tried to remember; so much had happened in the last twenty-four hours. Maybe her illness had shorted out her memory. "I don't think so. After Joe confronted Legs with the weapon, and he denied owning it, the so-called Smiths went up to bed. We did, too, and never left the bedroom until we got up around six."

J. J. nodded in his jittery fashion. "So the safe was unguarded after you went downstairs. Where is it, by the way?"

Judith pointed to the cherrywood cupboard. "There, on the other side of the bathroom door. There's a false panel inside."

J. J. shook his head. "Shame on Joe. Too obvious. First place burglars look."

"It was my idea," Judith retorted. "I had that safe put in when we expanded the attic after I moved back home."

"Sorry." J. J. pressed his fingertips together, as if he were begging Judith's forgiveness. "Still, somebody could've come up here early this morning while you and Joe were downstairs, taken the gun, shot Legs, and brought it back. Didn't find the body until after seven-thirty, right?"

"Right," Judith admitted. "But they would have had to unlock the door to the third-floor stairs."

J. J. made a dismissive gesture. "No problem. Anybody who could've opened the safe could've picked the lock." He gave Judith a shrewd smile. "Hear you're not so bad at that sort of thing yourself."

"Right, I'm a real whiz." Judith felt downcast. Was it possible that someone actually had removed the gun from the safe? "They'd have to come and go outside via the front door," she said out loud. "Otherwise, Joe and I would have seen them from the kitchen."

"Who else knew Joe had the gun?" asked J. J.

"No one," Judith responded. "That is, Darlene knew. She was with Legs when Joe questioned him about it."

"Darlene." J. J. scowled. "Where the heck is she? We've got the car. What'd she do? Ditch it and take a bus?"

J. J.'s ruminations encouraged Judith to probe further. "Have you run her through the computer? She must have left prints somewhere. Like the glass on the nightstand."

J. J. drew back as if Judith had waved a gun at him. "The glass? Right, the glass. We took it in." His eyes roamed everywhere around the room, except in the direction of Judith.

"The glass." Judith narrowed her gaze. "What was in that glass, J. J.? It didn't look quite right to me."

Once again, J. J. seemed at war with himself. "You're right. Rich thought it seemed kind of cloudy. Had it analyzed. Some kind of sleeping drug."

"I wondered," Judith said. "Darlene was very hard to rouse. So what about prints?"

"Haven't heard yet," J. J. said, then glanced at his watch. "Hey—got to go. Let you know what to do about these other guys tomorrow."

"But J. J.," Judith pleaded, leaning forward in the bed, "you haven't told me why Barney would kill Legs. With a nickname like Fewer Fingers, I have to assume he's a gangster, too."

"Assume correctly," J. J. said, but kept on going.

Exasperated, Judith threw off the covers and got out of bed. The recurring dizziness was still with her, but she attributed it to frustration. Judith needed a bath, a nice, long soak in the tub. She needed to change into her nightgown. She needed to eat something other than toast.

But most of all, *she needed to know.*

*   *   *

Renie returned while Judith was still in the bathtub. "Are you decent?" she called through the door.

"Since when did I take a bath with my clothes on?" Judith shot back. "Can you make me some chicken noodle soup?"

"Sure. Crackers?"

"Please." A bit shakily, Judith got out of the tub and called out to Renie. "Hey—did you check the Malones' car?"

"Yep," Renie replied. "Full of junk. Well, not exactly junk, but all the stuff you'd haul along for a cross-country car trip."

"Okay. Thanks." On wobbly legs, Judith toweled herself off. "I could drink more tea, if you didn't mind."

"I don't mind. I'll bring a tray, just like the maid. You want a rose stuck somewhere?"

"I can guess where you'd stick it," Judith called back, then heard Renie snicker as she left the bedroom.

Judith still felt weak by the time Renie brought the soup, crackers, tea, and the guest register to her bed. "Here are the signatures you requested, Madam. Deduce, if you will."

Excitedly, Judith opened the register. "Were they co-operative? Did anyone balk?"

"Only Mal and Bea Malone," Renie answered. "But they balk at everything."

"What I'm banking on is that none of these signatures will match those notes," Judith said, gazing at the entries, then opening the drawer on the bedside table and taking out the two small slips of paper. "I made copies of these on my computer," she noted. "Just in case. You see, I figure they were written by John Smith."

"Legs, you mean?" said Renie, getting a grip on the soup bowl lest Judith's movements upset the contents.

"Right. I keep forgetting to call him that, which isn't—wasn't—his real name anyway . . . Hunh." She stared at the notes and the signatures. "I was wrong," Judith said with a troubled expression. "There *is* a match." She shoved the register and the pieces of paper at Renie. "Both those notes were written by Roland du Turque."

Renie agreed. There was no mistaking the similarities. "Why," she asked, "would Roland want to meet Barney? He's not a musician."

Judith had fallen back against the pillows. "Damn! I feel so . . . out of it. My poor logical mind seems to have skipped out on me. In fact, logic doesn't apply to this case. J. J. started to tell me some things, but then he clammed up. I don't know when I've felt so frustrated."

Renie was still studying the notes. " 'Legs-Hoffa-Provenzano,' " she read. "What did Legs Benedict have to do with Jimmy Hoffa? And who's Provenzano?"

"How should I know?" Judith sounded grumpy. "Maybe Legs—who was a professional killer—whacked Jimmy Hoffa. But what does that have to do with Roland and jazz?"

"Good point." Renie chewed her lower lip. "Giacalone," she said suddenly.

"Same to you." Judith started to taste her soup.

"No." Renie bounced on the bed, causing Judith to grip the soup bowl. "Giacalone and Provenzano were the guys Hoffa went to meet when he disappeared. Bill and I watched an A&E biography on Hoffa awhile ago. I don't know why I remember the names, except that Provenzano reminded me of *'Di Provenza il mar.'* "

"No kidding. Coz, are you feeling dizzy, too?"

Renie shook her head. "Not at all. It's an aria from *La Traviata.* Anyway, that's what I thought of, and Giacalone reminded me of *La Gioconda.* You know, the Ponchielli opera."

"I don't know," Judith said, but decided that maybe Renie, whose knowledge of opera far surpassed her own, wasn't crazy after all. "Were those two guys mobsters?" She didn't attempt to pronounce their names.

"I think so. One of them—I forget which—had alleged

mob ties. The other was definitely a crook. They were from Detroit. I think.''

Nibbling on a cracker, Judith grew thoughtful. ''Admit it, coz. Americans are fascinated by gangsters, going back to the highwaymen. Killers like Jesse James and John Dillinger were heroes, in a way. Heaven knows, I've always been intrigued. But when they're under your roof, there's nothing glamorous about them. It's just plain scary.''

The phone rang on the nightstand. ''My mother?'' Renie said as Judith reached for the receiver. ''Tell her I went to Antarctica to catch some rays.''

But it wasn't Aunt Deb who was on the other end; it was Mike.

''Hi, Mom,'' said the familiar, cherished voice. ''Hey, we've got a favor to ask.''

''Sure,'' Judith replied, then mouthed ''Mike'' to Renie. ''What is it?''

''Can you put us up for a few days? The doctor told Kristin today that the baby may come early and he'd like to have her stay closer to a hospital. It's an hour from here at the park ranger lodgings, and that's in light traffic. Okay?''

Judith's jaw dropped. ''Ah . . . When would you arrive?''

''Tomorrow,'' Mike replied. ''We thought of coming in tonight, but Kristin was tired from going in to see Dr. Fendall and we've still got to pack up some things.''

''Sure,'' Judith gulped. ''Come ahead. You can stay in your old room.''

''Great. We'll see you around noon.'' Mike paused. ''How's everything?''

''Umm . . . Great. Everything's just . . . great. Love you.'' Hanging up the phone, Judith burst into tears.

''Coz!'' Renie was alarmed. ''What's wrong?''

''Everything,'' Judith wailed.

''Huh?'' Renie grabbed a Kleenex from the box on the nightstand and handed it to Judith. ''Everything's not great then,'' Renie said under her breath, waiting for Judith to calm down.

"Mike and Kristin are coming tomorrow to stay until the baby gets here." Judith wiped her eyes and blew her nose. "Joe won't come near me because I'm sick. Mother is driving me insane because I don't know whether she is—or not. The FBI thinks she's a Nazi. And some Mafia hit man got whacked right in front of my birdbath and who knows how many other mobsters are wandering around my dear old family home?" Judith burst into fresh tears.

"Hmmm." Renie's expression was unusually sympathetic. "It's a mess, all right," she finally said. "But you know things will work out. Come on, coz—you're the one who always sees the bright side of things. As Grandma Grover would've said, 'Keep your pecker up.' ''

Judith glared at Renie from swollen eyes. "A lot of good that did her. Grandma's dead, isn't she?"

Renie gave a start. "Well . . . yes, but she lived to be almost ninety."

"How can I let Mike and Kristin stay here with all these mobsters? How can I get rid of these awful people? How can I convince the FBI that Mother was never at Auschwitz? How can I do anything when I'm sick?"

"I guess you can't," Renie said, unable to remain sympathetic for more than a couple of minutes at a time. "You might as well just roll over and croak."

Judith blew her nose again and gave Renie a sharp look. "You're mean."

"Yep." Renie lay down at the foot of the bed and yawned. "How soon do I put the guests to bed?"

"You don't." Judith's face softened as she dabbed at her eyes with a fresh Kleenex. "Are you tired?"

"I'm tired of *them*," Renie replied. "You know I always stay up late."

"Maybe I'm just tired, period," Judith said in a hollow voice. "It's only the start of the tourist season, but I really haven't had a break since January. The B&B was full up for most of the spring."

"You're run down," Renie said, sitting up again. "When Arlene gets back, why don't you ask her to take over for a few days? Now that the two of you have cut out the catering business, she'd probably be glad to fill in."

"Maybe." Judith knew that Renie might be right. The catering arm that Judith and Arlene had run for several years had become too demanding and not as necessary to Judith's income after she married Joe. Then Carl Rankers had retired, and Arlene needed more free time. But Judith's friend and neighbor enjoyed being busy. It was very likely that she wouldn't mind running Hillside Manor for a few days while Judith and Joe slipped off to the ocean or to Canada.

Carl's retirement reminded Judith of Renie and Bill's key club. Though the thought horrified and puzzled Judith, she had to ask. "Tell me more about this hobby of yours," Judith said, giving her nose one last blow. "What kind of key club is this that you and Bill joined?"

Renie shrugged. "The usual. Trading spouses. There are problems, of course. Sometimes you get somebody who can't deliver. They talk the talk, but they can't walk the walk. So to speak." Renie yawned again.

"I see," Judith said, and wished she didn't. Maybe it was better to talk of murder. "Are you sure you don't mind staying here tonight with these goons?"

"They may not all be goons," Renie pointed out. "Still, it's a good thing those cops are on duty. Even if J. J. had let me stay on the second floor, I think I'd have passed. Who wants to sleep next door to Bad Manners Malone or Pop 'Em Off Perl?"

"Good point," Judith agreed, finally finishing her soup. "How are we going to confront Roland du Turque about those notes?" She used her spoon to indicate the two slips of paper resting on the down comforter.

Renie scratched her head. "Well—the smart thing to do would be to turn them over to J. J."

"Aside from that," Judith said.

Renie sighed. "Do you want me to give it a try? Roland

was playing Uncle Corky's old ukulele the last time I saw him.''

Judith considered. "No. I'd like to see his reaction in person.'' Reaching into the nightstand drawer, Judith took out her notebook and a pen. "For now, let's try to determine how everybody ended up here. As I've said all along—and I was right—it wasn't a coincidence that these people booked themselves at the same time.''

"You're dreaming,'' Renie said, though she grinned at her cousin. "You must be feeling better.''

"A little.'' Judith passed the notebook and pen to Renie. "Use your God-given artistic talent. Draw a map of the United States.''

Renie looked askance. "How detailed?''

"Rough—just so we can fill in the cities where these people came from.''

With quick, sure strokes, Renie drew a recognizable map. "Now what?''

Judith leaned forward, smiling appreciatively. "Good work. Start with Legs in New York. Then go west to Detroit.''

Renie drew a line from the east coast to Lake Erie. "Legs and Darlene arrive to find that Barney and Min have already skipped town, right?''

"You got it. Barney makes a reservation for Hillside Manor. Why here? Why make a reservation at all?''

Renie was studying her own handiwork. "Because of the overnight deliveries, we know that Barney, as well as Legs, left Royal Oak Friday. It's a long haul from there to here. When we've driven back to visit Bill's family in Wisconsin, we've always spent three nights on the road. But we take our time.''

"It's doable,'' Judith said. "There were two drivers in each car. They probably traded off. The question is, how did Legs know Barney was headed here?''

"Somebody squealed?'' Renie suggested.

"Maybe. Somebody squealed on Legs and his mission to kill Barney.'' Judith paused, her brain clicking away.

"The FedEx envelope! You use FedEx quite a bit. When you've scheduled a pickup and have to leave the house, you put it in your milk box. I've seen you do it when we've gone somewhere together."

"Sure," Renie responded. "I just tell them on the phone where I'm leaving it."

"So if Barney did the same thing—and he certainly would have been in a hurry to get out of town—Legs might have come along and found the envelope addressed to me at Hillside Manor. That means he knew where Barney was headed." Judith gave Renie a triumphant smile.

"Brilliant, coz," Renie said with a grin. "What about the others?"

Judith's smile faded. "That might tie in to whoever tipped off Barney. In terms of geography, Pam and Sandi were closest to Legs. Isn't Newark right across the Hudson River from New York?"

"More or less," Renie said. "Close enough, anyway." She looked again at her makeshift map. "Geography may have nothing to do with it. The telephone, E-mail, all the marvels of modern communication are at the disposal of contemporary crooks as well as honest working stiffs like us. You've got the Santoris in Miami, Roland in Kansas City, the Malones in Chicago. Any one of them, along with Pam and Sandi, could have tipped off Barney, and Barney could have reciprocated by telling them where he was going."

"Don't forget, the Malones didn't make a reservation." Judith rested her chin on her fist. "Again—why did Barney come here?"

"The most unlikely place to look for him?" Renie offered. "A cozy little B&B tucked into a neighborhood hillside? A big city not associated with gangsters?"

"You're forgetting one connection, coz," Judith noted. "The Teamsters. Hoffa. And before him, our own Dave Beck."

"Maybe. But Beck goes back forty years or more," Renie pointed out. "Hoffa took over from him—when?"

The early sixties? And Hoffa was never associated with this area.''

Judith sank back against the pillows. ''True. But it was a thought.''

Except for the constant patter of rain against the dormer windows, the room was silent for a few moments. The twilight had almost faded into darkness, and Judith had turned on the bedside lamp, which cast a golden glow under the eaves. At last, she sat up again and regarded Renie with a curious expression. ''We're forgetting somebody.''

''Who?''

''In the original batch of reservations made last Friday, there was one that was canceled later in the day,'' Judith explained. ''Meanwhile, Roland called—or someone did, requesting Monday and Tuesday nights.''

''That's right,'' Renie said. ''I remember that when I scrolled down and found your reservation list there was one for somebody who isn't here. It wasn't a very common name. What was it?''

''Doria,'' Judith replied. ''From Las Vegas. Who do you suppose he really is? And,'' she added ominously, ''did he cancel—or was he canceled?''

ELEVEN

"DAMN!" JUDITH EXCLAIMED. "I can't remember Doria's first name. And of course it got deleted when somebody dumped the reservations from the computer."

"A first name might not help," Renie noted. "Las Vegas is a huge city these days. If it was a common Christian name, there might be more than one of them in the Vegas phone book. Then again, it could be an alias."

"I don't recall much of anything about the man's voice," Judith said, "but it was perfectly normal, no accent of any kind. I do remember that the woman who called in the cancellation sounded kind of husky."

"Disguised?" Renie suggested.

Judith gazed at Renie. "Possibly." She flexed her legs under the covers, then batted at her temple in a frustrated gesture. "I should have gotten Caller ID for me, not just for Mother. She doesn't need to screen her calls in the toolshed as much as I need to know who's called here at the B&B."

"I think," Renie said, "I mentioned it at the time."

"I know, I know. Sometimes I tend to put things off." *How long had it been? Two, three years?* Judith silently chastised herself for procrastinating.

"Couldn't live without my Caller ID," Renie chirped.

Then, seeing Judith sink into gloom, she mustered a bit of compassion. "Stop beating yourself up. It might not have showed the number. Sometimes long distance calls come up only as out-of-area. Besides, you really don't know if this Doria fits into the rest of the puzzle."

"True," Judith acknowledged, taking her watch from the nightstand. "It's not quite nine-thirty. I feel a need to apologize to my guests for this inconvenience."

"Why? You didn't shoot Legs."

Judith's gaze narrowed. "Don't be dense. I want to talk to these people."

"You're sick." Renie fixed Judith with a hard gaze.

"I'm convalescing," Judith replied, stare for stare. "Bring them up. Start with Roland."

"Jeez!" Renie threw up her hands. "Okay, okay. What if they don't want to come? What if they're afraid of germs?"

"They *are* germs," Judith retorted. "At least some of them may be. Hint that I might be willing to refund some of their money. Not that I will. Tell them I have spells. Quinsy. That's always a good one, if only because nobody knows what it is anymore."

"Did we ever?" Renie responded, but dutifully headed for the door.

Five minutes later, Roland du Turque appeared, looking concerned.

"You gave us quite a fright," he said, gingerly seating himself on the dressing table bench. "Are you feeling better?"

"Much," Judith replied, then went into her personal apology for upsetting Roland's plans.

"Oh, no," he assured her. "I'm not bound by a fixed schedule. There's no need to reimburse me. Writers are their own bosses, you know. Except when it comes to deadlines." He grimaced slightly.

"Yes," Judith said vaguely, then reached into the drawer and removed the two small slips of note paper. "Which reminds me—I believe you mislaid these?"

Roland got up and came over to the bed. A bit warily—or so Judith thought—he put on a pair of wire-rimmed glasses. "Oh, my," he murmured, "so I did. Do you mind telling me where you found them?"

"I found only the one with the names on it," Judith said. "It was under the piano. The other was retrieved by my cleaning woman."

"Indeed." Roland's smile was thin. "Do you know where she found it?"

"Somewhere on the second floor," Judith answered blandly as she held out her hand. "If you don't need them anymore, I'll put them in the wastebasket."

Roland hesitated. "Why no. They're of no use to me now," he responded, lowering his gaze and putting the glasses in the pocket of his blue dress shirt. "Thank you. I hate to be so careless."

Judith feigned consternation. "Oh, dear—then whoever you asked to meet you outside never got the note. Is that a problem?"

Roland's brown eyes had hardened, though he tried to sustain his smile. "Not at all. It turned out that the person I hoped to speak with had no knowledge whatsoever about Fats Waller."

"Oh—yes," Judith said with a big smile. "You write about music, I hear. Have you been published?"

Roland's manner was self-deprecating. "In a small sort of way. You probably couldn't find any of my work in stores or libraries."

"That's a shame," Judith responded. "I would have enjoyed reading what you had to say about jazz."

"A minor contribution," Roland shrugged.

"A major loss," Judith said. "For me."

Roland sketched a bow. "You're too kind. Thank you for finding my notes." He started for the door.

"One thing," Judith called after him. "What does Hoffa have to do with music?"

Roland turned ever so slightly, not quite meeting Judith's gaze. "Detroit, the Motown recording industry. I've been seeking a connection between Hoffa and the music business. There've been rumors, you see.''

"Rumors," Judith echoed. "You mean the Teamsters tried to take over Motown Records?''

"As I said, rumors." Roland sketched another small bow and made his exit.

Drumming her nails on the bedclothes, Judith wondered about those rumors. It was possible, of course. Certainly Hoffa had been head of the Teamsters in Detroit while Motown Records had surged to the top of the charts. She was still trying to figure out whether or not Roland was lying about Hoffa, about the note that had been found in Barney's room, and maybe just about everything else when Pete and Marie Santori entered the room.

"I feel terrible," Judith declared as the couple sat down pressed against each other on the dressing table bench. "This episode has ruined your honeymoon."

Clinging to Pete's arm, Marie simpered. "We'll make up for it during the next fifty years."

"No problem," Pete said, squeezing Marie's knee. "Maybe we can head out tomorrow."

"For where?" Judith inquired, in what she hoped was a casual tone.

"Canada," Marie replied.

"California," Pete answered at the same time.

The couple looked at each other and burst into laughter. "I guess," Pete said between chuckles, "we have irreconcilable differences."

Marie leaned her head on Pete's shoulders. "Shall we get a divorce, Pooky-wooky?"

"Why not, Sudsy-wudsy?" Pete said, rubbing noses with Marie. "Then we could get married all over again."

"I gather," Judith said, still trying to maintain her casual manner, "that you had no planned itinerary."

Taking Marie's hand and getting to his feet, Pete shook his head. "We figured this would be a good jumping-off point. Canada, California—about now, I'd prefer some sun. How about you, Cutsey-wootsey?"

Marie toyed with the gold chain around Pete's neck. "Sure. Carmel. Santa Barbara. San Diego. Sounds good, Doodily-woodily."

"Then that's where we'll go," Pete said, steering Marie through the door. "Thanks, Mrs. Flynn. You've been great."

"But . . . wait," Judith said, no longer sounding casual. "I have a couple of other questions to . . ."

Pete waved a hand. "Not to worry. We won't bother you any longer. You've been sick."

The Santoris exited the bedroom. Judith swore under her breath. "A washout," she muttered, then wondered if that was true. The Santoris had no idea where they were going after they left Hillside Manor. Perhaps they intended to go back to Miami. Honeymoon or not, Heraldsgate Hill might have been their destination point.

Judith was still mulling over the Santoris when Pam and Sandi all but skipped into the room.

"A is for apple," Sandi chanted. "A is for animal, A is for April, A is for . . ."

"Arrest," Pam filled in. "Isn't that something? About Mr. Schwartz, I mean."

"A is for agreement," Judith said dryly. "As well as for apology, which I offer you now. I hope all of this hasn't completely spoiled your visit."

The preschool teachers glanced at each other. "Applesauce?" said Sandi, and Pam broke into the giggles.

"Sorry, Mrs. Flynn," Sandi said, giving Pam a playful little shove. "We were still on A. Honestly, though, it's been kind of a thrill. Sometimes our world shrinks to the size of three- and four-year-olds."

"Really," Judith breathed. "I think it's rather charming. Alphabet games are fun. How about H? As in H is for headcrusher?"

Sandi blanched and Pam cringed as if she'd been struck. "That's not a word we teach our kids," Pam declared with a hint of anger.

"I don't even know what it means," Sandi said with indignation. "Is it like bonecrusher?"

"I'm not sure," Judith admitted. "It just suddenly popped into my head. Maybe I thought it was an East Coast colloquialism. It's interesting how we speak the same language, but different parts of the country have different expressions and terms."

Sandi's pretty face had grown hard. "Is that why you asked us up here? To discuss regional idiosyncrasies?"

Pam's eyes had narrowed. "If you have something to say, say it. Just because we teach preschool, do you think we're really stupid?"

With an ironic smile, Judith shook her head. "No, I don't. Far from it. Look, I know both of you recognized Pete and Marie Santori. Why is that such a secret?" Sandi and Pam exchanged quick, sharp glances. "We knew him in high school," Pam said in a rush.

"It had been at least ten years since we last saw him," Sandi put in. "It was such a surprise to find him here."

"We weren't even sure it was him," Pam added. "We'd never met Marie. She's not from Jersey."

Judith was certain they were lying, but there was no point in pressing the matter. Instead, she recalled the notes that Renie had taken, and resorted to surprise tactics. "What happened to Isaac?"

Pam covered her mouth with both hands; Sandi's soft features sharpened, green eyes glinting like a feral cat.

"Who are you?" Sandi demanded, the growl in her voice a full octave lower than usual.

"What do you mean?" Judith asked innocently.

Pam's hands fell away from her face, and she jabbed a finger at Judith. "Are you the reason Legs came here?" She took a menacing step towards the bed. "Are you Doria?"

Judith was flabbergasted. The dizziness returned. The cozy bedroom, with its yellow and green tulip motif seemed topsy-turvy, as if a mad gardener had planted the bulbs upside-down.

"Doria?" Judith echoed, her voice sounding far away. "Doria, from Vegas?"

"You know Doria." Pam's face wore a shrewd, calculating expression. "But are you Doria?"

"No. No," Judith added hastily, trying to gather her wits and her equilibrium. "Doria canceled."

The young women again exchanged glances. "I'm not surprised," said Sandi. "Doria's reputation is erratic."

"Why," Judith began, "don't you tell me who Doria is? And about Isaac?"

Resignedly, Pam sat down at the far end of the bed, while Sandi perched on the dressing table bench. "Doria's just a name, someone who seems to surface in some very sticky situations," Sandi said, her usually cheerful face troubled. "All we know is that he—or she—isn't somebody you mess with."

"I see," Judith said, though of course she didn't. "Isaac's quite another matter, I believe."

"He certainly is," Pam sighed. "Or was." She paused, turning her head away from Judith. "I'm not sure why we should tell you about him, except that you know more than you ought to. How come?"

Judith raised both hands in a helpless gesture. "This is my house. My husband's a cop. I've already had an accused killer try to take me hostage under my very own roof. Not to mention finding a corpse in my backyard. Why wouldn't I try to find things out?"

"That's a good point," Sandi allowed, looking more like her usual harmless self. "We hadn't thought about it from your perspective."

Pam nodded. "Mrs. Flynn—you really are Mrs. Flynn?" She waited for Judith's nod. "Anyway, Mrs. Flynn's caught in the middle. It's not fair to keep her in the dark."

"So enlighten me," Judith urged.

Sandi squirmed on the bench. "I don't know . . . It's not a pretty story."

"That's not *our* fault," Pam retorted.

"But," Sandi persisted, "it might give Mrs. Flynn the wrong impression."

Judith shook her head. "I'm fairly good at zeroing in on the truth."

Sandi remained dubious, but Pam leaned back on her elbows, eyes on the low dormer ceiling. "First of all, Isaac is dead. He wasn't a criminal, but he got in a bind over some business debts several years ago. He was in import-export, mainly leather goods. He made the mistake of going to the mob for money. When things improved for him, he was able to start paying them back. But they didn't want the cash as much as they wanted his services. Isaac was in a position to launder money for the mob. And that's what he did, until he couldn't stand it anymore and wanted out. What he didn't realize was that you don't get out—ever. Foolishly, he quit. Just quit. And what was even worse, he threatened to go to the police." Sadly, Pam shook her head. "The mob had him killed last year." There was a catch in Pam's voice. "Isaac—Isaac Perl—was my father."

Judith's condolences were heartfelt. "Was the term 'headcrusher' a reference to whoever killed your father?" she asked after her sympathy had been expended.

"Not exactly," Pam said. "A headcrusher is an enforcer. The headcrusher came around a couple of times before my father was killed. Of course Papa tried to keep all of this to himself, but my brother and I could see the bruises. We began to piece together what was going on."

"And your mother?" Judith asked.

Pam shook her head. "Mama died six years ago. Cancer. That was when Papa got into financial difficulties. He was spending so much time taking care of her that he let the business slide."

"I'm so sorry," Judith murmured, then remembered some of the other phrases from the notes Renie had taken while Pam was being interviewed by J. J. "Would I be wrong if I guessed that the killer—the stone killer, I believe is the term—was Legs Benedict?"

Pam's eyes widened. "No. How . . . Are you sure you're not Doria?"

Judith winced. "Of course I'm sure. Maybe you'd better tell me about this Doria."

Once more, Pam and Sandi looked at each other. "We can't," Sandi finally said. "It's not that we don't want to, it's that we're not exactly sure who Doria is. All we know is that Doria was supposed to be here and didn't show."

Pam gave Judith a strained smile. "We do have a confession to make, though. Yesterday, we couldn't figure out why Doria wasn't among the assembled guests. We went into the kitchen when you weren't around and looked at your computer. By accident, we deleted some of your database."

"I see." Judith wondered if the deletion had in fact been an accident. "Did you also swipe the disk and rip the pages out of the guest register?"

"No," Pam replied, looking startled. "Why would we do that?"

"Somebody did," Judith said in a dry tone. "Tell me this—how many of these people did you know before you got to Hillside Manor?"

"Pete," Pam replied. "That's all. Except we knew Legs was coming here. We had never met him, though."

Judith was dubious. "Not Barney?"

Sandi shook her head. "I've never heard of him."

A terrible suspicion had crept over Judith. If Barney hadn't killed Legs, somebody else had committed the crime. Pam Perl had a motive. And she and Sandi had had a gun. They had flown from Newark in a private plane. There was money somewhere. Perhaps it had come out of the family import-export business. But maybe it had come from a more sinister stash.

"How did you know Legs was coming to this B&B?" Judith asked.

"Somebody called us," Pam answered. "It was a woman."

"We *think* it was a woman," Sandi put in. "She had a

really husky voice. Pam took the call, but we don't know who it was. But she—the woman with the deep voice— told Pam that Legs was arriving here Monday.''

"When did you get this call?" Judith inquired.

"Friday," Pam said. "We flew out of Newark Sunday afternoon and stopped off in Chicago. We got here Monday afternoon. You know that."

"Chicago?" Judith cocked her head at Pam. "Why Chicago?"

"I'm a licensed pilot," Sandi said. "The plane belongs to Mr. Perl's company. I'd never flown cross-country before, so since we didn't have to be here until Monday, we decided to break up the flight and not do it in one day."

The explanation made sense, though niggling doubts remained. Chicago was Malone territory in Judith's mind. Yet Mal and Bea would have been on the road by then. Maybe the teachers were telling the truth.

"I still don't understand the purpose of your trip," Judith said, moving around in the bed in an attempt to get more comfortable. "Why did you want to meet Legs here? You were just a few miles from him back in Newark."

Sandi pushed a stray lock of blond hair from her forehead. "That's true. But you don't know New York. You can lose yourself a lot easier there than in a city like this. Especially if you want to get lost."

Judith uttered a short, impatient sigh. "That still doesn't explain what you intended to . . ." She stopped as Vivian Flynn came through the bedroom door.

"Judith!" Herself cried, flying across the room. Renie, looking annoyed, was right behind her. "Joe told me you were at death's door. How can I help?"

It was ten o'clock, but time meant nothing to Herself. She was a night person who blossomed after dark. Renie looked as if she'd liked to have nipped Vivian in the bud.

"That's very kind of you to offer," Judith said in a beleaguered voice, "but we're doing fine. And I'm better. Really."

Herself sat on the bed, next to Pam. "Oh, dear—I hope

so. You look absolutely *awful*." The gloating tone annoyed Judith, but Vivian didn't skip a beat. "Pale and wan, peaked and drawn—poor thing, I hear this whole tragedy has been a dreadful ordeal. Joe told me all about it. Imagine! Gangsters!" She darted quick glances at Pam and Sandi. "Are they . . . ?"

"We're preschool teachers," Sandi put in, looking perky. "Pam teaches the threes. I have the fours." She stood up and went over to Pam, their customary girlish guises back in place, apparently for the benefit of Herself.

"May we go now?" Pam asked.

"Ah . . ." Judith grimaced. "Yes, I guess so." It would be hopeless to try to interrogate the teachers with Vivian on hand.

The teachers left, practically bumping into each other as they made for the door.

"The young," Herself murmured. "So naive, so impressionable, so pretty. Well." She sat up straighter on the bed and placed a hand on Judith's. "This is all too thrilling. I can't believe I missed everything this morning. Luckily, Joe filled me in. If you want help, I'm right down the street. In fact, I'd be glad to give you any advice you need."

"Advice?" Judith was forced to leave her hand under Herself's, though her fingers seemed to have taken on a life of their own and were wiggling like so many minnows. Mercifully, Vivian had switched to a different perfume. Judith had feared that Eau de Muskrat might make her throw up again.

"Yes." Vivian patted her platinum locks with her free hand. "You see, I've known some of these types from my days on the nightclub circuit. Especially in Florida. They can't pull the wool over these eyes." The false lashes fluttered wildly.

It was a temptation, but even Judith had her limits when it came to sleuthing. "Thanks, Vivian, but the police think they have a suspect in custody," she said, trying to summon up a grateful smile. "Or didn't Joe tell you?"

"Of course he did," Herself replied, finally removing

her hand. "He tells me everything. But apparently there's some doubt. I saw him talking outside earlier this evening with that lean, nice-looking detective. J. J., isn't it? I met J. J. ever so many years ago when Joe and I were married. I remember once when J. J. and his wife—what was her name? A tall, blond Scandinavian girl. Brigitta. I always figured she'd run to fat. Anyway, we were all sitting around having drinks and . . ."

"I'm going to get the Malones," Renie broke in. "I'll be right back."

Judith gave Renie an appreciative nod. For the next five minutes, she laid back and listened to Herself's reminiscences about the Martinezes' visit to the Flynns. The memories shouldn't have galled her—but they did. Joe and Vivian had been married for over twenty years, and Judith still resented what she considered an extended intrusion on her own life. As Herself rambled on, Judith thought of the wasted decades with Dan, sitting not with J. J. and Brigitta Martinez, but with her husband's drunken cronies from the restaurant he'd owned and lost. In a more perfect world, Dan and Vivian would have married each other, and spent the rest of their lives in drunken oblivion.

"Then Joe got Woody Price as a partner," Herself was saying. "A good-looking fellow—I've always had a weakness for black men—but much too serious. On the other hand, he was never as nervous as J. J. Indeed, I've often wondered if Woody has any nerves at all. I recall one time, when we went to the annual departmental picnic, Woody . . ."

Renie returned with the Malones. "Mal and Bea had to be coaxed," Renie said in a tone that suggested she'd persuaded them with the threat of a fireplace shovel. "They're worn out," she added, glancing meaningfully at Herself. "They'd like to get to bed as soon as possible."

"Of course." Judith sensed her smile was phony. "Vivian, I'm sorry, but I have to speak with these guests. If you'll excuse us . . . ?"

Herself offered Mal a coquettish glance. "Certainly. I

understand. Now don't tell me these two are on *their* honeymoon?'' Getting up from the bed, Vivian went over to the Malones and pinched their chubby cheeks. "Cute! No wonder you want to go to bed. 'Night, all.'' With swinging hips, Herself left.

"Sheesh! Who's that broad?" Mal demanded, rubbing at his right cheek as if stung by a bee.

"A neighbor,'' Judith said. "She means well. I think.''

"Hunh,'' grumbled Bea. "She looks like a hussy to me.''

"Flamboyant,'' Judith said, somehow feeling a need to defend Herself.

"Where's the money?'' Mal demanded.

"Money?'' Judith blinked. "Oh—the refund. We'll work that out later. Right now I wanted to apologize for all the inconvenience. It's possible that you'll be able to leave tomorrow. If you do, I'd like to make up a nice picnic basket for you to take on your way to . . . Sorry, I don't know your next destination.''

"The ocean,'' Mal replied. "That's the whole point of this trip. Me and Bea have never seen the ocean.''

"A lake's a lake,'' Bea put in, catching a glimpse of herself in the dressing table mirror and patting her untidy curls. "Oh, sure, Lake Michigan's big and you could pretend it's the ocean. But it's not.''

"True,'' Renie murmured from her post by the bureau. "The ocean's bigger.''

The irony was lost on the Malones. "Look,'' Mal said, jabbing a finger at Judith, "we'd better get out of here tomorrow. Yeah, yeah, everybody says this is a nice city, but it rains all the time and we can't see much of it holed up in this place of yours.''

"The beach,'' Bea said, her voice starting to quaver. "We dreamed of the big waves and all that driftwood and those tidepools full of funny-looking little animals. We were going to take Corelli with us. We knew how much he'd love the beach. But . . .'' Bea bit her lips, buried her face in her hands, and burst into tears.

Renie, who only cried when her favorite baseball team didn't make it into the postseason, let out a little hiss of annoyance. "Come on, Mal," she said, "don't get left out. Everybody cries tonight."

Mal, who had put an arm around his wife, shook a fist at Renie. "Don't be a smartass! You got no feelings?"

Wide-eyed, Renie looked all around her person. "I got some somewhere. Now where did I put them?"

Judith, naturally, was moved by Bea's distress. "Please— ignore my cousin. She has a heart of brick. What happened to Corelli, Mr. Malone?"

Mal lifted his bulbous chin. "He was shot, that's what happened." Turning back to Renie, Mal made a gesture that emulated the squeezing of a trigger. "You get that, big mouth? You think that's funny? Sheesh—Corelli was our baby boy, our own dear son."

Bea collapsed in Mal's arms.

Judith began to cry again.

Renie went into the bathroom and slammed the door.

TWELVE

BETWEEN SOBS, JUDITH realized that her cousin hadn't barricaded herself in the bathroom, but had gone to fetch some water for Bea.

"Here," Renie said, thrusting the glass at the grieving woman. "I'm sorry I shot my face off."

It was the wrong thing to say. "That's what happened to Corelli! He had his face shot off!" Bea shrieked and clawed at her husband's chest.

"I'm gettin' her outta here," Mal grumbled. "You dames make me wanna puke." Clumsily, he gathered Bea close to him and virtually dragged her out of the bedroom.

Judith was wiping her eyes. "You *are* a big pain," she said to Renie between sniffs. "You went too far. Sometimes you take after my mother instead of Aunt Deb."

Renie shrugged. "It's some kind of syndrome, a refutation of what our mothers represent that we don't like about them. As Bill would say, we become just the opposite. You act like *my* mother, all sentimentality and bleeding hearts. It's a form of rebellion, and ..."

"Oh, shut up!" Judith glowered at Renie. "I'm in no mood to listen to your long, drawn-out rehash of Bill's brilliant insights. Didn't you hear what the Malones said? *Their son was shot.* It must have happened while they were driving from Chicago.'' The tears had stopped, and Judith was sitting up very straight. ''It can't be a coincidence that one of our guests is shot here, and another was shot en route.''

Looking vaguely chagrined, Renie perched on the edge of the bed. ''Okay, you're right about that. But I'm not apologizing for my attitude. The Malones are a pair of jackasses, and I suspect they were that way even before Sonny Boy got whacked. Besides, it isn't always what you say, it's what you do. In case you haven't noticed, I'm here.''

It was Judith's turn to look sheepish. ''I know.'' She pressed her fingers against her swollen eyes. ''You usually are. But you have to remember that no matter how odious these people may be, they're still my guests.''

''This bunch is beyond odious,'' Renie stated with a grim expression. ''What did the teachers have to say for themselves? And Roland?''

Judith recapitulated the conversations. Renie listened, if not with sympathy, at least with patience. ''So Pam's dad— Isaac Perl—got whacked by Legs, providing Pam with a terrific motive. And someone wanted Pam to know where she could find Legs, away from his natural habitat.''

''Put like that,'' Judith said, casting a shrewd eye at Renie, ''it makes sense. Here on the other coast, Legs had no goons to protect him. He was out of his element.''

''And out of luck,'' Renie noted. ''Still, I hope the police and the FBI are right. It makes perfect sense for Barney to have shot Legs in self-defense.''

Judith stared at Renie. ''You're right. So if Barney killed Legs, why didn't he claim self-defense instead of denying what happened?''

''Hmmm.'' Renie paused in thoughtful concentration. ''Do you know if the cops are sticking to J. J.'s theory that Barney somehow retrieved his gun from your safe?''

''It'd be a pat solution,'' Judith replied, then looked past Renie as Joe poked his head into the room.

''I'm saying goodnight,'' he said with a slightly embarrassed expression. "If you need me, I'll be in Mike's old room."

"Not for long," Judith retorted. "Mike and Kristin will be here tomorrow. The baby's due any minute."

Joe inched a bit further into the room. "Really?" His grin was a trifle lopsided.

"Really. Which also means that J. J. and Company better have this homicide solved in the next twelve hours," Judith asserted. "I don't want Mike and Kristin under the same roof with these creeps."

Joe held up both hands. "Hey—it's not my case. You can't rush these investigations, especially when you're dealing with cross-jurisdictions."

Judith remained firm. "You'll see J. J. before I will. Tell him I want this mess cleaned up. Quick."

Joe bristled. "Are you nuts? You know better."

"Do I?" Judith glared at Joe. "I'm beginning to think I know more than your homicide squad and the FBI combined."

"Really." Joe's green eyes grew frosty. "Over the years, I'll admit you've gotten lucky a couple of times. But you're no detective, Jude-girl. Now go to sleep and lose the disease. G'night." He shut the door with a bang.

Judith had turned pale and her fists were shaking. "Jerk! He's jealous. He won't admit I've been smart as well as lucky." She blinked at Renie. "Or have I?"

"A bit of both, coz. Mainly," Renie went on as she rose from the bed, "it's your knack with people. They open up to you. For instance, who else could have gotten Pam and Sandi to spill everything?"

Judith regarded Renie with a wry expression. "Did they?"

"What do you mean?"

Judith sighed. "On a scale of ten, they opened up at about a six. In fact, no one has told me everything, and everybody is telling some lies. I just wish," she said wearily, "I knew who was doing what."

*   *   *

After a rather rocky start, the cousins got settled for the night. Judith slept like a log, and Renie slept like she usually did, which meant she didn't wake up until nine o'clock.

"Good grief!" Judith shouted in horror. "Did you sleep through the alarm?"

"Hunh?" Renie rolled over. "Alarm? What alarm? Fire alarm?"

Judith reached for the clock-radio on the nightstand. "The six o'clock alarm. Damn! You forgot to set it."

"Never set alarms," Renie mumbled. "Alarm clocks are . . . dumb."

"*You're* dumb," Judith shot back as she threw off the covers and got out of bed. "The guests must be enraged. Why didn't Joe wake us?" In a frenzy of motion, Judith went into the bathroom, then returned to throw on some clothes. "A good thing I took a bath last night," she grumbled. "Get up, you lazy butt. I need help."

"No fire," Renie murmured into the pillow. "Goody."

Judith ripped the bedclothes off of Renie. "Come on! Mother must be wild. Let's go."

"Hey!" Renie opened her eyes and groped in vain for the covers. "I can't wake up that fast. I have to go at it slowly. Very slowly."

"Phyliss will be here any minute," Judith said, quickly running a brush through her hair. "She'll wonder what on earth has happened to me."

"Blast." Renie staggered out of bed. "Now I'm too awake to be asleep. Okay, okay, I'll be with you in a minute. Blast." She headed for the bathroom, then turned around. "You're better?"

"Yes, I'm fine. I'll see you downstairs." Judith hurried out of the bedroom.

To her astonishment, the guests were all seated at the dining room table, finishing the last of what appeared to be a bountiful breakfast. The Malones were lapping up pork sausage patties, Roland was polishing off a Belgian waffle, the Santoris were taking the last pieces of toast from the toast rack, and the preschool teachers had fried eggs on their heads.

"Chicken," they chanted, "chicken or the egg? Cluck, cluck, cheep, cheep, we must beg. Tell us chicken, which came first? Which is better, which is worst?"

Seeing Judith, Pam and Sandi began to giggle. "Don't worry," Sandi said, regaining control, "we've got napkins under the eggs. Oops!"

Sandi's egg slid off her head and into her lap. Pam practically fell out of her chair, laughing merrily. "Sandi . . . Sandi . . . not . . . so . . . dandy," she gasped between gusts of laughter.

"Bonkers," muttered Mal. "Just plain bonkers."

"High-spirited," put in Roland. "Very refreshing."

Marie was gazing at Pete. "Someday," she said in a dreamy voice, "we'll have little ones to send to pre-school."

"Ah . . ." Judith tried to gather her aplomb. "Who made breakfast?"

Bea made a slashing gesture with one hand. "Your old man. Not bad, either. Where'd he learn to cook?"

Judith gulped. "Joe's always been an excellent cook. He learned how . . . um . . . while he was single." Joe had, in fact, learned to cook before he was married. His mother had died while he was in his teens, and the skill had served him well when he discovered that Herself couldn't serve anything that didn't come in a bottle with ingredients marked a hundred and fifty proof.

"I'm glad you've been taken care of. So to speak," Judith added, remembering her audience. Turning tail, she headed for the toolshed.

Agent Dunleavy opened the door. Judith's jaw dropped. "You're back?" she gasped.

"I am." Dunleavy stepped aside. "Your mother has just finished breakfast."

Gertrude waved from her favorite chair. "Your lunkhead husband brought me my vittles. Not bad, I have to admit. Tell him next time, I'd rather have links than patties. Why don't you bring some extra coffee for my nice visitor here?''

Dunleavy intervened. "I'm fine. Don't bother. But thank you all the same." He cleared his throat and offered Gertrude his most boyish expression. "As we were saying, about your responsibilities at Auschwitz . . ."

"Hold it!" Judith shrieked, then stepped in front of Dunleavy. "If you persist in this foolishness, I'm going to call somebody and tell them how off-base you are. My congressman, if necessary," Judith added, wondering who had the authority to call off an FBI investigation.

"Just a few more questions," Dunleavy replied, ankling around Judith and sitting in a ladderback chair he'd pulled up to the card table. "Your mother and I are doing just fine."

"Go back to your loony guests," Gertrude ordered, waving a hand at Judith. "This young man and I have plenty to hash over."

"No, you . . ." Judith began, but Gertrude rapped her knuckles on the card table.

"Cut that out! Can't you see we're having a nice visit? How often do you sit around and chew the fat with me? How often does anybody do that? Take a hike, twerp."

Seething, Judith stomped out of the toolshed. If, in a very short time, she had found it difficult to go up against an FBI agent, she also knew from a lifetime of experience that it was impossible to win an argument with her mother.

Still, she couldn't resist leaving the door ajar.

". . . With the prisoners?" It was Dunleavy, speaking amiably.

"Prisoners are bad people," Gertrude replied. "You have to rough 'em up sometimes."

"In what way did you accomplish this?"

"Well . . . that depended. How would you have done it?"

"According to our files, you supervised torture and inflicted other inhumane means."

"Torture. Hmmm." Gertrude's tone was musing. "Like playing loud music?"

Clapping her hands to her head, Judith continued on into the house. The situation was impossible, Agent Dunleavy was impossible, her mother was impossible. Still fuming, Judith entered the kitchen and found Renie making a fresh pot of coffee.

"I'm up," Renie announced, "and doing. How long do you want me to hang out around here?"

Judith considered. She was definitely feeling better, though still a bit weak in the knees. Nor had her appetite returned. And, though she wouldn't admit it out loud, Judith needed Renie for moral support.

"Noonish?" she temporized.

Renie glanced up at the old schoolroom clock, which showed twenty-five after nine. "Okay, I guess I can manage. The Boring Company can wait."

Judith put both hands on Renie's shoulders. "Thanks, coz. I really appreciate it." Over the top of Renie's disheveled chestnut curls, Judith saw J. J. Martinez trying to get through the dining room. The guests, particularly the Malones, were buffeting him with questions.

"Later," J. J. shouted, coming through the swinging door. "By noon, maybe." He nipped into the kitchen and stepped out of the guests' line of sight. "Whew! They sure want to leave. Are they tired of the rain?"

"Maybe they're just tired," Judith said with a small smile. "I am."

"You're better?" J. J. glanced around the kitchen, spied the coffee pot, and made a stabbing gesture. "May I?"

"Sure," Judith replied, going to the cupboard and taking down a clean mug. "What's up?"

J. J. poured his coffee before responding. "Police at the airport picked up Minerva Schwartz—that is, Minerva Schlagintweit—this morning. She was headed for Brazil."

"My goodness," Judith said in surprise. "She was leaving the country?"

J. J. nodded in his jerky fashion. "Tickets for her and Fewer Fingers were bought four days ago, originally booked for New Zealand. That flight doesn't leave every day from here, so they had to wait until this morning. But Minerva cashed in Barney's ticket and exchanged hers for a Rio flight. Now you know why they came here first. The connections are better from the West Coast to Down Under."

"Except Minerva changed her mind, and was leaving without Barney. That sounds odd," Judith said.

J. J. shrugged. "We got nothing on her. Technically, she could have taken off. But she's a witness, and we want to question her."

Judith was still looking thoughtful. "So you still suspect Barney—I mean, Fewer Fingers—of killing Legs?"

J. J. cleared his throat. "We're working with the FBI on that." Moving nervously around the kitchen, J. J. looked for the phone, then spotted it in its cradle on the counter. "May I?"

"Of course." Judith turned back to Renie, who had lighted a cigarette and was drinking coffee. "They're not sure," she whispered. "It must be the part about how Barney got the gun out of the safe."

Renie gave a faint nod, but said nothing as Judith strained to overhear J. J.'s phone conversation. Between the monosyllables and the occasional grunt, she couldn't figure out what he was saying or to whom he was speaking.

J. J. finished the call, then handed the phone to Judith. "Sorry. Someone rang on your second line. Couldn't hang up on my call." He hurried out through the back door as Sweetums scooted between his feet and came down the hallway.

Judith checked the messages that had accumulated since the previous day, which totaled four. Two were for reservations in late July and mid-September. The third was from Mike, saying that he and Kristin would be late as they wanted to stop at the mall and pick up some last-minute baby items. The fourth and the last call, which had interrupted J. J., was from Phyliss Rackley.

"The demons must have got you," Phyliss said in a mournful voice. "Glory be. I suppose I'll read about it in the papers. By the way, I'm sick. If the good Lord permits, I'll see you tomorrow. Unless you've gone to your heavenly reward."

"Great." Judith erased the last two messages, but took down the number of the out-of-state caller. "Now I have to clean this place by myself."

Renie blew out a big cloud of smoke. "No, you won't. I'll help. Where do I start?"

"Ohhh . . ." Judith rubbed her temples. "I don't want you cleaning house. That's beyond the call of duty."

"Stick it," Renie said, putting her cigarette out in a clean saucer. "You've been sick, your wack-o cleaning woman probably caught it from you, no doubt I'm next, so take advantage of this opportunity before I keel over."

With a sigh of resignation, Judith gave in. "You start with this floor, including the breakfast things. I'll take care of the guest rooms."

Renie stopped halfway into the dining room. "Aren't you going to eat something?"

Judith shook her head as Sweetums jumped onto the kitchen counter. "Not yet. My stomach's still unsettled." She grabbed the cat and put him on the floor. "What about you?"

"I never eat until after eleven," Renie replied, heading through the swinging doors. "My brain may be in gear, but my body's still asleep."

Sweetums's growls had deteriorated into pitiful mews. Judith opened a fresh can of Feline Feast and left the cat happily swilling down his breakfast. Collecting a load of cleaning equipment, Judith headed up the back stairs.

J. J. met her outside of Room Six. "One last check," he said, looking sheepish. "Sorry."

Out of breath, Judith set the hand vacuum and the dustmop against the wall. "I thought you finished searching the guest rooms yesterday."

"Never hurts to be sure." J. J. checked his watch, which looked as if it should adorn the wrist of a commercial airline pilot. "Anyway—nothing."

"Okay, J. J.," Judith said, grabbing the dustmop and making a churning gesture with the handle, "what's really up with Barney?"

J. J. ground his teeth. "Waiting to hear from the FBI. If not murder one, a grand jury in Detroit has already indicted him on organized crime charges."

"Barney doesn't strike me as being very organized," Judith sniffed. "What kind of crime is he involved in?"

"Hot cars," J. J. replied. "Sells them off his dealership's used car lot."

"Why don't they take the dealership away from him?"

"Maybe they tried. Maybe he convinced them it was a bad idea."

"Barney sent in the headcrushers?"

J. J. looked startled. "How'd you know about guys like that?"

"I read a lot," Judith answered with a wry smile. "So what did Barney in Detroit have to do with Legs in New York? Was Barney part of the Fusilli mob?"

"The Fusilli family was trying to get a piece of the action in Detroit. An illegal gambling operation," J. J. said with a pained expression. "Shouldn't be telling you all this. But it'll come out sooner or later. Anyway, some of Fewer Fingers's—Barney's—pals were running the gambling show. The Fusilli family tried to muscle in on the action. Fewer Fingers didn't like seeing his pals get hurt. He sent in some enforcers."

"Goodness." In a gesture of dismay, Judith shook her head. "It all sounds so . . . seedy."

"It is." J. J. gave Judith a bleak expression. "Lucky for us we live here, not in some of those other cities. Wouldn't want to deal with these people on a regular basis."

Judith agreed. "So you'll continue to hold Barney until the FBI says otherwise?"

"Guess so." J. J. didn't seem very happy about the idea.

"Which means," Judith said, taking a deep breath, "you don't know who killed Legs Benedict."

J. J.'s dark eyes seemed to have trouble meeting Judith's. "You might say that. Then again, you might not. Can't rule him out."

"Oh, shoot." Judith tossed the dustmop against the wall and fixed J. J. with a rueful expression. "I've got something for you," she continued, unlocking the door to the stairs that lead to the third floor. "It probably doesn't mean much, and I can't believe Roland du Turque is involved, but . . ."

On the way up to the family quarters, Judith explained about the notes. "I kept them," she said, entering the bedroom and retrieving the notes from the nightstand, "after I showed them to Roland."

J. J. carefully studied the small slips of paper. "You say this one about meeting someone outside was intended for Fewer Fingers?"

Judith nodded. "Phyliss found it under the rug in the Schwartzes' room. By the way, does Minerva plan to come back here? I really don't have room for her or any of these other people."

"What?" Intent on the notes, J. J.'s head snapped up. "Minerva? Mrs. Schlagintweit?"

"Yes. I assume you're not going to hold her in the jail."

"No. No, no." J. J. pocketed the notes. "Thank you. Should have seen these sooner." He gave Judith a vaguely reproachful look.

"I forgot," Judith fibbed. "I got sick."

"Right. Oh. Mrs. Schlagintweit wants to be put up at a downtown hotel. Probably the Plymouth," J. J. said.

"Good." Judith replied, leading the way out of the bedroom. "Why don't you put the others there? I've got a houseful tonight."

J. J. sighed heavily. "Have to check with the boss.

Where'd you say you found the note about Hoffa?''

"Under the piano." Judith and J. J. started downstairs. "Do you have any idea what it means?"

"Sort of," J. J. replied, a step behind Judith.

Reaching the second floor, she turned to look at the detective. "Like what?"

"Like several things." J. J. hesitated. "Maybe you guessed."

"What?" Judith asked, perplexed.

"Like du Turque." J. J.'s eyes darted around the empty hallway. "He's not who he says he is."

Judith was surprised, though she knew she shouldn't have been. Nobody was what they seemed to be, and in her present uncertain state of mind, she could picture Gertrude in an SS uniform, saluting Hitler, and herding prisoners at Auschwitz.

THIRTEEN

ROOM SIX WAS still occupied by the Malones. Bea and Mal weren't particularly tidy, though Judith had seen far worse in her years as an innkeeper, including the couple from Iowa who had managed to sneak a pot-bellied pig named Gustav into Room Three.

After stripping the bed, Judith rearranged the lace curtains and flowered drapes. She put fresh linen on the bed, ran the dust mop around the room, and vacuumed the hooked rug that Gertrude had made before her eyesight began to fail. Then, because she was there and couldn't resist, she went through the drawers and the closet.

The only thing of interest that she found was a roll of unprocessed film. She debated with herself for a full minute: The film did not belong to her but to the Malones. The Malones had behaved badly during their entire stay at Hillside Manor. Taking the film would be a theft. Taking the film might provide insight into the Malones, and perhaps even into the homicide case. The Malones had suffered a terrible loss on their trip from Chicago. Judith offered up a prayer for them. And took the film.

Room Five, with its clusters of pink rosebuds, was also still occupied. Pete and Marie Santori were surprisingly neat visitors. Even the bed was partially made up. Their clothes, which were few in number, hung on hangers in the closet. Two pairs of slacks and a cashmere sweater made up Pete's wardrobe. Marie also had two pairs of slacks as well as two blouses and a cotton turtleneck pullover.

"There you are," Renie said from the doorway. "I thought I'd better let you know that your guests have left."

Judith whirled around. "Left? What do you mean?"

"It's stopped raining," Renie explained as she came inside the room and closed the door behind her, "so J. J. told them they could take off for a few hours as long as they came back here by three. I got the impression that he was having them all tailed. Meanwhile, those uniforms—or their replacements—are outside again. Not to mention what looked like some reporters and at least one TV crew."

With a disgruntled sigh, Judith sat down on the bed. "Damn. I was so hoping they'd be sent somewhere else. I thought J. J. might find other accommodations for them. What am I going to do with the new guests?"

Renie shrugged. "Maybe J. J.'s working on that. He's gone, too. The guests would have to come back here anyway to collect their belongings."

"That's true." Judith's eyes strayed to the open closet. "Speaking of which, what's wrong with this picture?"

Renie turned. "The closet?"

"What's in the closet. Or isn't in it, I should say." Judith folded her arms across her bosom and waited for Renie's response.

"Cashmere," Renie remarked, feeling the sleeve of Pete's pale blue sweater. "He's wearing one just like it now, only in cream. No shirt, just the sweater and all those gold chains."

"Go on."

Renie rubbed at the fabric of Marie's lime turtleneck. "Cotton. Cheap. These slacks are polyester." Renie looked stunned. "You're right—this is all wrong. No wife should ever wear clothes that are inferior to or less expensive than her husband's. It's shocking and probably violates the constitution.''

Judith's smile was wry. "So what do you deduce?''

Leaning on the walnut bureau, Renie grew thoughtful. "What you suspected all along—they're not married. Where are the frilly negligees and sexy underthings?''

Judith bent down to pick up a pair of bunny slippers, one of which was missing an eye, and the other had no whiskers. "Not romantic.''

"So who are they?'' Renie asked.

Judith set the slippers down on the floor. "We're told Pete went to high school with Pam and Sandi. Do we believe that?''

Renie shook her head. "Probably not. Did you find anything in here that might suggest who they really are?''

"Nothing. Although,'' she went on as she stood up and went over to a laundry bag that was sitting on top of the Santoris' suitcase, "I didn't look in here. Oof!'' Judith juggled the bag, almost dropping it. "It's heavy. What . . . ?''

Digging among the soiled items, Judith hauled out a gun case. The gun, a Sig Sauer P220, was still in it.

Gingerly, Judith dropped the gun and its case back into the laundry bag. "I don't get it. J. J. and Rich searched these rooms thoroughly. In fact, I'm sure J. J. told me that everyone staying here had a gun, and they'd all been confiscated.''

"Well . . .'' Renie assumed a puzzled look and tapped her foot. "I can't explain it, unless the Santoris had two guns, and ditched one of them somewhere else in the house.'' Brightening, Renie made one of her futile, noiseless attempts to snap her fingers. "The garage! That's where we saw Pete with Sandi. Could he have hidden this gun out there?''

Judith considered the suggestion. "Possibly. But Joe's in and out of there every day with his MG, and those uniforms have been all over the place. It'd be tricky.''

Renie gestured at the laundry bag. "What are you going to do about the gun?''

"I'm not sure," Judith replied, fingering her chin. "The Santoris have gone off without it, and J. J. left. Maybe I should ask Joe. Even before Legs was shot, Joe was quick to confiscate what turned out to be Barney's gun."

In the end, Judith left the Sig Sauer where she'd found it. Perhaps there was some logical explanation. Pete and Marie might be someone other than the honeymooners they pretended to be, but they didn't seem unreasonable. Still brooding, Judith went into Room Four, which Phyliss had cleaned the previous day before Barney's arrest and Minerva's flight. The room had been swept clean of personal items.

"Minerva must have taken their stuff with her," Judith said to Renie, who had followed her down the hall. "I'm still not sure if she'll be back, so I guess I won't change the bed. Yet."

"I finished up downstairs," Renie said as they entered Room Three. "Want me to check the other two rooms?"

Judith was standing in the middle of the room that had been occupied by Legs Benedict and the woman known as Darlene Smith. Like Room Four, Phyliss had tidied it up.

"No, I'll go with you," Judith replied, moving to the bureau, then the closet, and finally the bathroom. "Nothing here. Let's check Pam and Sandi's room."

Room One was cluttered with clothes and cosmetics and magazines. At first glance, it reminded Judith of trips she had taken with Renie when they were both still single. According to the ship steward, their state room on the voyage to Europe had set a transatlantic record for disorder.

"What do we expect to find?" Renie asked, searching the closet. "You already know why Pam and Sandi are here."

"True," Judith replied, going through the drawers on the mirrored bureau. "But are they really Pam and Sandi?"

"Good point," Renie responded. "So what are we looking for? False passports?"

Judith shot Renie a sardonic glance. "Hardly. We're looking for . . ." She stopped, staring at a copy of *Vogue*.

"Names, like this one," she continued, reading from the magazine's mailing label. "Pamela Perl, 309 Parker Street, Newark, New Jersey. Or," Judith went on, picking up two *New York* magazines, "Cassandra Williams, same address. They must be roommates."

Renie, who had been looking through the teachers' luggage, gave a nod. "So it seems. And they are definitely Sandi and Pam. Pam has a motive to kill Legs. Pam and Sandi do everything together. They are as close as . . ."

"Cousins," Judith put in, and grinned at Renie. "Would you kill for me, coz?"

"That depends," Renie replied. "Who'd you have in mind?"

Judith, who had suddenly grown serious, didn't answer directly. "Why was Sandi in the garage with Pete Santori? The teachers claim they hadn't seen him since high school, they barely recognized him. Yet they both pitched a fit when he and Marie were checking into the B&B. At first," Judith went on, sitting down in one of Grandma Grover's old rocking chairs, "I thought they were frightened. Then, when we saw Pete and Sandi in the garage together, fear wasn't the emotion that leapt to mind."

"It wasn't," Renie agreed, adjusting the mirror on the oak bureau. "In fact, there was a sense of intimacy. Or so I felt."

"The Santoris and the teachers don't talk to each other much," Judith pointed out. "You'd expect Pete and Pam and Sandi to reminisce about the old days. Most people who went to high school together would do that."

"In other words," Renie said, "you don't think high school is the connection."

Judith shook her head. "No. And not only do I not think that Pete and Marie are on their honeymoon, I'm not even convinced that they're married. They're too phony. It's all an act."

Renie agreed. The cousins worked together to put the room back in order, then moved on to Room Two, where Roland du Turque was staying.

"Another Not-Who-He-Seems-To-Be," Judith sighed. "But where does he fit in? I don't associate black people with the mob."

"Gangs," Renie put in. "Younger. Drugs. Definitely not Roland's sort of thing."

Judith surveyed the long, narrow room with its curtained bed in the far nook. Roland was extremely neat, and it took only a couple of minutes to check out his belongings. The satchel and the briefcase were locked, but Judith found a notebook on a wicker stand next to the bed. It was much larger than the one from which the slips of paper had been torn, and appeared to be filled with Roland's handwriting.

"Listen to this," Judith said, sitting on the edge of the bed and twitching with excitement. " 'Alfonso Benedetto, aka Legs Benedict, born 1956, the Bronx, New York. Started as a booster in Detroit'—what's a booster?" Seeing Renie's blank expression, Judith continued, " 'Returned to New York, joined Fusilli mob circa nineteen seventy-nine. Bag man. Married Elena Fusilli, nineteen eighty-four'."

Renie evinced surprise. "Legs married into the Fusilli family? That must have given him—excuse the expression—a leg up. But what's this stuff got to do with jazz?"

"I don't know." Judith continued reading. " 'Leg-breaker, circa nineteen eighty-seven. Assassin, nineteen ninety—. Cool customer, remorseless, can be patient, but has trigger temper. Weakness—women, fast cars, Sinatra ballads. Alleged hits—seventeen since ninety.' What do you think of that, coz?"

"I think he's left more bodies than breadcrumbs in his path," Renie responded, now looking grim. "I hate to say it, but I'm glad he's dead. You wouldn't have wanted his return business anyway."

"True." Judith flipped through the rest of the notebook. "This thing's full of notes, apparently on other mob members. 'Teddy Fucillo—Boston, elder statesman, etc. Johnny Grasso—owned race horses, bookie. Joseph (The Fat Man) Magliocco—Profaci's underboss, also his brother-in-law.

Sam (Momo) Giancana—Chicago boss, fled to Mexico to avoid Feds.' '' Judith looked up from the notebook. "I recognize his name. Didn't he sleep with some woman who slept with everybody else?"

"Right," Renie said dryly. "Her name was Judith."

Judith gave a little snort. "No relation." She turned another page. "Listen to this: 'Cosa Nostra members are solely of Italian-Sicilian origin, often referred to as the Mafia.' " Judith frowned. Barney Schwartz—Bernhard Schlagintweit—isn't an Italian name. The Mafia should be sued for discrimination."

Renie agreed. "Or defamation. They certainly give a bad name to all the rest of the Italians. I could weep when I think of great musicians like Puccini and Verdi and Caruso and Toscanini and Tebaldi being tarred with the same brush. It makes me want to become a bonecrusher or whatever they call them."

Judith gave Renie a brief glance of sympathy. "Of course. But that's not my point—it's about Barney trying to muscle in on the Fusilli family. Maybe it's about turf, not nationality." Pausing, she leafed through the rest of the notebook. "Everything in here seems to be about organized crime, not jazz. What's Roland up to?"

"No good?" Renie's expression was as puzzled as Judith's. "Maybe he's doing some kind of tie-in, like a connection between music and crime."

"Some of the music the kids listen to today *is* a crime," Judith murmured. "What if . . . ?" She let the question dangle, replaced the notebook on the wicker stand, and hurried from the room. "Come on, let's call my friend Blanche Rexford at the library."

In years gone by, when Judith hadn't been tending bar at the Meat and Mingle, she had worked as a librarian at the Thurlow Street branch in the neighborhood where she and Dan had lived their dreary existence. Blanche Rexford, who was now head librarian at the Heraldsgate Hill library, had trained with Judith some twenty years earlier. Using the phone provided for guests in the hallway, Judith dialed the local branch.

After a rather long preamble, involving a dozen queries from Blanche about the murder at Hillside Manor, Judith asked her old friend to check on books about organized crime, especially those written by someone with a name like du Turque, Turquette, Roland, Orlando, or some sort of variation. It took Blanche less than a minute to bring up a title called *Cosa Nostra: Not Our Thing*.

"It was published in 1991," Blanche said in her wispy voice. "The author is Ronald Turk."

Judith gave Renie a thumbs-up sign. "Is there a picture of him?"

"I'm reading this from *Books in Print*," Blanche said. "Do you want me to check the shelf?"

"Would you?" Judith said in a plaintive tone.

"Of course. I'll be right back."

Judith gave Renie a full explanation. "It's got to be Roland. Ronald, Roland, Orlando—they're too similar to be a coincidence. Not to mention Turk instead of du Turque or Turquette."

Blanche came back on the line. "The dust jacket's been removed. You know how it is—even with plastic coverings, they get badly worn after a couple of years."

"Yes," Judith said, then asked another question. "Is there an author blurb inside the book?"

"I'm afraid not," Blanche said, the wispy voice tinged with regret. "It must have been on the jacket, too."

Thanking Blanche profusely, Judith hung up the phone. "Maybe we can eliminate Roland or Ronald or Orlando or whatever his real name may be. He's a writer, doing research."

Renie was walking aimlessly back and forth in front of the large linen closet between Rooms Four and Five. "That sounds harmless enough."

Judith started to nod, then bit her lip. "Does it?" She looked up from the settee. "What motivated Roland—let's keep that name to avoid confusion—what motivated him to write organized crime books in the first place? Academic interest? Some kind of personal involvement? Or a vendetta? The pen, I've heard, is mightier than the sword.''

''So they say,'' Renie conceded. ''But Roland seems so . . . pleasant. I can't imagine him shooting anybody.''

''But he had a gun,'' Judith reminded her cousin. ''It may have been for self-protection, but Joe says you shouldn't carry a weapon unless you're prepared to use it. And don't forget, someone notified him about Legs coming here. Who? Why? And did you notice the Amtrak tag on his satchel? It was from Oakland. Roland must have come here from the Bay Area, not Kansas City.''

''A fairly short trip,'' Renie remarked. ''Less than twenty-four hours. Roland wouldn't have needed much advance warning.''

''But someone knew how to get hold of him,'' Judith pointed out. ''Was it one of the other guests? Or someone . . .''

She was interrupted by a voice calling from the stairway. ''Yoo-hoo! Yoo-hoo! Are you up there, Judith?'' Vivian Flynn's platinum coiffure appeared through the banister railings.

''Hi,'' Judith said weakly. ''Renie and I were cleaning the guest rooms. Phyliss is sick today.''

Attired in magenta silk lounging pajamas and matching wedgies, Herself grabbed the dust mop that was leaning against the settee. ''I'll take that.'' She paused, staring at the dust mop. ''What is it?''

Judith, who knew from Joe that Herself considered housework a step below digging ditches on a Georgia chain gang, started to reply. Vivian, however, waved a hand that featured long, crimson nails. ''Never mind, I'll figure it out. Judith, you've been ill. You should still be in bed. I told you,'' she went on in a scolding tone, ''to let me know if you need help. Now you go rest your poor self while I finish up here. Shoo, shoo. You look positively ghastly.''

Judith and Renie exchanged irked glances. ''We're almost done,'' Judith said, getting up from the settee.

"Renie's been helping me. Really, Vivian, you needn't bother. Don't you have a house guest?"

Herself was running the dust mop on the sections of bare floor not covered by a colorful pink, green, and yellow runner. "DeeDee's sleeping in. We talked far into the night, and she's worn out, poor darling. Maybe this evening you and Joe could stop in and meet her. If you're up to it, of course." Herself paused and eyed Judith critically. "If I were you, I wouldn't push it. Your color is perfectly dreadful and those bags under your eyes could hold a week's worth of groceries."

"Thanks," Judith said faintly, then started to protest Vivian's endeavors once more. Renie, however, poked her cousin in the ribs. "Okay," Judith relented. "Everything but the hall and the communal bathroom has been cleaned. Phyliss did Room Three yesterday."

"Not to worry," Herself said airily. Then, holding the dust mop as if it were a dance partner, she began to twirl around and sing, " 'I could have danced all night . . .' "

Judith and Renie scampered downstairs. "Is Vivian coming here just to tell me how awful I look?" Judith hissed when they reached the entry hall. "Since when has she offered to be so helpful?"

"Well . . ." Apparently Renie was trying to be reasonable. "She does call on your mother. That's helpful."

"That's treason." Judith surveyed the living room, which, to her relief, was empty of guests. "I mean, sometimes I think she keeps friendly with Mother just to annoy me. Furthermore, if she thinks I'm going to drag Joe over to her house to watch her and DeeDee Whoever suck down a fifth of Old Jolt, she's mistaken."

"Goodness," Renie said in mock dismay, "now who's being uncharitable?"

"Oh, shut up." Judith started for the kitchen just as the phone rang. "Damn! I left the cordless on the counter." She raced through the dining room, ran the length of the kitchen, and grabbed the receiver just as it trunked over to the answering machine. "Double damn! I've never figured out how to break in once I miss the actual call. Now I'll have to wait until the message is recorded.''

"No, you don't,'' Renie said in a calm voice. "You simply speak over the clicks and beeps. The only glitch is that your conversation gets recorded.''

"That wouldn't bother me,'' Judith said, watching for the red light to show that the message had been completed. "I'll try it next time. Ah—it's finished.''

She poked the message button and heard Mike's agitated voice, "Where are you, Mom? Kristin's in labor. We're at the hospital. They're wheeling her . . . My God, the baby . . . !''

The message stopped. Judith could hear only the buzzing of the line. For a moment, she thought her heart had stopped and that the buzzing was in her ears.

"Let's go,'' Judith shouted, racing for the back door.

The cousins ran past the toolshed, where Gertrude presumably was still being interrogated by the FBI, raced by two startled uniforms who remained on duty, brushed off a pair of reporters who yelled at them to stop, and flew down the driveway where Renie had parked her car.

They never looked back. If they had, they would have seen Minerva Schwartz pulling Barney's white Cadillac into the cul-de-sac.

FOURTEEN

THE HMO HOSPITAL that had served members of the Grover clan for almost fifty years was located across town, about five miles from Hillside Manor. Mike had been born there, as had two of the three Jones offspring, and Donald Grover had died in the old wing, which had since been demolished.

After Renie totaled the Joneses' big blue Chevrolet on a mountain pass two winters ago, she and Bill had bought a new Toyota Camry they lovingly called "Cammy." Judith, who wouldn't have dreamed of calling her Subaru "Suebby," found the nickname cloying.

She also found Renie's careful drive to the hospital frustrating, as well as uncharacteristic. Usually, Renie drove like she was waiting for the checkered flag at the Old Brick Yard in Indianapolis. But on this cloudy June afternoon, she exercised extreme caution, even waiting for hesitant pedestrians to cross at unmarked corners and pausing for vehicles to pull out of driveways.

"Come on, coz," Judith urged, "I'm about to have a stroke. Can't you put the pedal to the metal?"

"Cammy only likes to go fast on the freeway," Renie responded. "She has excellent manners in business and residential areas. A courteous car is Cammy."

Judith tried to relax as they skirted the edge of downtown and headed up the hill to Central Hospital. Her heart was still pounding, however, and she felt a throbbing headache coming on. The buzzing in her ears had been replaced by a different sound, which at first she couldn't identify.

"Your car is making a weird noise," Judith said.

"Cammy doesn't make weird noises," Renie snapped. "Cammy purrs."

"That's what it sounds like." Judith listened for a moment. The sound was still there, only louder. Then, just as Judith was about to turn around in an attempt to track down the noise, a large ball of fur flopped between the front seats and landed on the gearshift console.

"Sweetums!" Judith shrieked. "Good God! How did he get in here?"

Renie was so startled that she momentarily lost control of the steering wheel. The Camry veered to the right, just missing a blind man and his guide dog.

"Get that damned cat out of here!" Renie yelled. "He'll get Cammy hurt!" Grappling with a hissing, clawing Sweetums, Judith finally managed to put him in her lap. "He doesn't like to ride in cars," Judith muttered. "He thinks he's going to the vet."

"I wish he were going to the pound," Renie asserted, finally picking up speed as the white brick bulk of the hospital came into view. "He must have sneaked in through the window. Since it wasn't raining, I put it down so Cammy could get some fresh air."

"Honestly," Judith said in exasperation, "you treat this car as if it were a pet. It's a *car*, dammit."

Renie took her right hand off the wheel long enough to jab at Sweetums. "You treat that thing as if it were a person. It's a pain in the butt, if you ask me."

"You should talk," Judith shot back. "You make a fool over yourself with that rabbit. Who else tucks their bunny in at night and reads him a bedtime story?"

"Clarence is special," Renie asserted. "And I don't read to him. I only sing him a little song."

"I don't dote on Sweetums like that," Judith declared.

"I'm not one of those people who invest all my love and affection into an animal. But if I did, it wouldn't be as dumb as calling my car 'Suebby.' Unlike a pet, a car is not a surrogate child."

Renie turned the corner by the hospital so fast that three people dove for safety behind a phone pole. "Cammy isn't a surrogate child. Bill and I have three children of our own, as you well know."

"Grandchildren, then," Judith said, sounding waspish. "You're jealous because Joe and I are about to become grandparents."

"Bunk." Renie honked at an ambulance that was pulling away from the hospital's emergency entrance. "We take good care of our cars so they'll last forever, not to mention that they're our first line of defense when it comes to highway safety." Running up over the curb, Renie swerved around a "Do Not Enter" sign, and drove down the exit lane into the hospital's underground parking garage.

"Hey!" the attendant yelled from his kiosk, "you're going the wrong way, lady!"

Renie leaned out the window. "The hell I am. I'm in the parking garage, aren't I?" She rounded the corner and pulled into an empty spot. "How about this for convenience?" she said, her tone again chipper.

"It says 'Reserved for Staff,'" Judith pointed out.

"So?" Fending off Sweetums's claws, Renie removed a notebook from her handbag. "Today, I *am* staff. Are you forgetting I designed the HMO's outpatient surgery booklet?" She scribbled a note and placed it on the dashboard. "Let's go."

Carefully, Judith put Sweetums on the floor in front of the passenger seat. "Be good. We shouldn't be gone . . ."

"Whoa!" Renie was outside the car, glaring at Judith. "Get that cat out of there. He'll rip the upholstery."

"What? I can't take him into the hospital." Judith's patience, along with her nerves, had begun to fray.

"You'll have to," Renie declared, a dogged expression on her face. "Bill would pitch a five-star fit if you left that cat in Cammy. Come on, get him out of there.''

Judith couldn't risk arguing. She was too anxious about the baby. Cursing under her breath, she scooped up Sweetums and followed Renie to the elevators.

They reached the OB ward before anyone stopped them. A middle-aged nurse wearing scrubs and a weary expression barred the cousins' way to the main desk.

''You can't bring an animal in here,'' she said in a firm voice. ''Please take—'' The nurse paused as Sweetums's yellow eyes narrowed, his back arched, his fur stood on end, and he let out a menacing hiss. ''—that thing outside.''

Beset by murder, illness, a baby's birth, the FBI, and Herself, Judith balked. ''No. Tell me about Mrs. M . . . Mc . . . M . . . Monigle first.'' She had stumbled over the name, never having quite come to terms with the concept of another, much happier Mrs. McMonigle.

The nurse, whose nametag identified her as June Driscoll, glowered at Judith. ''The cat goes first,'' she insisted, as two other nurses and an orderly watched with curiosity.

''Here,'' Renie snapped, yanking a squalling Sweetums out of Judith's arms, ''I'll take care of the cat. I'll meet you back at the car.'' She started to turn around, but had a last word for June Driscoll. ''I don't know why you object to animals in this place. The last time I was in here for kidney stones you served me boiled warthog. At least that's what it tasted like. It sure as hell wasn't real meat.'' Renie stalked away with Sweetums under her arm, his plumelike tail waving furiously.

June Driscoll eyed Judith with distaste. ''What was the name?''

''McMonigle. Kristin McMonigle. Mrs. Michael McMonigle.'' Judith's mouth had gone dry. ''Please, I'm very worried. I'm Mrs. McMonigle's m-m-mother-in-law.'' She stumbled again, still not used to the role, and well aware of all its pejorative connotations.

''I'll check.'' Wrinkled scrubs flapping, June Driscoll strolled off down the hall, her attitude exuding indifference for Judith's concern.

Taking in her surroundings, Judith realized she was not only by the main desk, but that there was a waiting room off to her left. Glancing into the room, she saw that it was empty. Mike must still be with Kristin. He had promised to watch the delivery, though Judith had doubts about her son's ability to endure the process. She went over to the main desk, where a male nurse was sorting through charts.

"I'm waiting for word on my daughter-in-law," Judith said in the most amiable voice she could muster. "Have you heard anything about a Mrs. McMonigle?"

The young man, who wore a trim mustache and fair hair cropped close to his scalp, regarded Judith warily. "You had a cat."

"What?" The statement startled Judith. "Oh—you mean I *brought* a cat. I thought you meant that my daughter-in-law . . . Never mind. Do you have any information on her?"

The young man sorted through some more papers. "She was admitted at eleven-twenty." He glanced at his watch. "That was almost an hour ago. There should be some news shortly." He turned back to his charts.

Judith refused to sit in the empty waiting room. Instead, she began pacing the hallway. The clock above the main desk showed twelve-fifteen. Gertrude would be expecting her lunch. Searching for quarters in her wallet, Judith asked the nurse where the pay phones were located.

"There's a courtesy phone in the waiting room," he replied without looking up.

Despite the fact that a no smoking policy had been in effect for years, the waiting area still smelled like cigarettes. Some of the magazines were older than the smoking ban, and decades of frayed nerves seemed to linger on the stale air.

Judith called Joe first, but had to leave a message. He was probably out to lunch with Woody, Judith thought as she dialed her mother's number. As usual, Gertrude let it ring and ring . . . and ring. Just as Judith was about to slam down the receiver and let the old girl starve, Gertrude answered.

"Why are you calling me from the hospital?" she rasped. "Are you really that sick?"

"What?" Her mother's response startled Judith. "Oh—you saw the hospital's number on your caller ID. I'm okay, but Kristin is having the baby."

"Kristin?" Gertrude sounded puzzled. "Who's Kristin?"

"Your granddaughter-in-law," Judith said, trying to be patient. "Mike's wife."

"Who's Mike?"

Judith was about to explain when she heard Gertrude chortle. "Okay, okay, Toots, I get it. How soon?"

"I don't know," Judith replied.

"Surprise. You never know much, kiddo. When's lunch?"

"When I get home," Judith said, then remembered that Herself was probably still in the house. "Or, call my number and see if Vivian answers. She's helping out today and she'll fix you something."

"Vivian, huh? Haven't seen her for awhile. Okay, I'll ring her up. Say, how'd I leave Germany?"

The question took Judith aback. "What? You mean as a child?"

"Whenever. I told that nice young man from the government that I took a bus," Gertrude said. "Think that's right?"

In all the other excitement, Judith had forgotten about Agent Dunleavy. "Is he still there?"

"Nope. He left about an hour ago. But he'll be back." Gertrude sounded pleased by the idea.

Judith groaned. "What on earth for? Mother, are you leading him on?"

"Nope. Just answering his questions. Hey," she said in an excited voice, "here's Vivian now. Hello, sweetheart. Come right in, take a load off . . ."

The phone went dead in Judith's ear. She tried not to be

irked with Herself, who, for once, was being genuinely helpful. Getting up from the worn faux leather chair, she caught a glimpse of Mike, rushing past the open door.

"Mike!" she yelled, racing out of the waiting room. "Wait!"

Mike turned just before heading to the elevators. "Mom!" He was all smiles. "Are you here to meet your grandson?"

In midstep, Judith halted and stared at her son. "My grandson!" She reeled at the news.

Mike nodded and enfolded his mother in a bear hug. "He came so quick, downstairs, in the hall, we couldn't get up to delivery in time. Sorry I had to hang up on your machine, but . . ."

"Slow down." Judith realized she was gasping for breath, too. "The baby's already here? It's a boy? Is he okay? How's Kristin?"

"Fine, great, everybody's terrific." Still beaming, Mike released Judith. "I tried to call you again, but Mrs. Flynn— the other Mrs. Flynn—answered. She didn't know where you'd gone."

"I'd gone . . . here," Judith said, feeling dazed. "Oh, dear. Can I see the baby? And Kristin?"

"Sure." Mike took his mother's arm and led her back down the hall. "It's not far to the nursery. Then we'll go to Kristin's room. She's kind of tired, though."

"Of course." Relief swept over Judith. She squeezed Mike's arm as they approached the big windows of the nursery.

There were five babies in all. Two were black, one was Asian, and another seemed to be of Middle Eastern ancestry. Even if the McMonigle infant hadn't been the only Caucasian lying in the tiny isolettes, Judith would have recognized him. He was chubby, wrinkled, and had strange tufts of red hair sticking up all over his head.

"Oh! He's beautiful!" Judith burst into tears.

"Isn't he? Look, his eyes are open. See, he's waving his fists. Do you think he's trying to talk?" Mike was leaning so close to the window that his breath clouded the glass.

For several moments, Judith said nothing. She wished Joe were with them. "Wonderful," she murmured between sniffles. "Amazing. Have you picked out a name?"

Mike finally turned away from the window. "Yes. You're going to love it, Mom."

"I'm sure I will." She dabbed at her eyes with a Kleenex. "What is it?"

"What do you think?" Mike was beaming again. "Dan McMonigle, the second."

Judith cried even harder.

Renie seemed happy for Judith, though equally appalled at the name Mike and Kristin had chosen.

"I know, I know," Judith said in a rather fretful voice. "But it's their decision. And Mike really was close to Dan."

"You couldn't get close to Dan," Renie retorted. "He was too damned fat."

It was only when the cousins were getting into the Camry that Judith realized Sweetums was nowhere in sight.

"What did you do with my cat?" Judith demanded, backing out of the passenger seat and eyeing Renie over the car roof.

"I subdued him," Renie replied, ducking down to get behind the wheel.

"Where is he?" Judith's voice was strident.

"He's fine," Renie insisted, turning the key. "Come on, get in. Let's go."

But Judith refused to budge. "I want to see him. Alive."

Renie uttered a strangled sigh. "Okay, okay," she said, leaning down to flip the latch to the trunk. "Check him out. He's back there."

Hurrying to the rear of the car, Judith lifted the trunk lid. There was no sign of Sweetums. Then she saw the heavy cardboard box that the Joneses used to hold their emergency equipment. The box was upside down—and jiggling.

"Sweetums!" Judith cried, lifting the box.

His eyes were bright; indeed, blazing would have been a better word. Except for a few missing patches, his fur stood straight up and the growl that came from low in his throat was ominous. Taking a chance, Judith grabbed the cat, slammed the lid of the trunk, and got into the car.

"You mangled the poor little guy," Judith said in reproach. "How could you?"

"It was either me or him," Renie said, backing out of the parking place. "I chose me. Don't you dare let him get out of your lap."

There was no use arguing further with Renie, so Judith dropped the subject, preferring to talk about how beautiful the baby was, how alert, how utterly extraordinary. Renie had listened with apparent interest, though Judith noticed that her cousin had caressed Cammy's steering wheel several times during the drive home.

By the time Renie dropped Judith and Sweetums off at Hillside Manor, the TV crew and the reporters had left. The officers who remained on duty were sitting at the curb in their squad car. Judith recalled that the guests weren't required to return until three o'clock. There was no other sign of activity in the cul-de-sac, which came as a relief.

As usual, she entered the house through the back door. Sweetums, obviously relieved to be on his own turf, leaped out of her arms and ran for cover in the Rankerses' hedge. Judith was heading for the phone when Vivian appeared in the kitchen.

"Are you a grandma?" she asked with a big smile.

Judith nodded. "A boy, named Dan." It took willpower not to gulp at the name. "Eight pounds, nine ounces. He's adorable."

"Of course he is!" Vivian hurtled the length of the kitchen and hugged Judith. "Grandma Flynn! How I envy you! And how you look the part! Granny!"

Judith wriggled free. "Maybe," she said with a touch of asperity, "some day Caitlin will finally find a man and provide you with grandchildren."

"Caitlin," Vivian said, referring to the daughter she had had by Joe, "is a dedicated career woman who has found plenty of men but not one who suits her. She's terribly fussy."

Unlike her mother, Judith thought, and for once, didn't regret being mean-minded. "I thought one of your two sons by your first and second husbands had married."

"They did," Herself replied airily. "Both of them. Twice. But so far, no kiddies. It's just as well—I'm too young to be a grandmother." She waved a magenta-clad arm and simpered at Judith.

"Mm-mm," Judith murmured, keeping her thoughts buttoned up. "Did Mother have lunch?"

Herself nodded. "She ate a beautiful meal. Turkey, dressing, mashed potatoes, cranberry sauce, peas. She lapped it up and said she'd never had better."

A TV dinner, Judith thought. And, in fact, Gertrude actually enjoyed them. Unless she pretended she did, just to be contrary. Judith refused to serve her mother frozen meals.

"I'm off now," Herself declared. "I must see if DeeDee would like to go shopping. She and I used to buy out the stores in Florida."

With Joe's money. But again, Judith kept the thought inside. "Thanks for everything," she said, and hoped she sounded as if she meant it. "I really appreciate it. I know Mother does, too."

"Of course." Herself examined her crimson nails. "Your mother and I had such a nice visit. She's in quite a chipper mood. I think it's all the company she's had the past few days. Guests cheer her immensely. I tried to get that Minerva to join us, but she's stuck up, isn't she?"

Judith gave a little start. "Minerva?"

Herself nodded. "The one whose son was arrested for killing that gangster. She came by right after you left. Of course I didn't realize you'd gone, so I looked all over for you, but . . ."

"Minerva came here?" Judith interrupted. "Why?"

"She wanted her money back for last night, since neither she nor—Barney, is it?—stayed here," Herself explained calmly. "Minerva was—oh, I don't know where, she's very closed-mouth. Anyway, she was somewhere, and Barney was in jail. By the way, she dropped off a raincoat she borrowed."

"Did you give her credit?" Judith asked, thinking that Phyliss would be relieved to have her coat back.

Herself chuckled. "Are you serious? I know all about motels and hotels and inns and such. From traveling," Herself added hastily, lest Judith get the wrong idea, which of course she already had. "You have a cancellation policy, I'm sure. They are never retroactive. I put a flea in her ear and sent her on her way."

Once again, Judith was forced to feel grateful to Herself. "Thanks, Vivian. Do you know where she was going?"

"To hell in a handcart, for all I care," Herself retorted. "Don't get me wrong, I like people, they make great audiences. But that woman's a pain."

Judith couldn't disagree. But she wished that Vivian had extracted more information from Minerva Schwartz. "Did she mention Barney?"

"The son?" Herself patted her platinum curls. "Is he worth mentioning?"

"You mean . . . ?"

"Looks, Judith. Build. Endurance. All the important things when it comes to men." Herself's tone was faintly patronizing.

"Barney's a crook," Judith said.

"Nobody's perfect."

"He's homely."

"Oh." Herself shrugged. "That's different. No, I don't think that even his mother thought he was worth mentioning. I must dash. Stand by, I may call you tonight to see if you and Joe can come over to meet DeeDee."

Judith didn't bother to protest, though she assumed that Joe would want to go up to the hospital to see the baby. Finally getting a chance to check her messages, she saw that her husband had called while she was out. Judith dialed his number; he answered before the first ring had finished.

"We're grandparents," Judith said, the excitement rekindling. "A boy. He's adorable."

"Wow." Joe sounded awestruck. "Maybe I'll swing by the hospital on the way home. Have they named him?"

"Uh . . . yes." Judith swallowed hard. "Dan McMonigle II."

Joe didn't respond for what seemed like a long time. "Okay. That figures." He laughed, a wry, sharp sound. "Who does he look like?"

"You."

"Then I guess that's my revenge."

"It's your immortality."

"Damn. I still wish . . . Never mind, Jude-girl. This is great news. I'll see you later."

Judith stood by the phone for some time. She had made her decision when Mike and Kristin were married. Her son would never know that Joe Flynn was his real father. Despite Dan's faults, Mike had idolized him, especially in death. They had a bond, in name, in fact, and in deed. It was as deep as blood, as imperishable as memory. Despite Joe, Judith's respect for Dan's sense of duty as a father could not be revoked.

But that didn't diminish Joe's pain. Though he had unknowingly left her pregnant and eloped with Vivian, he still longed for the intimacy with Mike that a stepfather could never have. His feelings stabbed at Judith's heart, yet she couldn't change the past. The wound lay deep inside, an old scar that never quite healed, and festered at times like this, when blood was indeed thicker than water.

J. J. Martinez was at the front door, looking abject. "Couldn't get permission to put the witnesses up at a downtown hotel. They should be back in an hour or so."

"*What*?" Judith was aghast. "You mean that you haven't cleared them as suspects, either?"

"Right." J. J. shifted from one foot to the other on the welcome mat. "Tomorrow, maybe."

Judith shook her head several times. "That won't do. I have all the rooms taken for tonight. The new guests will start arriving any time. You've got to do something, J. J. I have only two rooms available. I wouldn't have that many if Minerva Schwartz hadn't checked out this afternoon."

"Minerva Schwartz?" J. J. looked startled. "She was here?"

Judith nodded. "But I wasn't. Didn't your uniforms tell you?"

J. J.'s response was to race off the porch and out to the curb where the officers sat in their patrol car. Still angry over the dilemma the police had put her in, Judith watched with a wary eye.

J. J. trotted back to the house. "Said they thought it was okay, as long as she came back by three," he said, obviously annoyed. "When we let her go downtown, she told us she was going to spend the night here. Suppose she came back to get her things."

"She'd already taken them," Judith said, then frowned. "Why *did* she come back?"

J. J. gave a nervous shrug. "Couldn't say. That is, if she didn't check back in. Darn."

Perhaps Minerva had returned merely to get credit for the unused room. But Judith wasn't entirely convinced. The only good news was that Minerva's departure freed up a room.

"Come on, J. J.," she urged. "You've got to help me. Where am I going to put all these people? Or should I call the chief?"

J. J.'s dark eyes opened wide. "No! Can't cause trouble. Besides, it's not just us. It's the feds. Have to walk a narrow line on this one." His gaze darted toward the vacant Rankerses' house. "Any chance of putting them up over there while your neighbors are out of town?"

"Heavens, no," Judith shot back. "I wouldn't dream of imposing. I'm not even sure when they're coming back. It could be today."

"Well . . ." J. J. fidgeted, his eyes still darting around

the cul-de-sac. "What about the other B&Bs around here? They full, too?"

"Find out," Judith said, her chin jutting. "Let me know by three-thirty." She backed into the house and slammed the door in J. J.'s startled face.

The phone was ringing. Judith rushed into the kitchen to grab the receiver.

Blanche Rexford was on the line. "You made me curious, Judith," she said in that faintly wispy voice. "I looked up Mr. Turk in *Contemporary Authors* and *Who's Who*. I thought you might be interested in what his biographies say about him."

"I am," Judith assured the librarian.

"I won't read the whole pieces," Blanche said, "but I'll summarize them for you. Mr. Turk's real name is Orlando Turquette, born in New Orleans. After graduating from college—LSU—he moved to Kansas City. His parents joined him there, where his father opened a night club. Apparently, he'd had one in New Orleans as well. His father's first name, by the way, was Parnell. Eight years ago, he was murdered. The killing was never solved, but the tragedy motivated Orlando to write about organized crime. Is that of any help?"

"It could be," Judith allowed. "Poor Roland. I mean, Orlando. I can see why he took to writing about criminals. Or does it say specifically if his father's slaying was gang-related?"

"It was suspected, but never proved," Blanche replied. "I flipped through Mr. Turk's book. He mentioned the Fusilli family. Does that mean anything to you?"

Judith said that it certainly did.

FIFTEEN

JUDITH IMMEDIATELY ASKED Blanche to put aside *Cosa Nostra: Not Our Thing*. She promised to check it out as soon as possible. Then Judith listened to the other messages that had accumulated in her absence. Fortunately, none of them was of immediate importance.

A trip to the grocery store was required, however. She could stop at the library on the way back. But first she went to the front door and peeked outside. The patrol car was still there, but Judith couldn't see any sign of J. J. Martinez or his unmarked city vehicle.

After closing the door, she bent to straighten the throw rug in the entry hall. On Wednesdays, Phyliss usually shook out the area rugs. While Judith didn't intend to go through the house to freshen up the rest of the rugs, she decided she might as well take care of the one in the hall. It got more wear than any of the others.

She opened the front door again, then picked up the rug, which was a small Oriental that matched the larger carpets on the rest of the main floor. She lifted the pad as well, then stopped and stared.

A small round object that looked like a gold coin lay just under the edge where the pad had rested. Judith opened the screen door, dumped the rug and pad on the porch, and came back to examine what turned out to be a small medallion.

Her first reaction was that it had religious significance, a St. Christopher or a Miraculous Medal. But upon close inspection, she recognized the figure as a cupid. Turning the medal over, Judith saw an inscription: "CW2RP." A tiny heart had been engraved beneath the letters and the number.

It was possible, of course, that the medal might have lain under the pad for some time. But Judith didn't think so. Phyliss was very thorough. Pocketing the medal, Judith finished with the rugs, replaced them, and headed for Falstaff's on top of Heraldsgate Hill.

Half an hour and a hundred and forty dollars later, she was back at the B&B, unloading groceries. The phone rang again as she was putting milk and butter in the fridge.

"It sounds," said Ingrid Heffleman of the state B&B association, "as if you're in a bind."

"Oh, Ingrid, thank goodness," Judith said in relief. "Can you help me?"

"I suppose I'll have to," Ingrid responded in her customary dry manner. "The authorities have stepped in. Honestly, Judith, you have more problems than any other innkeeper in the Pacific Northwest. I marvel that you stay in business."

"Well, I do," Judith retorted, stung by the criticism. "My occupancy rate is one of the highest in the area."

"Baffling," Ingrid murmured. "All right, this Martinez person says you need four rooms in the vicinity. Would they be smoking gun or nonsmoking gun rooms?"

"Very funny, Ingrid," Judith snapped.

"With or without a view of the crime scene?" Ingrid seemed to be on a roll.

"Please, Ingrid," Judith pleaded. "It could happen to anyone."

"But it usually happens to you." Ingrid's voice had sharpened. "Okay, I've got two at Marvin Gardens, one at Cozy Nook, and another at Apple Blossom House. They're not as close to downtown as you are, but as you know, they're first-rate.''

"Yes, they're excellent," Judith agreed, feeling a need to humble herself. "Ingrid, can you find two more?"

"Why?" Ingrid asked, not unreasonably. "Mr. Martinez said you had two vacancies."

"I do," Judith admitted, "but I'm not sure that . . ." She bit her tongue before saying *innocent people.* ". . . That newcomers should have to mingle with the holdovers. You see, they're witnesses in the homicide case."

"So Mr. Martinez indicated," Ingrid said in that familiar, dry tone. "In other words, you're afraid the new guests might be in danger?"

"Well . . . not exactly. But," Judith added, "they might feel uncomfortable."

"Like with a hole through their heads?" Ingrid's sigh was audible. "All right. But we'll have to go much further out, almost to the city limits. I'll let you know as soon as I find some vacancies. It's almost three o'clock, so some of your guests could be arriving at any time."

Not to mention returning, Judith thought, then wondered if indeed the current crew would show up at all. Maybe she should have waited. But that wouldn't be fair to the incoming visitors.

Thanking Ingrid profusely, Judith disconnected, then called Renie. "Coz," she began, at her most obsequious, "can you do me a huge favor?"

"Again? In the same day? What now?" Renie's exasperation wasn't entirely feigned.

"I went to the store and forgot to swing by the library to pick up Roland's book. I'm anxious to read it, and Blanche is holding it for me." Briefly, Judith recounted what the librarian had told her on the phone. "Could you pick it up for me and drop it off?"

"No, I could not," Renie retorted. "I am not allowed on the premises of the Heraldsgate Hill library. Our children—some or all of them—borrowed my card several years ago, and I owe two hundred and forty dollars in fines and lost materials, including a video on *How to Raise Your Own Ant Farm*, not to mention the sequel, *What to Do When Your Ants Get Out.* I refuse to pay for something I didn't do. Thus, I am barred.''

Judith ground her teeth. ''Then would you fill in for me here while I go get the book?''

A long silence ensued at the other end of the line. ''Okay,'' Renie said grudgingly. ''It's a good thing the wheels turn slowly if at all at the Boring Cómpany. I'll be over in fifteen minutes.''

The first of the new guests, a couple from Augusta, Maine, arrived before Renie did. Judith apologized, and sent them off to Cozy Nook. Renie pulled into the driveway just as the Malones entered the cul-de-sac.

''Return of the suspects,'' Renie said as she entered through the back door. ''I'll handle them. You take off for the library.''

The Heraldsgate Hill branch was only five minutes away, which meant that Judith should have been back in a quarter of an hour. But Blanche was full of questions, and it took twice as long for Judith to get back home. It was almost three-fifteen when she came through the back door of the B&B.

''The so-called Santoris are here, too,'' Renie said. ''They've gone upstairs. So have the Malones. No Roland or preschool teachers yet.''

''They're late,'' Judith said, frowning at her watch. She remembered the medal she'd found under the hall rug and reached into her pocket. ''What the heck . . . ?'' She let out a little gasp as she pulled out not the medal, but the roll of film she'd found in the Malones' room. ''Damn! In all the excitement about the baby, I forgot about this film. Now where's that . . . ?'' Digging into her other pocket, she produced the medal.

''What do you think?'' she asked Renie after explaining where she'd found it.

''I think you're right,'' Renie responded, turning the gold piece over in her hands. ''It probably hasn't been there for more than a few days. Shall I guess as to its owner?''

''Pete Santori?'' Judith cocked her head at Renie. ''He's the only one in this group who wears gold chains and medals.''

''Exactly.'' Renie handed the medal back to Judith. ''But what does CW2RP stand for?''

''CW2RP,'' Judith repeated. ''As in, CW to RP? Sandi's last name begins with W.''

''But her first name is Sandi, which I assume stands for Sandra,'' Renie noted. ''And who's RP?''

''P for Perl?'' Judith gazed at the medal. ''What was the man's name that you overheard when the teachers were being interrogated? The one that seemed to upset Pam?''

Renie grimaced. ''Dick? No, Rick.''

Judith's lips curved into a faint smile. ''Rick Perl? Pam's brother?''

Renie also smiled. ''Who is really Pete Santori?''

Judith's smile widened. ''Which would explain a lot. Pete is Rick. Rick is Pam's brother, and also Isaac Perl's son. But who,'' she continued, the smile disappearing, ''is Marie?''

Renie sat down at the kitchen table and lighted a cigarette. ''Not his sister. Not his wife. Not his girlfriend—maybe.''

''But pretending to be,'' Judith put in, finding an ashtray in the cupboard. ''Coz, when are you going to quit?''

''I've barely started,'' Renie said, then waved a hand.

Judith made a face, then snapped her fingers. ''We're wrong about Sandi. Her first name is Cassandra. Remember the mailing label on that magazine? Sandi and Pete—or maybe Rick—in the garage. Sandi and Pam lying about how they knew Pete—or Rick. But why?''

Renie exhaled a trail of smoke. ''We know about the connection between the teachers and Legs. If we're right, and Pete is really Rick, the brother of Pam, and son of Isaac, then he was involved in their father's death, if only as an innocent bystander. Pam came here as herself. Why couldn't Rick?''

"We're guessing," Judith cautioned.

"Since when did guesswork bother you?" Renie retorted. "Besides, it's all we've got."

"True. Okay," Judith relented, "let's see where it goes. For some reason, Rick had to change identities and add a bogus wife. Under what circumstances would a man go to such extremes?"

Renie considered. "To start a new life." She shook her head. "To hide out. To lose yourself."

Judith nodded in appreciation. "To hide from the authorities, or . . . ?" She let the question dangle.

Renie eyed Judith with a knowing expression. "The mob."

Judith started to speak, then heard the front door open. Hurrying into the entry hall, she saw Roland du Turque.

"The sun came out for a bit," he observed with a small smile. "I strolled the waterfront."

Judith nodded. "Very different from the Louisiana bayous, I imagine."

Roland's surprise was almost imperceptible. "That's true. New Orleans is a fascinating place. So much rich music history."

Judith wavered, then took the plunge. "It must have been wonderful growing up there. Is that why you became so interested in music?"

Roland seemed to relax, but his eyes were wary. "Of course. Music is such a big part of history. I literally grew up with the rhythm and blues movement. Professor Longhair—his real name was Roy Byrd—was the pioneer in the field right there in New Orleans." Roland paused and lowered his voice. "How did you know?"

"I used to be a librarian," Judith said.

The implication had the desired effect: Roland put a hand to his high forehead, then gave Judith a sheepish look. "You mean—*Cosa Nostra: Not Our Thing*?"

Judith nodded slowly. "It's been a popular work for some time. Until today, I didn't realize that you were Ronald Turk. Which isn't your real name, either."

"If you know the book so well," Roland said, squaring his shoulders and assuming a dignified air, "then you know why I don't write—or travel—under my real name."

"Yes, that explains it," Judith said quietly. "You can't afford to let your subjects know who you are. Like Legs Benedict, for instance."

"Legs." Roland expelled a great sigh. "Whoever shot him saved the state a great deal of money. Not to mention lives."

Judith was aware that Renie had followed her as far as the dining room doorway. "Do you know who killed him?"

Roland shook his head. "Not for certain. Fewer Fingers—Barney—is certainly a possibility. But it could have been anyone, including an outsider. Your guests aren't necessarily the only suspects."

Judith thought that Roland had a point. If most of the guests at the B&B had been alerted to Legs's destination, why couldn't other interested parties have been notified?

"I hope the police are considering that," Judith said, then changed the subject. "You wrote that note to Barney and slipped it under his door. Why?"

Roland had begun to perspire. He pulled a neatly folded handkerchief from the pocket of his jacket and mopped his forehead. "To get his slant on Legs. I knew there was trouble between Fewer Fingers and the Fusilli family in Detroit."

"But you didn't have a chance to talk to him because he never got the note," Judith pointed out.

"That's right," Roland agreed. "Then Fewer Fingers was arrested. I assumed the authorities had the right man. But now . . ."

"Now what?" Judith urged.

"I have my sources," Roland said, sounding a bit defensive. "There's some discrepancy about the weapon, I believe."

"There is," Judith said. "But the police still have Barney in custody."

"Naturally. The FBI must have finally found grounds to hold him. Other than for murdering Legs."

Now that the barrier had been broken between them, Judith had a dozen questions for Roland. But a glance outside revealed Sandi and Pam running out of a taxi cab and hurtling toward the front porch.

"Tardy isn't smarty," Pam announced at the door.

"Being late isn't great," Sandi chimed in.

"Whew," Pam sighed in relief, "we were afraid that Mr. Martinez would give us a time out."

"We couldn't find the right bus stop," Sandi explained, "so we had to take a cab."

"That's fine, you're here," Judith said with a smile. "If you'll excuse us, Mr. du Turque and I were about to adjourn to the living room."

Roland, as well as the teachers, looked faintly surprised, but he dutifully followed Judith into the living room. Renie followed Roland. The cousins settled into one of the sofas by the hearth; Roland sat down in its mate on the other side of the glass-topped coffee table.

"Would you care for a drink?" Judith asked, ever the hostess.

Roland shook his head. "I'm not much of a drinker," he replied. "Liquor is the root of innumerable social problems. It's incredible how many great musicians have been cut down early by drink. And drugs, of course."

Renie, however, rose from her place next to Judith. "I think Mrs. Flynn could use a stiff Scotch," she said. "She became a grandmother today for the first time."

Roland's round face brightened. "Marvelous! Congratulations!"

Judith murmured her thanks as Renie returned to the kitchen. "I know," she began, "that there was a tragedy in your family, and that it may have been connected with Legs's gang, the Fusilli family. I hate asking you this, but did Legs Benedict kill your father?"

Roland's dark eyes moistened. "No," he said calmly. "It wasn't Legs. It was someone else in the organization.

I tried very hard to find out who, not to mention why. But I never did. The deeper I dug, the more I became convinced that it was a personal, rather than a professional crime. My father never had any connection to organized crime, not in Kansas City, not in New Orleans.''

"Why did he leave New Orleans then?'' Judith asked as she heard Renie going to the front door.

Roland sighed. "My stepmother wanted to move. She was from Chicago, and she never liked the South. For years, she begged my father to go back north with her, but he loved New Orleans. Finally, after I moved, they compromised and joined me in Kansas City. I must admit, I felt responsible for my father's death. If he hadn't left New Orleans . . .'' Roland made a helpless gesture with his hands.

"Hey,'' Renie yelled from the entry hall. "Where do the widows go?''

Startled, Judith jumped up from the sofa. "Widows? Oh—the four ladies from Vermont.'' She rushed to greet them, apologized profusely, and gave them directions to Marvin Gardens. Somewhat dazed, the quartet of older women departed Hillside Manor. At least, she thought as Ingrid Heffleman's caustic comments came back to haunt her, they wouldn't become victims.

Back in the living room, Judith tried to console Roland. "It wasn't your fault. Your stepmother was the one who wanted to leave New Orleans.''

"That's true,'' Roland agreed, though he still looked wistful. "Italian women are very strong-minded.'' He stopped and uttered a rueful little laugh. "An ethnic generalization. How wrong of me to say that.''

Judith glossed over the apology. "Your stepmother was Italian?''

"Second generation,'' Roland said as Renie appeared with the drinks. "She was born in New York but had lived in Chicago for several years. My own mother died when I was three. I really don't remember her very well, and Rita was—is—my mother. She married my father when I was five.''

The wheels were turning in Judith's head. ''You said the murder could have been personal, yet you mentioned the Fusilli family in your book. What do you mean?''

Roland paused, thanking Renie for bringing him a glass of apple juice. ''Oh, my. I didn't dare speculate further in print, but . . .'' He ducked his head, then gave Judith and Renie an embarrassed look. ''I've never told anyone except Rita what I'm about to say. Why am I doing it now?''

''Because,'' Renie put in, ''everybody unloads on my cousin. She has that kind of face. And heart.''

Roland brightened. ''She does. I mean, you do,'' he said directly to Judith. ''It's rare. And wonderful.''

''I like people,'' Judith said simply. ''At least, most of them.''

''That's obvious,'' Roland said. ''Otherwise, you wouldn't be in this business.''

The phone rang, and Judith dashed to the cherrywood table where the living room extension rested. The caller was Ingrid Heffleman, informing Judith that she had found two more B&B vacancies, at the Cedars and Chez Moi. Judith conveyed her profound gratitude and returned to the sofa.

Apparently, Renie had been encouraging Roland to tell his story. As soon as Judith sat down, he leaned forward on the other sofa and resumed his confidences.

''My stepmother's maiden name was Pasolini,'' he said, his soft voice even softer, though there was no one to overhear. ''But she had married earlier, when she was still in her teens. His name was Ernesto—Ernie—Doria.''

Judith froze. ''Doria?'' she echoed.

''Yes.'' Roland gave Judith a curious look. ''You know the name? Other than the ship and the great Genoese admiral for whom she was named?''

''Let's say,'' Judith said cautiously, ''that it rings some sort of vague bell.''

''Hmm.'' But Roland took up his tale. ''Ernie Doria had a suspicious background, and her parents had forbidden

Rita to see him. She defied them, however, and they eloped. The marriage was short-lived, as you might imagine. Rita left him after less than a year and returned—in tears—to her parents. To avoid the shame, they sent her to live with an aunt and uncle in Chicago. That's where she met my father. He'd gone there to audition some musicians for his club in New Orleans.'' Roland paused to offer the cousins a self-deprecating smile. ''My interest in music is very real. But I'm sure you've gathered that by now.''

Judith nodded. ''We have. You're extremely knowledgeable.''

Roland eschewed the compliment. ''In my research, I found out that Ernie Doria worked for the Fusilli family. I came to the conclusion that somehow, over the years, they had taken offense because a woman who had married into the family—in the gangland sense—had left one of its members, and worse yet, had then married a black man.'' Roland shut his eyes tight for a moment before continuing. ''I believe that my father was killed because he married Ernesto Doria's former wife. What's even stranger,'' he went on with an apologetic grimace, ''is that I think Ernie Doria may have killed Legs Benedict.''

SIXTEEN

QUESTIONS TUMBLED FROM both cousins' lips. Roland held up his hands, gently begging them to slow down.

"No," he responded to the one query he had managed to single out, "I don't know what Ernie Doria looks like. My stepmother destroyed his pictures right after she left him. She's described him, of course, and said he'd be about seventy by now."

Judith and Renie exchanged blank looks. "None of these guests are that old," Judith said, "except Minerva Schwartz, and she's a woman."

Roland conceded the point. "That's what I meant earlier—whoever killed Legs might not be a guest. Legs may have agreed to meet someone outside before he got here, or perhaps he made the arrangements over the phone in the upstairs hall."

Neither Judith nor Renie spoke for a few moments. Finally, Judith made up her mind to tell Roland about the canceled reservation for someone named Doria.

Roland was stunned. "Do you recall the first name?" he asked.

Judith shook her head. "I'm not even sure whether it was for a man or a woman. All I know is that the address was in Las Vegas, but that it got dumped when Sandi and Pam were fooling around with the computer."

"Sandi and Pam." Roland repeated the names under his breath. "Do you . . . ?"

Judith nodded. "They told me their story. At least some of it. Do you know who Pam's brother is?"

"Rick Perl," Roland replied promptly. "Why do you ask?"

"Would you recognize him?"

"No. I don't actually know Pam or Sandi, rather, not until now. But," Roland continued, polishing his glasses with his handkerchief, "I've spoken with Pam on the phone. I tracked her down because of her father's slaying. My interviews with her were part of my background for my book on mob assassins like Legs Benedict."

The conversation was interrupted by the arrival of another pair of guests, this time a newlywed couple from Omaha. Unlike Pete and Marie, they struck Judith as the real thing: As soon as she regretfully informed them they would have to stay at Apple Blossom House, they immediately began blaming each other for the unexpected change of plans.

Back in the living room, Judith asked Roland if he knew what had happened to Rick Perl after the death of his father. Roland replied that when he had posed the same question to Pam, she had evaded it.

"In fact," he amplified, "I didn't get much out of her after that. Since running into her here, we haven't had much opportunity to speak privately. This is a lovely house, but you never know when someone will come upon you without any warning."

"You must have been surprised to see her and Sandi at Hillside Manor," Renie remarked.

"Oh, no," Roland responded. "She was the one who called me in San Francisco to let me know that Legs Benedict was on his way. Pam Perl had tracked me down through my publisher."

Judith and Renie stared at Roland. "Pam called you? Why?" Judith asked.

"Because she knew it would be a rare opportunity for

me to have personal contact with Legs," Roland explained.
"There was no way I could get to him as long as he was
in New York. I know, I'd tried." He cleared his throat.
"You must realize that the kind of writing I do is . . . del-
icate. Which brings up that note I dropped under the piano.
I feel I owe you an explanation."

"Yes?" Judith leaned closer.

"For years, I've researched the Hoffa disappearance,"
Roland said in his quiet voice. "It's possible that the truth
will never be known, but it's a fascinating subject. Recently, I learned of a young man who was allegedly connected to Provenzano and Giacalone, who supposedly met
with Jimmy Hoffa the night he vanished. The young man's
name was then Alfonso Benedetto." Roland paused, smiling wryly. "Yes, Legs Benedict, before he became a made
guy, as they say, or a member of the Mafia. He was op-
erating out of Detroit in those days. So this alleged connection was all the more reason for me to meet Legs."

"Would he have talked?" Renie asked, lighting another
cigarette.

Roland sat back, his arms extended across the top of the
sofa. "It's hard to say. Sometimes these people will, if ego
is involved. I sensed that Legs might somehow be that
type."

Judith absorbed the information, then steered the conversation back to the preschool teachers. "How did Pam
know where Legs was headed? His original destination was
Detroit."

Roland gave Judith another of his self-deprecating
smiles. "That I couldn't tell you. There's a grapevine out
there when it comes to such things. As odd as it sounds,
gangsters lead very busy lives. If one of them—such as
Legs—goes out of town, he has to make sure that his areas
of responsibility are covered."

Judith winced, imaging just what those "areas of responsibility" might entail. Her brain, however, was busily
filing all the information Roland had dispensed, along with

the nuances and implications. "What about Darlene?" she asked. "Why did she come with Legs?"

Roland grimaced. "Again, I don't know. Darlene is a bit of a wild card in this situation. She may simply have been his girlfriend."

Given the evidence of the so-called Smiths having slept separately, Judith didn't think so. But she kept the doubts to herself. "So you have no idea where Darlene might have gone? The car has been found, but she's still missing."

"Yes," Roland said, sipping at his apple juice. "That indicates she used some other mode of transportation to make her getaway. A second rental car, perhaps, though I believe the police haven't had any success checking out the local agencies. In fact," he went on, lowering his head, "I called on Detective Martinez at headquarters this afternoon. That's why I was late getting back."

"You spoke to J. J. about the case in general?" asked Judith, surprised. "Does he know who you really are?"

"Oh, certainly," Roland answered. "I told him early on that I wrote about organized crime."

The doorbell rang, and Renie jumped up. "I'll take care of this bunch. Where do I ship them?"

"That depends," Judith replied. "This is one of the last two reservations. If it's the couple from Santa Cruz, send them to Chez Moi. The directions are on the little desk in the hall. If it's the nuns from Milwaukee, they'd probably prefer the Cedars."

Renie hurried off to the front door. Roland resumed speaking.

"I've worked closely with the authorities in several cities, though mainly in the East and the Midwest," he said. "I gave Mr. Martinez my bona fides. He was helpful in some very small ways, but he's certainly a nervous fellow, isn't he?"

Judith started to agree, but Renie interrupted. "The nuns," she yelled. "Should they take the freeway or Highway 99?"

Judith glanced at her watch. It was almost four. "The

freeway should be okay until rush hour starts. Are they driving a rental car?''

"They've got a Humvee," Renie called back. The nuns could be heard giggling. "It's bright red," Renie added.

Judith didn't know if her cousin was kidding or not. She turned back to Roland. "That's an important point," she said, gesturing toward the entry hall. "Travel routes. There are really only two main north-south arteries in this town. Minerva could have taken several routes to the airport and ditched the car in that huge parking garage. It would take some time to find her, but I suspect they tracked her down through the car."

Roland grew thoughtful. "I mentioned Darlene's disappearance to Mr. Martinez. He seemed quite baffled."

Renie returned to the sofa. "Police baffled? How unusual," she said, her voice dripping with sarcasm.

"Hey," Judith said, on the defensive, "Joe is rarely baffled."

Renie smirked, but made no further comment. Roland said that J. J. Martinez had informed him the Chrysler Concord driven by Legs and Darlene had been rented from a New York agency in Queens.

"That's why the police felt Ms. Smith—for lack of a real name—might have rented a second car," Roland explained to the cousins. "Since they haven't been able to track her through the agencies, Detective Martinez thought she might have used her real name and worn some sort of disguise."

Mal and Bea came into the living room and stopped, standing like a pair of homely watchdogs on the other side of the sofa where the cousins were seated.

"We're going to sue," Bea announced.

"Sue who?" Renie asked, and grinned at the unintentionally rhyming query.

"Everybody," Mal responded, obviously not sharing Renie's mirth. "This place. The cops. The feds. We've had it."

"I take it you didn't enjoy your outing today?" Judith inquired, trying to remain pleasant.

"Sheesh," Mal blurted, "what's to enjoy in this burg? You got water, we got water. You got tall buildings, we got tall buildings. You got bums, we got . . ."

"I'm sorry," Judith said, leaning over the back of the sofa, "but I think you're wasting money to file a lawsuit."

Draining her cocktail glass, Renie stood up. "Stop picking on my cousin," she ordered. "None of this is her fault. Mrs. Flynn feels terrible about your loss. It seems to me that you should be angry with whoever killed your loved one. Why don't you take out your sorrow and wrath on them?"

To Judith's surprise, the Malones looked at each other long and hard. "Too little, too late," Mal murmured. The bereaved couple left the room. Quietly.

"Where'd they go?" Renie asked when the cousins had concluded their chat with Roland and had gone into the kitchen.

Judith pointed to the window above the sink. "Right out here, between the flower bed and Rankerses' hedge. They're just sort of standing around, looking pathetic. Bea may be crying, I can't really tell. You're right—I feel very, very sorry for them. All that rough, tough talk is a coverup for their real feelings. Mal and Bea are probably very nice people."

"I don't think so," Renie countered. "Bad things sometimes do happen to bad people."

"Their grief is real, though," Judith said, watching the couple with a sympathetic eye. She finally turned around. "Can you stay for just a few more minutes while I check on Mother? I've been ignoring her since this morning. I wonder if she'd like to go see the new baby."

"Sure," Renie responded. "I don't have to get home. Bill's doing a Key Club exchange this afternoon. I canceled my part of it—I just wasn't in the mood."

Judith pressed her fingers against her temples. "Coz,

you're going to have to explain all this to me pretty soon. With everything else going on, I don't think I can take it right now, but promise that you will eventually.''

"Sure," Renie said again. "Go see your mother. When do you expect those other guests?''

"There's no way of telling," Judith replied, heading for the back door. "They paid by credit card, so they can arrive any time right up until ten o'clock. Chez Moi, remember?''

"Got it." Renie sat down at the kitchen table and began leafing through the evening paper which had just arrived.

Gertrude had dozed off in front of the TV. She gave a start when Judith entered the toolshed.

"Help!" she cried. "I'm being attacked!'' Fumbling for the TV remote, she pointed it at Judith and clicked several times. "Bang, bang! You're dead!''

Judith hurried to her mother's chair. "It's me, Mother. You've been watching an old western on TV.''

Rubbing her eyes, Gertrude blinked at Judith. "What? Where've you been? California?''

"Why would I be in California?'' Judith asked, taking her mother's empty water glass to the sink for a refill.

"You've been gone long enough to be in Europe,'' Gertrude declared. "Where's that nice young man from Washington, D. C.? He said he'd be back.''

Judith didn't comment. "I thought,'' she said, putting the glass on Gertrude's side table, "you might want to go up to the hospital to see your new great-grandson.''

Wincing, Gertrude rubbed her knees. "I don't know, kiddo. I'm kind of stiff today. Maybe tomorrow or the next day.''

"They don't keep mothers and babies in the hospital very long,'' Judith pointed out. "I wouldn't be surprised if they sent Kristin home by then. They'll be staying here, you know.''

"Two weeks,'' Gertrude said. "You stayed for two weeks. Fact is, I stayed longer than that. I had some problems. But you wouldn't remember. You were asleep most of the time.''

"Everything's different now," Judith said, turning off the TV and sitting down on her mother's small couch. "When I had Mike, they let me stay for five days."

"Two weeks," Gertrude repeated. "You had time to get yourself together. What's with doctors these days?"

"It's the insurance companies," Judith said vaguely. "Mother, aren't you anxious to see . . ." She gulped. ". . . little Dan?"

Gertrude made a disgusted noise. "Dan! What a dopey idea to call the baby after that lunkhead. Why not Donald, for your father?"

Judith made a helpless gesture. "It's their business. I don't like it, either."

For several moments, Gertrude shuffled the jumble puzzles and the candy wrappers and the magazines around on her card table. "It's kind of strange, isn't it?" she said, seemingly from out of nowhere.

"What is, Mother?"

"Babies. Birth. Death." Her voice dropped on the last word. "I've lived almost this whole century. This new little guy'll probably live through the rest of the next. Two hundred years between us." She paused and gave Judith a bleak look. "And what will we have to show for it?"

Judith took a deep breath. "Living. Coping. Being part of a family. In the long run, there's not much else."

Gertrude uttered a little snort of laughter. "You, too, huh, kiddo? I guess we'll never be rich and famous."

Getting up, Judith crossed the short distance to hug her mother. "Even if we did, it wouldn't matter. It's about love. It's about *us*." She felt Gertrude shudder in her embrace. "Hey," Judith asked softly, "what's wrong?"

The voice that answered was not at all like Gertrude's usual rasp. "I'm scared. I'm old, I'm useless, and I'm scared."

Judith tightened her hold. "We're all scared. But you're tough, Mother. If you weren't, you wouldn't have gotten to be so old. Now you have a great-grandson, you've got something new and wonderful to live for."

"Hunh." Gertrude gave a little shake of her head. "So what next?" Judith started to respond, but the old woman answered her own question. "I just keep getting older, right?"

"That's what you do," Judith said trying to keep the catch out of her voice. "That's what we all do."

"Older," Gertrude repeated, leaning against her daughter. "Older and tougher. I guess I can do that."

"You're doing it now," said Judith, and felt her mother hug her back.

The garden seemed peaceful under the late afternoon sun. Judith paused by the small patio and the statue of St. Francis. Foxgloves stood taller than she was, almost all of the rose bushes were in full bloom, the Oriental poppies provided brilliant splashes of red, pink, and orange. By the back fence, the dahlias were coming up, the Peruvian lilies were leafing out, and spears of gladiola leaves were showing above the soil. The three remaining cherry trees from the old Grover orchard were in blossom, though crooked with age and unlikely to bear much fruit.

There was no sign of the Malones, and the Rankerses' house still looked empty. Judith went back inside to find Renie talking to Pete Santori.

"Pete is repeat," Renie said, obviously annoyed. "He insists he's really Pete Santori, and has papers to prove it."

Judith stood next to Pete's chair. "We think we know better." She reached into her pocket and pulled out the medal. "CW2RP. This is yours, isn't it?"

Pete seemed to pale under his tan as his hand automatically flew to the gold chains around his neck. "What? No, of course not. I've never seen it before."

Judith pocketed the medal. "Okay. I'll ask Sandi about it. Or should I say Cassandra?"

"Whatever." Pete's finely chiseled chin was thrust out. "I don't need this crap. Marie and I want to get the hell out of here."

Pulling out the chair next to Renie and across from Pete,

Judith sat down. "Look," she began, trying to sound reasonable, "as long as guests are well behaved and discreet, I don't pry. It doesn't matter to me if you and Marie are married or not. But the least you can do is spare us the phony—and sickening—lovebird stuff. Okay?"

Not only did Pete's color return, but it heightened. He cuffed the can of beer in front of him and stared at the table. "We're not doing anything wrong," he muttered.

"Define 'wrong,' " Renie put in.

A harsh laugh escaped from Pete's lips. "You define it. I mean, morally."

"How about legally?" Renie retorted, and gave Judith a nudge under the table.

"Let's try ethically," Judith said, on cue. "As in bringing guns here. That's not allowed by the management, which is me. I understood that a gun had been confiscated from you and Marie. But there's still a weapon in your room. How come?"

Pete's gaze, hostile and challenging, locked with Judith's. He took a big swallow from the beer can, set it down hard on the table, and stood up. "Ask your old man about that," he said to Judith, and exited the kitchen.

The cousins were left staring at each other. "Joe?" Judith said in a puzzled tone. "Did he mean I should ask Joe?"

Renie shrugged. "He wasn't talking to me. Anyway, I doubt that Bill would have an answer to that one."

Judith went to the cupboard to refresh their drinks. "Speaking of Bill, if he's . . . ah . . . um . . . out this evening, do you want to have dinner with Joe and me?"

"Oh," Renie replied with a wave of her hand, "Bill will be finished by dinnertime. He's not one to linger after the deed is done. Besides, the kids will be home tonight."

Judith handed Renie her bourbon. "How do your kids feel about this Key Club thing? Or do they know?"

"They like the idea," Renie said. "They thought that when Bill retired, he might get bored, even though he retained some of his private patients and still serves as a consultant to the university. But Tom and Anne and Tony all feel that the Key Club has perked up our lives. The kids were afraid that Bill and I would just park ourselves in our respective places at night in front of the TV and never budge. As Anne puts it, we have a whole new energy force going for us. After all, variety is the spice of life.''

Judith turned away, lest Renie see her appalled expression. As soon as the current crisis at the B&B was resolved, Judith intended to take her cousin to task for such a moral lapse. Adultery—Judith refused to call the Key Club encounters by a gentler name—was totally out of character for the Joneses. She couldn't imagine what had made them stray from their usual virtuous path.

But for now, Judith held her tongue. ''Well . . . that's . . . nice.'' She took a big sip of Scotch and sat back down at the kitchen table.

''So,'' Renie went on, ''I'll finish this drink and be off. You have to get dinner, too, not to mention the appetizers for those fun-loving guests.''

''I'd rather skip that tonight,'' Judith said, then frowned. ''I assume they'll be allowed out for dinner. I have no intention of feeding them.''

Renie looked up at the old school clock. ''It's almost five now. Say, do you want me to drop off that roll of film?''

''Oh!'' Judith slapped at her temples. ''I forgot again. Damn. Yes, would you? I wonder how soon they can get it back to me? The Malones may look for it. It's three-hour service when you get it in by four o'clock.''

Renie shook her head. ''Too late. You won't have it until tomorrow morning.''

''But it'll be early, won't it?'' said Judith, looking anxious. ''I'll go up to the camera shop right after I serve breakfast.''

Polishing off her drink, Renie stood up as Judith handed her the film. ''They open at eight,'' Renie said, slipping the roll into her big purse. ''Good luck, coz. I'll talk to you tomorrow.''

Judith walked Renie to the back door and watched her go down the walk to the driveway. The clouds were moving in again, and the air felt faintly humid. More rain was on the way. As if to justify the prediction, Judith saw a rainbow in the eastern sky. The graceful arch of soft pastels did nothing to cheer her.

Neither, for that matter, did the Scotch.

Joe came home shortly before six, just as Judith was carrying the appetizer tray out to her grumbling guests. She ignored their complaints and went back to the kitchen to greet her husband.

"I stopped by the hospital," he said, after kissing Judith. "The baby's great. I'm going to call him Mac."

"That's a good idea," Judith said. "Maybe I will, too. It's better than—gag—Dan."

"Most things are," Joe said, washing his hands at the sink. "By the way, I talked to J. J. The department has agreed to pay for the displaced reservations."

"I should hope so," Judith said. "None of this is our fault. Now please tell me they're also paying for their dinners."

"I don't know about that," Joe said, stretching and yawning. "The budget's tight these days."

Judith started to fume. "They'd better be out of here tomorrow. I can't go through another day of uncertainty like this one. We still have one pair of guests who haven't showed up yet. Not to mention that Minerva Schwartz—I won't even attempt to pronounce her real name—came by this afternoon while I was gone, and then left again. Do you know where she went?"

"No idea. The last I heard, she was trying to finagle some kind of deal with the FBI. Don't ask me what it was, because I don't think J.J. knows," Joe said, getting out a bottle of gin, and gesturing at Judith. "Martini?"

Judith shook her head. "I got a jump-start today. I needed it." She waited for Joe to pour the vermouth and find an olive in the refrigerator. "Why would Minerva want to cut a deal with the FBI? Does that mean she was in on her son's illegal operations?''

"Could be," Joe allowed. "From what little I saw of her, she seemed like a very capable woman. Maybe she had a business background, maybe she kept the books for Barney. Who knows?''

Judith certainly didn't, so she changed the subject. "What's this about Pete and Marie still having a gun in their room?''

Joe's shoulders tensed as he manned the martini shaker. "A gun? We took their gun. It was a Beretta.''

"That was Gun Number One," Judith said, her patience fraying. "Gun Number Two is a Sig Sauer. Don't pretend you don't know. Pete informed me that you did.''

Joe uttered a one-word expletive under his breath. He didn't respond until after he had poured his martini, added the olive, and taken a deep sip. "How'd you know it was a Sig Sauer?'' he asked.

"It said so. I can read," Judith snapped.

Joe gave a faint nod, then grew silent as he took another sip from his drink. "The Beretta belonged to Pete," he finally said, leaning back in the captain's chair at the kitchen table. "We're hanging onto it until they leave.''

"What about the Sig Sauer? Don't tell me it's Marie's," Judith said, her eyes narrowing.

"Okay," Joe replied. "I won't tell you.''

"It *is* Marie's, isn't it?''

"You said not to . . .''

"You know I didn't mean that.'' Judith had grown tight-lipped, a preface to anger.

"So it's Marie's," Joe said calmly.

"Why does she get to keep it?'' Judith demanded.

Joe sighed. "Because," he finally answered, "as you've probably guessed, she's not Marie Santori. She's Mary Lou Desmond, and she's entitled to keep the weapon under any circumstances. Mary Lou, you see, is a U. S. Marshal.''

SEVENTEEN

JUDITH DEMANDED AN explanation. It was clear that Joe was reluctant to give one, but having opened the door a crack, he couldn't slam it shut.

"Mary Lou Desmond works out of the Justice Department's Miami office," Joe began after Judith had poured another finger of Scotch into her glass. "As you probably know, given your inquiring mind when it comes to criminal activities, federal marshals are assigned to people who have gone into the . . ."

"When do we eat?" It was Bea Malone, holding the swinging doors open with her broad behind. It looked to Judith as if she'd been crying.

"Eat what?" Judith snapped, aware that coupled with the aggravating guests, the Scotch might be taking a toll on her disposition. Noting the grief in Bea's eyes, Judith was immediately repentant. "I'm sorry, I'm a bit jumpy. What did you say?"

"I said dinner," Bea shot back. "Those doodads with the shrimp and the mushrooms and the funny cheeses with all those little holes aren't what I'd call filling."

"I'm afraid no one told me you'd be here for dinner," Judith said in a truculent tone. "Aren't you allowed out this evening?"

Pam had come up behind Bea. "We only got afternoon recess," she said.

Judith had planned a simple meal of ham-filled crepes and salad for herself and Joe. A stuffed pork chop was already baking for Gertrude, along with a potato.

"I don't have anything prepared," Judith finally said, as her brain took a hasty mental inventory of the freezer. "I hadn't planned on dinner for seven extra people."

"Hunh," snorted Bea. "You mean you want us to starve on top of everything else we've gone through?"

"Well . . ." Judith took pity. "I went to the grocery store today, so I . . ."

But Joe had picked up the phone. "Hold it, Jude-girl," he urged. "Hello? Four large, the works, and seven Caesar salads." He gave the name, address, and phone number for Hillside Manor. "Thirty minutes? Fine. Thanks." Hanging up, he looked at Judith. "Problem solved by Athens Pizza. Not to mention your mate. Come on, let's go."

"Go?" Judith asked in surprise.

"To dinner," Joe responded, polishing off his martini.

"Pizza?" Bea said, making a face. "Deep-dish, Chicago style?"

"Greek," Joe responded, getting his jacket from the peg in the hallway. "Via Heraldsgate Hill. You'll love it." The tone of his voice suggested that Bea wouldn't dare do otherwise.

"Pizza!" cried Pam. "Sandi and I love pizza. We make them in class, and our students help. You wouldn't believe what they use for toppings."

"Yeah, I would," Bea said in a caustic voice. "Pizza. Hunh."

The two women left the kitchen area, however. Judith turned to Joe. "I have to get Mother's dinner. Can you wait five minutes?"

"Sure," Joe said. "I'll be out in the car."

Judith quickly opened a can of string beans and heated them on the stove. Five minutes later, she was in the tool-shed where Gertrude accepted the meal with a minimum of criticism. The stuffing in the pork chop was nowhere nearly as tasty as what Gertrude herself used to make. It wasn't as good as Grandma Grover's, either, and if Gertrude had to tell the truth, even her daughter made better dressing, at least for turkey and chicken.

Judith joined Joe in the red MG at exactly six-thirty. "Who's paying for the pizza?" she asked as he backed out of the driveway.

"They are," Joe replied. "Even a Mafioso wouldn't stiff Stavros. Haven't you ever wondered why Athens Pizza has such big ovens?"

Judith smiled. "No, but I've watched customers who dared to complain get thrown out onto Heraldsgate Avenue. When it comes to the no-nonsense business approach, he's right up there with Cal the Cobbler. About now, I wish I had their nerve."

"It should be over by tomorrow," Joe said, turning right onto the avenue and heading down the very steep hill that led to the lower Heraldsgate business district. "Those guests can't be held indefinitely. Shall we try Freddo's?"

"Uhhh . . ." Judith grimaced. "I'm not in the mood for Italian tonight. How about T. S. McSnort's?"

"Sounds good." Joe braked for the light at the bottom of the hill. "I'll finish my federal marshal tale when we get there."

Luck was with them. A parking space right in front of T. S. McSnort's opened up. Two minutes later, Judith and Joe were seated in a wooden booth, directly across from the usually noisy bar. On this Wednesday night in June, however, the restaurant was comparatively quiet.

After ordering their drinks, Joe resumed telling Judith about Mary Lou Desmond's role in what the police department was calling—unfortunately—the Hillside Manor Case.

"Let me back up a bit," Joe said, keeping his voice down. "When J. J. and Rich Goldman conducted their search of the guest rooms, they found both guns. Pete allowed us to hold his Beretta, but Mary Lou refused. She knew the local laws, and that she was allowed to retain a handgun as long as she had a carry permit. She was right, of course. That's legal in this state. But this was a homicide investigation, which changed the rules. The weapon had to be confiscated in case it turned out to have fired the shots that killed Legs Benedict.''

"But," Judith interrupted in an effort to keep her train of thought from derailing, "it was the Glock that had been fired.''

Joe nodded. "But, as it turned out, that wasn't the gun that was used to kill Legs.''

"It wasn't?" Judith's eyes widened. "But I thought . . .''

"It was a natural assumption, until the ballistics report came back," Joe said, glancing up at the TV over the bar, which showed a baseball game underway. "A Colt .45 was the weapon. The bullet casings were found by the body. But the gun has never turned up.''

Judith was shocked. "You mean . . . Legs really might have been killed by someone who wasn't staying at the B&B?''

"Yes. But," Joe added quickly, "let's not get side-tracked. When J. J. demanded the Sig Sauer, Marie showed him her badge. The story came out then, but J. J. had to agree to keep it to himself and continue treating Mary Lou as a suspect. The only reason he told me is because he felt a personal responsibility. He wanted me to know that at least one of these people staying at the B&B wasn't a crook. And the only reason I'm telling you now is so that you know the gun belongs to a law enforcement officer.''

Judith paused, sorting out this new information in her mind. "But why is Marie—Mary Lou—here in the first place?''

Joe grimaced. "What do you know about Pete Santori?''

"That he's not Pete Santori," Judith replied. "And frankly, I didn't think Marie was Marie, either. They didn't fit as a couple. Opposites may attract, but despite all the goo-goo cuddle talk, they came from different planets.''

Joe gave a slight nod. "Okay. So maybe you know who Pete really is."

"Rick Perl, Pam's brother, and probably Sandi's boyfriend." Judith couldn't help but look smug.

Joe grinned over the rim of his martini glass. "You do amaze me sometimes, Jude-girl. So why are he and Mary Lou posing as husband and wife?"

"Well . . ." Judith gazed into her Scotch. "If Mary Lou is a federal marshal, she's on the job. Said job has something to do with Pete—Rick—but he's not a cop, or he could have kept his gun, too. Neither of them is using their real names or identities. Thus, I'm left with the impression that Pete—Rick—might be in the witness protection program."

The gold flecks in his green eyes danced as Joe nodded. "That's right. Can you guess why?"

The waiter, a young man named Kevin with a blond crewcut and two spots of high color on his cheeks, arrived to take the Flynns' dinner order. Judith ordered the steak and mushroom pie; Joe opted for the prime rib. Neither could resist starting with T. S. McSnort's delicious clam chowder.

"My guess?" Judith said after Kevin had left. "Rick somehow got involved in the murder of his father, Isaac Perl. I don't mean that he was an accomplice, but he must have done something that made him go into hiding from the Mafia, or more specifically, from the Fusilli family."

Joe selected a slice of rich dark bread from the basket that Kevin had brought earlier. "Excellent. Every so often, it occurs to me that you could have been a detective."

"How often?" Judith asked, unsure whether or not her husband was teasing her.

Joe, however, avoided the question. "After Isaac Perl found himself under the Fusilli family's thumb, his son, Rick, tried to infiltrate the mob. Naturally, I haven't talked to Rick about this—in fact, I've hardly talked to Rick and Mary Lou at all—but according to the FBI, Rick was successful in the beginning. Under an assumed identity, he became a mechanic, or a shill for some of their illegal gambling operations. It was a hopeless idea. He was only what is known as a half-assed wise guy who was probably never going to become a made guy, or an actual mob member. Consequently, Rick couldn't figure out a way to get his father unconnected from the mob, let alone to save Isaac's life. Rick was still working as a mechanic when his father was murdered. Somehow his cover was blown after Isaac was killed, and Rick was forced to go into hiding. End of story."

"No, it's not," Judith asserted. "It doesn't explain what he's doing at Hillside Manor with a federal marshal to protect him."

Pausing as Kevin delivered the chowder, Joe offered Judith a speculative glance. "Do you think I know that?" he finally said after the waiter had left.

Judith was disappointed. "I thought you might. Shall we conjecture?"

Joe shook his head. "I never speculate. And it's not my case." He broke a couple of wafer crackers into his chowder.

"It's not my case, either," Judith retorted, "but it *is* my B&B. And I *do* speculate. Here's how it goes: Pam and Sandi told Rick that they were heading out west to confront Legs. Or, maybe it was the other way around. Anyway, the siblings wanted revenge for their father's death. But Rick can't travel without federal protection, so Marie has to come along. They pose as honeymooners. Then, either Rick or Pam kills Legs. How's that?" Judith gave Joe a self-satisfied look.

"Fair to poor," Joe responded, as the baseball game on TV heated up along with the customers at the bar. "Are you saying that Pam or Rick would be dumb enough to kill somebody with a federal marshal watching them like a hawk?"

Judith wasn't daunted by her husband's quibble. "Human emotion drives people to do stupid—and self-destructive—things. I know, you're trained to look only at evidence. If I ever thought about playing detective—'' Judith paused and gave Joe an arch little smile, ''—it would be because I'm interested in people and what makes them tick. You and I work in opposite ways, Joe. I'm Mrs. Inside, you're Mr. Outside.''

''Intuition,'' Joe murmured, setting aside his empty martini glass. ''We're discouraged from relying on that at the police academy.''

''Exactly,'' Judith said. ''Which is probably wise, especially when you're young. But I believe in it, and sometimes it works.'' Before Joe could interrupt, Judith waved her soup spoon at him. ''I'm not ruling out Sandi in this mix. It would be clever of Pam and Rick to have her commit the crime, and she had motivation, too. Isaac would have become her father-in-law, assuming the romance was serious. And, if you want to know the truth, I still consider Marie—I mean, Mary Lou—a suspect.''

''Interesting,'' Joe remarked. ''Fascinating. And absurd.''

''Why?'' Judith countered. ''Her job is to protect Rick Perl. She realizes he wants revenge. Legs is a known criminal. Why not whack him and eliminate the temptation for Rick?''

''Why not say so?'' Joe asked. ''Anyway, you're wrong. Mary Lou allowed J. J. to check her weapon. It hadn't been fired recently.''

Judith's face fell. ''And nobody else's gun at the B&B had been fired, either. Except Legs's own weapon, which wasn't the one that killed him.''

''That's right,'' Joe agreed as Kevin showed up with their entrees. ''Which is why I figure they'll either release Barney tomorrow, or hold him on other criminal charges. That's up to the feds, not our department.''

''Then they'll also have to let the rest of them go?'' Judith asked after thanking Kevin for serving their entrees.

''Yes. Your troubles should be over in a few hours,'' Joe said with a wry smile.

"But the mystery will remain," Judith said in a melancholy tone.

"It won't be your mystery anymore," Joe noted. "Or does that make you sad?"

"I hate a lack of resolution," Judith replied as she opened the flaky crust of her steak and mushroom pie. "I'd certainly like to know who killed Legs."

"So would J. J.," Joe said, his eyes straying to the baseball game.

Judith followed her husband's glance. The hand that held the fork that conveyed a large chunk of tender beef halted in midair. "Joe," she whispered, nodding toward the bar, "that's Agent Dunleavy over there."

"Who?" Joe turned to the customers who were lined up along the brass rail.

"Agent Dunleavy. The young man from the FBI who's been interrogating Mother about her alleged connection with the SS or whatever."

Joe chuckled. "Oh, yes. Dark suit, white shirt, muted tie. I should have guessed. When is he hauling her away? Shall I buy him a drink?"

"Don't be nasty, Joe," Judith chided. "He's on a fool's errand." She removed her napkin from her lap and placed it on the table. "Actually, I'm going to speak to him. Maybe I can convince him he's wasting his time."

Sliding out of the booth, Judith approached the bar. "Agent Dunleavy," she said pleasantly, "I'm Mrs. Grover's daughter, remember?"

"Of course," Dunleavy replied, though his youthful face looked surprised.

Judith gave the agent a faint smile. "I hope you've figured out that Mother isn't the Gertrude Hoffman you're looking for."

"Not at all," Dunleavy responded. "She's been most cooperative. Naturally, I realize she's elderly and therefore confused about some things. Not to mention that she doesn't remember certain specific situations."

Shaking off the bartender's inquiring glance, Judith

stared at Dunleavy. "That's ridiculous. Tomorrow I'm going to the federal building, or wherever your offices are
located, and show your superiors Mother's records. For one
thing, she and my father were married before the war, right
here in this very city. I was born here, two months to the
day before Pearl Harbor. My father, Donald Grover, had a
rheumatic heart and couldn't serve in the armed forces, so
he was an air raid warden during the war. My mother
worked with all sorts of volunteer organizations, and received several certificates of commendation. All of this is
stored in the house someplace. I can even find their ration
books from the OPA.''

Dunleavy, who was drinking very dark beer, grimaced
slightly. "As I told you, those things can be forged. Believe
me, it's happened with many war criminals. How else do
you think they've eluded the law for so long?''

Frustrated, Judith slammed her hand on the mahogany
bar. "That's idiotic. What exactly has she told you that's
so blasted helpful?''

"I'll give you an example," Dunleavy said in his reasonable manner. "There were two sisters named Greenberg
at the women's camp at Auschwitz. They came from a very
illustrious Jewish family. Your mother remembered them,
and how she and an accomplice tortured them until, as she
put it in her own words, 'They threw in the cards and
crawled off to die.' ''

"Greenberg?'' Judith gaped at Dunleavy. "Esther and
Hannah Greenberg? They were in Mother's bridge club
years ago. They had a system of signals, and Mother and
Aunt Deb wanted to get back at them for cheating. Neither
Mother nor Aunt Deb would dream of cheating in return,
so they devised a bunch of diversions, like snapping their
girdles and singing Gershwin songs off-key and spilling
lemonade in the Greenbergs' lap. Naturally, Esther and
Hannah finally dropped out of the bridge club. And yes,
they came from money. Their father had a carpet store
south of downtown.'' Judith gave Dunleavy a pugnacious

stare. "That's how the Greenberg sisters threw in the cards. Literally."

If Dunleavy was taken aback, he didn't show it. "A very glib explanation."

"If you don't believe me, ask Aunt Deb. She still has all her marbles. Or most of them," Judith amended.

"I intend to canvass the neighbors for background," Dunleavy said, as if he hadn't heard Judith. "Frankly, the agency is more interested in how your mother got out of Germany after the war. That information has been somewhat difficult to extract from her. So far, I've learned that she took a bus to some place called Corafatale. It must be in Italy, which is very odd. I can't find it on a map."

Glancing over at the booth where Joe was calmly eating his meal, Judith sighed. The steak and mushroom pie must be getting cold. It was useless to argue with Agent Dunleavy. He would never believe anything she said, including the fact that Corafatale wasn't a place, it was a person. Grandma Grover's nickname had been Cora Fat Tail, for reasons that had never been explained to Judith or Renie, no doubt because the grandchildren were never allowed to use it.

Without another word, Judith turned away and went back to the booth. "Hopeless," she said, and resumed eating her steak and mushroom pie.

She was right. It was cold. So, suddenly, was she.

For the first time since opening the B&B, she had forgotten about her guests. No provision had been made in case the last of the Wednesday reservations showed up in her absence. Leaping out of the booth, Judith announced that they had to go home at once.

Joe hadn't quite finished his prime rib. "Why?" he asked, mildly surprised.

Judith explained. Joe shrugged. "So? The other guests know you'll be back. The new ones will just have to wait."

"But that's wrong, that's terrible," Judith asserted. Then, a slightly unsavory idea popped into her head. "Never mind. I'll call Herself."

The pay phone was beyond the bar, near the rest rooms. Vivian Flynn answered on the third ring. "I hate to ask." Judith said, at her most humble. "But would you mind . . . ?"

The request was brief and to the point. Herself said she'd be delighted. "DeeDee's making dinner, so I'm free as a bird. I'll tell her to put everything on the back burner. Oh, by the way, can you and Joe stop in tonight?"

"I don't think so," Judith said, then, because she didn't want to be rude since she'd asked a favor, she added, "but thanks anyway. I've been derelict in my duties as it is. I'd better stick around the B&B the rest of the evening."

Herself seemed satisfied with the excuse. "You should come tomorrow night then," she said. "I don't think DeeDee will be staying much longer."

Judith mumbled an ambiguous reply, then returned to the booth. Her steak and kidney pie was gone.

"I told Kevin to warm it up for you," Joe said, wiping his mouth with a green linen napkin. "He's a nice kid."

Judith reached across the table to pat Joe's hand. "You're a nice husband," she said with a fond smile. "Usually."

After Judith and Joe returned from T. S. McSnort's, Judith stopped off to see Gertrude and take her dinner things away. "Mother," she began, trying to sound stern, "if that FBI agent comes around again, I don't want you talking to him. He has no right to question you. Just refuse to answer, okay?"

"You mean Bruce?" Gertrude asked. "Why shouldn't I talk to him? He's good company. Nice manners. His mother raised him right. He knows how to treat old people." She shot Judith a reproachful look.

"That's not the point," Judith sighed. "You know darned well this is a case of mistaken identity. It's not fair to you, it's not fair to him. He's wasting his time, and by leading him on, you could get him into serious trouble."

Gertrude's answer was to turn up the volume on the TV. "Can't hear a word you say. You know I'm deaf."

Realizing that arguing with Gertrude was as hopeless as arguing with Agent Dunleavy, she decided she might as well let them have at each other. It would serve them both right. But she still planned to call on Dunleavy's superior.

Carrying Gertrude's plate and silverware out of the tool-shed, Judith jumped when a figure hurtled over the back fence. Blinking into the shadows, she caught her breath as she recognized O. P. Dooley.

"Hi, Mrs. Flynn," he said, bounding across the lawn. "You miss me?"

"Huh?" Judith juggled the dinnerware and her handbag. "Have you been gone?"

O. P. nodded. "I got the flu, too. I wasn't on the route today. Did you know the police finally towed that Chrysler Concord away from our place?"

"Do you know if they found anything of interest in it?" Judith asked.

O. P. shook his head. "I was sick in bed when it happened last night. In fact, I got sick right after I left your place. Anyway, the police wouldn't search it there, right? They'd do that at headquarters."

"That's probably true," Judith conceded. "What's puzzling is that Darlene would leave it in the neighborhood. How did she get away?"

"There's a bus stop on Heraldsgate Avenue," O. P. pointed out. "That's only three blocks away."

"People don't go on the run by taking a bus," Judith noted as the first drops of rain began to fall. "There's no pay phone nearby to call a cab."

"She could have walked up to the top of the hill," O. P. suggested.

"Yes," Judith said, "she could have. It's not that far. But why not park the car up there and save the hike?"

"Maybe she ran out of gas," O. P. said.

Judith uttered a heavy sigh. "Maybe. People do such inexplicable things. Thanks for telling me," she added with a big smile. "I've got to get back to my guests. I hope you feel better, O. P."

"I will," he replied, heading for the fence. "I already do. I'll be back on the route tomorrow. Meantime, I'll keep my eyes open."

"You do that," Judith called as the boy climbed back over the fence and disappeared.

Music assailed her ears as she entered the house. Heading for the source, which seemed to be the living room, Judith saw Roland playing the piano and Herself lounging on top of it, belting out a smoky-voiced version of "St. Louis Blues." Joe and the guests seemed enthralled, with the exception of Bea Malone, who was jabbering in her husband's inattentive ear.

Led by Pam and Sandi, enthusiastic applause followed the rendition. "More, more!" the teachers shouted.

Herself bowed modestly. "I was just telling Roland that all we need is a sax player. Then we could do a really great set."

"What fun," Judith said, hoping she sounded as if she meant it. "Did the other guests come?"

"Not yet," Vivian responded airily, then signaled to Roland. "How about some Ma Rainey? 'Jelly Bean Blues' will do."

Roland plied the piano and Herself burst into song. Judith went into the kitchen to check her messages. Sure enough, there was one from the tardy Santa Cruz couple. They had stopped for dinner in the state capital, and would be late. Judith dialed the number for Chez Moi, which, unfortunately, was located in the south end of the city, and meant that the latecomers would have to backtrack. After alerting the Chez Moi innkeeper, Judith looked out the window over the sink.

It was drizzling, and the clouds that had moved in made the evening seem much darker than it should have been at eight o'clock in June. Judith went out to the garage to get a pair of garden clippers and a box of slug bait. The clippers weren't where she'd left them, which was on a peg next to the shovels and trowels. Groping around on the garage's cement floor, she found them behind one of the larger shovels. As she tucked the box of slug bait under her arm, she was reminded of her dad and Uncle Cliff, Renie's father, arguing over the merits of various methods of eliminating slugs. Donald and Cliff, whose resemblance was noticeable only in their heights and builds, had stood out on this same porch on a spring evening over forty years ago. Judith's father, who was scholarly by nature, had read that a shallow plate of beer would entice slugs and lead them to a merciful, possibly happily inebriated, death. Uncle Cliff, with one hand in his pocket and the other holding a cigarette, had responded that he wouldn't buy a beer for a slug. Judith could still see him putting out the cigarette, picking up a flashlight and a sharp shovel, and moving with his seaman's gait into the garden's deep shadows. He'd always count the slugs he'd killed, returning to the house to announce the toll in his terse, droll manner. "Eighteen." "Twenty-two." And if there had been no rain to bring the pesky gastropods out, a somewhat muted "Six." Donald Grover never fared half so well with his saucers of beer.

This evening's light rain was barely noticeable to a Pacific Northwest native such as Judith. She wore no covering for her head, and hadn't bothered to put on a jacket. As she worked her way along the backyard, she could hear Herself and Roland through the french doors. Judith was forced to admit that Vivian had a decent voice, in a typical torch singer's style. She also had to admit that the singer, if not the song, still seemed to intrigue Joe Flynn. Her mind flitted back to the first—and fatal, from Judith's point of view—meeting, which must have been a scene very like the one that was being reenacted in her living room. After putting two teenagers in body bags, Joe had gone to a downtown bar where Herself had been draped over the piano. He drank, she sang. They eloped a few hours later to Vegas. Judith spotted two slugs under one of the azalea bushes by the second living room window. She poured an extra measure of bait onto them and smiled grimly.

Going around to the front of the house, she clipped a few errant branches from the lily of the valley shrub and a couple of rhododendrons. At the far corner by the front porch, she stopped to trim the huge camellia that had been covered with lush pink blooms earlier in the spring. When she finished, Judith stood back to admire her handiwork.

"Not bad," she murmured to herself. "The garden's beginning to shape up for the summer."

Starting around the corner of the house, she paused. The ever-present squad car was still in the cul-de-sac, but now parked at the far corner, by the Steins' house. Judith's eyes strayed to the Malones' Ford Explorer, which stood at the curb. Judith moved toward the vehicle, wondering if Renie had overlooked anything when she'd given it the once-over the previous day.

The rear end, as well as the passenger seat, was jammed with belongings. Clothes on hangers, a big cooler, three more suitcases, a set of golf clubs, a big duffel bag, and some smaller items, including a steel fishing tackle box, a dirty brown blanket, a water dish, a mismatched pair of hiking boots, a pile of opera tapes, and several magazines filled the Explorer. There was no doubt that Bea and Mal had planned a lengthy car trip.

Judith continued spreading bait alongside the part of the house that was shielded by the Rankerses' hedge. Someone, probably something, like the Dooleys' dog, Venerable Bede, had been digging in the damp earth and had trampled two of Judith's snapdragons. It wasn't the first time the animal had made a nuisance of himself, but Judith never complained. The Dooleys were wonderful neighbors.

The snail bait was used up by the time she had come full circle. Dumping the empty box into the recycling bin by the porch, she headed for the garage to get a trash bag for the garden clippings.

As usual, the double doors were open. They were the originals, and one of them had been off its hinge for over three years. Joe had promised Judith to have an automatic door installed, but he hadn't gotten around to it. Like Bill Jones, Joe Flynn wasn't particularly handy around the house. Which, Judith thought with a frown, was also why

Joe hadn't replaced the garage light. Circumventing her Subaru and Joe's MG, she started to move toward the shelf where the trash bags were kept.

Something moved at the far end of the garage. Judith gave a start and peered into the shadows.

She could see the outline of a man, and he appeared to be holding a gun.

EIGHTEEN

JUDITH SCREAMED, WHIRLED around, and started to run. She tripped over a shovel, and caught herself on the Subaru's trunk. Panicked, she regained her balance. A hand reached out and grabbed her shoulder.

"Mom," Mike shouted, "it's me. What's wrong?"

Judith froze. "Mike?" she breathed, daring to turn her head. "Oh my God! What are you doing in the garage with a rifle?"

"A rifle?" Mike juggled the long, slim item he'd been holding in his hand. "It's one of those umbrella strollers. You gave it to Kristin at the baby shower Aunt Renie threw, and we stored it, along with some of the other stuff she got, in the garage, remember?"

In relief, Judith slumped against the Subaru. "I couldn't see . . . It was so dark in here . . . Oh, dear." She stood up and hugged her son. "When did you get here?"

"About five minutes ago," Mike replied, grinning and shaking his head at his mother's panic. "I spent most of the day at the hospital. Kristin and little Dan may come home tomorrow, and she wanted me to find the umbrella stroller. We've got the big, fancy one her folks gave us up at our place at the summit."

Judith had collected her wits. "You should have

brought the other one. Newborns can't sit in one of these things. They have to be five, six months old because there's not that much support. You might as well put the stroller back for now.''

"Damn," Mike breathed. "Okay, I'll just grab that carton marked 'Blankets, clothes, etc.' Hold on.''

It took Mike only a moment to make the exchange. With one arm cradling the carton and the other around Judith's shoulders, he steered her toward the house. "How come you're so jumpy, Mom?''

Judith had hoped that she wouldn't have to tell Mike about the unfortunate situation at Hillside Manor. Obviously, he hadn't had time during the last two days to read the papers or watch TV. When Mike had announced that the baby was on the way, she had prayed that the guests would be, too. But they remained, and now Mike and his family were moving in for a few days. Judith had promised to help with the baby for the first week while Mike went back to work.

"We need to talk," Judith said, leaning against her son. The shrubbery clippings could wait. The rain was coming down harder, and Judith was tired. Maybe she'd overtaxed herself before fully recuperating from the flu. "Have you eaten dinner?''

Mike nodded. "In the hospital cafeteria. It was pretty lame." At the porch steps, he broke away from Judith. "Can I unload the car first? I haven't gone in the house yet. I came out to the garage because I was afraid if I didn't do it first, I'd forget the stuff that was stored." He tilted his head and gave Judith a lopsided grin. "It's been a crazy kind of day.''

You don't know the half of it, Judith thought, but she tried to smile back. "Sure, go ahead. Take your time. The guests are all in the living room, but we can talk upstairs.''

Mike went down the walk and around the corner of the house, the carton of baby items tucked under his arm. With a lump in her throat, Judith watched him disappear. It seemed like only yesterday that he had hurtled around that corner, carrying a G.I. Joe doll; later, it was a football; then it was the Blonde du Jour, one of many young girls who had preceded Kristin.

Inside the house, Judith started for the living room. The music had stopped, and Vivian was being shown to the door by Joe and Roland du Turque.

"DeeDee will be wild if I don't get home before dinner burns up," Herself said, placing a hand on each of the men's shoulders. "You've all been too kind." She noticed Judith and reached out to embrace her. "You poor thing. You still look drawn and haggard. Do take care of yourself."

Judith withdrew from the embrace. Herself was still wearing a more subtle scent, one which suddenly struck Judith as familiar, though she couldn't quite place it. "Thanks for your concern," she said without enthusiasm. "And thanks for coming over." It wouldn't do to make a snippy rejoinder; Vivian really had been helpful.

"Anytime," Herself said in her breezy manner. "What are neighbors for?" She wagged a finger, the nail of which glistened with crimson polish. "And don't forget, tomorrow night for certain. I called DeeDee and tried to coax her into coming over here, but she couldn't leave her bouillabaisse. Ta-ta, all."

Roland returned to the living room, but Joe started up the stairs. "Tonight's the beginning of 'The Best of Eastwood' festival on channel thirty-two. Want to spend some time with Clint and me upstairs?"

"In a bit," Judith replied. "I still have to wait for the couple from Santa Cruz. Mike's here. He's unloading his things."

"Good. I'll see him as soon as he's finished." Joe made a thumbs-up gesture and headed upstairs. Judith went to the doorway of the living room. Bea and Mal were flipping through some of the magazines on the coffee table. Pam and Sandi had gone out through the french doors to the back porch. Roland had abandoned the piano bench to browse through the records and tapes and CDs that filled one of the tall bookcases. Marie and Pete were sitting in the windowseat, looking glum.

Judith went through the dining room and kitchen, and out onto the back porch. "I hear you may be able to leave tomorrow," she said to Pam and Sandi.

The teachers turned, their usually lively faces wary. "We might as well head back," Sandi said. "I hope the weather's good across the country."

"That's right, you're flying your own plane," Judith said. "Tell me, Sandi, will you and Rick be getting married now that . . . this is over?"

Sandi turned pale. "How did you know?" she gasped, clinging to Pam.

Judith's smile was wry. "I have my sources," she said. "Will you go into hiding with Rick? How does that work?"

"What does it matter at this point?" Sandi sighed, struggling to regain her aplomb and dismissing Pam's warning glance with a wave of her hand. "We're leaving the country. Rick's cover is blown. He risked everything to come here."

"Why?" Judith asked, no longer smiling.

"To finger Legs Benedict for Mary Lou," Pam put in before Sandi could reply. "She was going to arrest him."

"I don't believe you," Judith said, though she wasn't quite certain why the words had tumbled out.

"It's true." Pam's expression was hostile. "Rick was there when our father was murdered. He was the witness. He won't have to testify now because there won't be a trial."

Judith was puzzled. "I thought Rick was in the mob at the time," she said.

"He was," Pam responded. "But he'd come home that particular night. He saw Legs heading for the house, so he hid. I begged Dad not to let Legs in. But Dad was fearless. He thought that Legs had come just to talk, that he was simply an intermediary. Dad made me go upstairs, which I did. But Rick stayed downstairs, in the coat closet. Rick had a gun, and he figured he could handle any trouble.'' Pam halted for a moment, her face stricken as she relived the tragic memory. "There was no talk. Legs stood on the threshold and opened fire. Then he was gone, and Dad was dead before he hit the floor. Rick never had a chance to take aim.''

"Good Lord,'' Judith murmured. "How horrible.''

"But Rick had seen Legs clearly,'' Pam went on with obvious effort. "He recognized him as one of the Fusilli hit men. Thank God he knew better than to chase Legs out into the street. There was a car with more armed men waiting for Legs. They would have mowed Rick down without a second thought.'' Pam bit her lips and her eyes glistened with tears. "The only good part was that Legs never saw my brother.''

"That's when Rick went into the witness protection program,'' Sandi put in, patting Pam's shoulder. "But trying to get somebody like Legs Benedict arrested isn't easy.''

Pam swallowed hard and nodded. "When we heard Legs was coming out here, we saw this as our chance to nail him.''

"Who told you he was coming here?'' Judith asked. "That wasn't his original destination. He was headed for Detroit to kill Barney Schwartz.''

"Fewer Fingers?'' Pam nodded again. "We found out right after he and his mother fled Detroit and Legs went after him.''

"So who told you?'' Judith persisted.

The teachers exchanged glances. "Doria,'' Sandi replied. "He always knows everything.''

"Who is he?'' Judith asked, surprised at the response.

"Honestly, we're not sure,'' Pam said. "Rick thinks he may have some connection with the Fusillis. While Rick was working for the mob, he heard the name mentioned several times.''

"How did you get in contact with him?'' Judith inquired, marveling at the complexity of relationships in the Legs Benedict case.

"He called Rick originally," Pam said, "to tell him to get lost, that the Fusillis were onto him."

"Have you met this Doria?" Judith queried.

Pam shook her head. "No. I told you, I'm not even sure if it's a man or a woman. We call him 'he' because it's easier. Doria's voice is very soft, almost a whisper. I've often wondered if Doria is female just because a woman might be more concerned for Rick's safety. Even if he is my brother, he's very good-looking."

For a few moments, Judith mulled over what the young women had told her. She was almost sure that whoever Doria was, he—or she—must somehow tie in with the man Roland du Turque's mother had married for such a short, unhappy time. But this wasn't the moment to mention her surmise. Judith didn't want to sidetrack Sandi and Pam.

"Why were you so shocked to see Rick when he arrived here?" Judith asked.

Sandi gave a slow shake of her head, and Pam put her hand over her heart. We honestly hoped Rick wouldn't come," Pam said. "He was putting himself in harm's way. Just seeing him in the entry hall made me realize what might happen."

Sandi nodded. "Not to mention the shock of seeing him with a strange woman. It's a wonder I didn't collapse instead of Pam."

That explanation satisfied Judith. The preschool teacher antics might have been exaggerated, but there was no doubt that both young women were high strung.

"By the way," Judith inquired, "what was it you wanted to put in the safe?"

Sandi flushed. "It was nothing, really. Well, I guess it was." She reached inside her poplin shirt and fished out something that gleamed. "It was this. Rick and I exchanged these medallions just a week before his father was killed."

Judith examined the medallion that matched the one she had found under the rug, except for one difference. Sandi's was inscribed RP2CW.

"I couldn't bear to part with it," Sandi confessed, returning the medallion to its place of safekeeping. "I tuck it inside my bra, next to my heart."

Judith smiled softly at Sandi. "Here," she said, reaching into her pocket. "You may want to hang onto this for Rick. He was still keeping up pretenses when I showed it to him and told him I'd found it under the rug in the entry hall."

Sandi beamed. "Thanks. Thanks so much." She tucked the second medallion inside her shirt.

Judith, however, had another question for the young women. "You say that Marie—Mary Lou—came here to arrest Legs. That sounds iffy to me. What's more likely," Judith went on with a grimace, "is that Rick wanted to get revenge by killing Legs."

"He didn't kill Legs." The words shot out of Sandi's mouth.

"How can you be so sure?" Judith asked.

"Because," Sandi replied, her eyes narrowing at Judith, "we spent the entire night together. Mary Lou switched rooms. She stayed with Pam."

"That's right," Pam acknowledged. "Rick has an air-tight alibi."

Judith made no comment. In her opinion, no alibi given by a woman in love was worth ten cents.

Mike came out onto the back porch. "You wanted to talk to me, Mom?" he asked.

"Yes, let's go upstairs." Judith paused long enough to introduce Mike to the teachers, then mother and son went back inside. "They seem nice, don't they?" she asked, halfway up the back stairs.

"Sure," Mike replied. "Why shouldn't they be nice? Most of your guests are nice, aren't they?"

Judith sighed. Filling Mike in was going to take some time.

Joe had managed to break away from "The Beastwood Festival," as Judith called it, to help her relate the events that had engulfed Hillside Manor for the past three days.

By turns, Mike was horrified, terrified, and—to Judith's dismay—amused.

"The mob is *here*, under this roof?" He had clutched at his stomach and rolled around on the settee in the den. "Those good-looking girls I met may be killers? That rocks!"

"Not the term we were thinking of," Joe said calmly. "What's important here is that you're aware that these aren't ordinary guests. They should be gone by the time Kristin and the baby arrive, though. Meanwhile, just to be on the safe side, try to avoid these people."

"The mob," Mike breathed. "Wow. And some guy got whacked on Granny's doorstep?"

The front doorbell, which rang on the third floor, sounded. Judith excused herself, but not before she gave a final warning to her son. "This isn't funny. As Joe told you, they made an arrest, but they have no real evidence against Fewer Fingers. It's very likely that the killer is still at large."

"And Granny was a Nazi?" Mike grinned at his mother. "I'm going out to see her now. I want to hear some of her concentration camp stories."

Muttering, Judith went downstairs. The couple from Santa Cruz had been let in by the Malones.

"You wouldn't want to stay in this dump anyway," Mal was saying. "I'd rather be in a slave labor camp."

"Funny you should mention that," Judith said under her breath. "Excuse me, I have to handle this."

It took several minutes of apology, directions, and humbling herself before Judith was rid of the would-be guests. They left, dazed and confused, at precisely nine-thirty. The last thing she heard was the husband ask the wife why the cops were at the corner.

"To protect the guests?" the wife suggested.

Judith firmly closed the door.

Judith couldn't resist calling Renie. Since all of the guests except Roland were still in the living room, she went into the kitchen to seek privacy. As she dialed her cousin's number, she glimpsed Mike, going out the back door to visit his grandmother. Judith smiled. The bond between the generations was strong. Gertrude's propensity for sharp-tongued criticism seemed to have skipped her grandson.

"So," Renie said after Judith had recounted the evening thus far, "Mike scared the bejeezus out of you. Can't you screw in a lightbulb?"

"I can, but why should I?" Judith responded in a defensive tone. "I do everything else around here, including the garden. It wouldn't hurt for him to take on some of the simpler chores."

"I tell you," Renie said, and Judith could picture her cousin shaking her head in despair, "when Joe retires, you'd better join our Key Club. It's certainly reduced the frustration quotient in my life."

"Come on, coz," Judith said, irritated. "Joe and I wouldn't go along with that sort of thing."

"You're being silly," Renie chided. "Frankly, you could use Bill's services right now. I hear the need in your voice."

"Coz! I wouldn't! I couldn't!" Judith was practically shaking with indignation.

"You aren't doing so hot on your own this time," Renie asserted. "Bill could bail you out."

"How?" Judith demanded. "Why can't Joe—as you so crudely put it—bail me out?"

"Because he's a cop, not a psychologist," Renie said, sounding reasonable.

"Huh?" For once, Judith didn't seem to be on Renie's wavelength.

"Bill could talk to those people in a different way than Joe or J. J. do," Renie went on. "Isn't that why they have psychologists and psychiatrists on the force? I'll bet Bill could tell whether or not someone was capable of murder."

"What," Judith said slowly, "are you talking about?"

"I'm talking about the Key Club," Renie said, her usual impatience surfacing. "Every member has a skill or a talent. Unless you haven't been listening for the past thirty years, Bill's gifts aren't limited to teaching and psycho-analysis. He also understands people and counsels them. For example, if somebody in the club has a troubled teen-ager, Bill talks to the kid and tries to figure out what's going on. In return, the husband checks out our wiring. Or whatever.'' Renie's voice suddenly sharpened. ''What the hell did you *think* I was talking about?''

''Uh . . . you know. Sex,'' Judith gulped.

''Oh, good grief!'' Judith could now visualize Renie twirling around in a frenzied circle. ''I can't believe you could be so dim. In fact, I'm insulted.''

''Coz,'' Judith said in a pleading voice, ''you never ex-plained how the Key Club worked. What was I to think?''

''Something terrible, apparently,'' Renie snapped. ''You know Bill hates household tasks. He's like Joe. Several of the couples in the club can't afford appliance repair calls or counseling or auto maintenance or a trip to the dentist. My contribution is design advice, like what color to paint your house or putting together a brochure for the Senior Service Center. If you and Joe join, he could offer safety tips or even provide security. You could cater an event or donate a room for an anniversary getaway. It all evens out, and saves money, especially for retirees on fixed incomes.''

Now that Renie had explained the Key Club, it made perfect sense. Feeling weak in the knees, Judith leaned against the refrigerator. ''I'm so sorry, coz,'' she said meekly. ''I knew it didn't sound like you and Bill. But you never clarified your . . . ah . . . duties.''

''Skip it,'' Renie said, still irked. ''I'll get over it. In about twenty years.''

''Do you want to hang up on me?'' Judith asked, still meek.

''No. Why did you call in the first place?'' Renie asked, her tone softening slightly. ''Go ahead, tell me. Bill's watching Clint Eastwood blow away a bunch of scumbags. I've seen all these movies a hundred times, and Clint never misses.''

"I know the feeling," Judith murmured, then finished recounting the evening's events.

"You've had quite a time of it," Renie remarked when Judith had finished. "Do you really believe they'll be gone by tomorrow?"

"Yes," Judith replied with conviction. "I see no legal way the police can insist on them staying."

"So where did Minerva end up?" Renie asked, sounding more like her normal self.

"I have no idea," Judith answered. "A downtown hotel, maybe. I can't understand her running out on Barney, though. I guess she had to be mixed up in his criminal activities. Still . . ." Her voice trailed off.

"Still, she's his mother, right? Would we leave our mothers in prison?" Renie chortled a bit.

"You know we wouldn't," Judith said. "We might fantasize about it, but we'd never do it. In fact, we'd raise hell about it." She paused. "I wonder if Minerva has done as much for Barney. How do we know she really is his mother?"

"We don't," Renie replied. "Maybe," she added, chortling again, "she's his girlfriend."

"You know," Judith admitted, "I don't know when I've been involved with a case where I felt so at sea. The irony is, this murder happened on my own premises, with my own guests. And yet, I'm utterly—I hate to use the word—baffled."

"It's not your job," Renie said.

"But you know me," Judith protested. "I like to try. It's not always so difficult, especially if you understand people and apply logic. And sometimes I succeed."

"Coz," Renie sighed, "you're not a professional detective. Oh, sure, you've had some terrific successes, but you're an innkeeper, you've been a caterer, a bartender, a librarian, and while going through college, you sold roller-skates. Now you've got a new job. You're a grandmother. Knowing you, you're going to love it."

Judith smiled into the receiver. "That's true. I will.

Thanks, coz. You made me feel better. Right after you made me feel worse."

"That's what I'm here for," said Renie.

Judith didn't sleep well that night. Maybe it was the excitement of having the new baby coming home or her reluctance to give up on the Legs Benedict case or her anxiety over getting the current guests out of the B&B. Perhaps it was even the aftermath of the flu. For whatever reason, she tossed and turned and woke Joe up twice. If Mike hadn't been sleeping in his old room, she would have slept there and left Joe in peace. Instead, from four o'clock on, she tried to lie as quietly as possible until the alarm went off at six.

Finally, she decided that waiting was pointless. At five-thirty, she got up, showered, dressed, and went downstairs. Breakfast would be simple: eggs, bacon, toast, juice, and coffee. Judith didn't care to expend any extra energy or expense on the lame-duck visitors.

She heard Rob Simon, the regular morning carrier, send the newspaper against the front door screen around six-fifteen. Rob was already pedaling out of the cul-de-sac when she retrieved the latest edition. Skimming the front section and the local news, she saw no mention of the "Hillside Manor Case." Relieved, she sat down to drink her first cup of coffee.

Forcing herself not to think about Legs Benedict, Judith tried to concentrate on the rest of the paper. Joe would be down shortly. The bacon was already sizzling on the stove and two eggs sat side by side on the counter. She shifted her thoughts to little Dan. Mac. She liked that much better.

What other baby items were in the garage, she wondered? First-time fathers didn't realize what was involved with newborns. Sometimes the mothers didn't either, as in the case of the umbrella stroller. Judith realized that they had no cradle. The white wicker bassinet, which had first held Renie, then Judith, and eventually the cousins' children, was out there, together with the stand that Uncle Cliff had made for his only child.

Judith went outside. It was too early to check on Gertrude, who usually woke around six-thirty. At least officially. Judith's mother often spent restless nights, her arthritis making it difficult to find a comfortable position for sleep.

It was still raining, a gloomy morning that felt more like January than June. Summer was only two days off on the calendar, but Judith knew the damp weather could continue until the Fourth of July.

She entered the garage, recalling that the bassinet and the stand were in the loft that Uncle Cliff had built sixty years ago to house a small rowboat that he and Grandpa Grover had eventually abandoned on a fishing trip to a lake with a virtually impassable trail. Getting out the step ladder that leaned against the wall, Judith set it up and began climbing the six steps to the loft.

Peering into the gloom, she saw a man with a rifle. Judith laughed. "Mike, what are you doing here with that stroller? Didn't I tell you . . ." The words stuck in Judith's throat.

It wasn't Mike.

It wasn't a stroller.

It was Agent Dunleavy, and Judith heard him cock the rifle and aim it straight at her.

Judith almost fell off the ladder. Her hands gripped the edge of the loft as she tried to steady herself.

"It's me," she squeaked, her knees shaking and her mouth dry. "Mrs. Flynn. What are you doing?"

Dunleavy lowered the rifle. "Go back down," he said. "Get the hell out of here." His usually soft voice had deepened and even in the gloom, Judith could see that his youthful features had hardened.

Clumsily, Judith obeyed. Then she moved under the shelter of the loft. "What on earth are you doing up there?" she asked, still barely able to speak.

"Go back in the house." Dunleavy didn't sound as if he were in the mood to argue.

"Not until you tell me what's going on," Judith declared, summoning up every ounce of courage she possessed. "Are you going to shoot my mother?"

"Maybe," Dunleavy said evenly, "I already did. Shouldn't you check on the old bat?"

"Oh my God!" On trembling legs, Judith hurtled out of the garage and staggered toward the toolshed. The door was locked; she hadn't brought her key. Racing back to the house, she grabbed her purse, then fumbled in it for the ring that contained the key that opened her mother's so-called apartment.

It seemed to take forever before the lock turned. Judith fell across the threshold and rushed into Gertrude's bedroom. The old woman was lying in bed, her head turned away from Judith.

"Mother!" Judith cried. "Are you okay?"

A muffled grunt came from under the covers. Judith gently pulled back the sheet, the electric blanket, and the comforter that Gertrude required even during the warmer months. There was no sign of blood. Judith expelled a sigh of relief.

"What now?" the old woman demanded, though the words were slightly indistinct. "Whath with thith crack-of-dawn vithitor thuff the latht few dayth? Whereth my teeth?"

"Here, Mother," Judith said, handing over the glass in which Gertrude kept her dentures. "I'm sorry. I got up early, and I thought I'd check on you. I'm sorry," she repeated, aware that her voice was shaking.

"You can all thop it right now," Gertrude declared before putting in her teeth. "I'm thick of it."

"Don't worry, I'm going," Judith said, patting her mother's shoulder. "I'll be back soon with breakfast. You stay put."

The dentures were in place. "Where else would I go, you moron?" Gertrude rasped. "You think I got a motor scooter in here and I can take off whenever I feel like it?"

"Yes. No. Of course not." Judith was inching out of the

tiny bedroom. She didn't dare call the police from Gertrude's phone lest her mother become upset. Or worse, interrupt with another flurry of questions. "I have to go now."

She had reached the living room when she heard several popping noises. Had some of the neighborhood kids gotten hold of illegal fireworks? It wouldn't be the first time, as Judith recalled the unfortunate episode that had reduced the original toolshed to rubble.

Slowly, she edged her way outside. Judith couldn't remember if the squad car had been parked in the cul-de-sac when she was on the front porch taking in the newspaper. If the watch had finally been canceled, Judith would call Homicide and hope that J. J. Martinez or Rich Goldman were in. Agent Dunleavy's situation had to be explained. Certainly it had nothing to do with Gertrude.

The rain had let up and the skies were brightening. Judith paused halfway down the walk between the toolshed and the house. If she moved just three steps to her right, she could see into the garage. In order to inform the police, she needed to know if Dunleavy was still there.

He was. It was easy for Judith to see him. His head, upper body, and arms dangled over the loft's edge.

Without getting closer, Judith was certain that Dunleavy was dead.

NINETEEN

JOE WAS PUTTING bacon, one rasher at a time, in the frying pan when Judith came tearing into the kitchen. "What the hell . . . ?" He yanked the pan off the burner and rushed to meet his wife.

The words that tumbled from Judith's lips were so incoherent that Joe had to give her a little shake. "Calm down. What is it? Your mother?"

If there was a trace of hope in Joe's tone, Judith didn't notice. She shook her head emphatically, then took a deep breath. This time Joe was able to make some sense of what she said.

"Jesus!" he breathed, racing for the back door. "Get the uniforms," he shouted over his shoulder.

Judith steadied herself against the counter, then walked shakily to the front door. There was no sign of the squad car. She picked up the pace and went halfway down the cul-de-sac to see if the officers had moved their vehicle around the corner.

They hadn't. Judith hurried back into the house and called 911. After giving the pertinent information, she asked the dispatcher to transfer her to J. J. Martinez.

J. J. wasn't in yet, which didn't surprise Judith, who then requested that he be paged. The voice on the other end was reluctant until Judith revealed that she was the owner of Hillside Manor and the wife of Detective Joe Flynn.

By the time Judith hung up, Joe still wasn't back. She went outside, carrying the cordless phone with her in case J. J. should return her call immediately.

Joe was in the driveway when he saw Judith. "Get inside," he called, then jogged toward the house. "I have to get my weapon. We don't know if the killer is still out here."

Judith stood uneasily in the entry hall as Joe strapped on the holster that he'd hung on its usual peg prior to leaving for work. "Dunleavy *is* dead, I take it?" Judith asked.

Joe nodded. "No pulse. He's been shot. I'm going to check out the vicinity."

"No!" Judith cried. "The uniforms are gone—they must be changing shifts. Wait until the other officers get here. It's too dangerous for you to go it alone. J. J. is supposed to call us back. Please wait." Still trembling, she clung to his arm.

"I can't wait," he said. "I'm a cop, remember?"

"I don't care," Judith said stubbornly. "You're my husband. You might get shot, too. Oh, Joe, when will this nightmare end?"

Joe shook Judith off. "Where I work, we call it a job. Stop fussing, I'll be careful. You stay right here and wait for J. J. to call." He gave Judith a long, hard look and went outside again.

Frantically, Judith glanced at the old schoolhouse clock. It was twenty to seven. Unless the commotion had awakened them, the guests might not be down for another hour. Noticing that the burner for the bacon was still on, Judith clicked the dial to off. Then she collapsed into a chair and held her head.

In less than two minutes, she heard sirens. Jumping up, she went to the front porch as a patrol car pulled into the drive. She was about to join the officers when the phone rang in her hand.

It was J. J. Judith quickly explained what had happened.

"Will you come over?" she asked when she'd reached her breathless conclusion.

"On my way," J. J. said, and rang off.

A second siren sounded as Judith started for the back door. An ambulance, perhaps, though there was no need to rush. Judith was going out onto the porch when a voice called from behind her.

"Who's dead now?" It was Mal Malone, unshaven, and wearing a gaudy bathrobe over striped pajamas.

"It's not a guest," Judith said, trying to force a reassuring smile. "No need for alarm."

"Sheesh." Mal passed a hand over his high forehead. "I never been in such a lousy place. Is there a fire?"

"No, no." The smile felt peculiar on Judith's lips, probably because they were twitching with nerves. "It's nobody you know. Go back to bed, breakfast won't be ready for an hour."

But Bea had joined Mal. "I heard a shot," she said. "Who got whacked this time?"

Was there any point in keeping the tragedy a secret? Judith decided there wasn't. The police—and the FBI— would be interrogating the guests. Again. Judith groaned. The sun was barely up and the day had already disintegrated around her.

"An FBI agent was murdered," Judith said, swallowing hard. "No one connected to this case," she added feebly. "As far as I know."

Mal looked taken aback. "One of them guys who hauled off Barney Whatshisname?"

Judith shook her head. "No. Someone who was working a different investigation." *How in the world could she have two, maybe three, separate investigations going on at the same time in what was supposed to be a quiet, restful B&B?* Contrary to what Joe had said, the last few days were definitely a nightmare. Judith felt it was about time to wake up and laugh it all away. Indeed, she felt a wave of hysteria coming on, but managed to fight it off. "Excuse me, I have to see what's happening . . ."

Behind the Malones, Judith saw Marie Santori. Or Mary Lou Desmond. Judith felt it was almost impossible to keep everybody straight as their real names emerged. Maybe she should still think of her as Marie, since the federal marshal didn't want her cover blown with the other guests.

"What's going on?" Marie asked in a sharp tone.

Judith noticed that Marie was dressed, and had on a cotton jacket that could easily have concealed a weapon. "See for yourself," Judith said, taking a chance that the Malones wouldn't follow Marie.

They did, however, but only as far as the back porch. They remained there, huddled in their ugly bathrobes, looking like a pair of toadstools.

"I know who you are," Judith said under her breath as she and Marie approached the garage where Joe, the patrol officers and the ambulance attendants had gathered. "It's okay. Joe told me."

"Keep it to yourself," Marie said in a much deeper voice than Judith was used to hearing. "I'm still Marie Santori as far as you're concerned."

"Sure. Fine." The smile of acknowledgment that Judith tried to give Marie didn't quite materialize.

Agent Dunleavy's body still hung from the loft. Now that the initial shock was over, the sight seemed even more sickening to Judith. She took a couple of backward steps, then caught Joe's eye.

"J. J.'s on his way," she said.

"That's what we're waiting for," Joe replied, his manner brusque.

"Who is this guy?" Marie whispered to Judith.

Judith explained how Bruce Dunleavy had been sent on a fool's errand to question Gertrude. "Of course my mother was never a Nazi," Judith said, still finding the situation incredible. "I can't imagine that the FBI would waste its time and resources on such a silly quest." She glanced up at the loft. "And look what it led to. A needless tragedy. I can hardly believe it."

"Then don't," said Marie, and walked away.

*   *   *

Before J. J. arrived, Pete, Pam, and Sandi had also come outside. The officers, who had turned out to be Mercedes Berger and Darnell Hicks, herded the guests inside, including Marie. There was no sign of Roland, but as his room faced the front of the house, Judith thought he might not have been disturbed.

J. J. showed up at exactly seven o'clock, just as Gertrude came out of the toolshed on her walker. The last thing Judith wanted her mother to see was Bruce Dunleavy's body.

"Mother," Judith said in her most compassionate voice, "you shouldn't be out here in the damp. It's bad for your arthritis."

Gertrude clumped forward, using the walker to nudge Judith out of the way. "What's all this hullabaloo?" she asked. "Shoo, I want to see what's going on."

"No, you don't," Judith said, putting a firm hand on the walker. "Go back inside. I'll come with you."

"Where's my breakfast?" Gertrude demanded, though she didn't try to move any further.

"It's going to be a little late," Judith said, taking her mother by the arm. "Come on, I'll try to explain what's happened."

Back in the toolshed, Judith settled her mother in her favorite chair. "There was an accident this morning." It would be futile to keep Gertrude completely in the dark. Her mother's questions would drive Judith crazy. "Agent Dunleavy got hurt. He won't be coming by again."

Gertrude's face fell. "He won't? But he was such good company."

"I know, Mother. But he's . . . off the assignment. Because of his injury."

"What injury?" Gertrude's gnarled hands clawed at the card table's edge.

"He got hurt in the garage." Judith hesitated, then continued. "And he decided you weren't a Nazi."

"I wasn't?" Gertrude's wrinkled face was puzzled.

"Of course not."

"Hunh. Well, maybe not. I've always been a lifelong Democrat," Gertrude said. "I don't suppose you can be both."

"No, you can't. You wouldn't want to renounce your Democratic party membership, would you?" Judith asked slyly.

"Never," Gertrude responded. "I'm voting for FDR."

"There you go." Judith rose from the arm of the sofa where she'd been perching. "I'll be back in just a little while with your breakfast."

"You better be," Gertrude said darkly. "I'll miss that boy. He had such nice manners. Did I tell you that?"

"Yes, you did." Judith smiled at her mother.

"What day is it?" Gertrude asked suddenly.

"Thursday," Judith replied.

The answer seemed to satisfy Gertrude. "What a week. Lots of company. It's been nice. Except for the early wake-ups. You scared me half to death this morning. Just like the other day."

Judith paused at the door. "I didn't wake you up early the other day."

"Yes, you did," Gertrude insisted. "Monday, it was. Or Tuesday. I forget."

Tuesday had been the day that Judith had found Legs Benedict's body outside the toolshed. But she hadn't wakened Gertrude, who had probably been up by then, anyway. Judith had gone straight back into the house to tell Joe.

As always, it was pointless to argue with her mother. Judith merely smiled again. "I promise not to do it anymore," she said.

But she wondered just how confused Gertrude really was.

According to J. J., Agent Dunleavy had been shot from a distance of at least thirty feet. That meant, Joe explained, that his killer probably had been standing in the driveway or even on the sidewalk further down the cul-de-sac.

"I don't get it," Judith said. "How many shots were fired?"

"One," Joe replied. "It went straight to the heart."

Judith shook her head. "That's not true. I mean, I heard more than one pop. Or shot. Three, maybe."

Joe stared at Judith. "Why didn't you say so?"

"Nobody asked me," Judith said, annoyed. "I haven't even talked to J. J. yet."

J. J. was still outside. Joe hurried from the kitchen, apparently seeking his fellow homicide detective. Judith resumed frying bacon. All the guests had now gathered in the living room, including an astonished Roland du Turque. They were drinking coffee and engaging in bewildered conversation.

Five minutes later, just as Judith was dishing up fried eggs, Joe and J. J. returned. "Can you wait?" she asked. "I'd like to get these people fed. It'll only take three minutes."

Joe poured coffee for J. J. while Judith served breakfast in the dining room. Then she begged for another two minutes while she took Gertrude's plate out to the toolshed. At precisely seven-thirty, she was back in the kitchen, having seen the ambulance carry away Agent Dunleavy's corpse.

Since neither Joe nor J. J. had eaten, she served them as well. Grabbing a piece of toast and a rasher of bacon, she finally sat down at the kitchen table.

"Three shots?" J. J. asked. "You sure?"

"I'm sure there were more than two," Judith said. "There might even have been four."

"Weird," J. J. remarked. "Got the uniforms combing the area for stray bullets. We'll see. Tell me exactly what happened." His knee was jiggling so hard that he actually raised the table.

Judith recounted the morning's events. To her surprise, J. J. and Joe didn't seem surprised when she told them how Dunleavy had seemed to threaten her when she'd found him in the loft.

"It was like he was a different person," Judith said, then noticed J. J.'s eyes snap. She leaned across the table. "What do you know that I don't?"

Joe and J. J. exchanged quick glances. "Not much," J. J. answered. "When I called the local FBI office to tell them that Dunleavy had been killed, they told me they'd never heard of him."

It was Bruce Dunleavy who had told Judith several times that papers and documents could easily be forged. Maybe she should have guessed. Had he not been on a fool's errand after all? Or had Judith been the fool? Why had he come to Hillside Manor in the first place? Judging from Marie's attitude, Judith suspected it had nothing to do with Gertrude.

"All right," she said, gazing from Joe to J. J., "who was he? If he was a phony, then questioning Mother was just an excuse to hang out on the premises. Do you two have any ideas?"

Joe was shaking his head and J. J. started to answer when Judith heard another siren.

"What's that?" J. J. jumped out of his chair, dropping his napkin.

"It sounds like an ambulance," Joe said. "Maybe they dispatched a second crew by mistake."

"Why not a fleet?" Judith asked, her voice unnaturally high. "The Red Cross, too, with field tents and truckloads of wounded and . . ."

Reaching across the table, Joe put a firm hand on Judith's arm. "Calm down," he said in what Judith assumed was the voice he used on hysterical witnesses.

"I'm calm," Judith said, swallowing hard and feeling bug-eyed. "I'm very calm."

The siren stopped short of Hillside Manor. "It's somewhere out in the cul-de-sac," Judith squeaked, then managed to lower her voice. "I'm going out the back way so I don't have to answer the guests' questions."

J. J., however, was already in the lead. Judith and Joe

followed. Berger and Hicks were running down the street, past the Ericsons' front gate. The ambulance had stopped in front of Herself's house, and the attendants were hurrying inside with a gurney. As Judith, Joe, and J. J. began to run, yet another siren sounded, and a medic van roared into the cul-de-sac.

Judith's initial reaction was to burst into gales of laughter. Then, struggling for control, she visualized Vivian Flynn, drinking herself into a coma. But Vivian was standing on the back porch, frantically waving her arms.

Joe held Judith and J. J. back to allow the medics to precede them. Once again, Judith recognized Ray Kinsella. With a sinking feeling, she felt he'd become a regular in the neighborhood, like O. P. Dooley or Cecil, the mailman.

Vivian started to follow the medics inside, but Joe yelled to her. "Hey! What happened?"

Wringing her hands, Herself leaned over the porch railing. "It's DeeDee. She's been shot."

Herself disappeared through the back door.

Joe and J. J. took the steps two at a time. Judith followed them, but Joe barred the way. "Stay put. That's an order."

For once, Judith didn't argue. Her head was swimming and her eyes seemed out of focus. She leaned against the wall next to the back door and took several deep breaths. Mercedes Berger and Darnell Hicks were nowhere in sight. Maybe they had gone inside, too. Judith felt faint.

Mercedes Berger was the first person to come back outside. She glanced at Judith and kept going. Stopping by the driveway that Herself shared with the Ericsons, Mercedes bent down and picked something up. Judith tried to focus. The officer turned around and Judith saw that her index finger was balancing a gun by its trigger guard.

"Mrs. Flynn?" Mercedes said in a tentative voice, now recognizing Judith. "Are you okay?"

Judith gave a slight nod. "I think so. It's just that I'm so mixed up. Where did that gun come from?"

"I don't know," Mercedes replied. "But Darnell thought

I should see if there was a weapon around here someplace. I'm not even sure what happened. Darnell's inside." She nodded at the house. "Maybe he knows."

The exchange with Mercedes had given Judith an opportunity to collect herself. "You'd better give that gun to J. J. Martinez," Judith said.

"Of course," Mercedes responded, her blue eyes widening as she saw Rich Goldman hit the brakes in the middle of the cul-de-sac. "Or to Detective Goldman. Gosh, I'm glad he and Detective Martinez are here. Darnell and I aren't used to . . . you know . . . like . . . real crime. This is usually such a . . ."

". . . Quiet neighborhood," Judith finished. "Yes. Usually." She stared at Herself's back door. Vivian Flynn had bought the place at a bargain price because a particularly grisly crime had been committed there three and a half years earlier. Judith wondered if the house was hexed.

Rich Goldman practically flew up to the porch. "J. J. told me to get here ASAP," he panted, then saw the gun dangling from Mercedes's finger. "Whoa. Let me get an evidence bag for that. Where'd you find it?"

As Rich and Mercedes exchanged information, Judith slipped inside the house.

A tiny entranceway led into the kitchen and down the basement stairs. Judith stood on the top step and peered around the corner. A smear of blood marred the floor between the back door and the middle of the kitchen. The ambulance attendants were standing by the sink, the gurney supported between them. Ray Kinsella and the other medic were working over a prone form that Judith assumed was DeeDee. J. J. and Darnell Hicks stood by the kitchen table. Judith could hear Joe and Herself's voices coming from the living room.

"Okay," Ray was saying, as he stood up. "That's it for now. Let's get her to the hospital. I think she's going to be okay."

The medics stepped aside as the ambulance attendants took over. Judith could hear DeeDee's soft moans as she was moved onto the gurney. Moments later, the injured woman was being rolled out the door. Judith glanced down at her face.

Several sensations simultaneously assaulted Judith. The scent of jasmine, the sound of pain, the expression of misery on the victim's face.

The face. It didn't belong to a stranger, as Judith had assumed. She stared at the gurney.

It was Darlene Smith.

Herself was trying to explain. "She's Darlene Daniels," Vivian insisted, clutching a Bloody Mary that Joe had fixed for her. "I met her eight, nine years ago, when she was working her way through college. She liked to be called DeeDee. It was a childhood nickname. How was I supposed to know she was some kind of suspect? She's an old friend, we sang together, we did the circuit, we were a hit along the Gulf and in the Florida Keys."

Joe was looking grave. "Okay, okay. So what happened this morning?" He looked up as J.J. and Rich Goldman entered the living room. "This is official, Viv. Take your time."

"I don't know what happened," Herself pouted. "I was in bed." She ran her hand the length of the deep blue silk robe. "I woke up when I heard DeeDee scream. I came out of the bedroom—it's right there," she noted, pointing to the little hall which, as Judith well remembered, led to two bedrooms and the bathroom, "and saw DeeDee crawling across the kitchen floor, bleeding and looking like death. I called nine-one-one, and did my best to stanch the bleeding in her shoulder. I didn't know she'd been shot then."

"She say anything?" J. J. asked, pacing back and forth in front of the fireplace.

"Yes." Herself paused to take a deep drink. "She said she'd been shot."

"Anything else?" J. J. queried, as Rich Goldman took notes.

"Umm . . ." Herself ran an agitated hand through her

disheveled platinum locks. "Yes. Just before she passed out, DeeDee said she'd been shot by someone named—this sounds so silly, maybe she was delirious—by someone named Baby Face Doria."

Judith had the feeling that things should be coming together. But she didn't know what it all meant. The logic of the case still proved elusive. Herself's account seemed to puzzle J. J., who promptly went out into the kitchen and used his cell phone to get in touch with the FBI.

Judith couldn't hear what he was saying. She turned to Joe, who was sitting next to Herself on a black leather couch. "I must tell J. J. about Doria," Judith said.

"What?" Joe gave a little shake of his head, as if he hadn't heard properly.

"Someone by that name made a reservation for last Monday and then canceled," Judith explained. "That someone is known to Pam and Sandi and . . . I'm not sure who else."

Joe swore. "Did you ever, even for two seconds, think of telling J. J. this before?" He was all but shouting by the time he finished the question.

Judith drew back in the rattan armchair where she was sitting. "There was never a reason to tell him. Doria's name didn't come up in the official investigation." She jabbed a finger in the direction of the kitchen. "J. J. didn't know anything about a man named Doria. He just said as much."

"How many times," Joe said, his expression severe, "have I warned you about the dangers of playing detective?"

Herself placed a hand on Joe's arm. "Now, Joe," she purred, "don't go off on your poor wife. Can't you see she's been sick? She's aged ten years in the last few days."

Judith felt a low, angry growl trying to escape. She suppressed the urge, however. "Don't worry about me, Vivian," she said. "I'm fine. When did Darlene get here?"

"DeeDee?" Herself paused to put a cigarette in a long ebony holder. "What's today? Thursday? It was Tuesday then, well before noon. I'd just gotten up. She came in a cab."

"Did you see the cab?" Judith asked.

Herself was inhaling deeply. "No." She blew four perfect smoke rings, then looked at Joe as if for approval. He smiled. Thinly, Judith thought. "The cab had left, I guess," Herself went on. "DeeDee insisted it took forever for me to come to the door."

"There was no cab," Judith put in. "DeeDee's car— Legs Benedict's car—was parked by Dooleys'," Judith said. "DeeDee simply drove around the block—or maybe she cruised the neighborhood for awhile—and ditched the car before she came back here. I'll bet she came in through the backyard. There's a fence, but it's not very high."

Joe appeared glum; Herself was looking aghast. "She drove Legs Benedict's car? The man who was murdered?" Vivian chewed on the cigarette holder. "What next, musicians who aren't on drugs? Hookers who give it away? Men who like women for their personalities?" Dazed, Herself shook her head over and over.

J. J. returned to the living room and addressed Vivian. "Agents Terrill and Rosenblatt are on their way. They'll question you about DeeDee, aka Darlene. Got to hold off talking to her until she's out of surgery. Okay?"

Herself blew some more smoke rings. "I'm available," she said, blinking several times before she realized her false eyelashes hadn't yet been attached. "As I recall, J. J.," she continued, running her fingers through her hair, "you're partial to blondes."

J. J. jigged a bit on the hearth. "Wife's a blonde. Married for thirty years. Happy. Very happy."

"Marvelous." Herself beamed at J. J., then patted the leather cushion next to her. "Now why don't you sit here and we'll talk about DeeDee."

Judith rose from the rattan chair and left the room. She caught a faint whiff of Herself's latest perfume. She realized it was jasmine, and felt like a fool for not having made the connection between Darlene Smith and DeeDee Daniels. Darlene had been wearing the scent when she'd stayed at Hillside Manor. Obviously, she had lent some of it to Vivian. Maybe, Judith thought disconsolately, she really wasn't much of a detective after all.

The guests had barricaded themselves in the front parlor. Chairs had been shoved against both doors and a fire had been lighted in the grate, lest someone try to come down the chimney. Apparently led by Bea and Mal Malone, they refused to be questioned again by the police or the FBI.

"We were told we could leave this morning," Pam shouted at Judith through the locked door. "We either want our lawyers or we're out of here."

"It's not my fault," Judith yelled back. "Is Marie in there?"

"Yes. So what?" retorted Pam.

"I'd like to speak with her for a moment. Please." Judith winced at the whining tone in her voice.

"Screw it," Marie said, yanking the door open. "I'm tired of being undercover. It doesn't matter anymore. What do you want?"

"Just that," Judith gulped. "I mean, why can't you leave?"

"Because I haven't discharged my duty," Marie snapped with a glance in Rick Perl's direction. "I have to see what this idiot plans to do next."

The phone rang. Judith hesitated, then dashed into the kitchen. It was Phyliss, declaring that she was about to meet the Lord.

"Pain. Suffering. Agony," the cleaning woman groaned. "I can hear angel wings flapping over my bed."

"That's too bad, Phyliss," Judith said in a distracted manner. "Do you think you'll be resurrected by tomorrow?"

Phyliss was indignant. "What? Are you blaspheming?"

"No, but with the weekend coming up, it would be nice if you could make it since your regular day doesn't come again until Monday."

"I won't be alive by Monday," Phyliss snapped. "I told you, the Lord is reaching down to me. I can hear the trumpets."

"That's someone honking in the cul-de-sac, Phyliss." Rich Goldman hadn't yet moved his car out of the middle of the street. "Okay, if you can't come, that's it. Let me know if you ever recover." Judith hung up in an uncharacteristic show of impatience.

Joe was in the kitchen, making a pot of coffee. He had called in to say he'd be late, perhaps not arriving until noon. It was now nine-fifteen. To Judith, the day already seemed like it should be ending.

"What did you find out?" she asked. "I couldn't bear to stay and watch Herself vamp J. J."

"We came up with the obvious conjecture," Joe replied, pouring coffee for both of them. "DeeDee must have seen Dunleavy approach the driveway. We assume she recognized him as Baby Face Doria. She got her gun, which I suppose she'd managed to sneak out of the B&B before she went on the run Tuesday morning and before J. J. and Rich searched the guest rooms. Anyway, DeeDee must have gone outside where she spotted Doria in the garage— as you know, there's a direct line of sight between that loft and the sidewalk and street in front of Herself's. Or, he saw her, opened fire, and she returned it. She's a hell of a shot, but after listening to Vivian and checking with the national criminal information records, I can see why."

"What do you mean?" Judith asked with a puzzled frown.

Joe sat back in his captain's chair and shook his head. "Darlene Daniels, aka DeeDee aka Darlene Smith aka about five other names, is a hit woman for the Fusilli family. Now tell me, Jude-Girl, had you already managed to deduce that one?"

Judith hadn't. Her sense of failure soared while her self-confidence plunged to a big, fat goose egg.

*   *   *

Herself had some vague idea that her friend DeeDee's singing career was merely a blind. During her senior year at Florida State, the younger woman had far too much spending money at her disposal. Since Vivian knew precisely how much their act was bringing in, she had wondered at first if DeeDee came from a rich family. Later, she had learned that DeeDee had no family. She was an orphan, from New York.

"It was none of my business what she did on the side," Herself had told Joe and J. J. "A bit of lucrative naughtiness is small potatoes compared to getting an education. I wish I'd had the chance to go to college. It makes one even more . . . well rounded."

When told what her old friend actually had done to pay for books and tuition, Herself had laughed uproariously. "Think of the money she's saved the police and the courts by getting rid of all those crooks," Vivian had said between bursts of husky laughter. "She's a one-woman social service. Bless her heart!"

Joe and J. J. hadn't argued.

Judith wasn't quite as amused. "Are you saying," she asked Joe, "that DeeDee came here to kill Doria? And who was he, anyway?"

Joe spread his hands. "Give me a chance, I'm getting to that. Baby Face Doria—again, according to our computer—was also a hit man for the Fusilli family. What J. J. and the FBI are figuring is that DeeDee was sent along with Legs to whack Barney. Legs was probably told that DeeDee was a decoy, to lure Barney with her womanly charms. But in reality—and this is conjecture because we'll have to wait until DeeDee can talk—after the hit in Detroit, DeeDee was supposed to knock off Legs. The mob often works that way. For whatever reason, the original hit man also has to get hit."

"So DeeDee shot Legs and Doria?" Judith asked, her dark eyes wide.

"That's what it looks like," Joe said. "But Doria wasn't her part of her assignment. He was sent to whack her."

Judith didn't comment for a few moments. "So," she finally said, "why didn't DeeDee keep going after Legs was killed and she left the B&B?"

Joe shrugged. "She must have known Herself was in the neighborhood. I gather they'd kept in touch. Maybe DeeDee wanted to keep an eye on what was happening with the investigation. Hiding in plain sight, so to speak, probably struck her as a smart idea. She was safer there than if she'd tried to skip town. Minerva Schwartz got caught that way."

"No wonder DeeDee wouldn't come here to meet us," Judith said, still marveling at the complexity of mob family ties. "What if we'd accepted Vivian's invitation and gone over there?"

"DeeDee probably would've developed a headache," Joe said.

"I guess." Judith was still thinking. "Last night at T. S. McSnort's, Doria mentioned canvassing the neighborhood. He must have known DeeDee was still around here somewhere. Maybe he saw the car parked by Dooley's."

"Possibly," Joe conceded. "He may also have known her M.O."

"Yes. Yes." Judith's tone was very vague before she remembered to tell Joe about the connection between another man named Doria and Roland du Turque. "Do you think they're related?" she asked.

Joe shrugged again. "Why not? This mob stuff is all about families. Baby Face could be that other Doria's son or even a grandson. But I doubt he came here because of Roland."

Again, Judith was silent. "She could have gotten away," she said at last.

Joe made a face. "What do you mean?"

"DeeDee. Minerva got caught because she tried to skip the country. She was at the airport, which the police always check, along with the bus depot and the train station and the major highways. DeeDee had a half-hour, maybe forty-five-minute head start on the APB, I forget exactly. But she could have ditched the car, even left it here, and still have disappeared. This is a big city.'' Judith leaned forward, both fists on the table. "Why didn't she?"

"Because she had an obligation to finish the hit on Barney?'' Joe suggested. "She may have figured he'd be released.''

"Will he?" Judith asked.

Joe shook his head. "Dubious. The feds have put together a pretty tight case based on his organized crime connections.''

There was a spark in Judith's eyes as she sorted through Joe's explanation. "Darlene must be savvy enough to know that. As for Doria, he hadn't shown up yet. She stayed here because she had to find out what was happening. I'm not arguing she didn't intend to kill Legs Benedict, but she didn't do it. She had to stay here because she needed to know who did.''

TWENTY

JUDITH KNEW THAT Joe was humoring her by not scoffing at her conjecture. "Does that mean these people can leave?" she asked, gesturing toward the front parlor.

"J. J.'s checking on that," Joe replied. "As soon as he's talked to DeeDee, I imagine he'll say they can go."

Judith's shoulders slumped. "Thank goodness. I think."

"What?" Joe had picked up the morning paper and was peering at Judith over the sports section.

"Nothing." Judith rose from her chair just as Mike appeared. In all the excitement, she'd actually forgotten that he was staying in the house. "Mike!" she cried, startling both men. "Are you okay?"

"Sure, why shouldn't I be?" He grinned at his mother, then thumped Joe on the shoulder. "Man, I slept like a cedar stump. I was so tired after yesterday that I just put my head down and died."

Joe and Judith exchanged quick glances. "Have a seat," said Joe, pulling out the chair next to him. "I think I'd better fill you in."

Judith decided that Joe could go it alone in Round Two of the ongoing Legs Benedict saga. She headed for the front parlor to try to reassure the guests.

Halfway through the dining room, she stopped. If the

255

guests were really going to leave, Judith had to retrieve the Malones' film. They might not check their camera gear, but they'd miss the roll eventually. Turning around, she headed back through the kitchen, telling Joe and Mike that she was going to run a quick errand on top of the hill.

"I might be gone when you get back," Mike called after her. "I have to be up at the hospital by eleven to get Kristin and Dan ready to come home."

"That's fine," Judith shouted over her shoulder. "I'll be here by the time you get back."

The rain had started again, with the gray clouds hanging low over Heraldsgate Hill. In the rearview mirror, Judith could barely see the bay, which was almost obliterated by the rain. Now that she had a moment to take in her surroundings, she realized that it was another gloomy June day. Judith also felt gloomy. She had a feeling that a murderer was about to get away with what she could only consider the perfect crime. The lack of justice, the absence of conclusion, and her own ineptitude made her feel depressed. The usual logic, by which she set such store, had deserted her.

The photography store was on her left, where only diagonal parking was allowed. This morning the spaces were already filled. Over the years, Heraldsgate Hill had become a fashionable neighborhood. The situation was ironic: The location was close to downtown, yet the hill itself was comparatively isolated. Many of the homes were large, suitable for families. Singles flocked to the apartments and condos that had sprung up in the last two decades. Yet another attraction was the low crime rate. Except, Judith thought with remorse, at Hillside Manor. She felt like a one-woman blight.

Three blocks along the avenue, she spotted a parking place on the opposite side of the street. Driving into Falstaff's lot to turn around, she recklessly went down the exit lane, hoping to avoid anyone entering from the other direction.

She'd made a mistake. A champagne-colored car was coming toward her at an alarming rate of speed. Judith put on the brakes. So did the other driver. They missed colliding by about three inches.

"Hey, you half-wit!" the other driver shouted before getting out of the car. "You can't go this way! You're . . ."

"Coz," Judith said in a docile voice. "Hi."

Renie leaned against the hood of the Camry. "Good grief. What on earth are you doing?"

"What are *you* doing? It's only ten o'clock," Judith said, catching her breath.

"Those damned Bulgarians woke me up," Renie said. "If they don't stop that renovation project across the street, I'm going to dynamite the damned place."

"We've got to talk," Judith said, checking behind her to make sure she hadn't gotten boxed in. "Meet me at Moonbeam's."

Luckily, the parking place was still available. It was exactly halfway between the photography shop and Moonbeam's, so after retrieving the film, Judith walked the distance to meet Renie.

Her cousin was already settled into a big armchair by the fireplace. "Latte for you, mocha for me," Renie said.

Judith smiled in gratitude. Then, as she sat down in another big armchair, she struck her head with her palm and let out a little yip. "I can't believe I was so stupid," she cried.

"What now?" Renie asked, stirring two extra packets of sugar into her mocha.

Aware that a middle-aged man reading the *Wall Street Journal* and a young college-age couple had turned to stare, Judith lowered her voice. "I had the film *developed*. I can't replace the roll. All I've got are the actual photographs. How will I explain that to the Malones? What was I thinking?"

"You thought there was a clue in the photos, or one that might show Corelli," Renie said calmly. "Wasn't that the whole point?"

Judith stared through the big front window where the outside seating had been abandoned on this rainy June morning. "Was it? It seems silly now that Doria's dead and we know that DeeDee was . . ."

"*What*?" Now it was Renie's turn to make heads swerve. "Slow down, coz. I'm about ten miles behind."

With a sheepish smile for the other caffeine addicts, Judith spoke to Renie in a whisper. She recounted the most recent events while her cousin's eyes grew huge.

"So that's it," Judith said, wrapping it up. "It looks like DeeDee killed Legs. But I'm not sure I believe it."

Renie was oblivious to the puddles of mocha she'd left on the low marble-topped table. "Let me get this straight. Baby Face Doria contacted Pam and Sandi after he learned that Barney had managed to escape Legs in Detroit and was headed here."

"That's my guess," Judith said. "Pam and Sandi told Pete—Rick, I mean, and Marie had to come along to protect him. But I don't think Pam and Sandi expected Rick to join them. I guess they thought Marie or some other fed would show up. Rick could ID Legs after he was in custody. But Rick—alias Pete—came along, and that's why they were so shocked to see him at the B&B."

Renie frowned. "You mean they were afraid that Rick might do something foolish?"

"Of course," Judith replied. "They warned Rick *not* to come. Or else they were afraid he would, and they had to come along, too, just in case."

"To keep him from said foolish act," Renie noted. "What a mixup, with possible tragic results."

"Talk about a tangled web," Judith remarked with a shake of her head. "As for Roland, Pam and Sandi also got hold of him so he could interview Legs. Or try to, before Legs got whacked. And that's how they all happened to make their reservations at the same time."

"But Doria canceled." Renie was wearing a mocha mustache, which she haphazardly tried to wipe away. "How come?"

"He must have had second thoughts," Judith said. "As part of the Fusilli gang, he would have been recognized by Legs, and maybe Darlene and Pete. I mean, Rick Perl. Somehow he came up with the idea of posing as an FBI agent. He couldn't pretend he was part of the real team, so he had to think of some other reason to be around the action. Doria might have had time to do some homework on Hillside Manor and our family. He never came inside the house, only to the door when he first arrived, and then he always came straight to the toolshed. It was an excellent gig, because we were overrun with law enforcement types. One more, no matter how absurd the premise, didn't seem to stick out. His presence was more of a nuisance than anything else, and we were all too caught up with the murder to check on him."

"Wild," Renie remarked. "So if DeeDee didn't kill Legs, who did?"

"Barney seems the most likely suspect," Judith said. "For all we know, he's plea-bargaining with the FBI. He could claim self-defense, but he'd still need to avoid a long prison term for his involvement in organized crime."

"What about Hoffa?" Renie asked as two mothers pushed strollers past them on their way to the barista, who was busy tending the coffee urn.

"Hoffa," Judith echoed. "I'd forgotten about him. Maybe Barney was involved somehow. But I doubt that it plays a part in this case, except as background for Roland's book."

Renie had finished her mocha. "Let's see those pictures. I've got to get to Falstaff's, which is where I was headed when you tried to mow me down."

"I feel silly," Judith said, taking the packet of photographs out of her purse. "How will I ever explain this to the Malones?"

"You'll think of something," Renie said with a sly look.

"Here are the Badlands in North Dakota, with Bea and a dog looking wind-blown," Judith noted as she went through the photos one by one. "I like it when they put dates on pictures. Maybe I'll get Joe a camera like that for his birthday in August. Mike and Kristin already have one, which is great now that the baby's here. Okay, now we have Mal and the same dog in front of the lodge at the east entrance to Glacier National Park. More Glacier, Going to the Sun Highway. This is all Montana, taken late last week. Now they're at Lake Coeur d'Alene in Idaho. Oh, Lordy, Bea in a bathing suit. Bad idea. Dog holding life preserver in its mouth. Mal on water skis. Mal sinking into Lake Coeur d'Alene on water skis. That was Sunday.'' She was almost to the last few pictures.

"Where's their son?" Renie asked. "Had Corelli already been killed?"

Judith made a face. "Didn't they say they'd lost him on this trip? Surely they wouldn't have . . . I don't get it. There are no photos of Bea and Mal together. There should be, if Corelli was with them and had been using the camera. Maybe I didn't hear right, maybe Corelli was shot earlier, and they came west to get away from it all."

"Did you ever remember those other names Mal mentioned on the phone?" Renie asked as she reapplied lipstick.

"They were all Italian, except for an Irish name. McCormack. Of course it could be Scots," Judith added.

"Hmm." Renie was scowling. "Interesting."

Judith turned sharply. "Why?"

"Never mind for now," Renie said. "What else have you got?"

"A rest stop, somewhere in the eastern part of the state. Bea with a dog." Judith stopped, then locked glances with Renie. "Go back to what you just said."

"That was interesting?" Renie leaned over to peer at the photo. "A black lab. What's the last picture?"

It was of Mal, on his haunches, scratching the ears of the dog. "That's it," said Judith, then gave a start. "Coz, am I crazy or could Corelli be the dog?"

Renie gasped. "My God! of course! And maybe McCormack and those Italians you can't remember were dogs, too. They were named after opera singers. Franco Corelli, John McCormack, and whoever else they mentioned.''

"They had opera tapes in their car," Judith said, excitement mounting. "Remember what we were saying yesterday about kids and pets and cars? Some people treat animals as if they were children. As in sons and daughters.''

"Somebody shot their dog," Renie said. "Somebody shot several of their dogs. Is this making sense? Do the Malones have a criminal record? Or just enormous bills at the vet?''

"No one has mentioned a criminal record to me," Judith admitted. "Look, we've already figured that those names belonged to animals, not people.''

"So how do you ask the Malones if their son was a dog?" Renie broke in.

Judith waved a hand. "Look at this picture. They had a dog on Sunday.''

"Do we know it's *their* dog?''

"Yes," Judith declared. "They have a water dish in their Explorer. I saw it last night, but it didn't sink in. They may have more pet-related stuff under the rest of their belongings. If a child, a person, had been killed along the way, the Malones would have turned around and gone back to Chicago.''

Renie had stood up and slung her handbag over her shoulder. "How about this? The Malones are insane. Period. With any luck, the Malones will also be gone in an hour or two. Got to run, coz. Let me know what happens.''

When Judith returned home, she found Joe in the entry hall, arguing through the closed door with the guests in the front parlor. They didn't believe that they'd be allowed to depart by one o'clock. In polite tones, Roland conveyed the message that, after a discussion of J. J.'s announcement, there had been unanimous agreement that it was a trick to get them to come out. Apparently, even Marie didn't trust her fellow law enforcement officials.

"They'll get hungry eventually," Judith said grimly.

"They ate breakfast early, and it's already going on eleven. I'm going to check on Mother. Meanwhile, could you get that bassinet and the stand down from the loft now that the corpse has been removed?"

Joe gave Judith an ironic smile. "Sure. Anything else?"

"The box with the receiving blankets and baby clothes," Judith replied, heading for the back door. "Oh, if you see another carton marked 'Bottles Etc.,' get that. I assume they'll send formula home from the hospital. Kristin has decided not to nurse."

Halfway down the walk, Sweetums darted out from behind the statue of St. Francis of Assisi and sidled up to Judith. "Did I forget to feed you?" she asked wearily. "Stick with me, this won't take long."

Gertrude looked up from her game of solitaire. "Well, aren't I the popular person these days?" she asked in a sarcastic manner. "Where are all my other guests? I feel deserted."

"Arlene's still out of town," Judith replied. "Vivian is . . . ah . . . busy this morning. She's had company, you know. And, as I mentioned, Bruce Dunleavy is . . . gone."

"What about that German woman? We had quite a time, talking about our arthritis." Gertrude peered at her cards. "Drat. Old Nick beat me again."

"German woman?" Judith stared at her mother. "Who do you mean?"

"Minnie, or whatever her name was." Gertrude reshuffled the cards. "Another widow. Why do all these men have to die on us? Your father was way too young to peg out when he did. I've never forgiven him."

"Right," Judith said vaguely, having heard the undeserved indictment of Donald Grover many times. "When did Minerva visit you, Mother?"

Sweetums jumped on top of the card table just as Gertrude laid out the first row of cards. "Hey!" the old woman shouted. "Get out of there! You can't play cards. I know, I tried to teach you cribbage." She gave the cat a shove.

"Worthless animal. When was the last time he caught a mouse?"

"Friday," Judith replied as Sweetums jumped onto the floor and gave an indignant swish of his tail. "Tell me about Minerva. Please."

"Minerva?" Gertrude frowned. "Oh. Minnie. Nice woman. When's lunch?"

"*Mother.*" Judith's patience was ebbing fast. "When did you talk to Minerva?"

"The other day." She paused to straighten the cards that Sweetums had disarranged. "Monday. Or Tuesday. I forget."

"Think hard," Judith urged. "Please."

Gertrude finished laying out the hand. "Okay. Tuesday. Right after Bruce left. The first time, that is. Why isn't he coming back?"

"Because you're not a Nazi," Judith said, and knew she sounded irritable. "Why did Minerva come to see you?"

Gertrude drew back in her chair. "Because she's neighborly. Nice woman. We had a good visit. I figure she's had a hard life. Left with a boy to raise. He sounded like trouble. But aren't you all for us poor widows?"

As usual, Judith was fighting an uphill battle. "Barney, right?"

"Yep." Gertrude had started playing her cards. "A real handful. Unlike that other kid, Coronary or whatever."

Judith stepped around Sweetums and leaned on the card table. "Whose kid?"

Gertrude waved a hand. "That other woman. Kind of gruff. But that's okay. What's wrong with being gruff?"

"Was her name Bea?" Judith asked.

"Could have been," Gertrude conceded. "Or Cee or Dee or . . ."

"Mother!" Judith broke in. "This is important. I'm asking about a guest, a Bea Malone from Chicago. Did she come to see you in the last few days?"

"Chunky woman. Chunky and gruff. Didn't stay long."

Gertrude paused, peering at her cards. "Where's that black eight? I còuld've sworn I uncovered it."

"When was this? Please try to remember." The sharpness was gone from Judith's voice, now she was pleading.

"The other day. I figured she might come back," Gertrude said, playing up the ace, deuce, and trey of diamonds. "People sure are funny."

"Was Bea here Monday? Tuesday?" Judith was practically on her knees.

"She came before Bruce. That must have been Tuesday. That's right," Gertrude said, more to herself than to Judith. "That was the big day for company."

Only now did Judith recall how her mother had mentioned having visitors that day. The old woman had used the plural. Judith should have known that her mother wasn't referring to Joe and J. J., following the discovery of Legs Benedict's body. In Gertrude's world, Joe wouldn't count as a guest. Neither would J. J., if he appeared to be a friend of Joe's.

At last, Judith remembered what her mother had mentioned earlier in the day. "You told me this morning when I woke you up that I did the same thing one other time this week," Judith said carefully. "It wasn't me. But someone obviously did. Do you recall who?"

Gertrude was winning the hand. Her arthritic fingers fumbled a bit, but she played up every card until only the kings were showing on top of their respective suits. "Got it," she announced in triumph. "Now can I go two in a row?"

"Mother . . ." The patience that Judith had reined in with such difficulty began to fray again.

Gertrude swept all the cards into a pile. "It wasn't you, huh? Then it must have been that man."

"What man?"

"The one who got me out of bed. To tell the truth," Gertrude went on, again shuffling the cards, "I wasn't asleep. He brought me a present. But he said I couldn't open it until the Fourth of July."

Judith took a deep breath. "Where is this present?"

"I put it in my bureau," Gertrude replied, setting out another game of solitaire. "You know, where I put all my special candy. Under my old girdles."

Judith bolted into the bedroom. "It's not wrapped," Gertrude called to her daughter. "But it's a nice box."

There were half a dozen worn-out girdles in the middle dresser drawer. Though some of them were probably older than Mike, Gertrude refused to throw them out. Molded by the Great Depression, Judith and Renie's mothers hoarded all sorts of bizarre, useless items, from paper bags to rubber bands to hair nets they hadn't worn since Eisenhower was president.

The precious candy boxes were another matter. Gertrude reserved the more expensive chocolates for special occasions. There were five boxes under the girdles, all unopened. One was wrapped in Christmas paper, two were heart-shaped, from St. Valentine's Day, and another bore a yellow ribbon with a small Easter bunny cut-out.

Next to the plain sealed two-pound box of Dolly's Dark Delights was a black leather case. At first, Judith thought it might be her father's old shaving kit. But the case was too long and too narrow. Judith flipped the clasp open and gazed at the contents.

Nestled against a soft cloth background was a Colt .45. Judith slammed the lid shut, tucked the case under her arm, and, without giving Gertrude an explanation, ran from the toolshed.

Joe had given up on the guests in the front parlor, and J. J. had gone back to Herself's house where Agents Rosenblatt and Terrill had arrived to conduct their own interrogation.

When Judith showed Joe the gun, he swore out loud. "You mean this freaking thing was in your mother's freaking drawer this whole freaking time?"

Judith nodded. "And I think I know who gave it to her."

"Who, dammit?" Joe was glaring at Judith, his face almost touching hers.

Judith backed away. "We have to do some checking first. I'll take the closet in Room Three." She offered Joe a coaxing smile. "While I'm doing that, could you go out to the garage and get a shovel?"

Joe opened his mouth to lash out at Judith, then clamped it shut. "A shovel," he said at last. "What do I do with it? Slam you in the backside?"

Judith's smile wavered. "Of course not. You use the shovel to dig. And here's where you do it and what I expect you're going to find."

Despite his skepticism, Joe agreed to cooperate. "So far, this isn't making much sense," he said, over his shoulder.

Judith had reached for her handbag, which was sitting on the kitchen counter. "You may be surprised. When you come back in, I think we'll both know who shot Legs Benedict."

TWENTY-ONE

MIKE, KRISTIN, AND the baby arrived at Hillside Manor five minutes after the lame-duck guests had finally departed. Judith's reaction upon seeing the dark green Isuzu Trooper pull into the drive brought a lump to her throat. No more Ford Explorers from Chicago, Cadillac Sevilles from Detroit, Chrysler Concords from New York; no aliases, no concealed weapons, no deceptions. Just a mother and a father in the front and a newborn in the back, securely strapped into a high-tech car seat. Judith welcomed the trio with tears of joy.

The new parents' first stop was at the toolshed, where Gertrude was introduced to her great-grandson, Dan McMonigle II.

"Wasn't one enough?" Gertrude had rasped. But her wrinkled face had shone with pleasure when Kristin placed the baby in the old woman's arms. Lifting one of his tiny hands in hers, the new great-grandmother gave a shake of her head. "Look at those little bitty fingers. So small and perfect." She held up her own gnarled hand. "See what time does. My, my." But Gertrude still managed a smile.

Renie dropped by half an hour later. "Bill couldn't come," she said. "He's doing the housework today and he hasn't finished the list."

"List?" Judith gave her cousin a puzzled glance.

"Right," Renie said. "When it's his turn for housework, he makes a list for the kids. You know—Tom: Vacuum first and second floors; dust. Anne: Clean bathrooms. Tony: Clean kitchen, including refrigerator."

"That's it?" Judith responded, still puzzled.

"Of course," Renie said nonchalantly. "It takes time. First, he has to divvy up the work in fair amounts. Then he has to make sure everything is done right. If it isn't, he has to call the kids back, give them hell, and make them do it right. When it's his turn and there's a long list, Bill gets exhausted by the end of the day."

After Renie had taken her turn at holding little Dan, the baby had become fussy from all the excitement. Kristin and Mike took him up to the third floor to change him and put him down for a nap.

"Maybe Bill can stop by this evening," Judith said as she and Renie sat down in the blessedly empty living room. "Joe had to leave before they brought the baby home, so our husbands could do a male bonding thing after dinner."

"Good idea," Renie noted, sipping from a can of Pepsi. "Now tell me about the arrest."

"It was very quiet," Judith replied. "Anticlimactic, really. Joe wasn't surprised. But then he's had so much experience with murderers. He told me that when a perp feels vindicated by killing someone, the frequent reaction to arrest is indignation."

Renie gave a little shake of her head. "Still, in this particular case, I would have expected something more volatile. And frankly, coz, it's not going to be easy to prove which of them did it, is it?"

Judith smiled wryly. "Not when they both say they fired the shot. But," she went on, bemused, "I suppose when you've been married as long as Mal and Bea Malone have, you truly feel as one. Maybe we'll never know which of them fired that Colt .45 and put an end to the life of Legs Benedict."

Once more, Judith showed Renie the photographs she'd

had developed. "You see, there in the background at that rest stop is Legs Benedict. This was taken Monday. The date is right there. As Bea was perfectly willing to explain, they'd stopped to give their dog, Corelli, a run before heading over the pass and into town. She admitted that the dog could be annoying."

"You and Dan had a black Lab when you lived out on Thurlow Street," Renie pointed out. "Oliver. He was awful. The first—and only time, thanks to Bill's No Oliver Allowed decree—you brought him to our house, he ran across the living room, got behind Bill's favorite chair, and did something exceedingly nasty on our new carpet."

"I know," Judith sighed. "He ate our drapes, the screen door, and our landlord's prosthesis." The memories of the shoddy neighborhood in the city's south end made Judith cringe. "Anyway, Bea admitted that Corelli could be a nuisance, which I translate as vicious. All their dogs—Corelli, McCormack, Albanese, Tagliavini—were Labs."

"And thus," Renie put in, "caused problems for other people. By the way, the opera singers they named the dogs after were Franco Corelli, John McCormack, Licia Albanese, and Ferrucio Tagliavini. If you'd remembered those other names, I might have gotten on the right track much sooner."

"Make me feel bad," Judith said sarcastically. "Don't you think I had already begun to wonder if my brain wasn't disintegrating?"

Renie grinned at Judith. "It wasn't. Its wheels just slowed down a bit because you got sick. Go on, tell me more."

"At the rest stop," Judith said, taking up her tale as told to her by the Malones, "Mal went to use the restroom while Bea tended to the dog. Corelli started bothering Legs. Or Mr. and Mrs. Smith, I should say. Bea had let him run, and the dog was barking and jumping all over Legs and Darlene. Finally Legs told Bea that if she couldn't control her pet, he would. Bea didn't scare easily, despite the fact that back in Chicago, two of their other dogs had been poisoned by neighbors—I think that would have been Albanese and McCormack—and a third had simply disappeared.''

"Maybe they should have gotten a Chihuahua," Renie mused.

"What happened next," Judith continued, "was that Corelli bit Legs—in the leg, I might add—and tore his very expensive trousers. I noticed the tear when he and Darlene arrived, but of course I never paid any special attention. I did check the closet, which still contained Legs's clothes. The tear definitely could have been made by a dog." Judith paused as Renie digested the information. "Anyway, according to Bea, Corelli's attack so infuriated Legs that he whipped out his gun and shot the dog. That, in turn, explains why Legs's gun—the Glock—had been fired recently."

Renie winced. "What a mean thing to do. Unless," she added wryly, "Legs was wearing Armani."

"He was," Judith responded. "Mal, who had his gun with him, came out of the restroom just as Legs and Darlene got into their car and roared off. Bea had left her weapon in the Explorer, so all they could do was follow Legs into the city. He and Darlene may have known they were being followed, but they probably just laughed it off. Anyway, the Malones lost the Chrysler after it turned off Heraldsgate Avenue. However, they assumed he was headed for some sort of lodging since his car had out-of-state plates. It turns out that they came into the cul-de-sac only to turn around, but then O. P. ran into their Explorer, and the Malones saw Legs's Chrysler. That's when they asked me if there was somewhere to stay nearby."

Renie set her Pepsi down on the glass-topped coffee table. "Are you saying they planned from the start to shoot Legs?"

Judith gave a sad little nod of her head. "The Malones were childless, maybe even friendless, given their harsh manner. Their pets meant everything to them. As we mentioned earlier, a dog can become a child, a son, the focus of thwarted affection. They'd already lost three animals.

Then Corelli was gunned down before their very eyes. Something snapped, I guess. They were out for revenge. By chance, the Malones and the Smiths—Legs and Darlene—didn't cross paths here at the B&B Monday evening. In the middle of the night, Bea and Mal got up and went outside. Do you remember that J. J. said there was fresh dirt on their shoes?''

"I'm not sure I ever heard that," Renie said.

"The Malones had wrapped Corelli in that dirty brown blanket I'd seen in the Explorer. They borrowed a shovel from the garage—I noticed last night that my garden tools had been disturbed—and buried the poor dog in the flower bed between the kitchen and dining room windows."

Renie gave Judith an inquiring look. "You didn't see any sign of digging out there?"

Judith's expression was sheepish. "I did, but it was getting dark and it was raining, and I assumed that the Dooleys' dog had been rooting around out there. He does that, you know."

"Farky was the worst," Renie put in, referring to the Rankerses' pesky dog of many years past, who had also met a suspicious end.

"Yes," Judith agreed. "Anyway, I asked Joe to dig out there—I couldn't bear to do it myself—and sure enough, he found Corelli. Then I showed him the torn trousers and that last photo from the Malones' roll. Joe saw Legs in the background. That was when he began to think that maybe I wasn't crazy."

"You'd already found the Malones' other gun under your mother's girdles," Renie noted.

"The Colt .45," Judith said, still amazed by the discovery. "Mal told Joe that each of them always carried a gun when they traveled. Ironically, they considered rest stops and restrooms the most dangerous places on the road. Since they couldn't go to the restroom together, they each carried a weapon. As it turned out, they'd left the one locked in the car and brought the Colt .45 into the house. At this point, according to Bea, they hadn't yet figured out how to get to Legs. But he played right into their hands. J. J. found out from Darlene just a few minutes ago that Legs had made her write a note to Barney, asking him to meet her outside because she was planning to double-cross Legs and needed his help. Apparently, Barney didn't fall for it, and tore up the note in a fit of rage. But Legs didn't know that, and showed up in the backyard anyway. The Malones spotted him as they were putting the shovel back in the garage, and they shot him. End of story.''

Renie sat back on the couch, shaking her head. ''Amazing. All this conjecture about the mob and hit men and everybody chasing everybody else.''

Judith nodded. ''The crime turns out to be purely personal. Legs could have been a grocery store manager or an orthodontist as far as the Malones were concerned. The murder came straight from the heart, not from the mob.''

''So what were the Malones doing out by their car that morning?'' Renie asked.

''They knew there'd be a search for the weapon, which they'd already given to Mother and told her it was a present. They figured that the police wouldn't tear up an old lady's apartment. Oh, J. J. and Rich made a cursory examination that morning, but the Malones were right,'' Judith went on. ''However, they had carry permits for Illinois, which meant the police might wonder if they didn't have a gun. They kept the other weapon strapped under the SUV's carriage. They retrieved it and put it in their room so that it could be found, and yet wouldn't be the gun that killed Legs.''

Kristin, whose usually robust manner seemed lackluster, entered the living room with little Dan propped against her shoulder. ''He woke up,'' the new mother announced. ''I thought you might like to feed him. Grandma,'' she added, with a hint of her usual brilliant smile.

Judith reached out for the baby. ''I'd love to. You look as if you could use a nap.''

Kristin yawned and stretched. ''That's what I'm going

to do. Mike just left for work. He'll be back around seven. I'll get the formula out of the fridge.''

''No, you won't,'' said Renie, rising from the sofa. ''I'll get it. You go to bed. Grandma and Auntie have some experience with this sort of thing.''

With only a minor show of reluctance, Kristin trudged off towards the back stairs. Renie returned to the living room a couple of minutes later, carrying a four-ounce bottle filled with formula. If she was envious of her cousin's new status as a grandmother, she kept it to herself.

''Now tell me what Darlene told J. J.,'' Renie said after Judith had managed to get little Dan to suck. ''You were right about Legs having knocked her out that night, I gather.''

''Yes,'' Judith replied, smiling down at the baby's tiny red face. ''Darlene and Legs weren't lovers. She was supposed to be his backup in the hit on Barney 'Fewer Fingers' Schwartz.'' Little Dan hiccoughed; Judith put him against her shoulder and rubbed his back. ''Darlene was also the decoy to lure Barney. But Legs didn't trust her, so he put something in her water glass to make her sleep extra soundly. He didn't want her waking up and interfering when he met Barney outside.'' Little Dan turned his head away from the bottle and began to cry. Judith patted him some more. ''Legs was right, according to Darlene. She had orders to whack Legs after he whacked Barney.'' Little Dan swung his small fists and spit up on Judith's shoulder. ''What she didn't know was that Baby Face Doria had orders to whack her,'' Judith went on as she used a spare diaper to mop herself up. ''He impersonated an FBI agent so he could find Darlene. Obviously, he'd seen the car parked by Dooleys' and assumed she was still around.'' Little Dan began to calm down. Judith resumed feeding him. ''What wasn't clear to him was who had really shot Legs. Doria finally decided that even if Darlene hadn't pulled the trigger, Legs was dead, and he'd better carry out his assignment. Thus, they exchanged fire this morning, and Doria was killed.'' Little Dan pulled his head away from the bottle and emitted some rather alarming bodily noises. "As for Darlene, she had to find out who killed Legs in order to inform the Fusilli gang. That's why she hid at Herself's house. And, I might add, used her unwitting hostess to keep her apprised of what was happening here." Little Dan had become quite furious, screaming and waving his arms. "I think he needs changing," Judith declared, wrinkling her nose. "I put some diapers and a package of wipes out on the kitchen counter."

Renie was gone less than a minute. "Funny how you forget the gruesome part about babies," she said, handing Judith the needed supplies. "That kid's a real gas bomb."

"He's merely adjusting to his new menu," Judith said with a smile. "Not to mention the whole world around him."

"It's a much more peaceful world this afternoon," Renie remarked. "Say, did you ever figure out what happened to your disk and those pages that were torn out of the guest register?"

"No," Judith admitted, as the baby emitted a belch that seemed too loud to have come from such a small person. "I can only guess that it was Minerva. Maybe she wanted to cover her tracks."

The doorbell sounded. "I'll get it," Renie volunteered. "I could use some fresh air."

"It can't be the new guests," Judith said, trying to keep Little Dan from squirming all over the sofa. "It's only two o'clock."

"It's a Mr. Harwood," Renie announced from the entry hall. "Dare I bring him in?"

"Mr. Harwood?" The name was vaguely familiar. Judith turned slightly, but kept a firm grip on the baby. "I'll be there in just a sec. What does he want?"

"I don't know," Renie replied. "He says he's from the FBI."

Judith carried the freshened infant into the parlor and invited Mr. Harwood to have a seat. Fortunately, Joe had put the room back in order after the guests had finally agreed to come out.

"I must tell you straight off," Judith began as little Dan sucked happily on his bottle, "the case is closed. You should contact Agents Rosenblatt and Terrill."

Harwood chuckled. "Please call me Glenn. This isn't a formal visit. I've already spoken with Terrill and Rosenblatt. That's why I'm here. I felt I should apologize. Do you recall when I phoned the other day and asked for your mother?"

"Oh!" Judith gave a start, briefly unsettling little Dan. "Of course. I thought you were a salesman," she added with a sheepish grin.

"My, no," Harwood smiled back. "Though it's not a bad cover in my line of work. I'm in the bureau's division that tracks down war criminals. I'd gotten a tip last Friday that a certain Gertrude Hoffman we've been looking for since 1945 was going to be in the vicinity. When I did some checking before I left Las Vegas, I discovered that a woman by that name actually lived here. It was very confusing, but as soon as I talked to her on the phone that morning, I realized she wasn't the person we were looking for."

Judith recalled that Gertrude had mentioned something about a census. Glenn Harwood's questions had undoubtedly led Judith's mother to such a conclusion.

"However," Harwood went on, "the tip was accurate. We've finally found the other Gertrude Hoffman, who was notorious for her dealings with women prisoners at Auschwitz. All these years, she's been in this country under another name."

Carefully cuddling little Dan, Judith leaned forward in her chair. "Dare I ask?"

Harwood gave a single nod. "Certainly. Don't worry, she's being held prior to possible extradition. Though her married name was Schlagintweit, you would know her as Minerva Schwartz."

*   *   *

By chance, Glenn Harwood and Baby Face Doria had been on the same Vegas flight Monday morning. They had sat next to each other and had fallen into the usual superficial chit-chat. Trained to be discreet, Harwood hadn't offered any information about his profession. Needless to say, Harwood added drolly, Doria hadn't talked about his own livelihood, either.

"My reticence seemed to pique my fellow passenger's interest all the more," the FBI agent explained. "After I came back from the restroom, I noticed that some of my belongings had been disturbed. Naturally, I keep my briefcase locked, but I'd been going over some of the data about Gertrude Hoffman that had been faxed to me from our Detroit office. Now that I've learned that this Doria impersonated someone from the bureau, I realize that he must have used that information to make his story credible."

Judith gave the agent a rueful smile. "It also explains why Doria canceled his reservation that day. He decided it would be better not to come here as a guest where some of the others might recognize him. If he stayed away from the house and called on Mother, the others wouldn't notice him. He was free then to collect whatever information he could."

Harwood agreed, but only in part. "According to Terrill and Rosenblatt, Legs Benedict was already dead by the time Doria showed up here. I'm also told that Doria wasn't a member of the Fusilli family. His grandfather, Ernie Doria, had worked for them up until his death a few years ago. But the grandson was freelance, and had been hired so that there would be no connection between him and the Fusillis. But of course there was still a chance that he might have been recognized by Legs Benedict."

"The mob is a complicated organization," Renie remarked. "I ought to know. Bill's watched *The Godfather*, Parts One and Two, about a hundred and fifty times."

Harwood acknowledged Renie's comment with a slight smile. "The mob is a business, a big business. But getting back to Legs's death, Doria may have assumed at first that

Darlene had killed him, which meant he had to get rid of her. But I gather she'd fled by the time he arrived."

Judith nodded. "But your trip wasn't in vain. It's lucky that Minerva was caught before she left the country. Dare I ask how you got onto her after all these years?"

Harwood gave the cousins a small smile of satisfaction. "You must remember that when it comes to some of the more minor figures from World War Two, efforts aren't concentrated. When we have a break between current investigations, we go back to our long-standing cases, such as the search for Minerva Schlagintweit. Even after more than fifty years, the evil perpetrators must be brought to justice. Not to mention that when one of them is found, it's a reminder to younger generations of what the Holocaust was all about, and why we must never forget it."

"My cousin and I were small children during the war," Renie put in, "but I remember seeing those first photographs of the concentration camp prisoners. To this day, I see those stark, ghastly faces in my mind's eye and feel a sense of horror all over again."

Harwood paused, his pleasant features suddenly harsh. "I was born right after the war, but I've talked to so many victims and relatives of victims over the years. Their stories give people like me an incentive that goes far beyond just doing the job. Of course," he went on, making an obvious effort to put aside the appalling accounts that clearly haunted him, "many of those war criminals are dead by now. But when our criminal bureau was digging into Fewer Fingers's operations, they discovered Barney Schwartz's real name and eventually IDed his mother. You see, she'd married a man right after the war who was able to get her out of Germany. Minerva was pregnant at the time, and Barney was born in this country. Mr. Schlagintweit apparently stayed in Germany where no trace has ever been found of him. One has to wonder, of course."

Judith gave Harwood a questioning look. "You mean, once he got her papers and passage, she may have . . . ?"

"She may," Harwood said in confirmation. "Minerva—

Gertrude Hoffman—was a ruthless woman.''

"She came back here yesterday while I was gone," Judith said. "Do you suppose she was checking on Dunleavy? I mean, Doria?"

"It's possible," Harwood allowed. "She must have known that someone was after her, and assumed Doria was the real McCoy. It's even credible that having been thwarted in her attempt to leave the country, she intended to do away with him and destroy his records. Of course he didn't have any, only what he cribbed from my notes. I'm sorry he put your mother through such a bogus ordeal."

"Mother loved it," Judith said, standing up. "You really must meet her. She loves company."

Glenn Harwood expressed pleasure over an introduction to the other Gertrude Hoffman. As Judith and Renie led the FBI agent out to the toolshed, Renie murmured, "We should have guessed about Minerva."

"What do you mean?" Judith asked.

"When Barney was just a little kid, Minerva dragged him to Wagnerian operas. Anybody who does that *has* to be a Nazi."

Judith grinned at her cousin. "By the way," she said to Harwood, her hand on the toolshed's doorknob, "do you know how Barney lost his fingers?"

"Agent Terrill mentioned it," Harwood said. "As a teenager, Fewer Fingers got bit by a dog."

The rain stopped around dinnertime, and the sun came out just after seven o'clock. All of the new guests, a seemingly mild-mannered crowd, had arrived between four and six. Renie and Bill had showed up by seven-thirty, and Mike had returned from the ranger station at the summit. He insisted that everyone gather on the patio in the backyard to pose for family pictures.

Gertrude, who was seated in one of the lawn chairs, was given the honor of holding little Dan. Judith, Joe, Renie, Bill, and Kristin gathered around the chair and smiled for the camera.

"Great," Mike said, clicking off the first picture. "This time, how about you three ladies kneeling down in front of Joe and Bill, okay?"

The group shifted. Mike took two more shots before Joe suggested setting the camera timer so that the proud papa could also get into the frame. Then Kristin and Mike posed alone with the baby. Renie and Bill, looking vaguely wistful, took their turn.

Judith insisted that she should take a picture of Joe, Mike, and little Dan. "Three generations," she said, then winced at the gaffe. "I mean . . ."

"You mean four generations," Renie interrupted, with a sharp glance at Judith. "We span the century, don't we Aunt Gertrude?"

"You bet, Toots," Gertrude replied. "But let these men have their snapshot taken together. Who wants to see any more of my ugly old mug?"

Judith gave Renie a grateful look. Apparently, no one else had noticed the significance of Judith's remark. Bill was arranging the pose: Joe stood behind Mike, who got down on one knee and held little Dan.

After snapping two pictures, Joe and Mike stood shoulder to shoulder, the baby between them. The light had changed, and Judith had to adjust the camera settings. She looked up to see Mike staring at Joe's red head, then at little Dan's, and, finally touching his own. The realization that all three of them shared the same color hair showed in his eyes. It had never been more obvious than now, in the golden glow of the setting sun.

"Smile," she said in a voice suddenly gone breathless.

Joe smiled and the baby yawned. Mike's expression was part wonder, part awe. "Let's do that again," Judith said, still breathless. "Come on, Mike. Smile for your mother."

Mike's smile was uncertain, and he looked not at Judith, but at Joe.

Joe looked back at Mike, and grinned from ear to ear.

CHECK INTO THE WORLD OF MARY DAHEIM

WHAT COULD BE more relaxing than a well-deserved respite at Hillside Manor, the charming bed-and-breakfast inn set atop Heraldsgate Hill? Well, for Judith McMonigle Flynn, the ever courteous proprietress, hand-to-tentacle combat with an irritated octopus might, on occasion, seem like a quieter pastime than running her beloved inn.

Daily worries for Judith include whether she'll be able to pay the utilities bill, whether she'll be able to keep the inn at full capacity during the busy season, whether her supply of hors d'oeuvres will satisfy her guests, whether her crotchety mother will keep out of the way, but most importantly, Judith always worries where that next body will turn up . . .

It's not that she goes out in search of murders to solve— after all, she doesn't deliberately try to compete with her husband, Homicide Detective Joe Flynn, on his own turf— it's just that murder and mayhem seem to find her. And what's a gal supposed to do?

Grab her ravenous and reliable cousin Renie and hit the trail after the latest killer, before this energetic and entertaining hostess is put permanently out of business.

JUST DESSERTS

A WIDOW OF three years, Judith McMonigle decided to convert her family home into the charming—and therefore destined to be successful—Hillside Manor bed-and-breakfast, which will provide her with a steady income (she hopes) and a place to live for herself and her not-so-gracefully aging mother, Gertrude. In business for just over seven months, Judith suddenly wishes she hadn't gone out of her way to accommodate the Brodie clan . . . except for the fact that the corpse in her dining room, which may put her out of business, also brings the local police onto the scene. . . .

"She's pretty good at what she does," remarked Judith in an undertone. "I wonder if Oriana thinks she's getting her two grand worth?"

Over the flutter of unsettled noises, Madame Gushenka was speaking again: "Far off, bleak, isolated. A handsome bird in a concrete cage." Her voice rumbled into the very depths of her chest, then suddenly brightened. "There is music, too. Such pretty notes! Or are they? Greed, deception creep onto the stage." The tone had changed again, now overtly sinister. "Wrongs not righted, the past swept under cover, while over the

282

ocean, a crowd roars, then goes silent. Disaster strikes! The night goes black, the sky is empty, hush . . . hush . . . ssssh. . . .''

The last utterances had slowed, then begun to fade away. Judith and Renie almost banged heads trying to press closer against the door. They were steadying themselves when they heard the crash, the screams, and the sounds of chairs being overturned, crystal shattering and china breaking. Even as Judith fumbled for the kitchen light switch, the dining room sounded as if it had erupted into a stampede. Renie threw open the door.

The illumination from the kitchen showed a scene of utter confusion, with everyone clustered around the head of the table. Lance was struggling with something or someone, Ellie was whimpering and clutching at Harvey, Gwen was verging on hysterics, Oriana was deathly pale despite her makeup, Otto was swearing like a sailor, Dash was trying either to help or to hinder Lance, and Mavis was shrieking for order.

"The lights!" called Judith, and was amazed when Oriana immediately obeyed, bringing the chandelier up to full beam. Gwen stared at the blaze of shimmering crystal as if hypnotized and Lance stepped back, revealing Madame Gushenka, sprawled face down on the table, one hand on the cards, the other clawing at the azalea's vivid blooms. Her black hair spilled onto the Irish linen, and the brilliant veils seemed to have wilted like weary petals.

"She's out like a . . . light," said Lance, peering up at the chandelier.

"It must be a trance," Oriana said, but her usually confident voice was uncertain.

"Get back," Harvey ordered, assuming his best operating-theater style. "Give the poor woman room to breathe." As the others, including the distraught Ellie, moved away, Harvey felt for a pulse, first at the wrist, then at the neck. His sallow face sagged as his search for a vital sign grew more frantic. "My God," he exclaimed. "She's dead!"

FOWL PREY

JUDITH AND HER cousin Renie are heading north to British Columbia and the Hotel Clovia for a pre-Thanksgiving getaway. But when an addled and impoverished popcorn vendor is murdered along with his foul-mouthed parakeet, a local policeman's suspicions land on the visiting Americans, Judith and Renie. Meanwhile, the cousins suspect one of the "Sacred Eight"—a strange collection of showbiz glitterati gathered at the historic hotel. And unless Judith and Renie can find the murderer among the glitzy group, their goose will be cooked!

Renie was about to respond when the cousins both heard another noise, this time very faint—and very near. Their eyes darted to the bathtub where the shower curtain was pulled shut. With the poker again held aloft, Judith stood at one end of the tub while Renie guarded the other. Renie yanked at the curtain, revealing a cowering Mildred Grimm.

"Well, Mildred, first you show up half-naked in the middle of the night, then you come to take a shower with your clothes on. What gives?" asked Judith, putting the poker down.

"You'd never understand," whined Mildred, gingerly climbing over the mahogany surround.

"Could we try?" asked Judith, keeping her exasperation at bay.

Mildred stepped out of her low-heeled pumps, which apparently had gotten wet in the tub. "You wouldn't believe me," she said, not looking at either cousin.

"You'd be surprised what we'd believe about now," remarked Judith, as the trio emerged from the bathroom, went out through Renie's bedroom, and into the sitting room. "We presume this handiwork is yours, not the police's?" Judith made a sweeping gesture with one hand while replacing the poker with the other.

"Yes." Mildred drooped, a pitiful thing in her baggy blue sweater and pleated skirt. "I'm sorry, I would have put everything back if I'd had time."

Renie was already straightening the sofa cushions. "Sit down, we'll have a drink, we'll talk. What were you looking for, Mildred? More library cards?"

Whatever color Mildred possessed drained away. She collapsed onto the sofa like a rag doll. "How did you know?" she gasped.

"We were there," said Judith, closing the drawers on the end tables.

"Yes." Mildred sighed. "I saw you. But I didn't think you saw me."

Renie was at the phone. "What will you have, Mildred?"

Mildred opened her mouth, started to shake her head, then reconsidered. "A martini. Very dry. With a twist."

"Drat." Renie replaced the receiver. "No dial tone. I'll run downstairs and give the bar our order." She was gone before Judith could say "scotch."

With only one cousin confronting her, Mildred seemed to revive a bit. "I tell you, it's not believable."

"Let me decide," said Judith, sitting in the armchair opposite Mildred. "You owe us an explanation. You broke into our room, you ransacked our belongings. We could have you arrested.''

''I know.'' Mildred's face crumpled again. ''But that will probably happen anyway. Only on a more awful charge.''

''Of what?'' asked Judith, but the catch in her voice told Mildred she already knew.

The close-set blue eyes welled up with tears. ''Murder. Bob-o was killed with my gun.''

HOLY TERRORS

*CATERING THE ANNUAL brunch and Easter egg hunt is
enough of a hassle for bed-and-breakfast hostess Judith
McMonigle. Add to that, murder by a scissors-happy
fiend in a bunny suit and the return of her ex-beau, Lieu-
tenant Joe Flynn, and Judith is up to her elbows in some
serious unsolicited snooping . . .*

Joe's casual air masked his tenacious professionalism,
just as the well-cut tweed sports coat camouflaged the
spreading midriff Dooley had mentioned. His receding
red hair was flecked with gray, yet his round face retained its freshness, despite over two decades observing
the seamiest slices of life. At his side stood Woodrow
Price, a uniformed officer on the verge of thirty and his
next promotion. A stolid black man with a walrus mous-
tache, Woody Price had displayed a hidden reservoir of
talents during his previous adventure at Hillside Manor.

But it wasn't Woody Price's serious dark gaze which
held Judith mesmerized at the back door. Rather, Joe
Flynn's green eyes, with those magnetic flecks of gold,
turned her faintly incoherent.

"You're early," she blurted. "It's still two weeks to
go. But who's counting?" Judith giggled and mentally

cursed herself for sounding like a half-baked teenager instead of a poised middle-aged widow.

Joe's mouth twitched slightly, showing the merest hint of his roguish smile. "This is business, not pleasure. I've yet to bring Woody along on a date." He put a highly buffed loafer over the threshold. "May we?"

Judith actually jumped. "Oh! I didn't mean . . . Sure, come in, I just heard about what happened up at church . . ."

Gertrude's rasping voice crackled from the kitchen: "Is that Joe Flynn?" She didn't wait for confirmation. "Where's he been for six months? One lousy cribbage board and a box of chocolates won't buy this old girl! There was a caramel in with the creams, and it wrecked my partial plate! Get that bastard out of my house!"

As always, it was useless for Judith to argue over the legal rights of ownership to Hillside Manor. "Mother," she pleaded over her shoulder, "you know why Joe hasn't called on us since Thanksgiving. That was the bargain. Now he's here about Sandy Frizzell's murder."

"Baloney!" snarled Gertrude, wrestling with her walker as she tried to get up from the dinette table. "Joe's here because you got your hair dyed like a two-bit hussy! Out!" Her thin arm flailed under cover of a baggy blue cardigan. "Beat it, and take your chauffeur with you!"

"Mother!" Judith was aghast. "Don't be so ornery!" Agitated, she rushed to Gertrude's side. "Settle down. Do you want to be arrested for impeding justice, you crazy old coot?"

While she was still seething, Gertrude's voiced dropped a notch. "Justice, my foot! If there were such a thing, Joe Flynn would have spent the last twenty-odd years in prison for breach of promise! But you, you gutless wonder," she raged on, wagging a bony finger in her daughter's face, "you just rolled over and married Dan McMonigle! Is that justice, I ask you?"

DUNE TO DEATH

HAVING FINALLY MADE it to the altar, bed-and-breakfast hostess Judith McMonigle and Detective Joe Flynn head out for their overdue honeymoon. Settling into a cozy, costly cottage on Buccaneer Beach it seems like a dream come true. However, their newly wedded bliss is shattered when a dune buggy accident puts Joe in the hospital in traction and Cousin Renie shows up to keep Judith company. And to make a bad situation worse, the landlady shows up garroted to death in their living room . . . and Judith is on the case!

A soft mist had settled in on the MG's windshield when Judith and Renie reached the parking lot. The air was cool and damp, but the wind had died down. It was almost ten by the time they returned to Pirate's Lair. To Judith's relief, the house was dark, but she had remembered to leave a light on in the garage. The faint sound of music could be heard drifting from the We See Sea Resort next door. Judith decided they should build a fire in the cottage's stone fireplace. The cousins gathered wood and kindling to bring inside. Judith noticed that more boxes seemed to be missing from the garage. She gave a mental shrug—if Mrs. Hoke were moving her

belongings, that was fine—as long as she didn't keep popping into the house itself. Maybe, Judith thought with a
wry smile, she'd taken home a crate of dulcimers.

Renie was already in the kitchen, flipping on the lights.
"Have you opened the damper yet?" she asked, heading
for the living room.

"No," replied Judith as Renie switched on a table lamp
by the beige sofa that sat across from the fireplace. "Let's
make sure we do it right. I wouldn't want to set off the
smoke alarm."

The words were hardly out of her mouth when Renie set
off her own alarm. A piercing scream brought Judith vaulting around the sofa and across the floor. Renie stood frozen,
the kindling clutched in her arms like a newborn baby. At
her feet was Mrs. Hoke, long arms and legs at awkward
angles. At her side was the bright pink kite the cousins had
tried to fly in vain that afternoon.

And around her neck was the long, strong string. Her
face was a ghastly shade of purple and the gray eyes bulged
up at the cousins.

Judith and Renie knew she was dead.

BANTAM OF THE OPERA

As TIME GOES on, the bed-and-breakfast continues to do well, gaining a reputation that keeps Judith hopping for most of the year. In fact, Hillside Manor has begun to draw some high caliber celebrities, including obnoxious opera star Mario Pacetti, who threatens to eat Judith out of house and home. Judith's attempts to satiate the significantly statured songster seem of minor significance once the threats on his life draw his attention away from his next meal—which could possibly be his last. . . .

"Hey, Jude-girl," Joe called after his wife. "Where's my gun?"

Judith gnashed her teeth. During her four years of widowhood she had forgotten how men, even sharp-eyed homicide detectives such as Joe Flynn, couldn't find a bowling ball in the bathroom sink. Suppressing the urge to tell her husband to look in the vicinity of his backside, Judith opened her mouth to reply. But Joe had spotted the holster and was grinning with the pleasure of discovery.

"Hey, how'd it get there?" he asked in surprise.

"Gee, I don't know, Joe. I suppose it grew little

leather feet and walked, meanwhile tossing socks and shirts every which way. Are you taking that with you?'' It was Judith's turn to evince surprise.

But Joe shook his head. ''No need. I'll ditch it in the closet. Or what about that little safe you've got?''

Judith rarely used the safe, but considered it an excellent repository for Joe's .38 special. ''It's in the basement, behind the hot water tank. I think.''

''Right.'' Joe was filling his shaving kit; Judith headed out into the little foyer which served as a family sitting room. On her left, the door to Mike's room was closed. On her right, the door to Gertrude's former room stood ajar. As if, Judith thought with a pang, it was expecting Gertrude Grover to return at any moment. Judith consoled herself that by Monday she might have some good news for her mother. If the Swedish carpenter's estimates were relatively reasonable and his schedule wasn't too busy, Gertrude might be home for Christmas. Of course Judith must discuss it more fully with Joe, but not now, with his departure at hand.

She had just descended the short flight from the third floor when she heard a tremendous crash and a piercing scream. The sounds emanated from the front bedroom. Judith raced down the hallway and pounded on the door.

''Mr. Pacetti! What is it? What's wrong? Mr. Pacetti?'' Judith's heart thumped along with her fists. Fleetingly, she wondered if her insurance agent had already increased her coverage as she'd requested the previous day. It was a callous thought, she realized, since Mario Pacetti might be in a lot more trouble than she was.

A FIT OF TEMPERA

JUDITH AND RENIE are headed for their family's back-woods vacation cottage for some much needed R&R. But shortly after they've unpacked their bags they find out that someone has painted their world-renowned neighbor, artist Riley Tobias, permanently out of the picture—and has artfully managed to frame Judith for the crime!

"Let me make some coffee," Judith suggested, then remembered that the fire had gone out. "Or some pop? A drink? Ice water?" She grimaced slightly at the thought of chipping chunks off the ice block.

But both Kimballs declined the offer of beverages. Indeed, Ward was on his feet, fingering his beard and gazing out the window. Mount Woodchuck stood watch over the forest, the clouds dispersed along the river valley.

"I think I'll head over to see Iris," Ward said, touching Lark's shoulder. "The law should be gone by now, and if not, I'd like to hear what they've found out. If anything. Lark?"

His daughter shook her head. "I told you, I'd rather not play out a farce with Iris. She doesn't like me any more than I like her."

Ward Kimball sighed with resignation. "As you will, dear heart. I'll amble over there. I shouldn't be long." He sketched a courtly little bow and was gone.

"Come on, Lark," Renie urged, "have a beer. A sandwich? A couple of hot dogs?"

Judith heard the hunger pangs and made a face at Renie. "Don't force food and drink on people, coz. Not everyone is a Big Pig."

But Lark said she would like a glass of wine after all, if the cousins had any. They didn't. She settled for a beer. Judith and Renie joined her, trying to be companionable.

"I suppose," Judith mused as she sat down next to Lark on the sofa, "that Riley never married Iris because his first bout with matrimony was so unhappy."

To the cousins' surprise, Lark laughed. "No, it wasn't. Riley just didn't like the idea of the institution. Not when he was young, anyway. It wasn't part of his philosophy then. He was into Kerouac, and all those British Angry Young Men. But he changed. Riley matured late, but fully." She held her bottle of beer as if it were a case of jewels.

Renie cut to the heart of the matter. "Then why didn't he marry Iris?"

Lark's laughter took on a jagged edge. "He didn't love her." The beautiful, unworldly face turned from cousin to cousin. For one brief moment, Judith could have sworn that Lark Kimball was not only seeing but studying her hostesses.

"Did he tell you that?" Renie, as usual, had sacrificed tact.

"Of course he did. Why should he love her?" Lark sounded defensive. "She's well connected in the art community; she's supposedly glib, handsome, and articulate. Useful, in other words. But she's also a rapacious conniver. It didn't take him twenty years to figure that out."

"Yes, it did," retorted Renie. "They were still together when he died."

"That's only because he couldn't figure out how to get

rid of her.'' Lark's voice had risen and her face no longer looked so unwordly. Indeed, she was blushing, and her jaw was set in a hard line. ''Riley needed some time to tell her how he felt. How *we* felt.'' She flounced a bit on the sofa. ''He wasn't merely my teacher, he was my lover. And we intended to be married. As soon as he told Iris to go to hell.'' Lark Kimball sat back on the sofa, now smiling serenely.

MAJOR VICES

JUDITH AND RENIE would rather be boiled in oil than cater the seventy-fifth birthday party for their batty Uncle Boo Major, the billionaire breakfast mush magnate. But fortunately, their duties keep them in the kitchen and away from most of their contemptible kin—that is until the birthday boy is found blown away behind the locked den door. And now a plethora of wills are popping up all over the place making everyone suspect, Judith and Renie included.

Pandemonium broke out in the den. Aunt Toadie whirled on Jill, trying to tear the will out of her hands. Derek embraced his daughter, which wasn't easy, since he had to fend off his aunt's clawing fingers. Holly fanned herself with her hand and leaned against one of the radiators. Aunt Vivvie beamed—and fainted again. Judith called for Mrs. Wakefield and the smelling salts.

It was Renie, however, who showed up. "What the hell . . . ?" she muttered, encountering the chaotic scene.

"Derek won," Judith said in her cousin's ear. "Jill found the will."

"Well." Renie stared at Aunt Vivvie, who was lying on the parquet floor and making little mewing noises.

"Did you say smelling salts? I think she's coming around."

Renie was right. Vivvie was not only conscious, but also smiling, if in a trembling, anxious manner. "Oh, my!" she gasped out, allowing Judith to prop her into a sitting position. "Oh, my, my! Bless Boo! My son is so deserving!"

"Bunk!" shouted Toadie. "Let me see that will! It must be a phony!"

With an air of victory, Derek waved a hand at his daughter. "Let her read it, Jill. Let everybody read it. I always knew Uncle Boo loved me best." His off-center smile revealed his gold molar, making him look vaguely like a pirate.

Toadie snatched the document from Jill's grasp. She read hurriedly, then sneered. "This thing is three years old! He wrote this just after Rosie died. Do you really think he didn't make another will?" Toadie crumpled the legal-sized paper and hurled it at Derek. "I should make you eat that, you swine!"

Trixie's blond head bobbed up and down like a puppet's. "That's right, Mummy! Uncle Boo promised *us* his money! And the house! And . . ." Trixie took a deep breath, her cleavage straining at the deep ruffled neckline.

". . . *everything!* Let's go through those other books!"

Chaos reigned in front of the open bookcase. Shoving, pushing, and otherwise stampeding one another, the four Rushes, including a rejuvenated Aunt Vivvie, vied with the two Grover-Bellews. Books began to fly from the top shelf. Her librarian's sensibilities enflamed, Judith called a halt.

"Wait!" she cried, practically vaulting over the desk. "Stop!" To her amazement, the combatants did, staring at her with varying degrees of curiosity and hostility. Swallowing hard, she made a calming gesture with her hands. "I have an idea. There's a better way to find that will than to tear this place apart. Would all of you agree to a trace and to appointing Renie and me as neutral searchers?"

Aunt Toadie's face turned mulish. "We would *not*. Why should we trust you two?"

MURDER, MY SUITE

EVER SINCE JOE Flynn walked back into Judith's life and finally married her, Judith has begun to breathe a little easier. Life is good for Judith, who loves being surrounded by her devoted husband, her delightful son, her bosom buddy of a cousin, Renie, and even, in a rare tender moment, her mother. That is, until life takes a devilish turn when gossip columnist Dagmar Delacroix Chatsworth descends on Hillside Manor with a flurry of lackies and her yappy lapdog Rover, who seems to think he owns the joint. But Judith is ever the professional, gritting her teeth and bearing the barrage, even when things become fatally frenetic. . . .

Judith was at a loss. She abandoned guessing at Dagmar's veiled intentions. "You certainly cover everybody's peccadilloes. Do you ever get threatened with lawsuits?"

For a brief moment Dagmar's high forehead clouded over under the turban. "Threatened?" Her crimson lips clamped shut; then she gave Judith an ironic smile. "My publishers have superb lawyers, my dear. Libel is surprisingly hard to prove with public figures."

The phone rang, and Judith chose to pick it up in the

living room. She was only mildly surprised when the caller asked for Dagmar Chatsworth. The columnist already had received a half-dozen messages since arriving at Hillside Manor the previous day.

While Dagmar took the call, Judith busied herself setting up the gateleg table she used for hors d'oeuvres and beverages. At first, Dagmar sounded brisk, holding a ballpoint pen poised over the notepad Judith kept by the living room extension. Then her voice tensed; so did her pudgy body.

"How dare you!" Dagmar breathed into the receiver. "Swine!" She banged the phone down and spun around to confront Judith. "Were you eavesdropping?"

"In my own house?" Judith tried to appear reasonable. "If you wanted privacy, you should have gone upstairs to the hallway phone by the guest rooms."

Lowering her gaze, Dagmar fingered the swatch of fabric at her throat. "I didn't realize who was calling. I thought it was one of my sources."

"It wasn't?" Judith was casual.

"No." Dagmar again turned her back, now gazing through the bay window that looked out over downtown and the harbor. Judith sensed the other woman was gathering her composure, so she quietly started for the kitchen.

She had got as far as the dining room when the other two members of Dagmar's party entered the house. Agnes Shay carried a large shopping bag bearing the logo of a nationally known book chain; Freddy Whobrey hoisted a brown paper bag which Judith suspected contained a bottle of liquor. Another rule was about to be broken, Judith realized: She discouraged guests from bringing alcoholic beverages to their rooms, but a complete ban was difficult to enforce.

The bark of Dagmar's dog sent the entire group into a frenzy. Clutching the shopping bag to her flat breast, Agnes started up the main staircase. Freddy waved his paper sack and shook his head. Dagmar put a hand to her turban and let out a small cry.

"Rover! Poor baby! He's been neglected!" She moved

to the bottom of the stairs, shouting at Agnes. The telephone call appeared to be forgotten. "Give him his Woofy Treats. Extra, for now. They're in that ugly blue dish on the dresser."

Judith blanched. She knew precisely where the treats reposed, since she had discovered them earlier in the day, sitting in her mother's favorite Wedgwood bowl. Anxiously, Judith watched the obedient Agnes disappear from the second landing of the stairs. Rover continued barking.

"I thought the dog was a female," Judith said lamely.

Dagmar beamed. "That's because he's so beautiful. Pomeranians are such adorable dogs. Rover is five, and still acts like the most precious of puppies. Would you mind if he came down for punch and hors d'oeuvres?"

Judith did mind, quite a bit.

AUNTIE MAYHEM

JUDITH AND RENIE are taking in the London countryside for an unharried weekend at a real English manor. However they find the weekend anything but relaxing with Aunt Petulia, Ravenscroft House's aged mistress, holding court to her many relations. Then a box of sweets poisons Aunt Pet. Now Judith and Renie are up to their American necks in a murder most British.

Judith and Renie both recognized the neighborhood; some of the Grover ancestors had lived there in the late nineteenth century. "But you spend weekends at Ravenscroft House," Judith noted.

"Oh, yes," Claire replied with a tremulous smile. "At least some. London makes me nervy." To prove the point, Claire looked as if she were on the verge of an anxiety attack.

Renie was nodding. "We've got a cabin in the woods, about an hour outside of town." She referred to the ramshackle structure that had been built a half-century earlier by their fathers and Grandpa Grover. "Of course it's sort of falling down. We don't go there very often."

Claire put a hand to her flat breast and leaned back in the chair. "Oh! I know! These old houses are so stress-inducing! The heating, the electrical, the plumbing!''

"Actually," Renie murmured, "we don't exactly have plumbing. Or electricity or heating. The outhouse is collapsing, too."

Claire sympathized. "Outhouses! My! We call them outbuildings. But I know what you mean about repairs. Such a challenge! Judith—may I call you that, I hope? Thank you so. Margaret said you renovated your family home. The one in the city. Into a bed-and-breakfast. I shall hang on every word. I swear."

Judith assumed a modest air. "I'll do my best. Hillside Manor had some serious problems, too." Fondly, she pictured the Edwardian house on the hill, with its fresh green paint and white trim, the bay windows, the five guest bedrooms on the second floor, the family quarters in the expanded attic, and the enclosed backyard with the last few fruit trees from the original orchard. There was a double garage, too. And the remodeled toolshed where her mother lived. Gertrude Grover had refused to share a roof with her son-in-law. She didn't like Judith's second husband much better than her first one.

"It *was* a challenge," Judith finally said, thinking more of coping with Gertrude than of the renovations. "It's expensive. I had to take out a loan."

Claire's high forehead creased. "My word! A loan! Charles should hate that!"

Trying to be tactful, Judith made an effort to put Claire's mind at rest. "I'm sure my situation was different. I'd been recently widowed and had no savings." Dan McMonigle had blown every dime on the horse races or the state lottery. "My husband wasn't insurable." Dan had weighed over four hundred pounds when he'd died at the age of forty-nine. "We had no equity in our home." After defaulting on the only house they'd ever owned, the McMonigles had lived in a series of seedy rentals, and had been about to be evicted when Dan had, as Judith put it, conveniently blown up. "In fact," she went on, feigning serenity, "I had no choice but to move in with my mother. That's when it occurred to me that it didn't make sense for the two of us to rattle around in a big old house. My son was almost ready for college.''

''How true!'' Claire positively beamed, revealing small, perfect white teeth. ''That's precisely what I've told Charles. Why maintain a second home with so many expenditures and taxation? Why not turn it into something that will produce income?''

''Exactly,'' Judith agreed. ''The main thing is to figure out if you're going to run it or let someone do it for you.''

Claire's smile evaporated. ''Oh, no. The main thing is Aunt Pet,'' she insisted, her rather wispy voice now firm. ''First of all, she has to die.''

NUTTY AS A FRUITCAKE

WITH ALL THE comings and goings around the bed-and-breakfast, Judith finds it comforting to know that, should her aging mother require her assistance—beyond the meals she serves her every day and the errands she runs—Gertrude is right on the property, living in the converted toolshed. Although Judith and Gertrude have their moments, this mother-daughter relationship is an affectionate one, depending on how you look at it. . . .

"They're questioning the neighbors," Naomi said in a breathless voice. "First, Mrs. Swanson, then the Rankerses, and finally, me. Nobody else is home—except your mother."

"*My mother?*" Judith gaped at Naomi, then jumped out of the car to look down the driveway. She saw nothing unusual, except Sweetums, who was stalking an unseen prey in the shrubbery.

"They're questioning her now," Naomi added, backpedaling to her own property. "Don't worry, Judith. I'm sure she'll be treated with respect."

That wasn't what concerned Judith. With a half-hearted wave for Naomi, she all but ran to the toolshed. There wasn't time to think about the awful things Gertrude could say to the police, especially about Joe Flynn. Judith yanked the door open.

Patches Morgan was standing by the tiny window that looked out onto the backyard and the Dooleys' house. With arms folded, Sancha Rael leaned against a side chair that had originally belonged to Judith and Dan. Gertrude was sitting on her sofa, smoking fiercely, and wearing a tiger-print housecoat under a lime-and-black cardigan. She glared as her daughter came into the small sitting room.

"Well! Just in time, you stool pigeon! What are you trying to do, get me sent up the river?"

Judith's mouth dropped open. "What? Of course not! What's happening?"

With his good left eye, Morgan winked at Judith. "Now, now, me hearties, this is just routine. But," he continued, growing serious, "it seems that certain threats against Mrs. Goodrich were made by Mrs. Grover. You don't deny that, do you, ma'am?" His expression was deceptively benign as he turned back to Gertrude.

Gertrude hid behind a haze of blue smoke. "I make a lot of threats," she mumbled. "It's my way. I can't remember them all."

Judith stepped between Gertrude and Morgan. "Excuse me—who told you that my mother threatened Enid?"

Morgan's good eye avoided Judith. "Now, I can't be revealing my sources, eh? You know that anything we might regard as a threat has to be investigated when there's a homicide involved."

"It was years ago," Judith said, then bit her tongue. "I mean, it must have been—*I* don't remember it. Either," she added lamely, with a commiserating glance for Gertrude.

Sancha Rael stepped forward, a smirk on her beautiful face. "This threat involved a family pet. It had something to do with"—she grimaced slightly—"'sauerkraut.'"

Gertrude stubbed her cigarette out. She shot Morgan and Rael a defiant look.

Judith didn't know whether to grin or groan. She did

neither. "Look," she said to Morgan, "this is silly. I can't believe you're wasting the city's time interrogating my mother. Does she look like the sort of person who'd take a hatchet to somebody?"

Morgan eyed Gertrude closely. "In truth, she does," he said. "Where were you Wednesday morning, December first, between seven and eight-thirty A.M.?"

SEPTEMBER MOURN

JUDITH HAS AGREED to run a high school chum's bed-and-breakfast for a few days. So off she goes with cousin Renie for B&B sitting in the rustic splendor of Chavez Island. But when one odious blowhard tries to horn in on their dinner one night, Renie beans him with a china dish and moments later he takes a deadly tumble down a flight of stairs. Now Judith must find the real killer and prove coz Renie innocent.

Hodge bristled. "Lips that touch liquor will never touch mine."

Defiantly, Renie took a big swig of bourbon. "You can count on it, Burrell. I wouldn't touch you with a ten-foot pole."

"Let's all calm down," Judith urged, as she counted the simmering prawns. There were an even dozen. Divided by three, that made four apiece. Renie wouldn't be happy to share.

"We're having dinner for two," Renie asserted. "Beat it."

Though appalled by her cousin's attitude, Judith knew she had to side with Renie. "It's a rule," she insisted. "Mrs. Barber doesn't do dinner."

"Mrs. Barber isn't here," Hodge countered. "H. Burrell Hodge is." He wedged himself between the table and the matching bench. "Ah! Do I smell garlic? H. Burrell Hodge is fond of garlic!"

"Guess what?" Renie said, placing a knee on the bench next to Hodge. "I'm not fond of rude people who try to steal my dinner. You're not eating our pasta, but you might end up wearing it. Am I being clear?"

Hodge glared at Renie. "You're very maddening," he averred, picking up the silverware that had been intended for Renie. "H. Burrell Hodge doesn't give in to silly threats from mouthy women who drink too much. Where are my prawns?"

"That does it!" Renie was enraged. She snatched up the heavy blue-and-pink plate and cracked it over Hodge's head. The plate broke. Hodge let out a howl of pain. Clutching his head with one hand, he made a fist with the other.

"Damn your hide! I'm reporting this to the authorities! You assaulted me! I'll sue!"

Judith was staring at Hodge in horror, but the unrepentant Renie had gone to the cupboard to get another plate. "I'll use a skillet next time," she snapped. "Did you think I was kidding about the prawns? R. Grover Jones doesn't kid about *food*!"

WED AND BURIED

JUDITH McMONIGLE FLYNN'S son Mike is getting married and the Hillside Manor B&B is packed to the rafters with relatives. However, the joyous occasion is dampened for Judith when she spies a tuxedo-clad gent tossing a bridal-gowned beauty off the roof of a nearby hotel. Judith's determination to find the killer could put some stress on her own marital bliss with policeman husband Joe, but she's not about to take a honeymoon from amateur sleuthing until she's gotten to the bottom of the homicidal hanky-panky.

"I feel awful," Judith declared after they had driven around the block four times to find a parking place and waited ten minutes for a table. "I think it's the heat."

Joe was scanning the long list of microbrews that were written in various shades of colored chalk above the bar. The Heraldsgate Pub was crowded as usual, but Judith and Joe had been lucky—their table was at the far end of the long, narrow establishment, and, thus, not quite in the center of noise and bombast.

"The heat?" Joe replied rather absently. "Maybe." The green eyes finally made contact with Judith. "How about the corpse? You pegged the wrong one, Jude-girl.'' A faint smile touched Joe's mouth as he started to reach for her hands.

Abruptly, Judith pulled back. "Hey! I pegged *somebody*! You're ticked off because I knew there was a dead person at that hotel. You thought I was hallucinating.''

Joe's grin was off-center. "You're having one of your fantasies. Nobody was pushed off a roof. The dead man didn't die from a fall. He was stabbed.''

Judith gaped. "Stabbed? With a knife?''

Joe was noncommittal. " 'With a sharp instrument' is the way we put it. No weapon was found. Dr. Chinn says he'd been dead about forty-eight hours. He'll know more after the formal autopsy.''

"Stabbed,'' Judith echoed. Then the rest of what Joe had said sank in. "What do you mean? 'Whoever he is'?''

Joe shrugged. "Just that. The guy had no ID. He looked to be about thirty, just under six feet, a hundred and forty pounds, not in the best of health, signs of poor nutrition. But you're right about one thing—he was wearing a tuxedo.''

Judith's eyes sparkled. "So he was the man I saw on the roof.''

SNOW PLACE TO DIE

JUDITH MCMONIGLE FLYNN is more than ready to hang up her oven mitts, but her effervescent Cousin Renie needs help catering the telephone company's annual winter retreat. Judith gives in because the pay is good, never thinking that there would be a killer cooking up mischief on the premises. But when Judith and Renie discover the frozen garroted remains of the previous company caterer, they know that they are on the trail of a killer who would like nothing better than to put the two cousins in the Deep Freeze.

"When do you make your presentation?" Judith asked, forcing herself out of her reverie.

"Friday," Renie answered, no longer placid. "I told you, it's just for a day. Can't Arlene Rankers help you throw some crap together for these bozos? Bring her along. You'll be up at the lodge for about six hours, and they'll pay you three grand."

"Arlene's getting ready for her annual jaunt to Palm Desert with Carl, and . . . *three grand*?" Judith's jaw dropped.

"Right." The smirk in Renie's voice was audible. "OTIOSE pays well. Why do you think I'm so anxious to peddle my pretty little proposals? I could make a bundle off these phone company phonies."

"Wow." Judith leaned against the kitchen counter. "That would pay off our Christmas bills and then some. Six hours, right?"

"Right. We can come and go together, because my presentation should take about two hours, plus Q&A, plus the usual yakkity-yak and glad-handing. You'll get to see me work the room. It'll be a whole new experience. I actually stay nice for several minutes at a time."

Judith couldn't help but smile. Her cousin wasn't famous for her even temper. "How many?" she asked, getting down to business.

"Ten—six men, four women," Renie answered, also sounding equally professional. "All their officers, plus the administrative assistant. I'll make a list, just so you know the names. Executives are very touchy about being recognized correctly."

Judith nodded to herself. "Okay. You mentioned a lodge. Which one?"

"Mountain Goat," Renie replied. "It's only an hour or so from town, so we should leave Friday morning around nine."

Judith knew the lodge, which was located on one of the state's major mountain passes. "I can't wait to tell Joe. He'll be thrilled about the money. By the way, why did the other caterers back out?"

There was a long pause. "Uh . . . I guess they're sort of superstitious."

"What do you mean?" Judith's voice had turned wary.

"Oh, it's nothing, really," Renie said, sounding unnaturally jaunty. "Last year they had a staff assistant handle the catering at Mountain Goat Lodge. Barry Something-Or-Other, who was starting up his own business on the side. He . . . ah . . . disappeared."

"He *disappeared*?" Judith gasped into the receiver.

"Yeah, well, he went out for cigarettes or something and never came back. Got to run, coz. See you later."

Renie hung up.